DEDICATION

To Master Anthony Stevens, for his patience, guidance, and invaluable experience. (Told you I wasn't going to redshirt you!)

ACKNOWLEDGMENTS

To my hubby, who is definitely The World's Greatest Husband™, who put up with a blubbering workaholic wife during the initial writing process. He's probably my greatest supporter, and if it hadn't been for him pushing me to pursue my fiction, I might still be focusing on computer tutorials.

To Mr. B. He knows why.

To my friends and adopted family at the Sarasota Society, you are too numerous to mention. Thanks for inspiration, education, friendship and fellowship, and for making me laugh every time one of you asks (usually hopefully), "Will that end up in one of your books?" (Yes, it probably will end up in a book.)

And especially to Sir Vic and the spirit of Annie.

Lastly, although while alive she likely never would have read most of my books, but she would have been proud of my achievement for getting them published, for Granny. I wrote this book originally as a way of dealing with my grief over losing her the day before my birthday in 2008. Also, for Grandaddy, who we lost exactly three years to the day later.

Sometimes, life is truly stranger than fiction. There's a running joke in my family that I suck at remembering dates. Believe me, that one's etched in my mind.

THE RELUCTANT DOM

Tymber Dalton

MENAGE AND MORE

Siren Publishing, Inc.
www.SirenPublishing.com

A SIREN PUBLISHING BOOK
IMPRINT: Ménage and More

THE RELUCTANT DOM
Copyright © 2012 by Tymber Dalton

ISBN: 978-1-62241-545-8

First Printing: October 2012

Cover design by Harris Channing
All cover art and logo copyright © 2012 by Siren Publishing, Inc.

Printed in the U.S.A.

PUBLISHER
Siren Publishing, Inc.
www.SirenPublishing.com

AUTHOR'S NOTE

While this is a fictional story, the portrayal of a twenty-four/seven M/s relationship is not inaccurate. I have personally known people who use BDSM as a healthier, and safer, alternative to self-injurious behavior. I'm not saying it should be a replacement for medical intervention, but everyone makes their own choices in life. Being active in the BDSM lifestyle myself, I'm glad that I can write about it from a been there, done that point of view. This is, however, just one story, and a fictional one at that. There is a rich diversity to "the lifestyle" that most people never know about because their information comes from commercial BSDM fetish porn sites on the Internet. Try to define normal, either in a vanilla or kink relationship, and it's truly impossible.

You might be more "normal" than you think…

THE RELUCTANT DOM

TYMBER DALTON
Copyright © 2012

Chapter One

"I made her three promises when we got married, Seth. I would never lie to her. I would always take care of her. I would protect her, never let anyone hurt her ever again."

Seth watched his friend swirl the bourbon and ice in his drink. Kaden had laid his glasses on the table, and his face looked haggard and worn. There was something deeply wrong with his friend tonight. They'd known each other over forty years, since they were babies and their moms were best friends, and this was plain…

Wrong.

Kaden met his friend's concerned gaze. "I love her, Seth. She's my life. What am I going to do?"

"What are you talking about, dude? You're freaking me out."

Kaden sat back in his chair. "I went to the doctor today."

Seth felt a mental chill. "Are you gonna make me beat it out of you or what?"

Kaden took another drink. This was their weekly boys' night out, but Seth knew this was nothing like any other night. "I'm dying," Kaden whispered.

This had to be a horrible practical joke. Kaden was always looking for a way to get one up on Seth and sucker him in. "Dude, that's *not* funny. You don't fucking joke about something like that."

"Do I look like I'm laughing?"

Seth studied him, a cold, hard rock of emotion settling in his stomach.

"What the fuck?"

"I've got cancer. Best guess is a year or so."

"Well you need to go get a second opinion! Maybe the doctor's wrong. They can be wrong, you know."

Kaden looked at his glass again. "This was my *third* opinion. Pancreatic cancer. Inoperable."

Numb shock engulfed Seth. This man was his brother in everything except name and blood. There were a few years they were separated by distance while Seth was in the Army, and even then they'd e-mailed and talked on the phone as much as possible. Other than that, they'd been close.

"They've got medicine, radiation, chemo. There's got to be something."

"No. I refuse to spend the time I've got left like that. They said it'll only buy me a few months, if I'm lucky. I'd rather not spend it puking my guts up."

"But there's got to be something—"

Kaden shook his head. "I refuse to go out like my dad did. I go out on my terms." He took another sip of his drink.

What do you say in a situation like that?

Seth shook his head. "Fuck." He took a swig of beer. "How's Leah holding up?" he quietly asked.

"I haven't told her yet."

He stared at his friend in disbelief. "What do you mean you haven't told her?"

"I wanted to make sure before I did. I saw the first two doctors last week. They all agree on the diagnosis—and the prognosis."

Poor Leah. They'd been married nearly twenty years. Seth was overseas in the Army when Kaden met and married her in the span of three months. Seth had immediately liked her when he returned home and got to meet her. She was good for Kade.

Seth was lost in a swirl of emotions. Kaden had to repeat his question. "How's the apartment hunting going?"

What the fuck? Kade had just dropped the bomb that he was dying, and now he was asking about that?

Seth numbly shook his head while still trying to process Kaden's news. "I'm still looking. It's hard since I'm in school and shit. I'm sick of living at Ben's place and need to get back out on my own." Seth's older brother had insisted on him staying with them during Seth's divorce.

"So you're finally free of the bitch? I knew the papers had to be coming soon."

"Paperwork came through last week. I'm officially divorced. Only took two years and losing my ass." He looked at Kaden and refocused on the discussion at hand. "Quit changing the fucking subject!"

Kaden knowingly smiled. "I wasn't."

"You were."

Kaden sat back. "We need to have a talk."

"Fuck that. You need to get your ass home and tell Leah."

Kaden's grey eyes settled on his. "I need to talk to you first," he said, his voice dropping to a soft, steady tone. "Seriously."

Seth took a deep breath. "Okay, what?"

"I want you to move in with us."

Seth blinked. "What?"

"We've got plenty of room."

"What?" He'd wake up any minute from this nightmare. Or whacked-out dream, or whatever the fuck it was. This could not be real, couldn't be happening.

Kaden leaned forward and dropped his voice even further. "I need you to hear me out, without interruption. I don't want you to give me a yes or no tonight, okay? Can you do that for me?"

Seth slowly nodded.

Kaden's eyes never left his. "I need to tell you a few things about myself. About Leah. I need you to listen so you understand where I'm coming from, because this is hard enough for me to talk about without justifying myself to my best friend, okay? Promise?"

Seth nodded again. Kaden was the "still waters run deep" poster boy. They were close, but while Seth could dump everything on the table, Kaden played everything close to the vest. He always had. Maybe that was why he'd been happily married for nearly two decades and Seth was on his third ex-wife.

Kaden clasped his hands together. "You know I love Leah. She's my fucking life. I have never cheated on her, and she's never cheated on me."

Seth nodded. He knew. He'd seen and envied their obvious love and passion for years. Any moron could see how devoted they were to each other.

Lucky bastard.

"There's a few things I've never told you. About Leah's past. About how we met. Some of that doesn't need to be told tonight. You'll learn about it soon enough. Suffice it to say she was a fucking mess when we met. I probably saved her life. She had a horrible life before we got together."

Kaden took a deep breath. "Leah's not just my wife, Seth. She's my slave. I'm her Master, her Dom."

Okay, he was *definitely* being played. Seth fought and lost the battle against his grin, relief flooding in. "You're fucking with me. Goddamn it, you got me again, you son of a bitch! You really fucking had me scared there for a minute, dude. That was *so* not funny." That explained everything. Kaden had managed to pull the ultimate *Punk'd* job on him. Relief started to displace his fear.

Kaden's eyes, his serious gaze, never changed. "I'm not fucking with you," he softly said. "I need you to hear me out. You promised."

The hard, cold rock in Seth's stomach rolled over. He swallowed hard and nodded as his momentary relief retreated.

Kaden continued. Seth saw something for the first time in his life that nearly horrified him—

Tears in Kaden's eyes.

"We've been into it since a little after we met. It wasn't something we planned. It just happened. I didn't set out wanting to do it, but she needed it. It helped her heal. I know that sounds weird, but trust me, it did. If you'd seen her before..." He paused, took another drink. "If you'd known her when I first met her, you'd know what I was talking about.

"I promised her I would protect her and take care of her. That's what I've always done. I don't have a lot of time to put things in order because even though they found it relatively early, this form of cancer is aggressive and moves fast. I need to know that when I'm gone, there's going to be someone I trust with her life to step into my shoes and take over and keep those promises for me." That was when his eyes did tear up, and he angrily brushed them away. "I need to know that she's safe. I want to be sure she won't kill herself or go looking for what she needs and end up with some asshole who will abuse her."

Seth felt numb and wondered when the hell he'd wake up. This could *not* be real. His brain was not accepting that this was really happening. He knew his voice sounded soft and weak, emotional shock creeping in. "What are you asking me, dude?"

"I want you to come over for dinner tomorrow night. Don't call Leah. Just show up at seven. I need to talk to her and break the news to her and tell her what I want to do. I don't want your answer tonight. I want you to seriously think about this. I want you to move in with us. You can go to school and finish your degree, and I'll teach you what you need to know to take care of her." Kaden reached out and grabbed Seth's arm, his grip almost painfully firm. "Please. I need you to seriously think about this for me."

This was too much for Seth to process at one time. "You're dropping the bomb on me that you're dying, and now you're asking me to, what, fucking beat your wife for you after you die? Are you *shitting* me?" Not only couldn't he grasp that Kaden was dying, he couldn't process that his respectable, successful, soft-spoken and kind-hearted friend of forty years had a secret life Seth knew nothing about.

Kaden vigorously shook his head. "It's not like that at all. There's a lot of stuff I can't tell you unless you promise to help us because it's personal between me and Leah. And there's some stuff you won't understand unless you see it in person. It's not like the bullshit you see on the Internet. I mean, yeah, some people are into that, but it's not like that for us. We're twenty-four/seven. We live this. We're happy living like this."

Kaden took a deep breath. "Leah's healed because of it. But she needs things, Seth. She's always going to need certain things. I'm worried that when I'm gone, if she goes looking to others who don't know her, who don't care about her, it'll hurt her and put her back in that bad place emotionally where she could have died. If she doesn't kill herself to start with."

Kaden released Seth's arm. "I'm also a teacher. Those weekend seminars we go to? I do a lot of instructional stuff. I teach shibari."

Alternate dimension. That was it. He'd fallen through a fucking wormhole. "Shi-what?"

"Shibari. Japanese rope bondage." Kaden took another drink. "And a few whip classes. Please. Come to dinner tomorrow night. I can explain it better then. Show you. I've never asked you for anything before, man. I *need* you. *We* need you. Please."

Seth felt a wave of guilt. No, Kaden had never asked him for anything before. Ever. Kaden, however, had yanked his ass out of the fire more times than he cared to remember.

He thought about it for a long moment. "Okay. I'll come to dinner, but I can't promise you I'll tell you yes. I don't even know what you want me to do." Hell, he couldn't even promise he'd be sober after this bombshell.

Hope lit Kade's face. "That's all I'm asking for, just to hear me out."

"You don't know Leah will go for this."

"She will. Trust me, she will."

Chapter Two

Seth finished his evening back at his brother's house, alone in his room, with a few shots of tequila. When he awoke the next morning, hungover and blurry eyed, the prior evening's discussion with Kaden rushed back to him.

He closed his eyes and prayed he'd go back to sleep. A nightmare was preferable to thinking about his best friend dying.

Fuck.

Dinner.

Seth stumbled through his day, changing his mind about going at least once every five minutes. He barely made it through his morning classes and was glad that at least today he didn't have any labs.

Kaden and Leah had been his two biggest supporters when he decided to go back to college and get his nursing degree. After the Army he'd spent years in construction, but with the housing bust that was far from a great occupation. After the divorce from hell-bitch number three, he'd decided why not make a clean break in all ways? His credit wasn't totally fucked, so at least he'd been able to get a good student loan and a couple of grants for tuition. He'd had medic training in the Army and enjoyed helping people. Besides, it was one of the few occupations where demand constantly exceeded supply, especially in Florida.

At six o'clock, Seth took a deep breath and stepped into the shower. A steady diet of Tylenol and ginger tea all day had finally eased the worst of his hangover.

The bombshell pressed into his mind every few minutes. He'd be thinking about his classes, trying to run through things in his mind, then suddenly the thought.

Kaden's dying.

Trying to memorize something.

Kaden's dying.

Like a horrific heartbeat in his brain.

Kaden's dying.

What the fuck would he do without his best friend? He was closer to Kaden than he was to his own brother. Emotionally, at least. He knew Leah hadn't liked any of his three exes. Neither had Kaden, but they'd done their best to include the women into their close triad of friendship, welcomed them in.

How many times over the years had he wished he could find someone like Leah?

He wasn't excusing his own behavior. His first doomed marriage—Kelly—was, in retrospect, an attempt to find another Leah. She'd been the spitting image of his best friend's wife. Even Leah gently teased him about it in private.

Paula was a money-grubbing bitch who was more interested in how high Seth could raise her credit card limit.

Then, of course, there was Jackie. She'd sworn for richer or poorer, but when he told her he might have to file corporate bankruptcy because of the housing market tanking and his business going under, she'd taken off like a scalded cat.

Seth closed his eyes and rested his forehead against the cool shower tile.

Kaden's dying.

Fuck.

He'd fought the urge—and lost—to look up pancreatic cancer at the university library between classes. After five minutes of reading he closed the book and shoved it back onto the shelf.

No, Kaden wouldn't want to go out like his father had, wasting away in a hospital bed, sick for months before that from chemo and weakened by surgery to try to remove the tumors on his lungs.

As Kaden's friend, after sitting on the sidelines and watching it unfold, Seth couldn't blame him either.

Seth dug a pair of khaki slacks out of his closet and found a button-up shirt that didn't need ironing. Normally he would just wear shorts and a T-shirt. Tonight was different.

He wasn't sure what Kaden was asking of him. The knowledge that his best friends had this secret life for decades still shocked him. They were so...

Normal.

Kaden was a successful corporate lawyer, for chrissake. Leah didn't work, but she volunteered tirelessly for a couple of charities and nonprofits. Hell, when they went swimming in their pool she wore a one-piece bathing suit. He'd never seen her in anything racier than a sports bra and jogging shorts.

It'd shocked him several years ago when he'd seen a tattoo on Kaden's arm, circling his left bicep, an intricate vine pattern highlighting a small, round symbol of some sort. *Kaden* with a tattoo?

That was almost as shocking as seeing Santa in a lace bra and panties.

At the time, when Seth asked about it, Kaden had smiled and shrugged, said Leah liked it, and left it at that.

Seth sat in his car outside his brother's house, simultaneously trying to talk himself into and out of dinner. If he didn't go, maybe that would mean this wasn't real.

But he'd promised.

Over the years, Kaden and Leah had been better to him than he could have ever asked. They'd never asked for or expected anything in return.

Ever.

Was he really going to pull the chickenshit move now that Kaden was finally making a request of him?

Just to hear him out.

He pounded the steering wheel, which set off another round of throbbing in his iffy head.

Kaden's dying.

He didn't handle death well. Not his own grandparents or parents. And this was Kaden.

He started his car and pointed it toward Kaden's house.

* * * *

At the front gate, Seth punched in the code he knew by heart and drove in. The small, luxury-gated estate community was comprised of large, wooded lots of over five acres each. It was hard to believe there were fifty homes in the development. He'd built some of them, including Kaden's. Kaden and Leah's home sat far enough off the road you could barely make out the lights through the trees.

He parked his beat-up Mustang behind Leah's Lexus sedan. Kaden's new Ridgeline was parked to the side.

They'd never lorded their wealth over him. He'd never asked Kaden for money even though there were times Kaden hinted to him that if he needed a hand he'd help him out.

It was the last thing Seth wanted to do, ever, to bring money into their friendship. Even when Leah begged him to handle building their house he'd reduced the final price, not wanting to make a profit off his friends. Kaden had nailed him on that, too, asking why the cost was lower than the others he'd built and wanting to pay full price. Seth had refused to let him do that.

He'd managed to make it on his own and would keep figuring it out somehow. He'd asked Kaden for help with plenty of things over the years, but money was never one of them. And never would be.

The silence as he shut off the engine nearly deafened him and allowed the mental heartbeat to return.

Kaden's dying.

He forced himself out of his car and walked up the winding concrete path to their front door, rang the bell.

A moment later, Leah answered.

He noticed her normally beautiful green eyes first. Tonight they looked puffy, red, swollen. Kaden had obviously broken the news. His eyes traveled down her body…

Holy fuck!

She wore a short, black leather skirt that barely hung past the bottom of her ass. He didn't know she owned shoes like that—black, strappy, stiletto fuck-me pumps—much less ever wore them. He'd never seen her dressed in anything remotely like this. Obviously braless, her short crop top was cut low enough to nearly expose her nipples, which was ironic, because it was high enough that it barely concealed her breasts. She wasn't big-chested, just naturally perky, more than enough for a pleasant mouthful…

Holy fuck, what am I thinking?

She normally wore her shoulder-length brown hair either down, for dressier occasions, or pulled back into a plain ponytail. He rarely saw her wear makeup. Even then she was always very conservative. Tonight she'd not only set her hair in an alluring updo, but her makeup was just a few sexy breaths on the legal side of slutty. Around her neck she wore a dainty black leather collar, with a heart-shaped lock and small silver tag affixed to the buckle.

For the first time he realized she normally wore a delicate, intricately braided silver choker around her neck, with a small charm and tag attached.

A charm like the symbol in the tattoo on Kaden's arm. But tonight, she wore the collar.

"Hi, Seth," she softly greeted him.

Shock briefly overrode his ability to speak. He finally managed to open his mouth and make words come out. "How are you doing, sweetie?"

A weak smile caressed her face. He fought the urge to hug her like he normally would. He couldn't do it. Not tonight. Not when she was dressed like this, looking hotter than hell and…

Jesus, what sort of sick freak am I?

His dick throbbed in his pants anyway. He was only human. He'd been best friends with his right hand for over a year.

"I'm okay," she replied. Her voice sounded weaker than normal. He suspected it was from grief because she wasn't showing the slightest bit of discomfort from his eyes crawling all over her. The Leah he'd known all these years was a strong, feisty, playful woman, never mean or cruel. The two of them had developed a pleasant friendship, teasing, almost like brother and sister with a little more spice to it. He'd always carefully steered away from blatant sexual talk with her, because she was his best friend's wife.

But he'd be lying if he said he wasn't attracted to her. He'd always thought she was beautiful.

Especially tonight, dressed like this.

"Is he here, Leah?" Kaden called from the kitchen.

Leah motioned Seth in and closed the door behind him, started walking toward the kitchen. "Yes, Master."

Seth had started following Leah. At her words he stopped, as if plowing into a brick wall.

Master?

Holy fuck!

He had a feeling that would be a common expression for him tonight, if what he'd just seen was any indication.

As she continued walking he spotted her tattoo, one he never knew she had. Her skirt rode low on her hips, exposing her lower torso in a way he'd never seen. In the center of her hips, just above where he imagined the cleft of her ass started, she had a tattoo, a vine design similar to Kaden's, with the round insignia over her spine.

Leah apparently sensed he wasn't following and turned. "Seth? Are you okay?"

He dumbly nodded and followed her.

He still hoped that at any moment the two of them would break into broad, beaming grins and laugh that they'd really suckered him in this time, setting up the next round of practical jokes amongst them.

In the kitchen Kaden stood, barefoot and dressed in jeans and a chambray shirt. He chopped vegetables at the counter. He looked up and smiled as Seth walked in.

"There you are." He looked at Leah. "Are the steaks ready?"

She nodded. "Yes, Master."

He leaned over and kissed her. "Good girl. Go put them on, please." He wiped his hands on a dish towel and shook with Seth while Leah picked up a plate of steaks and took them outside to the screened lanai.

Seth's eyes followed Leah as she disappeared through the sliding glass doors. Realizing Kaden was watching him watch his wife, Seth jerked his eyes back to his friend.

Kaden smiled. "She's beautiful, isn't she?"

Seth dumbly nodded.

Kaden's smile faded. "Just hear me out, please. Watch and listen. At the end of the evening, maybe you'll understand a little more what and why I'm asking this of you."

Kaden's dying.

Stunned, Seth nodded again.

Kaden's smile returned. He clapped Seth on the arm. "Thanks, buddy."

* * * *

Seth settled on a barstool on the other side of the counter, his usual perch where he normally sat when he came over. He watched as Kaden prepped the rest of the vegetables. He skillfully and confidently chopped them with the large butcher's knife, the blade making *snick snick* sounds against the cutting board. Leah returned from the lanai and washed her hands, then smiled at Seth before shooting a pointed look at Kaden.

Kaden met her gaze and nodded.

She turned back to Seth. "Would you like a beer?"

"Yes, please." He suspected he'd need something a lot stronger than that when he got home.

She walked to the fridge and retrieved a bottle—his favorite brand, he realized—and she opened it for him before handing it over.

Leah always stocked his favorite brand. She always opened the bottle before handing it to him.

There were a lot of things, crazy puzzle pieces suddenly slipping into place, things he'd never noticed before and now saw in a new light.

When he'd had hernia surgery a few years earlier, between wives two and three, Kaden and Leah had insisted on bringing Seth home from the hospital to their home for a week. He'd spent the night before the surgery with them. Leah took him to the hospital the next morning, waited there for him, met him in recovery, and got all of the doctor's discharge instructions before bringing him back to their home. Back then they'd lived just south of downtown Sarasota. Seth hadn't noticed anything out of the ordinary between his friends in the time he'd stayed with them. They'd been perfectly normal.

Except the way Leah took care of him.

In a way his exes never took care of him.

The way Leah always seemed to focus on Kaden, as if anticipating his every need.

The way she focused on Seth, too, it seemed, when he was a guest in their home.

"Thanks," he muttered, watching them.

Kaden finished with the vegetables and poured them into a foil pouch, topped it off with some seasonings before he sealed it, and handed it to Leah. "Here you go, love. Stay out there with the steaks, make sure you don't let Seth's go too long. You know he likes his very rare."

"Yes, Master." She left again. Seth found himself unable to keep his eyes off her.

Kaden leaned against the counter and took a pull from his own beer, a different brand. "You okay?"

Seth nodded, numb.

"I've already told her about me, as I'm sure you've guessed. I've also told her about my plans."

Seth finally met Kaden's intense gaze. "You cannot tell me she's okay with this."

"Of course she is. Ask her yourself."

"You are *not* serious?"

He studied his bottle. "She's upset, of course. She doesn't agree with my decision to not get chemo. I'm sure she's mad about that, but it's something we'll work through. She also understands why I want to do this for her." He looked up. "Seth, she knows you. She likes you. You're the closest thing she's got to family besides me and mine. There isn't anyone else I would trust with her."

"I can barely keep my own shit together, Kade. How the hell do you expect me to take care of someone else? It's not like I've got a great track record."

Kaden's voice lowered, nearly a whisper. "Maybe you never met the right woman before. Did you ever think about that?"

Seth didn't answer. It was too close to a thought he'd had many nights over the years.

"She needs someone strong, Seth. I'm going to get sick, and I'm going to die." Kaden took a deep breath. Seth sensed his friend was once again close to tears. "She needs someone to get her through this. She's going to need someone to take care of her."

That didn't make any sense to Seth. "You realize lots of women lose husbands and go on to do just fine, right?"

Kaden shook his head. "Not Leah. You'll understand when you learn more about her, about us."

"I think you're underestimating your wife. She's a fucking strong woman."

"She's brilliant. She can do nearly anything she puts her mind to, and God help the person who gets in her way," Kaden agreed. "But there are things she needs that keep her...that keep her sane. That keep her grounded. And there are too many assholes out there who only want a willing sub to use. They wouldn't do for her what she needs done."

"You've lost me."

"You need to see for yourself." He took another drink from his beer. "I talked to my friend Tony this morning. He just moved back here from Denver a few months ago. If worst comes to worst he'll take her on as his slave, but he can't love her the way I do." His eyes met Seth's. "The way you do."

Seth reddened and dropped his gaze. "Fuck, man. She's your wife. I don't love her." That was a lie, and he knew it.

He just prayed Kaden didn't know it.

"I'm not a moron. You're not gay. You've got a hard-on right now. Admit it."

Seth felt his face redden even deeper. They never talked about sex. There was one drunken night after high school graduation, before Kade went to college and he went into basic training. A bottle of tequila and a willing coed later, they'd had an incredible three-way, yet over the years they never talked about their sex lives.

"Fuck, you parade her around here dressed like that, and I'd have to be dead not to notice her."

"She's wearing a lot more than she normally wears."

This couldn't be real. Seth looked at Kaden, who wore a sly smile.

Kaden continued. "Normally she's only got her collar on when we're home alone. The hair and makeup aren't normal when we're home. That's special for you tonight. I wanted her to look her best. Usually she wears a slightly longer skirt and shirt when we go to the club or private dungeon parties."

"Club?" *Dungeon parties?*

"Yeah. There's a private BDSM club we're members of up in Sarasota. We usually go once a week. You'll have fun."

Seth sat back and held up his hands. "Whoa. Dude, I said I'd hear you out. I never promised I'd agree to this. I don't think I can just...beat a woman." The thought turned his stomach.

The thought of Kaden beating Leah damn near made him sick. And angry.

Kaden's face hardened. "I do *not* beat my wife. I have *never* hit her."

Okay, now he was confused. And more than just a little relieved. "Then what the fuck are we talking about? Isn't that what BDSM is all about?"

"It's one of those things I have to show you. Trust me, there's a huge difference between what we do—which is carefully scripted and I've spent thousands of hours practicing so I don't injure her—and some fucking peckerhead who takes a swing at his wife."

He took another swallow from his beer. "As I was saying, Tony agreed that if worst comes to worst he can take her on as his slave, but there won't be the emotional connection for her. I'm worried it wouldn't be enough for her. If you agree to this, you can be there for her. I won't have to worry about her after I'm gone."

Kaden drained his beer. "I want you to move in with us. I want you to live with us, and I'll teach you. We'll teach you. She's nearly an expert in shibari, so she can take over teaching my classes. She's going to need your help taking care of me. After I'm gone, she'll need you to take care of her."

"I've got to eat, man. How am I supposed to do all this and go to school and work?" He was trying to find an excuse to get him out of this, one that Kaden would agree was valid.

One that wouldn't make him look like a total chickenshit asshole.

Kaden's dying.

"Quit your job. You're only working part-time, for crying out loud. I'll take care of everything. I'll even draw up an agreement. You take at least a couple of semesters off. We'll pay for your school, pay off your outstanding student loans, everything. You live here, help Leah, help me. Once..." His voice choked up. Seth felt something inside him die at the sound.

"Once I'm gone," Kaden finally continued, "you marry Leah and stay with her for at least a year. I'll draw up a prenup for you guys. After the year, if the two of you want to get divorced you can, as long as you promise you'll still be her Master unless she falls in love with someone else who is capable of taking over. You can make sure he'll take good care of her. If he meets your approval, then you can train him for her."

As crazy as this situation was, the thought of someone else being with Leah spun a strange, cold thread inside Seth. It knotted around his gut, drawing tight.

"Dude," he whispered, shocked, "you're asking me to *marry* your wife?"

"Well, not until after I'm dead." Kaden's practical smile chilled Seth. "It'll keep the government from taxing the hell out of you. You'll be able to access the assets, as her husband. Hell of a lot easier than trying to leave it to you."

Kaden was a control freak, meticulously planned everything, he always had. Probably one of the reasons he was such a damn good attorney.

This, however, stretched beyond the pale.

Apparently Kaden sensed Seth had reached his immediate limit for processing information. He went quiet and let his friend think things through. After a few minutes, Kaden quietly spoke. "She enjoys it. I didn't force her into this. She craves it. It's security for her. She knows I will always protect her. I promised."

"This isn't a cave where some other guy will drag her away by her hair, dude. Get real."

Kaden glanced through the sliders to the lanai, where Leah tended the steaks on the grill.

"I'm not going to tell you everything tonight. I will, however, give you a little insight. Leah grew up in foster care, spent most of her childhood there."

Well that made things clear as mud. "So?"

"Her biological father was sent to jail. Her mom died when she was two."

If Kade had a point, Seth wished he'd hurry the hell up and make it. "Again, so?"

Kaden took a deep breath. "He went to jail for raping Leah when she was seven."

Seth felt like the wind had been knocked out of him. "Holy fuck," he whispered.

Kaden nodded. "Her life went downhill from there, if you can imagine that." He walked to the fridge and got another beer. He held up one for Seth, who shook his head.

Maybe he shouldn't have a lot of alcohol tonight.

"That's why we've never had kids," Kaden explained. "Why she can't have kids. Between that and...other things that happened to her over the years. She didn't want to go through the surgeries and IVF and all that crap. I respected her decision."

Seth reeled. Leah seemed to be the most put-together person, besides Kaden, that he'd ever known. He'd never heard her talk about her past or her family beyond meeting Kaden. He just assumed she was estranged from them. He never would have guessed…

Holy fuck.

Kaden leaned over the counter and dropped his voice. "She needs things. It helps her cope. She doesn't feel or express emotional pain like you and me. She needs safety and security. She needs someone who will care for and about her and understand why she needs…things. Someone she can put her full trust in. It's how she's made it all these years."

Seth could barely stand the intensity in Kaden's grey eyes.

"Seth, I wouldn't ask you if I didn't think you could take good care of her."

"What 'things' are you talking about?"

"I'll show you after dinner."

* * * *

When Leah returned with the steaks and vegetables—Seth's steak cooked exactly the way he liked it, as always—he couldn't help but stare at her.

She managed a wan smile and looked at Kaden.

He nodded. "Tonight, that's one you don't have to worry about. Okay, love?"

Seth couldn't help himself. "One what?"

"Rule," Kaden replied, as if it was nothing. "Normally when we're formal she must ask for permission before speaking to someone unless I've already said it's okay."

Seth didn't know if it was his friend's words or the matter-of-fact tone that threw him. "Permission?"

Leah nodded. "Master takes very good care of me. He wants to make sure I don't talk with someone I shouldn't. I prefer it that way."

He'd seen this woman work a room full of hundreds of people at a fundraising banquet, Sarasota's movers and shakers, greeting guests and organizing the caterer and servers.

And she was asking permission to speak to *him*?

As if reading his thoughts, she smiled again. "I know it's sort of a lot to get used to."

"*Get used to*?" He stared at them. "I mean, I thought I knew you two! You're my best friends. How could I not know this was going on?"

"What was I supposed to say?" Kaden asked. "Hey, Seth, guess what? Want to hear what Leah and I do when the door's locked and the blinds are drawn?"

"You weren't doing this when I stayed with you after my surgery."

Leah nodded. "Yes, we were. We just weren't formal while you were with us, but we were still doing this."

"But…but you're so normal!"

Finally, a genuine, sly smile from Leah. "You'll be surprised who's into the lifestyle."

Kaden took over. "That's the whole point. It's not like what you see on the Internet. A majority of the people who are into some sort of kink, you'd never know it unless you ran into them doing it somewhere. It's not a bunch of horny freaks fucking anything that moves and wearing masks. I mean, yeah, there are some people like that. Most people are like us." He gently stroked Leah's cheek. Something about the tender gesture saddened Seth. "Well, maybe not like us. A lot of people aren't into it twenty-four/seven like we are."

Seth studied them. They both watched him. "Leah, are you telling me you're willingly his *slave*?" He already knew her answer. How many times had he envied her devotion to Kaden over the years?

A lot.

"Master takes very good care of me." Her voice choked up a little at the end as Kaden's eyes met hers. "He's always taken very good care of me," she whispered, nuzzling his hand when he stroked her cheek again.

"Let's eat before it gets cold," Kaden said as he removed his glasses and wiped his eyes with the back of his hand.

* * * *

After dinner, Leah cleared the table while Kaden led Seth to the back of the house, to a room he'd always assumed was Kaden's private home office. He hadn't been in there since construction was completed. Normally it stayed locked, a small electronic number combination pad just above the knob.

"You need to see this," Kaden said. "And I don't want you to be shocked or surprised."

"Too late for that," he muttered.

Kaden opened the door.

Inside looked like something out of a porn movie, only better quality and more tastefully decorated. A low, padded bench with leather cuffs attached at each end. An X-shaped frame. A large rack holding...

Holy fuck.

Whips, riding crops, and various other implements of torture.

The odd collection explained the keyless lock. During construction, Seth had asked him if he needed it because of his files.

"Something like that," Kaden had said with a smirk. "Keys are a pain in the ass. I'd rather have a combo lock. I don't want people wandering in here when we have guests over."

Seth hadn't questioned it at the time. He knew Kade had a lot of high-profile corporate clients. It made sense to him then.

Made perfect sense now, even if he was still in shock.

Kaden walked across the room to a bookshelf and pulled down a photo album. "Come here," he said.

His legs numb, Seth walked over while Kaden flipped through the pages, finding what he wanted.

"This is shibari." He pointed to a page of pictures of Leah trussed in intricate rope bindings, a ball gag in her mouth, looking...

Well, looking like she was enjoying herself.

Kaden flipped through page after page, naming the different rope configurations.

"She's my model and assistant during classes." He smiled, his finger trailing over one particularly intricate looking configuration. "And at home, of course, she's my practice model." He closed the album and put it back on the shelf before pulling down another one. This time he flipped to a page of pictures taken by someone else apparently, because Kaden and Leah were both in the shot. It looked like he was speaking to a gathered group of people. Leah was bound—naked—to a bench similar to the one in the room behind him.

Kaden wore jeans but was shirtless and holding a—

"Is that a whip?"

Kaden nodded. "Singletail. Specially made. That one's my favorite. Cost me nearly eight hundred dollars. This was a basic singletail class. Problem is, too many assholes think they can use one on a person when they really can't. I spend several hours a week practicing to get and stay as good as I am."

Maybe that explained Kaden's naturally muscled physique despite never going to a gym. Kaden wasn't ripped, yet he was firm and trim while Seth had managed to gain about twenty pounds and go soft since his best days in the Army.

Kaden put that album away and turned to Seth. He dropped his voice. "Have you ever looked at her arms?"

Seth hesitated before he nodded. He'd noticed the scars. Now he wondered if Kaden had done that to her. The possibility sickened him.

"She did most of that to herself before we ever met. Do you know what cutting is?"

"Not really." But relief crept back in.

Kaden glanced to the open doorway behind Seth, as if listening for sounds from the kitchen. Leah was still cleaning up dinner. Seth could hear her singing to herself at the other end of the house. Apparently satisfied that she couldn't hear them, Kaden lowered his voice and continued. "Some people, for various reasons, need pain. They use it. It's how they function, how they deal with their emotions. Some use it to help relieve intense emotional pain in an external way. Some use it to feel like they're connected to life again. Some just flat-out get off on it."

"There's medications for that kind of crap, dude."

"When you're a fourteen-year-old girl and being forced to give your foster brother blow-jobs and getting sodomized by him because he threatens to get you thrown out on the street, you don't exactly trot down to a shrink and ask for a pill."

Seth blanched, sickened. What kind of hell had she been through?

"She didn't take the news well last night, obviously. I needed to give her a long session last night to get her to cry. She's had two more today already. I took the day off from work. I knew she'd need me."

"She likes this?"

"She needs it. There's a lot I can't tell you tonight. You just have to see it for yourself. She's not a pain slut like some are. We have very specific routines and rituals we've developed over the years that help her stay calm and focused and deal with life." He motioned Seth over to a chair in the corner. Seth walked over and sat, his mind reeling.

"When we were first dating," Kaden continued, "she worked at a restaurant near USF. That's where we met. I went in after class one day. She was beautiful. I never believed in love at first sight until I met her. She claimed she was a klutz in the kitchen, always getting these weird injuries, mostly cuts and burns on her arms. She always had something. I had no reason not to believe her. Until I talked her into spending the weekend at my apartment and she got up to make coffee."

Kaden's gaze drifted, his mind's eye traveling back in time. "She didn't hear me get up. I walked into the kitchen and watched her take a knife out of the drawer and lay it against her arm. She closed her eyes like she was saying a prayer or something, and when I screamed, she jumped.

"I wanted to haul her to the hospital. I thought she was trying to kill herself. She was so upset I'd seen her, she got dressed and ran out. I panicked. I couldn't find her. She wouldn't answer my calls, wouldn't come to the door at her apartment. I finally staked out her workplace and made her talk to me.

"She wouldn't tell me why. She broke up with me right there even though she was crying and…it just felt like she didn't really want that. I can't explain it. I begged her to talk to me and she wouldn't. I knew I was in love with her, and it was killing me that she wouldn't talk to me. I knew she'd had a crappy life, but I didn't know everything."

Kaden wiped his eyes. This wasn't easy for him. "I went in every day after class and would sit and try to get her to talk to me. When she quit a few days later, I finally got one of the other waitresses to tell me where she went. Then she told me something else. 'She loves you, but she's scared of people. If you want her to open up to you, you need to prove you're not going anywhere and won't hurt her.'

"I was losing my mind. After three weeks I waited for her at her apartment one night and begged her to let me talk to her. She finally let me in, and she was like a fucking zombie, man. She looked like a dead woman. She told me she loved me, but that she couldn't see me anymore. I was sitting there on the couch trying to talk her into changing her mind when she got up and walked to the kitchen. Before I could get there, she'd cut herself."

"Fuck!"

Kaden nodded. "Then she started screaming. She screamed and cried, and she let me hold her. I sat there on the floor with her for an hour, and she finally told me about her father and the shit that happened to her growing up. What she did to deal with it. She told me she wanted me to find someone 'normal' who could feel emotions without cutting them out of her flesh." He studied his hands for a minute. "I told her I didn't care. I loved her. That I wanted to help her."

He took his glasses off and laid them on the bookcase. "She tried. Man, she fucking tried. I got her to move in with me. Every day I felt it building in her. Like a volcano. But the weird thing was, the more I felt it building in her, it's like the deader she got outside, right? She came home from work all happy one afternoon, and I saw she had a new burn on her arm."

He looked at Seth, his eyes glistening again. "I got so fucking scared and angry that she'd hurt herself. I just lost it. She'd promised not to do it anymore. I should have known better, that she couldn't stop herself. We got into a fight, screaming at each other. I grabbed her and hauled her into my lap, yanked her pants down and spanked the crap out of her."

"Fuck!" Seth couldn't imagine Kaden blowing his cool. He'd never seen his friend lose it, ever. *He* was the hothead, Kaden always coming to his rescue.

Kaden smiled. "I felt like shit, like fucking dirt. Then she fell off my lap, and she looked up at me and had this…absolutely gorgeous smile on her face. My hand hurt like a sonofabitch. I knew I must have bruised her a little, but she looked at me in a way I'd never seen her look at me before. She grabbed me and fucking kissed me and practically raped me right there on the couch. It was the hottest sex we'd had, and the sex was pretty damn good to start with.

"So I asked her after, when we'd finally made it to my bedroom a few hours later, what the hell that was about. She shook her head and said she didn't know. It was like something had just sort of popped free in her when I did that. So I made her a deal."

He frowned, working his hands again. "I told her if she could go the entire next day, just one damn day, without hurting herself, and that I would check every inch of her flesh for a new wound, I would spank her again the next night."

"Fuck!" Seth wished he could say something—anything—other than that, but that was all he could manage.

Kaden nodded. "Right. That's exactly what I thought. I was desperate. What the hell was I supposed to do? I didn't even know if it would work. So I get home from classes the next day and she gets home from work later and she runs in, I mean she's stripping her clothes off the second she gets through the door, asking me to look at her and check her over. I made her stand there and wait. She started to beg. I told her if she didn't behave, I wouldn't spank her.

"It's like she became a freaking statue, just waiting for me. I finished what I was doing and told her to go lie in bed. I get there and she's waiting for me. I start looking her over, taking my time, trying to be seductive about it, and I realize she's fucking wet. I mean, like you wouldn't believe. I asked her what was up with that, and she said she couldn't stop thinking about getting spanked all day."

"Did she ever hurt herself again?"

"A few times early on. After that, no. Not intentionally. We had a deal that if she got hurt, she would immediately tell me so I would know it wasn't intentional. I haven't had to worry about that for years now. That's because we have this. Usually she doesn't even need it every day, or just something light, not a full session. The deal was I would take care of that for her. I was in control of that. She began to beg for more. One day I had to threaten her again that if she didn't behave, I would make her wait another day before her next spanking. That made her even hornier."

Kaden smiled. "We'd been married for about a year when I found out about the local BDSM club and got hooked up with others. Learned a lot more. She was like a changed person since we'd started the spanking, but she wanted more. I wasn't doing it because I wanted her to feel pain. I was doing it because she wanted me to do it. She trusted me enough to let me into her life and take charge of that for her. She literally turned control of her pain over to me, not just physical but mental. Once we started doing that, it's like she was able to move on. It all progressed from there."

He met Seth's eyes. "You and me, we deal with emotional shit. No problem. She never had that, never learned it. She didn't have a family she could go to, someone to teach her safe and healthy ways to process her emotions. She was in survival mode for most of her life, and at the hands of the fuckers who were supposed to take care of her. I was literally the first person in her life she could trust not to hurt her. Well, I mean, you know what I mean. She went through a lot. Yes, I could have forced her into a shrink's office and made her go through years of therapy and medicated her out of her mind and maybe accomplished the same thing. What we do, she enjoys it. It helps her cope, and it keeps her happy. I love making her happy. Who am I to force her to do something we don't even know will work when we've got something we can do together that she loves?"

Seth looked into his friend's eyes. He would be the first to deck anyone who accused Kaden of not loving Leah. He'd seen their relationship firsthand all these years. Well, thought he'd seen it.

"What do you want me to do?" he quietly asked.

Kaden cocked his head to the doorway and listened, then called out. "Love, are you finished with the dishes?"

"Almost, Master. I'm wiping down the counters."

"Very good, love. Come here when you're finished."

Seth noticed something else, the term of endearment. He didn't remember hearing Kaden call Leah "love" before, although he'd heard him call her many other equally sweet things over the years.

"We have a sort of code," he explained to Seth. "You'll learn it. That's another reason I need you to move in. It's easier for you to learn it when you're living here. She's going to need you."

Leah appeared in the doorway a moment later. She stopped at the threshold and looked at the floor.

"Come here, love," Kaden said.

She walked over. He made a hand gesture. She dropped to her knees in front of him.

Seth felt weirded out, yet his cock throbbed in his pants again.

"Love," Kaden said, "I've told Seth we'll give him a demonstration."

"Yes, Master."

"Is that all right with you?"

"Whatever Master wants me to do."

"That was not my question."

"Yes, Master. It is all right with me."

"Prepare for me."

She stood, her entire body flushed. Seth first thought it was embarrassment then realized it was arousal.

She quickly undressed. Seth noticed she wasn't wearing any panties under her skirt. She neatly folded her skirt and shirt and laid them on a nearby shelf, then put her shoes on the floor underneath. When she wore nothing but her collar she turned and looked at Kaden, waiting for instructions.

Kaden was unbuttoning his shirt. "Are you all right, love?" he softly asked her.

"Yes, Master."

"Where are we, love?"

"Green, Master."

Seth wordlessly watched their exchange, his jaw slightly gaped. Her shaved pussy looked swollen, like she was...

Fuck.

Kaden draped his shirt on a hook apparently there for just that purpose. Seth had never paid attention before to how fluidly smooth his friend could move. And now he definitely saw the tattoos were matching.

"Love," Kaden said to Leah, "I'll let you choose this time. You pick what you want me to use."

Leah nodded and turned to the rack of implements. Without hesitation she reached for a coiled whip, one of several lying on a shelf.

Seth's blood ran cold, but he remained silent.

She walked over to Kaden and knelt before him, offering it up to him.

"The four-footer?" he said, almost sounding amused. "You don't want to take it easy on poor Seth tonight, do you?"

"Please, Master. I need to feel the bite." Her voice sounded choked, and her eyes looked red, like she was near tears again.

His face softened. He nodded and took the whip from her. "Of course, love," he said, his voice incongruously gentle. "Set of twenty?"

"Yes, Master. Please."

"Take your place, love."

She stood and walked over to the bench and lay across it, her arms and legs falling near the attached cuffs. Kaden walked over to her and stroked her ass. Seth, who felt he was now an outsider in this tableau, remained silent and still.

"Do you want the cuffs, love?"

Leah's eyes were closed. Seth had seen her tightly peaked nipples.

"Master's choice."

"Do you mind if we don't use them tonight? I think this will be intense enough for Seth without seeing that right now."

"I understand, Master."

Seth looked up as Kaden uncoiled the whip. He realized the ceiling in this room was higher than in the other bedrooms. While the living room and dining room had tall, vaulted ceilings, the other bedrooms were standard eight-foot ceilings. During the planning stage, Kaden had asked for this room to have a vaulted ceiling and no ceiling fan.

Now he understood why.

Kaden backed away from the bench and shook out the whip. He stretched his neck and rolled his shoulders, loosening up. His tone changed, firm, authoritative, sounding totally unlike Seth's soft-spoken friend. "Do you need to feel the bite, slave?"

From the bench, it looked like Leah actually wiggled her ass and hips at Kaden. "I need to feel the bite, Master."

"Set of twenty, love."

"Twenty, Master."

"Count."

Seth flinched, unprepared as Kaden nailed her with the whip, striking her squarely in the middle of her left ass cheek.

"One, Master."

His face a mask of concentration, Kaden slowly worked through the set, Leah keeping count with each strike. It was obvious Kaden knew what he was doing, making it look effortless and apparently striking his intended spot each time.

It was also equally obvious that Leah was…enjoying wasn't perhaps the best word, but she definitely wasn't upset about it despite the tears running down her face by the time he finished.

Kaden coiled the whip. "Where are we, love?"

"Green, Master."

"Very good, love." He walked over to her and knelt beside her, touching his forehead to hers, whispering to her. She nodded and cried. He pulled her into his arms and sat on the floor, holding her in his lap for many long, tender minutes as she sobbed, her agonized screams echoing through the otherwise silent house. Kaden remained silent as she clutched him, his face buried in her hair.

Now Seth felt even more uncomfortable. He wanted to get up and walk out and give them privacy, yet felt that would disturb them more than him just quietly sitting there.

Kaden nuzzled the top of her head, and that was when Seth spotted his friend's tears.

Leah eventually composed herself. Kaden whispered something to her, then tenderly kissed her temple. She nodded, stood, and left the room.

From his place on the floor, Kaden wiped his eyes and looked at Seth.

Taking a deep breath and knowing he could not refuse his friend, Seth softly said, "I'll do it."

Chapter Three

Kaden stood and turned his back to Seth for a moment as he wiped his face. He finally took a deep breath and then turned and nodded. "Thank you," he quietly said. "I can't begin to tell you how much I appreciate this. It takes a huge burden off me."

Seth felt emotionally drained. Not only from his own feelings, but from what he'd just witnessed.

He also worried he might not be able to step up and take over. Could he deal with that responsibility?

He was the perpetual fuck-up. Could he ever truly be strong and steady Kaden?

"You won't let her down," Kaden said as if reading his mind. "You'll do fine. I know you will."

Seth shook his head. "What am I getting myself into?"

"Let's go talk. Give her a few minutes to recover." He grabbed his shirt and glasses and led Seth back to the living room where they settled on the large sectional sofa. "Do you have early classes tomorrow?"

"No. I have one at eleven."

"Why don't you spend the night? I'm taking off the rest of the week for Leah. I need to finish up some things at work over the next few weeks, and then I'm going to stay home for her. I still have some projects going on that I need to wrap up or hand off. I can mostly work from here until they're taken care of."

Here he was, dying, and still talking about doing things for Leah.

Seth's eyes flicked to the hallway. "I don't know if I should spend the night tonight, dude. I mean…" He didn't know how to finish, so he didn't.

"Get used to seeing her naked. It's how she usually dresses. Unless it's chilly or she's not feeling well, she's usually wearing only her collar. I mean, how many times have you dropped by unexpectedly and caught her 'just out of the shower' and wearing only her robe?" Kaden used finger quotes around the phrase.

Seth mentally reeled. He'd joked with her that his timing always sucked and that she needed a new bathrobe. He caught her wearing it fairly frequently, always pulled high around her neck…

He closed his eyes. "Shit."

"Yep. Makes sense now, doesn't it?"

"Yeah."

"Come on, I mean, really. Did you honestly think she manages to take showers just when you show up?" Kaden laughed, amused. "That's why it's usually hanging behind the front door."

Seth flushed. He had noticed that on more than one occasion but hadn't thought anything about it. He assumed she left it there to put on in the morning when she walked down the drive to get the paper.

Kaden continued. "There's plenty of times when she thought you might be stopping by, or if she suspects anyone might be coming by, she'll keep a pair of shorts and a T-shirt by the door so she can slip them on quickly. Then she's usually wearing her day collar, not the one she's wearing now." He worked his wedding band around his finger. "Call your brother and tell him you're spending the night. You've stayed here before. That way he won't worry. We can talk, have breakfast in the morning."

"How am I supposed to get used to seeing your wife walking around here naked?" Seth didn't want to voice the last part of his statement.

Kaden smirked. "Buddy, you have to. Kind of hard to make love to her with her clothes on."

Horrified, Seth recoiled from his friend's words. "Dude! She's your wife! I can't…I can't ask her to have sex with me!"

"Why not? You're going to be her Master, her husband. She'll want it. I damn sure know you'll want it."

Seth tried to reconcile what Kaden had told him earlier. He dropped his voice to a hoarse whisper. "Dude, after what you told me—"

Kaden shook his head. "This isn't the same. You won't be forcing her, trust me. She likes you. She's attracted to you."

Seth fell silent, trying to process this information. He didn't know which shocked him more, the matter-of-fact tone Kaden used or his friend's obviously well-thought-out plans. Just when Seth thought he'd hit the high-water weird mark, Kaden raised the bar yet again.

Kaden's dying.

Kaden stretched back, an amused smile on his face. "We're married, not dead. No, we don't sleep with other people." His smile faded. "Before now. This will be a first for us."

"I'm *so* not doing you, buddy." How much more did Seth not know about Kaden?

And how much did he *not* want to know?

Kaden laughed. "Don't worry. I don't swing that way either." His voice softened. "Remember that girl that one time?"

Seth finally laughed. "Yeah. Jillian." He shook his head. "Man, she turned us every which way but loose that night. Well worth the two-day hangover that rotgut tequila gave me."

The men fell quiet again for a moment until Kaden broke the silence. "We talk, Leah and me. We use fantasy. You've played a starring role in hers more than a few times."

Seth reddened, simultaneously embarrassed and oddly pleased. "Yeah?"

Kaden nodded. "That's another reason I thought of you first. I know she can love you. She will be as good for you as you will for her."

Seth studied his hands. "I cannot believe you are telling me it's okay to fuck your wife."

"My life has changed a lot in the past few days, buddy. My whole way of thinking has changed." Kaden removed his glasses and closed his eyes, pinched the bridge of his nose, rubbed it. "I know her," he softly said. "If I don't hook the two of you up before... If something doesn't happen between you two, it won't. She won't let it. She'll feel too guilty, and that will leave her open to something horrible happening." He opened his eyes and looked at Seth again. "And let's face it. After, you'd normally not ask her out, right?"

Seth swallowed hard. "Right," he softly agreed.

Kaden sadly smiled. "I have to do this. I don't like that I have to make arrangements like this." His smile faded. "We should have had fifty or more years together." He closed his eyes and took a deep breath. "I want her to be happy, Seth. I want her to love and live and not spend her years in a black hole. Worse, I don't want her to kill herself."

"You think she'd do that?" One more worry on Seth's plate.

"Not if she has you. She'll have you to serve and take care of her. She'll hurt, she'll grieve, but if she has you she'll keep putting one foot in front of the other. She won't have a choice." He opened his eyes again. Seth saw he was near tears. "I'm not saying you've got to do anything with her tonight. I'm saying you need to let things happen between the two of you. And it will happen. It can't not happen."

Kaden glanced at the cable box, where the time was displayed. "You need to call Ben and Helen and tell them you won't be home tonight so they don't worry."

Seth numbly nodded and pulled out his cell phone to make the call. While he did, Kaden walked to the kitchen. He returned a moment later with two fingers of bourbon over ice and retook his place on the sofa.

"Let's get you moved in by this weekend, okay? I want you settled as soon as possible so I can get the two of you into a routine. She needs structure."

Seth had spent several nights at their house over the years, usually after a late-running card game or after having too much to drink after a cookout, but this felt different.

Weird.

The voice didn't sound like his own, Seth thought. "Okay."

"When does this semester end?"

Seth tried to force his brain to work. "A couple of weeks."

"Did you already register for the next one?"

"Not yet."

"You need to stop by the registrar's office and talk to them, find out the procedure for taking time off. If you still need to take one class at a time or something that's okay. You don't want a heavy class load for a semester or two at least." He looked away. "I doubt you'll miss many."

Seth stiffly nodded.

Kaden continued, his voice sounding hoarse. "I'll get the paperwork drawn up for you next week."

Seth shook his head. "I don't need paperwork. I trust you."

"I trust you, too. The problem is, Leah won't be able to function. I need someone with legal authority to make decisions and get shit done. I need you to have a power of attorney, medical proxy, DNR order, my living will has to be changed, bank accounts, all of that. I need you on all that paperwork for her, too. Might as well do it all and make it official. It'll make our lives easier later on. One less thing for me to worry about. Get it done and over with."

Seth numbly nodded. That even control-freak Kaden could think of all of this at a time like this…must be the attorney training.

Kaden took a deep breath. "I don't want to die in a hospital. I want to be here. We'll have to get hooked up with hospice when the time comes. At least you'll be able to practice your nurse training," Kaden attempted to joke.

Seth snorted, but Kaden knew it wasn't total amusement.

"Sorry, buddy." He paused a moment before he softly continued. "I want to be cremated. Whatever Leah wants to do with the remains is okay with me. You may have to help her make that decision. I'll have a few things prepared. I'll give them to my partner, Ed, so when it…happens, you can just call him and he'll set the other balls in motion for you. You can focus on her for the immediate time, and Ed will take over and handle that stuff for you both. Okay?"

Seth nodded. Surreal. Nightmare. Wormhole still looked like a viable option.

Kaden leveled his gaze at Seth. "I don't like talking like this. I don't like planning like this. I want it fucking done and out of my way. Out of our way. I want it handled now, so I don't have to think about it anymore. I want it done now, while I can think about it, so I don't forget anything and we can spend the rest of my time doing what needs to be done for Leah." He took a sip of his drink. "I don't want her reverting in her stress."

"What do you mean?"

"I know at first some of what I'll ask you to do to and for her might run contrary to what you think and feel is right. Remember, I know her and I know what she needs. You have to trust me. You cannot let her put up a wall. If she does, she'll hide behind it and then we'll lose her. She'll sink back into her old behaviors, and you won't ever be able to get her back once I'm gone."

"I thought you said you didn't have to worry about that anymore?"

"I also told you she's had three—well, now four—sessions in twenty-four hours. Usually she only gets them twice, maybe three times a week, if that, and sometimes I barely touch her. What you saw just now was mild compared to what she's already had today."

Stunned, Seth shook his head. "That was fucking vicious, man. You mean that was on the low end of the scale?"

Kaden nodded and sipped his drink, frowning. "You saw her ask for it. Physical pain like that helps her process emotions and ground herself." He met Seth's gaze again. "You can never let her emotionally detach. That's almost too far gone if she gets to that point. You'll learn to recognize her nonverbal cues, her body language. Sometimes all she needs is a barehanded swat to the ass to make her feel better. Sometimes she needs a lot more. Sometimes she'll ask if she recognizes what's going on. Your job is to spot the times when she's not cued in to herself and doing it for her."

"This is a lot to fucking learn, man. Are you really that worried she'll cut herself again?"

"Why do you think I was chopping the vegetables before dinner? I won't take the chance."

Seth heard their bedroom door open. A moment later, Leah walked into the living room, her hair down, face washed and free of makeup, apparently wearing nothing but her collar and a long T-shirt that hung to midthigh.

Kaden held his hand out to her. "Come here, love," he said.

She walked over and took his hand. She pressed her lips to the back of his hand before he pulled her into his lap. She curled there with her face buried against his chest, looking more like a lost child than a woman nearly forty years old. He kissed the top of her head, resting his chin in her hair, and met Seth's eyes.

"Thank you. For both of us."

Seth nodded.

* * * *

They sat silently for a few minutes. Kaden shifted position, and Leah sat up and looked at him.

"Love," he said, "Seth's said yes."

Her eyes teared up, but she nodded and looked at Seth. "Thank you," she whispered.

He nodded.

Kaden patted her on the thigh. "Let's go over a few ground rules, okay?"

She nodded.

"Are you comfortable calling him Master right now?"

She hesitated, but Seth answered for her. "Dude, *I'm* not comfortable with it yet. Can we wait on that? Please?"

Kaden thought for a moment. "How about 'Sir?' There needs to be a title."

Leah nodded. "That's fine, Master."

Kaden sadly smiled and stroked her cheek. "Maybe that is better, for now. Less confusion." He looked at Seth. "Okay with you?"

What was he supposed to say? He shrugged. "I can live with that, I guess."

"Good. It's important. Not all the time, just during play and when we're formal." He returned his focus to Leah. "We won't be totally formal for a week or so. Let's let things settle down. Seth's going to move in, and we'll start teaching him everything. You're going to have to help him learn, especially at first."

"Yes, Master."

Seth *so* could not get used to that.

"Very good, love." Kaden looked at Seth. "I think you've already noticed that. It's one of our codes. We can use it even if we're out with vanilla folks. We can still be formal in some ways and no one ever knows."

Seth dumbly nodded.

Kaden continued. "I know that might take you a little while to get used to, and that's okay. But it is important. Tomorrow night we're going to the club, and I want you to go with us. Might as well bring your stuff over, at least plan on spending the night." Seth started to protest, but Kaden intercepted him. "I'm not going to ask you to do anything tomorrow night except watch and learn. You need to see for yourself what we do, what happens."

Seth relaxed. "Okay."

Kaden looked at Leah. "Tell Seth our rule about your behavior."

She looked at Seth. "How I behave reflects upon Master. My behavior must always honor Master."

"And your behavior now will reflect upon Seth, too," Kaden said.

She nodded.

"Very good, love." Kaden kissed her temple. "He'll have to learn things for you. You will have to be patient with him, especially at first. If he says or does something that's contrary to what should be, you can red light and explain it to him. However, you need to understand, many things he won't do exactly like me. He's not me, and you will have to grow comfortable with that. Understand?"

She nodded.

Seth spoke up. "Red light?"

"Tell him."

She looked at Seth again. "Safe words. Red, yellow, green. Red means immediate stop of activities, or if we're someplace vanilla, it means we immediately switch to full vanilla mode until we can go somewhere private and talk about it. Yellow is caution. It means we need to check in with each other. Green is everything's okay."

Seth felt weird asking but knew he had to. "Is that what you were asking her back there?"

Kaden nodded as he stroked her hair. She closed her eyes and leaned into his hand, nuzzling him.

"You're going to get an eye-opening experience," Kaden said. "You're going to get over any bashfulness with her." His voice softened as he stared at Leah. "You're also going to learn things about yourself you never knew. You're going to have the time of your life, man."

Kaden stroked her cheek and turned her face to his. "You have to get used to listening to him, too. When you're alone with him, even if it's just at the store or something, it's as if you were with me. You must obey him."

She nodded.

"He will take care of you. I promise." Kaden's eyes flicked to Seth, and Leah looked at him.

Seth nodded, barely able to speak. "I promise."

Another sad smile. "Thank you," she said.

Kaden kissed her again. "You'll come to trust him the way you trust me. It'll take some time. That's why I wanted to start now with this, while we have time. I need to be able to spend time with him and show him."

She nodded.

"From now on, the rule about asking for permission to speak to someone doesn't apply to Seth. In fact, he can grant you permission to speak. He'll pretty much be going everywhere with us from now on, so his word is as good as mine."

She nodded.

"Seth's going to need some time to get used to the way you normally dress around here," Kaden said with a smile. He slipped his hand under her shirt. "In addition to not being totally formal, why don't you keep a shirt handy for a while?"

Seth couldn't get the memory of Leah's naked body and shaved mound out of his mind. "I doubt that's going to help," he grumped.

"I don't mind helping you with that," Leah softly said, blushing.

Seth frowned, certain he'd misheard her. "Huh?"

Kaden closed his eyes and kissed her temple. "It will happen sooner or later."

Seth felt like his body went numb. "Okay. While I'll admit there's part of me that wants to take you up on that right now, there's another part of me screaming bloody murder that I'm totally creeped out by you both being so okay with this."

"It's okay, Seth," Leah said. Her voice had dropped almost to a whisper. "Kaden and I talked." She took a deep breath, and her eyes brimmed again. Damn it, he hated seeing her so upset. "He's right that it will happen eventually. It's not fair to you to keep you hanging. I don't want to do that to you."

Seth started to speak then snapped his mouth shut again, speechless. He finally managed to string coherent words together. "Give me some time to get used to this, guys."

Kaden opened his eyes. Seth saw he struggled not to cry. "I don't *have* a lot of time. We don't have time for blushing bullshit. *I* don't have time. I know you're weirded out. I know it's uncomfortable." His hand stroked her hair again. Seth suspected it was more an unconscious gesture to comfort himself at that point. "There's no use dancing around the fucking issue. While I appreciate that you love me enough to not be a prick about this, you don't need to spare my feelings. After a couple of weeks with us I think you'll understand how and why I can do this."

Seth wasn't sure of that, but he nodded anyway.

As if to pull himself back from the brink of his emotional pain, Kaden took a deep breath. "Back to the rules." He looked at Leah. "No one is allowed to touch her—ever—except you and me. Only in an emergency."

Back to mass confusion for Seth. "She's hugged me before. And I've seen her hug and shake hands with people."

Kaden shook his head. "Sorry. I mean in non-vanilla circumstances. Or when we're vanilla-formal. Besides, a lot of the rules we have I've never applied to you. You're around so much, you're family. It wouldn't have been practical without outing ourselves."

Seth pinched the bridge of his nose. "Do I get a glossary of terms and a syllabus for this whacked-out course I'm cramming for?"

Leah actually laughed a little at that. When Seth looked at her again, her sad smile made his heart thump in a strange way. At least he'd made her smile in this whole crazy mess.

She shared a brief glance with Kaden. He nodded. She spoke. "Vanilla means, you know, everyday, plain, normal setting. Like what you used to see us as before all this. Vanilla formal means we're doing something but no one else knows what's going on. Like a private game in public. Formal is just that, how I address you and Master in public or private, how I dress, what you do with and to me. Informal is still we're playing but not with the protocols."

"Protocols?"

"You'll learn them," she quietly said. "It'll be okay. You'll do fine. I know you will."

"Do you ever, you know, relax in private?"

Kaden took over, nodding. "Usually, unless Leah's very stressed, she doesn't call me Master unless we're having a session. But for now…" He stroked her hair again. "It's comforting to her. It helps her cope."

She nodded but didn't speak.

Seth felt his heart break for both of them. How the hell was he supposed to help them through this and do what he was supposed to do *and* deal with losing Kaden?

Kaden's dying.

Kaden kissed her one more time. "We can deal with more stuff later. Go get the big guest room ready for him. We want him in there. It's got its own bathroom."

She nodded, climbed out of Kaden's lap, and kissed his hand again. She started to leave the room, then turned to Seth. "I know this isn't any easier on you than it is on us. I appreciate this. I really do."

Seth watched her go. He finally turned back to Kaden.

"You'll need to go to the doctor," Kaden said, low enough his voice wouldn't carry down the hall. "I don't want to sound like an asshole, but you need a full round of testing for HIV and STDs. Your last ex was a royal bitch. Frankly, I heard rumors she slept around on you. I also want you to get a full physical. I'll pay for it."

Seth felt his stomach roll in a bad way. He'd heard the same rumors but never wanted to think about them. "Okay," he hoarsely whispered.

"I'll have Leah make you an appointment with my doctor. She'll go with you and take care of the bill. I also want to make sure you're healthy. If you've got any issues we need to catch them early, get you taken care of. I know you've got VA, but I want you checked out now. It's bad enough I'm dying on her. She damn sure doesn't need to lose you, too." His voice choked at the end. Seth wondered at his friend's inner strength. If their positions were reversed, Seth suspected he'd be a blubbering mess by this point.

"What if I fuck this up?" Seth whispered. "What if I can't do this right for her?"

Kaden drained the last of his drink. "You can, and you will. I know you can. She won't let you fail. Neither will I."

"Glad you're so confident."

They sat in silence until Leah returned. She took Kaden's hand and kissed it before cuddling in his lap.

When Leah next spoke, it nearly startled Seth.

"I'm glad Kade asked you. If nothing else…" She choked up, paused, then spoke. "If nothing else, I mean, down the road…I know I can always turn to you, like that at least, even if you decide you want to move on. I know I can count on you. You guys have been best friends for so long. You're my best friend, too. You're my oldest friend. I mean that. You really are. I've always felt comfortable around you."

"Even that night in the Keys?"

She laughed, loud and genuine that time. "Yeah. Especially that night."

Kaden smiled. "She almost let the cat out of the bag that night."

Seth thought back, then remembered. "Wait! You did call her 'love' that night, I remember now. And you—"

She nodded. "I almost called him Master."

Seth remembered the night fifteen years earlier. They'd been on a lobster trip with some other friends, hitting the two-day mini season when every yahoo with a tickle stick and a lobster gauge was out on the water. Two of their buddies got into a bar fight. Kaden had gone to the bathroom before it started, and by the time he returned the whole place was involved.

Leah had gotten trapped in a corner behind two guys duking it out. When Kaden started her way, another guy jumped him. Seth, realizing what happened, immediately abandoned the friend he'd been trying to help and fought his way over to Leah, grabbed her, and ran outside to the car with her.

And in near hysterics when she'd seen Kaden fighting with another guy, she'd screamed for him, shouting, "Mas—Kaden!"

When Kaden finally fought his way out a minute later and ran to join them, he scooped her into his arms and called her 'love.'

Seth never would have admitted it, but later that night he lay in his bed in their rented condo and listened to them make love the next room over and thought how good it felt holding her for those few seconds, how good her hair had smelled, how protective he felt of her.

How envious he'd felt of Kaden.

"I made apple pie this afternoon," she said, bringing him back to the present. "I bought vanilla ice cream for you. Can I get you some?"

He blushed again. Leah taking care of him.

"Admit it," Kaden gently teased. "She takes good care of you already."

"How the hell do you read my mind like that?"

"I keep telling you. Maybe the problem all these years was that you hadn't found the right woman."

"I'll be honest with both of you. I'm not sure I can get used to having a 'slave' serving me hand and foot." Seth used finger quotes around the word.

"It's not like that," Leah insisted. "I get as much out of this as Kade does. With you, too." She blushed. "I mean, when I'm doing things for you. Like cooking dinner and stuff."

Kaden patted her thigh. "Go fix us some pie, please."

She kissed him and went to do it.

Kaden dropped his voice. "It's not about sex, either. That's tied into it, but in our case it boils down to giving her what she needs to function. Some people are in it for the sex. Yeah, the sex is hotter for us because of this. I won't lie. You'll find it's the hottest fucking sex you've ever imagined. But it's not about the sex. It's about fulfilling a need for someone. She needs to serve. She needs the structure, the safety and security. And the release for her emotional pain. Just keep an open mind. Have I ever lied to you?"

Seth shook his head. No, Kaden had never, as far as he knew, lied to him.

He was probably the one person Seth knew never would lie to him.

Kaden stood and motioned Seth to follow him to the kitchen. They took up two seats at the counter and watched while Leah finished the preparations. She even nuked Seth's a little to warm it before adding the ice cream.

The perfect way he liked it.

She handed Kaden his first. When she slid Seth's plate in front of him, she touched his hand and waited until he met her eyes.

"It's okay," she said. Then she gently squeezed his hand before letting go and fixing her own plate.

He hated himself that her touch made him harder than a rock.

"Any house rules I need to know about?" he asked, to distract himself more than anything.

Kaden shrugged. "Toilet seat down after you go, but you're good about that anyway."

"I figured you'd tell me rules about the dungeon," Seth snarked.

Kaden laughed, then sighed. "Honesty. Never lie. The only way this works is if we all talk to each other. It's going to feel weird and uncomfortable at first. It will get easier, I promise."

"Can't get much fucking worse," Seth muttered.

Kaden continued. "Whenever red is called, whatever's going on immediately stops without question, regardless of whether it's her or you or me calling it. You'll learn the routines and protocols as we go. It becomes automatic after a while. Oh, I'll give you keys in the morning. You already know the gate code, and the house alarm code is 1218."

"Leah's birthday." Seth didn't realize he'd spoken aloud until he looked up and saw her sad smile.

"You remember."

Kaden also smiled, to Seth's surprise. His friend clapped him on the arm, squeezing briefly before letting go. "See? You'll do fine."

They finished. Finally, Seth excused himself. "I need to go to bed, guys. I'm worn out. Frankly, my brain's fried. I don't know how I'm going to get through class tomorrow."

He walked to what was now his bedroom and closed the door behind him. Looking around, even though he'd stayed here before, he saw it for the first time. The bed was perfect, king-size, a helluva lot better than the rocklike mattress at his brother's. Not that he'd ever complain to his brother, because it had been free and a roof over his head. He always slept well when he spent the night at Kade's. The room was nearly twice as large as the one at his brother's, and the attached bathroom as large as many master bathrooms in smaller homes.

He'd started unbuttoning his shirt when he heard a soft tap on his door. He opened it. Leah stood in the hall. Kaden had apparently gone on to bed, because their door was shut.

Seth's heart hammered, panic threatening. "Leah, I meant it when I said I can't do anything—"

She shook her head. "No! No. I...I just wanted to say good night. And thank you." She looked up at him. "And you didn't give me my hug when you got here tonight."

He laughed but it came out sounding harsher than he intended. "You sort of caught me off guard with that outfit." This one wasn't much better, especially now that he knew what was under it. Or rather, what wasn't.

After a long moment, he opened his arms to her. Even though he tried to lean his upper body into it, to keep her away from his hips and feeling his hard-on that demanded attention, she pressed into him. Not lewdly or even seductively.

Desperately.

When he realized this, he relaxed and held her tightly, worried she'd cry. But she didn't, despite clinging to him like a drowning woman.

It took several minutes before she relaxed a little. "Thank you," she whispered. "I know this sucks for you. I'm sorry."

"Hey." He made her look at him. "Stop. If things were different and we were single, I'd..." Suddenly, that sounded like a really stupid thing to say under the circumstances.

But she smiled again. "Yeah. I would, too." She rested her head on his chest for a moment longer and he'd be lying if he said he didn't enjoy it.

"Just...go easy on me, okay?" he said. "You guys are going to fry my brain at this rate."

She stretched up and kissed his cheek. He was a little taller than Kaden's five eleven and knew that would be an adjustment for her.

"Just remember, I can and do have the ability to stop anything I don't like," she assured him. "I always have. There have been times in the past I've red-lighted a scene. Kaden usually does before I do, but I have. So don't ever worry about going too far. As long as you respect the safe word, you won't hurt me."

She left, quietly closing the door behind her.

* * * *

Seth got up around two a.m. to get a drink of water. Leah had left a robe hanging on the bathroom door for him. Instead of getting dressed he pulled that on. When he opened the door he heard a soft, strange, rhythmic noise he couldn't quite place.

The house was dark. A few carefully placed nightlights and his familiarity helped him make it to the kitchen without incident. The noise sounded louder now and almost sounded like...splashing?

He spotted a dark shape on the lanai. When he stepped out the kitchen slider, he saw Kaden standing in the shadows, staring at the pool and leaning against the wall near the sliders leading to the master bedroom.

The pool light wasn't on. In the dark water, Leah maintained a blistering pace down and back. He knew she swam a lot, one of the reasons Kaden had the large twenty-five meter pool built, but...day-amn.

Kaden didn't look at him, never took his eyes off the pool. He leaned in as Seth stood next to him. "Your first lesson. Never leave her alone when she's like this," he murmured.

"Does she know we're watching her?"

"No. If she cries before she gets out, she'll be okay. If she comes out looking like a fucking zombie, I'll immediately take her to the playroom."

Seth stared at Kaden. Kaden smiled in the dark. "Sorry. That's what we call it. Sounds better than 'dungeon,' don't you think?"

Seth stood vigil with Kaden for nearly an hour. He couldn't believe she was still going when she finally pulled up short at the shallow end and stood, gasping, leaning against the edge. She stood frozen for several minutes, then sank beneath the water.

A low moaning sound floated out of the pool, accompanied by a flurry of bubbles. She broke the surface and took a long, hitching breath before sinking below the water again.

Kaden nodded. "That's good."

"What the fuck?"

He looked at Seth. "She's screaming."

She repeated this for nearly ten minutes before resting her head on her arms on the pool's edge, softly crying.

Kaden nodded again and gently tapped Seth's arm, pointing to the kitchen sliders. They went inside and closed the door behind them.

"What the fuck?" Seth asked again.

Kaden shrugged. "She wears herself out in the pool, pushes herself to the point of physical exhaustion. I mean, she can't spank herself. She promised me she won't cut herself, although right now I'm scared she might not be able to keep that promise if we can't keep on top of things. She punishes herself. If it was daylight, she'd probably go run five miles or something. She hasn't had to do this in a long time. I thought she might do it last night but she didn't. She was too exhausted from crying."

"How will I know?"

Kaden looked grim. "You'll know. You might think you'll sleep through it, but you'll get to the point where if she rolls over in bed at night, you'll know it."

Seth glanced out the sliders, where in the soft moonlight he watched Leah crying in the pool. "Shouldn't we go out there to her?"

Kaden shook his head. "Not right now. Not in a case like this."

"Fuck."

"There will be times she'll come to you and outright ask to play."

"Play? Is that whips-and-chains-excite-me code?"

Kaden smirked. "Yeah. Whatever. There will be times she gets bratty."

"Bratty?"

"I know. It's a lot to explain. When she's bratty, sometimes she needs play, and sometimes she needs punishment."

"Whoa." Seth rubbed his forehead. "If whipping her isn't punishment, what is?"

"Withholding."

"Huh?"

"Not letting her play. You'll learn the difference about what she needs."

"You've so fucking confused me now, I'm lost."

"If a kid begs for ice cream in a store and pitches a tantrum, do you give it to them?"

"What the fuck do I know about kids?"

"Well?"

Seth sighed. "I don't know. I guess not."

"You don't give it to them. It's rewarding bad behavior if you do. A lot of times you'll know from her body language, how she's talking, interacting with you. You'll see her start to…I call it 'dull down.' It's like she's zonked out. Not just tired. Like she's detaching. It's fucking spooky. You'll learn to tell the difference between normal tired and that. Then she needs a session. Under normal circumstances our regular trips to the club are enough to keep her going without extra sessions. We might have very light play sessions here during the week.

"But now…" He looked out the sliders. "I'm hoping once the shock wears off and she's helping teach you that it will give her enough to focus on and I can back off on the sessions for a while. We'll have to keep a close eye on her."

It sounded both weird and right for Kaden to say "we" when talking about her. "Why aren't we out there with her right now?"

"Because when she does something like this and can find release on her own, it's better for her to handle it on her own. It's helping her cope in a healthy way. She'll come find me—or you now, too, I guess, depending on what's happening—if she needs aftercare."

Seth rolled his eyes. "Great. More vocabulary."

Leah climbed out of the pool. Now it registered in Seth's mind that she was naked. In the low light he hadn't noticed before.

Kaden headed for his bedroom. "I'll talk to you in the morning."

Seth finally got his drink of water and returned to his room in a daze.

What had he said yes to?

Despite his swirling mix of emotions, he knew he couldn't back out now.

Chapter Four

Seth awoke to the smell of coffee and…

Mmm. Bacon.

Leah was a great cook. He remembered his stay with them after his surgery, when she cooked every meal for him. They'd spent a lot of time talking while he was with them, with Kaden gone to work every day. Leah stayed home and took care of him. She was always comfortable to talk to.

He rolled over and looked at the clock. Seven thirty.

He was about to get up when he heard a soft tap on his door. He pulled the sheet back over him because he'd slept naked. "Yes?"

The door opened. Leah peeked in, smiling. Despite her puffy eyes the smile looked genuine. "Coffee."

He nodded. "Thanks. I'll come get some in a minute."

She pushed the door open. He was relieved to see she was wearing a long T-shirt in addition to the collar. "No, silly. I have your coffee." He realized she carried a steaming mug.

"Oh. Thank you." He nervously smoothed the covers to hide his morning boner, then realized that might have made matters worse.

She walked the mug over to him and set it on the bedside table. "You don't have to thank me."

"Um, it would be rude if I didn't, babe."

"I owe you, not the other way around." She took a deep breath as her smile faltered before she regained it. "I've got maple bacon, scrambled eggs, and I'm starting the French toast now."

"Jesus, Leah. I'm going to look like a water buffalo in a month."

Her playful grin finally reached her eyes. "Don't worry. I'll help whip you into shape."

She left him laughing.

* * * *

He'd take a shower at his brother's before he went to class. He dressed, then walked out to the kitchen. Leah stood at the stove. The place smelled great. He had to admit he'd really missed this. During his earlier stay, he'd quickly grown to love being with Leah and Kade.

It felt like a home. In a way he'd never felt, even with his ex-wives.

"Where's Kade?" He took his usual place at the counter.

"He'll be out in a few minutes." She walked over and took his mug without asking, poured him more coffee.

"Thanks."

She started to say something, but he held up a hand. "Listen. Y'all are just going to have to get used to me saying thank you." Leah smiled again. He studied her. "I'm still convinced this is a really whacked-out nightmare or something. No offense, hon."

He wished he'd kept his fucking mouth shut, because she looked sad again.

Kaden's dying.

She nodded. "I know," she whispered. "Me too. No offense."

They both froze, then nervously laughed. He stood and held out his arms. She went to him, and he hugged her. For once his cock decided to behave.

"You know," he said, "after a month you might get sick of me and toss me out on my ass."

She pressed tighter against him. "No. Never. We'd never get sick of you, Seth. I'll never get sick of you."

He retook his seat while she returned to the stove. "So what does one wear to a dungeon?"

She laughed. "You'd be surprised. Jeans are okay if you want, for tonight. Black jeans if you have them. I don't think Kade's will fit you."

"Don't feel like wearing clam diggers, even if I thought I could pull them over my gut."

"Hey, no short jokes. I can't help it you have long legs like a freak of nature." Kaden rounded the corner and clapped Seth on the back. "Sleep okay?"

He nodded.

Kaden crossed the kitchen and wrapped his arms around Leah from behind, kissed the back of her neck. "Good morning, angel."

"Good morning, handsome."

Seth felt a little uncomfortable and tried not to watch but couldn't help it.

He also couldn't help the thought that both sickened and excited him, that maybe she'd say something like that to him one day.

kaden'sdying

Crap.

* * * *

Seth tried to focus on what Kaden was saying and not on watching Leah at the stove. Even with the long T-shirt, he still made out the sweet curve of her ass beneath the fabric. Kaden reached into his shorts and handed Seth a set of keys.

"For the house, cars, everything. You need a set."

Seth hefted them. He currently had two keys, one for his car and one for his brother's house. It felt weird having a multitude of keys again. "Thanks."

"The playroom code is also 1218."

"I'm not ready to tackle that yet."

"You need to know it anyway."

They ate in relative silence. When they finished, Leah automatically cleared their plates and gently refused Seth's offer to help. She grabbed a personal organizer and pen from her purse. "What's your class schedule?"

Twenty minutes later, she had all the information she needed from him. Seth had to get moving to make it to class. He hugged Leah good-bye. Kaden walked him out to his car.

He looked aged, even from the day before. It saddened Seth to realize he wasn't going to grow old with this man, sharing stories about kids and grandkids on a front porch somewhere while they put mileage on their respective rockers. Somehow, the thought that Kaden wouldn't be around had never, before this, crossed his mind. If anything, he thought he would be the one dying first, strong and steady Kaden always there like the moon in the sky.

"What time do you think you'll be back?" Kaden asked.

"My class is over at one. I'll go back to Ben's and start packing." He snorted in disgust. "Won't take long. I don't have very much."

Kaden nodded at the Ridgeline. He'd bought it a couple of months earlier. "Why don't you take my truck? Make it easier on you."

Seth started to protest, then snapped his mouth shut.

Kaden's grey eyes met his and that fucking mental heart beat—

kaden'sdyingkaden'sdying

—threatened to take him over and drive him to his knees.

"Okay," Seth said.

"We'll have dinner before we go. We'll leave around eight for the club."

Seth nodded.

Then Kaden hugged him. He tried not to listen to the haggard, choked sound of his friend's breathing because Seth knew it would send him over the edge.

After a long moment, Kaden stepped back and wiped his eyes. "Thanks, man," he hoarsely said. "Seriously."

Seth looked at the ground. "I've got to tell you, I'm not comfortable with some of this. I mean… Okay, yes, she's beautiful. But she's your wife."

"Not anymore," he whispered.

Seth dumbly stared at him, horrified. "Dude, you're not dead yet! Please, don't rush things."

Kaden sadly smiled. "I decided the easiest way for me to get through this is to rearrange my thinking a little. It makes it easier that way. When I'm gone, she's going to be your wife. Right now, she's not my wife anymore, and she's not yours. She's ours."

"You are fucking whacked. Even for a goddamned attorney."

Kaden laughed. "Yeah, tell me about it. I'll be honest, when I thought about it that way, something inside me was okay with it. I felt so fucking jealous and angry that you'll have all these years with her that I won't. I knew I had to get through that somehow, because she needs me to teach you and I can't let my ego get in the way of that. When I thought about her being ours…" He wiped his eyes again. "Yeah, it's fucking whacked. Give me what I can hold on to, buddy. Okay?"

Seth nodded. "Okay."

Kaden helped Seth get his books and a few other things he needed and put them in the Ridgeline. It felt weird driving it, even though he'd driven it before.

It felt…

He shuddered.

kaden'sdying

* * * *

His sister-in-law had the day off from work. When Seth walked into the kitchen, Helen turned, smiled, and then her face fell. "Seth? What's wrong?"

He sat at the table, his head in his hands.

"Kaden's dying," he sobbed.

He barely felt her comforting arm around his shoulders as he cried.

* * * *

Somehow, Seth made it through class. Helen helped him pack when he returned. He didn't tell her everything about their new arrangement, only that Kaden and Leah had asked him to move in with them because of the obvious, that he wanted Leah to have help with him as his illness progressed. He did hint that Kaden was worried about Leah's state of mind and wanted Seth there to take care of her as much as to take care of him.

Helen looked sad. "They're so sweet. You guys have been friends for so long. Ben will be upset to hear about Kaden."

"I don't know how many people he's telling right now. Tell Ben not to tell anyone yet, okay?"

She nodded. "Right."

When all his stuff was crammed into the Ridgeline, Helen hugged Seth. "Give us a call. Don't be a stranger."

"I appreciate you guys putting up with me. I feel like the neighborhood stray dog everyone takes pity on."

"Hey, don't be hard on yourself. You've had a rough time. I'm sorry about Kaden."

He struggled not to cry again. It'd been hard enough to hold it together during class. He didn't want to break down in front of Leah and Kade.

"Thanks." It was after four when he started for their house. Halfway there, he pulled into a Publix parking lot and cried again. How was Leah holding it together? He was a fucking wreck.

After twenty minutes he put himself together and pulled into their driveway a little after five. Kaden walked out, smiling, as Seth backed up to the garage. He already had the tailgate down by the time Seth climbed out.

"Glad to see you, buddy. I sort of worried you might have second thoughts."

Seth snorted as they started unloading boxes into the garage. "I did. And third and fourth and fifth but I guess you're stuck with me. God only knows why you want me."

Leah walked outside wearing her collar and dressed in shorts and a T-shirt, much to Seth's relief. Her sad smile and welcoming hug set something spinning inside him.

"I'll take your clothes and get them unpacked for you." He handed her a suitcase and one of the several garbage bags holding his clothes. She took them inside.

"That's why I want you," Kaden said in a low voice. "That woman right there. She needs you."

Kaden helped Seth get the rest of the boxes neatly stacked in the garage while Leah took care of all his clothes. His ex-wife had ended up with the house and furniture. To avoid bankruptcy, he'd sold off everything relating to his business. That left him with a beat-up Mustang and what was now sitting in Kaden's garage, mostly books and some personal mementos.

"We'll get new bookshelves for the bedroom," Kaden offered, studying the boxes. "This weekend, we'll go out and get some."

"No, it's okay."

"It's *not* okay." Kaden turned to Seth and dropped his voice, angry. "What aren't you understanding? This is *your* home now. You live here. Yeah, it's my name on the deed, but you need to get used to the idea that you are lord and master of this fucking place, so to speak. The faster you can get that through your thick skull, the faster you can help her, because I don't have time for this kind of bullshit when you've got serious stuff to learn!"

Seth stepped back as Kaden closed his eyes and took a deep breath, calming himself. Had he thought Kaden was handling this remarkably well? Apparently not as well as Kaden tried to portray.

"I'm sorry," Kaden apologized. He stepped closer to Seth, his voice low and calm again. "When I...when it happens, you need to be at the point where you literally step in and fully take over in name as well as function. Leah needs to see you in that role by that time. It'll be too late to get her trust and faith in you by then."

He jabbed his finger at Seth. "That means you need to drop the bullshit, right now, and step up, buddy. I know it sucks. I know it's weird. I know it's contrary to every fucking thing you might feel right now. But you need to get used to pulling up in that driveway and looking at this house and thinking, 'I'm home. This is my house. That's my wife.' When you're doing that, she'll feel it, and it will help her."

Seth nodded, unable to think of a reply. Kaden returned to the house. Seth looked around. Leah had already taken all his clothes inside. He suddenly realized she'd also grabbed a bag containing dirty clothes.

He grabbed his guitar case and hurried inside. When he reached his bedroom she was still there, organizing his clothes for him, some things now neatly folded and stacked on his bed, dresser drawers open, the closet half-full. He anxiously searched for the bag of dirty clothes. When she looked at him, she laughed.

"I already got the dirty ones."

Stunned, his jaw dropped. "What, being into this stuff turns you psychic or something?"

She pointed to a pile on the floor in the bathroom. "You looked panicked. Don't worry, I figured it out as soon as I opened the bag."

He reddened, embarrassed. "I'm sorry, Leah. I'll go wash them." He started for the bathroom.

She frowned, firmly shaking her head. "No."

"What do you mean no?"

"That's *my* job."

"Leah—"

"No!" Her eyes widened. At her nearly frantic tone, Seth held up his hands in supplication.

"Whoa. Calm down, babe."

But she wasn't calm. "No! It's *my* job, Seth. *I* do that. I take care of Kaden, and I take care of you." Her whole body trembled. Kaden suddenly appeared in the doorway, a worried look on his face. He didn't speak, just stood there watching. Seth suspected Leah didn't know he was there.

Seth tried again, forcing his voice to stay calm. "Leah, honey, I don't expect—"

She stepped forward, almost in his face now, looking up at him. "It's *my* job. *Please*."

He glanced at Kaden, looking for help, but his friend stood there, unmoving, observing.

Swallowing hard, Seth finally nodded. He placed his hands on her shoulders and gently squeezed. "Okay, honey. It's okay. I'm sorry."

He heard her ragged breathing, watched her pulse thrum in her throat, her face flushed not from excitement but...

She stared at him, and he recognized the look from the night before. Barely constrained anguish fighting to bubble to the surface.

He suspected this was his second lesson.

Not sure what else to do, he grabbed her hands and gently squeezed them. "Babe, he told you to go easy on me. You've got to teach me this shit, remember?" He attempted what he hoped looked like a gentle smile. From the dangerous roll his stomach took, he wasn't sure he made it.

She finally took a deep breath, then stepped into him for a hug. "I'm sorry, Seth," she mumbled against his chest. "I know."

It felt weird to hug her like that, knowing Kaden was watching. But when Seth looked at his friend, Kaden nodded and offered up a smile before silently disappearing down the hall.

Seth figured he must have passed this test.

She clutched at him, the same desperation from the night before. He dared rest his face against the top of her head, inhaling her scent. She always smelled good.

"We'll get through this," he whispered. "I promise. I'm fucking lost and I might be stumbling and tripping all over myself, but I won't let you down."

"I know."

After a couple of minutes she stepped back, sniffling, and forced a smile. "Let me show you where I put everything." She finished putting his clothes away, showed him where she'd stowed his stuff, including his toiletries in the bathroom. When she finished, she turned. "Any questions?"

"What *do* you want me to do with my dirty clothes?"

"Just leave them on the bathroom floor for me. Do you normally take your shower in the morning or at night?"

That was a weird tangent. "Usually in the morning. I mean, I need one now after moving that crap but usually just in the morning."

"Before breakfast?"

"Um, I guess. No one's usually cooking for me."

She smiled. "Get used to it. What time do you need to be up in the morning?"

He shrugged. "It depends on if I'm working or have classes. Well, I guess working doesn't matter anymore." He'd stopped by after class to quit and pick up his final check. When he explained the basics of the situation, his boss understood and didn't give him any grief.

"I need to know so I can make sure you're up."

"Leah, you don't—" At her storm-cloud look he immediately backpedaled. "You don't have to do that all tonight. We can sit down this weekend and figure it out."

At that she relaxed.

Fuck.

His three ex-wives never doted on him like this. And he wasn't even sleeping with Leah.

Yet.

Fuck.

* * * *

Seth took a shower and joined Kaden in the den. Kaden sat on a stool as he idly strummed his guitar. Leah had already moved Seth's to the den, the case freshly dusted and leaning against the wall in the corner. Kaden didn't lift his head, but his eyes met Seth's.

Seth took a seat in one of the chairs and shook his head. "Fuck."

Kaden smiled and returned his attention to the guitar. "See why I needed you to move in? That isn't something I can explain."

"She nearly had a meltdown over my dirty clothes, for chrissake! Why the fuck didn't you come in and help me, asshole?"

He shrugged. "I watched. I was worried for a minute that she'd need to go to the playroom. You did good. That was smart, reminding her what I told her about teaching you."

Seth closed his eyes. "That wasn't planned, dude. I didn't know what else to say."

"But you said the right thing." He laid his palm over the strings to silence them and looked at Seth.

"I have to let you find your way with her as much as I can. It'll be too much of a shock for her to lose me and try to adapt to doing things your way all at the same time. There are some things you have to learn to do exactly right, and those I will work with you on. Those relate to safety and to her security. There's stuff like what happened earlier… There's not a lot of time, but we have enough for the two of you to work on some things on your own. I won't be there to help you out. You need to learn to deal with her in your way, not mine. To find things that will work for you and her. I can give you the map. You've got to make the journey."

"Thank you, Master Fucking Yoda."

Kaden smiled and strummed his guitar.

* * * *

Leah called them to dinner. Seth noticed she'd prepared his favorite foods. After dinner, he walked into the living room to watch TV with Kaden.

"This feels weird, to be able to sit back and relax," Kaden said.

"Relax?"

"Yeah, I know. Weird, huh?" He sighed. "New perspective. What's really important now. Usually I'd still be working on a night like this. Getting home about this time, wolfing down dinner and changing clothes so we could turn around and go to the club." He looked at Seth. "It changes a man's perspective, that's for sure. When you go back to school and get your degree and start working again, don't ever forget what's important."

They talked for a little while, then Kaden stood. "Time to get ready."

Seth wasn't sure he had the right wardrobe. "I've got jeans, but I'm a little short on latex."

Leah walked in from the kitchen and laughed. "I picked you up a couple of shirts this afternoon you can choose from. They're in your closet. Just wear jeans and your black sneakers."

They retreated to their rooms. Seth looked in his closet and, sure enough, found the shirts Leah had mentioned. Three button-up long-sleeved chambray shirts, nothing especially noteworthy. One black, one navy, one dark purple.

It didn't take him long to change. She'd apparently already washed and ironed them, because they smelled like detergent.

He nervously waited in the living room and debated having a drink but wasn't sure if that was a good idea. Kaden appeared first, a long duffel bag slung over his shoulder. He wore black jeans, black sneakers, and a button-up long-sleeved charcoal-grey shirt.

"Somehow, I always pictured leather vests and metal studs," Seth snarked.

Kaden set the bag on the sofa. "Yeah, leather's too damn hot. I usually take my shirt off anyway, keeps me cooler and more freedom of movement. I'm not in this to make a fashion statement." He glanced down the hall and dropped his voice. "Tonight, just watch. Don't object to anything we do, and don't act shocked at anything you see. The only time you think about stepping in is if she calls red, I call red, or I ask you in to help."

"You said I wouldn't have to do anything!" Seth felt panic clambering for a hold again.

"I hope I don't. But if I need help, I'd rather ask you than Tony or someone else."

"How are you explaining who I am to these people?"

Kaden shrugged, sadness in his eyes. "The truth. That I'm training you to be Leah's new Master."

Seth didn't think anything could break through the shock that Kaden's matter-of-fact tone had struck him with.

Then Leah emerged from the bedroom.

The stiletto heels set off her long legs and curvy hips. The black leather skirt was marginally longer than the one she'd greeted him in the night before but not by much. The black leather bustier pushed her breasts up. He suspected her nipples would be visible if it wasn't for the short white cotton shirt that barely concealed her cleavage. She wore a different collar, a little heavier looking than the one she'd had on before, still attached with a heart-shaped lock and with a small silver tag hanging from it. Makeup and hair the same as the night before.

She stopped in front of Kaden. With her head tilted to the floor, she lifted her eyes. "I'm ready, Master."

"Very good, love. You look beautiful. Doesn't she look beautiful, Seth?"

Seth nodded, finally croaked, "Yes."

She bashfully smiled, which Seth thought was weird considering what he'd already witnessed. "Thank you, Sir."

Shocked, Seth looked at Kaden. "We're in formal mode now," Kaden explained. He grabbed the duffel bag—Seth wasn't sure if he wanted to know what was in that—and took Leah's hand. "Let's go play, love."

Chapter Five

They took Leah's Lexus, with Kaden driving. Seth was going to sit in the backseat, but Kaden guided Leah there first, not releasing her hand until she was seated. Before she let go, she kissed the back of his hand.

"Thank you, Master."

"You're welcome, love."

Seth numbly slid into the front passenger seat and tried to quiet his racing brain.

The club was located in a nondescript mixed-use commercial complex east of Sarasota, not too far from the interstate. Several dozen cars were already parked outside. Kaden took his glasses off and left them on the dash, then reversed the procedure for getting Leah out after he grabbed the duffel bag from the trunk. He took her hand, and she kissed his before carefully stepping out.

Seth wouldn't deny he was as hard as a rock.

She held Kaden's hand while Seth trailed behind them. In the foyer, Kaden spoke to someone at the desk and then turned to Seth. "Here. Take her." He offered up Leah's hand.

Unsure what to do, Seth took it, offering no resistance when she kissed the back of his hand and looked at him.

"Thank you, Sir," she said.

He nodded. "Um. Uh-huh. Yeah."

Kaden took out his wallet and paid Seth's cover charge, gave them information on Seth, and went over the basic dungeon rules and etiquette with him. When they finished, Kaden took Leah's hand and she kissed him again. Seth followed them inside.

Seth hoped his jaw didn't hit the floor. At various equipment stations, several people were already scening. Kaden handed Leah off to Seth again and went to talk to someone. She stood quietly by his side, holding his hand.

What do you say in a situation like that?

He said nothing, just watched what was going on around them. That was difficult though, because he was having a hard time taking it all in.

She gently squeezed his hand. When he looked down at her, she smiled. "It's okay."

He nodded and continued looking around.

Kaden returned a few minutes later with another man. "Seth, this is Tony." The guy didn't look much different than Kaden, dressed like he could be heading to a sports bar instead of a dungeon in black jeans and a black shirt.

They shook hands. Unsure what to say, Seth simply said, "Nice to meet you."

Tony smiled. "I know. A lot to take in at once."

"You ain't kidding, buddy."

Kaden traded Seth the duffel bag for Leah. "We'll be right back. Restroom."

Seth nervously stood there, looking around.

"Kaden said it's your first time," Tony said.

Seth nodded.

"You'll get used to it."

"That's what he keeps telling me. I'm not so sure." Across the room from them, a naked woman was strapped to a large X-shaped frame. She screamed. Seth wasn't sure if it was pain or pleasure at first until he realized she had a vibrator strapped onto her.

Tony leaned in close and dropped his voice. "Kaden told me what's going on. I'm sorry you've got all this shit dumped on you at once."

Seth nodded. "Thanks."

"I've known them for years. They've always spoken very highly of you."

That shocked Seth more than the sights before him. Tony spoke again. "Kaden has my number. Don't hesitate to call me if you need to talk, or information, or anything."

Seth whispered, "How am I supposed to learn all this?"

Tony shrugged. "You learn what you have to. They're on the tamer end of the scale, all things considered." The woman screamed again, her whole body vibrating against her restraints. Another woman, dressed in what Seth imagined a Dominatrix would wear, stood nearby and watched with an impassive look on her face. Now the tethered woman was wearing nipple clamps, with a chain joining them and attached to her…

Fuck.

"Tamer end? He gave me a demonstration last night. That didn't look fucking tame to me."

"He's an artist with rope. Did he show you that yet?"

"Just pictures."

"Gorgeous what he can do. If you're ever here and need advice, feel free to hunt me down. I know this has to be scary."

"Scary isn't even in the same fucking universe as what I'm feeling right now, dude." Ball-crawling heebie-jeebies might come close.

Maybe.

Kaden and Leah returned. Kaden reached for the duffel bag. "Let's go play, love," he said to her.

Seth drifted behind them, Tony walking beside him, toward a low bench.

Tony leaned in again. "Remember, what they do is carefully scripted and totally consensual. She rarely uses a safe word. He reads her body, knows what she can take. There's a lot of wannabes and poser assholes out there who claim they're 'expert' Doms. If I had to point to one, your best friend really is. He can pick a goddamned fly off a wall with a singletail. You'll never hear him brag about it either."

Seth nodded and waited for someone to tell him what to do.

Kaden turned to Seth. "Important rules. Never leave her alone or out of your sight, except for the bathroom. Never turn your back on her when she's bound. Most importantly, no one besides you or me—*ever*—touches her unless it's an emergency and they're helping you get her free. Understand?"

Seth nodded.

Kaden turned to Leah and released her hand. He dropped the duffel bag and flashed the hand signal. She dropped to her knees before him.

Seth felt something tighten in his stomach, at war with his restless cock stirring at the sight of her kneeling there. Tony touched Seth's shoulder. They stepped a few feet back to the edges where a couple of others now stood, watching.

When Kaden spoke, the strength and authority in his normally gentle voice surprised Seth. "Tell me what you want, slave."

"I want to serve You, Master."

"And how do you wish to do that, slave?"

"However Master thinks is best."

"Do you need to feel the bite, slave?"

Her skin flushed. "I need to feel the bite, Master."

"Prepare for me then, if you need it so badly."

She jumped to her feet and walked over to the bench. She stripped, neatly folding her clothes and laying them nearby with her shoes. Left only in her collar, she turned to Kaden, who had stripped off his shirt, and knelt again.

He took something from the bag and quickly fitted it around her head. When Kaden straightened, Seth realized it was a ball gag. Part of him felt horrified seeing Leah like that but the look in her eyes…

It was pure devotion as she stared up at her husband.

Kaden pointed. "Take your place, slave. Don't make me wait."

She jumped to her feet and practically threw herself on the bench. Kaden already had something in his hands. Within a few breaths he had four heavy leather cuffs attached to her wrists and ankles and secured to the bench, her ass and bare mound open and exposed.

"Holy fuck," Seth whispered.

Tony leaned in. "Consensual. Remember that."

Seth nodded.

Kaden stepped back, never turning his back on her. "Where are we, slave?"

She made an okay sign with her right hand.

"Show me your hands and feet."

She wiggled them all, flexing her fingers and toes.

"Circulation," Tony said.

"Very good, love." Kaden took out a nasty-looking device from the bag.

"Soft flogger," Tony explained in the same low voice. "He's going to warm her up." From his tone, he could have been calling a golf game.

The *Twilight Zone* theme played in Seth's brain.

Kade stepped up to her and caressed her ass. She wiggled, squirming on the bench as he positioned himself. He rolled his neck and shoulders and the tone of his voice deepened further. "Are you ready to feel the bite, slave?"

She wiggled her ass at him and flicked a signal with her right hand.

"Sign language," Tony said.

Seth felt he had a front row seat at the weirdest show on Earth.

"Set of twenty, love."

She flicked another sign.

"That means yes," Tony said.

"Count."

With each swat of the flogger she twitched her ass, and with her right hand made a sign, apparently counting in sign language. Kade quickly finished the set and caressed her slightly pink flesh.

"Where are we, love?"

She flashed another okay sign.

"Set of twenty, love."

She signed yes.

"Count."

Kaden savaged her, or what Seth imagined was a savaging. Tony leaned in. "It looks a lot worse than it is," he assured him. "You could smack a kid with that flogger and it wouldn't hurt them. It's very soft. He's putting her in subspace. Building up to the harder implements."

Great. More vocabulary.

Kaden finished the set and switched to a paddle. After a set of twenty-five with that, Seth noticed Leah's eyes had closed and she'd been crying. He desperately wanted to go to her, comfort her, and knew he couldn't.

Next came a set of twenty-five with a harsh-looking riding crop. Seth flinched with each stroke that landed on her flesh. At the end of that set, Kaden leaned in close and said something too low for Seth to hear. She nodded and flashed him a sign. Kaden tenderly stroked her forehead and then returned to the duffel bag.

He pulled out a whip.

Tony grabbed Seth's arm and pulled him back a couple of feet, then waved a few other people back. When the area was clear, Kaden glanced at Tony, who nodded.

"Do you need to feel the bite, slave?"

She signed yes.

"Are you prepared to serve your Master, slave?"

She signed yes.

He flicked the whip at her, cracking it but not striking her. She flinched and wiggled her ass at him.

Seth thought she might have moaned.

"I don't think you want it badly enough, slave. I don't think you need it." The hard, firm edge to Kaden's voice twisted Seth's gut. He'd never heard his friend talk like that. Especially never to Leah.

Tony leaned in again. "He's trying to draw it out for her tonight. He's not normally this hard in a public scene with her."

Hard. Funny choice of words. As sick as his gut felt, Seth was harder than a rock.

She signed something at Kaden and wiggled her ass again. Again he cracked the whip over her, not striking her.

Seth flinched at the sound.

Kaden walked over to her and struck her ass with his bare hand, from the looks of it hitting her squarely between the legs.

Seth winced. Even through the ball gag he heard Leah's moan.

And it didn't sound like she was in pain.

Kaden struck her again. It looked like she tried to grind herself against her husband's hand. He whispered something to her, and she moaned again, louder.

Two more swats and her whole body trembled.

Kaden quickly stepped back and nailed her ten times in quick succession with the whip, each strike hitting her squarely in the center of her now-red ass cheeks.

She screamed around the gag, her hips bucking.

Holy fuck! Seth realized she was coming.

Kaden swatted her bare-handed several more times, followed by another round of ten with the whip. When he finished he said, "Where are we, love?" His tone had softened to the tender voice he'd used with her the night before in the playroom.

She panted but flashed an okay sign.

Kaden quickly coiled the whip and put it away, then knelt beside her, stroked her forehead. He whispered something, and she nodded and closed her eyes. He quickly released her from the cuffs and pulled her into his lap. He removed the ball gag from her mouth, and she cuddled in his arms, recovering.

Seth swallowed hard. He wished it was his arms around her. Couldn't he skip the beatings and go right to the recovery phase with her? That would sure as hell make his life easier.

He was watching them when he heard loud voices from another part of the dungeon. A middle-aged, overweight man dressed in tight leather pants and a leather vest dragged a young woman around by a leash. The woman had something that looked like a gag in her mouth, and her hands were bound behind her.

He berated her, swatting her on the ass with a crop. "Fuck, didn't I tell you not to embarrass me tonight? You stupid cunt."

Tony's face hardened. Seth wasn't sure if it was part of their play or something else but the energy he felt from the crowd watching them didn't set him at ease. Kaden's scene had felt controlled, disciplined, respectful even. This asshole looked like, well, an asshole.

From the disgusted looks on some of the other people's faces, Seth got the impression the man wasn't very popular.

"How the hell did he con someone into playing with him?" Tony muttered.

"Who is he?"

"Baxter. He's a real asshole. That's not just play, what he's doing. I mean, some people are into humiliation, and that's fine if it's their kink. This guy really *is* an asshole. He goes through subs like some people change their socks, sometimes more. He's a fucking poser."

"Why do they let him in?"

"He hasn't violated any rules…yet. I guaran-damn-tee you, the first time he does he's out on his ass."

Seth watched as the guy dragged the poor woman around. She fell to the floor, and even from where Seth stood he heard her scream something.

Baxter looked down at her. "You're shitting me? You're safe wording me? We haven't done anything yet!"

She screamed something else. Tony looked like he was about to go over there when one of the dungeon monitors stepped in and whispered something to the guy.

"Aw, fuck. Fine! I was going to let her up."

As soon as the woman's arms were free she ripped the gag out of her mouth and spewed a stream of obscenities at the guy. She yanked off the collar and threw it at him. "Fuck you, Baxter!" she screamed, then stormed off.

Tony laughed. "Well, another one bites the dust."

Seth turned his attention back to Kaden and Leah. He was speaking to her now. She nodded, stood, and started dressing while he unclipped the cuffs from the bench, wiped it down, and put their accessories away. He slipped his shirt on and looked at Seth, tipped his head at him, indicating for him to step over.

Leah finished dressing and knelt before the two of them.

"Thank you, Master," she said.

He reached out his hand to her and she took it, kissing the back of it. He pulled her to her feet.

Kaden was about to say something to Seth when Baxter walked over.

"Kaden! Do you still have room in that class next weekend?"

"No." He turned from the guy. Seth noticed that Leah had tensed.

"Well, how about the one after that?"

Now Kaden looked tense. "I'm cancelling my classes for a while. I'm taking some time off."

Baxter struck Seth as one of those kinds who couldn't take a hint, had maybe learned his social skills on the free porn sites. "Why are you doing that?"

Tony stepped in. "None of your business."

"I wasn't talking to you."

"Well, you are now. Leave them alone. They're not done with their scene yet."

"You're here, and that guy's with them. What's up?"

Kaden grabbed the bag. He motioned Seth to follow him and made a beeline for the exit, Leah's hand firmly clamped in his.

Seth stayed close behind them and glanced back to see Baxter hurrying after them.

"Hey, Kaden, wait up," Baxter called.

Kaden swore under his breath and tossed his keys to Seth, handed Leah off to him. "Get her in the car. Now."

Seth didn't question him. He hurried Leah to the car and put her in the backseat. Then he locked her in and returned to Kaden's side. He wasn't sure what this asshole's problem was, but he'd be damned if he'd let Kaden face him alone.

Baxter glanced at Seth standing behind Kaden. "Kaden, look, if I pissed you off I'm sorry. I just want to sign up for a class."

"I told you, I'm taking time off from teaching. You'll have to take a class from someone else."

Seth wanted to deck the asshole.

"What's going on?" Baxter asked.

kaden'sdying

"No offense but it's none of your business. Come on, Seth."

"Look, I want to learn to treat my subs the way you treat Leah. Everyone says you're the best—"

Kaden whirled, suddenly in the guy's face. Seth worried he'd have to pull Kaden back. "Don't you *ever* think what you do and what I do are even remotely related, Baxter."

"Come on, I told you, I'll pay a lot of money to have a private training session with her! Please?"

Kaden shoved the guy. Seth pulled him back, getting between them. "He's not worth it," Seth growled in Kaden's ear, now worried. He'd never seen Kaden blow his cool before. Ever. And if he didn't stay focused on getting Kaden in the car, Seth knew he would deck the slimy son of a bitch himself for even thinking about touching Leah. "Let's go, Kade. Dude, let's get Leah home."

That broke through Kaden's anger. He let Seth guide him to the car, then slipped into the backseat with Leah while Seth slid behind the wheel.

Baxter stood with his jaw gaping, watching them leave.

"Who the fuck was that?" Seth glanced in the rearview mirror. Leah was curled in Kaden's lap, his face buried in her hair.

"Baxter's a prick. Real estate attorney. He's one of the assholes I was talking about who abuses subs. I had him in one of my classes. He was only worried about how hard he could hit someone. He's a real jerk."

Kaden didn't have to say anything else. Seth fought the urge to turn the car around and pound on the guy himself. The thought of that bastard wanting to lay a finger on Leah…

At home, Kaden helped Leah from the car, then scooped her into his arms and carried her inside. Seth followed them and dropped the duffel bag on the couch, unsure where it should go. He started for the kitchen to pour himself a drink when Kaden returned from their bedroom. Without a word he hugged Seth. After a moment, he released him.

"Thanks, man."

Seth nodded. "Yeah."

Kaden stepped back and took a deep breath. "That's why I need you," he hoarsely whispered. "That's why *she* needs you. Assholes like him. Problem is, there's a lot of assholes out there who aren't as obviously obnoxious as Baxter, who can sucker a sub in and then they abuse them. Or they play and drop them. They look like nice guys on the outside."

"Is she afraid of him?"

He nodded. "Not just him. After a scene she's extremely vulnerable. We never hang around after. We go, scene, and I bring her home immediately. If we hang around, it's before, never after."

Seth understood. That made sense. He could feel it in her, the way she seemed so...docile wasn't the right word, but it was close.

"Tell her good night for me."

Kaden smiled. "You can go tell her, if you want."

Seth shook his head. "No. I'm good." His cock had finally softened. The last thing he needed to see was her in that outfit. Or wearing even less.

Kaden patted him on the back and returned to their bedroom.

Seth found a bottle of bourbon and started to get a glass, then took another look at it.

No, maybe this wasn't the best way to go tonight.

He walked to the den and closed the door behind him. His guitar was way out of tune. He hadn't played it in ages. It took him a little while to tune it. He spent an hour trying to remember his way through old favorites. Mostly folksy stuff like Gordon Lightfoot, and even some Jimmy Buffett.

It felt good to play again. Their moms had made Kaden and him take guitar together. While they fought it at the time, when they realized they were both decent at it and the girls loved it, they quit complaining and had fun with it.

How many hours had he and Kaden played together, Leah sitting at their feet and leaning against Kaden or even against him, singing together? Playing for her.

kaden's dying

His fingers fumbled the chords. He tried again, blinking back tears.

The soft snick of the latch startled him. The den door swung open, and Leah stood in the doorway.

"Hey," he said.

"Hey."

"Are you okay?"

She nodded and stepped into the room. She wore the smaller black collar and a long T-shirt. "I couldn't sleep."

"Neither could I."

"Can I come in?"

He started to say of course she could, it was her house, then he remembered Kade's advice.

He nodded.

She pushed the door shut behind her. "We've had some good times," she wistfully said. "Lots of nights singing together."

Seth nodded, feeling guilty that those times hadn't been as many lately as they once were.

kaden'sdying

How many more nights did they have? "Yeah."

She sat at his feet and rested her head against his knee. It was something she'd done countless times over the years, but now the gesture took on a poignant new meaning for him.

For her too, probably, he suspected.

"Play 'Come Monday' for me," she softly asked. "Please?"

One of her favorites. While he knew his voice wasn't as good as Kade's, he softly sang to her, trying not to cry his way through the words.

He realized at the end of the song that she'd fallen asleep. The door swung open again and Kade looked in.

"Is she finally out?" he whispered.

Seth nodded and carefully put his guitar aside, trying not to jostle Leah. "How long have you been standing there?"

"I knew she came in here. I wanted to make sure she was okay." He walked in and carefully scooped her into his arms.

Seth beat his jealous pang back into submission.

He didn't care what Kaden said. She was still Kaden's wife.

"Good night, Seth," he whispered.

Seth nodded and waited for a moment, until he was sure Kaden had returned to their room.

He quietly closed the den door and picked up his guitar again.

Chapter Six

Seth awoke the next morning, feeling drained and sluggish. He'd made it to bed a little after three a.m., but his sleep was anything but soothing.

So many conflicting emotions swirling through him—

kaden'sdying

—mixed with the fear he couldn't step up and be enough for Leah no matter what he promised her.

He had class at one. Thank God tomorrow was Saturday. He felt he'd need a couple of days to vegetate. It was a little after seven when he stepped into the shower. Not having to work, he could at least get some study time in this morning.

The image of Leah bent over that bench…

He closed his eyes and rested his forehead against the cool shower tile. He fisted his cock, stroking, trying to work out a little tension. He wouldn't deny he'd love to sink his dick into her or feel her lips around him, but she wasn't his.

Not yet.

Seth stroked, finally able to shove conscious thought out of his mind in lieu of physical pleasure. He pounded his cock. It didn't take long, and it surprised him that the memory of her coming while strapped to that bench and being spanked by Kaden was what pushed him over.

As he recovered, taking deep breaths, a knock on his bathroom door startled him. He jumped, slipped, nearly fell but caught himself.

"Yeah?" he hoarsely called.

The door opened. Through the opaque shower door glass he made out Leah's shape.

"I brought your coffee."

He reddened, embarrassed. "Thanks."

"Want me to scrub your back for you?"

Despite what he'd just done, his cock immediately stiffened. "No," he hoarsely said, "I'm good. Thanks."

"You sure?"

"Um, yeah. Thanks. It's just...you know..." He couldn't finish and prayed she wouldn't open the shower door.

"Too soon?" she offered.

"Yeah. Exactly."

"Did you want French toast or pancakes?"

He looked down at his soft paunch. He wasn't horribly overweight, but he wasn't happy with how he'd let himself go over the years. He'd need to get back in shape. Next to Kaden he looked fat. "I need to go on a diet."

She leaned against the counter. "You need to eat a good breakfast. I'll make you a salad for lunch."

What did it say about him that he could have a conversation with her like this?

He'd better get used to it.

"Pancakes, please."

She sounded happy. "Good. I'll have everything ready when you get out."

"Thanks."

She left. He seriously considered jerking off again, but by the time he finished his shower he'd softened. He shaved, then went to get dressed. He stopped in the bathroom doorway.

Something was off. But what?

He looked around and it hit him. Leah had made the bed.

A wave of guilt swept through him. He'd meant to do it after his shower.

He caught sight of himself in the mirror over the dresser. A week ago, he'd been stuck in his rut but at least with a plan. In the space of just a couple of days his life had taken a hard right turn. In some ways amazing. For the most part...

He wished he could go back. He would settle for his old sucky life if it meant Kaden would always be in it.

* * * *

Kaden sat at the counter, a plate of food and the newspaper in front of him. "Morning. How'd you sleep?" he asked Seth.

"Fine."

Leah took Seth's coffee mug and refilled it, then slid a plate of food in front of him.

Kaden pushed the rest of the paper toward Seth. It felt surreal on a bunch of levels. That last night he was watching…and this morning… Ozzie and fucking Harriet. Literally.

Weird.

"Go ahead and take my truck again today. I'm not going anywhere this afternoon."

Seth nodded. It was easier to agree than protest.

After breakfast, Seth spread out with his books and laptop at the dining room table. Kaden left him alone, retreating to the study Seth used to think was Leah's. Now he realized it was Kaden's. Leah quietly worked around the house, unobtrusively, leaving him alone.

He almost managed to keep his mind on his studies.

A little before lunchtime, Leah paused in the dining room doorway.

"What's up, hon?" he asked.

"Did you want grilled chicken or turkey for your salad?"

The question took him off guard. "What?"

"What kind of meat?"

"Don't go overboard for me."

She stepped inside the room, a hint of thunderclouds rolling through her green eyes. "I'm not. I'm taking care of you."

He bit back a reply. Wouldn't most guys kill for this? For their own personal slave?

"Whatever Kade's having."

That answer seemed to soothe her. "What time do you think you'll be home? So I can plan dinner."

"I'll just grab something." He stopped when she frowned again. "I don't want you guys waiting on me to eat."

"It's okay. If you think you'll be late I can make Kaden's and have yours ready. I don't want you to eat fast food."

"Why doesn't Kaden weigh three hundred pounds?" he snarked.

She smiled. "I keep him busy."

Something he could laugh about. And it looked good to see Leah smile.

He leaned back. Before all this shit hit the fan they'd had fun playfully bantering back and forth, gentle teasing that never quite reached outright flirting but still fun and friendly. Not so much during his own marriages or around his wives, just in between.

And there were plenty of times in between.

"You going to keep me busy?"

She flushed a little. It stirred his cock despite his best efforts. "I hope so."

He waved her to him and pulled her into his lap despite knowing it wouldn't help his situation. She put her arms around his neck.

"You guys said honesty, so I'll be honest," he said. "I don't know how crazy I can be. How…" He fought to come up with the right words. "If I can keep up a full-time Master act. I'll do my best to do whatever you need me to do, but I'm probably going to need downtime from that."

"I know. A lot of the time Kaden and I aren't doing that." She smiled. "Well, except for my collar."

"And running around naked."

Her smile widened. "I like it. Just because I'm naked doesn't mean you have to act any different than you normally do. Just…sometimes."

Hell, he'd had a hard enough time getting his ex-wives naked in bed, much less to run around that way all the time.

"That'll be good enough for you?"

"Yeah."

"I mean, I'm going to want to be normal, whatever that is, a lot of the time."

She nodded. "I know. Me too."

"Just normal naked."

She grinned. "Right. Normal naked."

He wished she was wearing more than the long T-shirt and collar. "I know Kaden said something about not being formal for a while. Could we be whatever passes for vanilla normal around here for a couple of weeks? I've got exams to study for. Once I get the semester behind me you guys can start showing me full-time formal or whatever you call it."

She frowned. "You really should start learning some of the whip stuff."

"I'm not talking about that. I'm talking just everyday stuff, like right now. I know we've got a limited window of time. I need to ease into this.

It'll make it easier on me in the long run."

That seemed to make sense to her. She nodded. "Does that mean I need to wear clothes all the time?"

He resisted the urge to stroke her thigh. "How about when I'm trying to study, you should dress like this, at least."

She grinned. "And when you're not?"

Man up, asshole.

He shrugged. "Give me a few days before you start springing the full monty on me again, girl."

She hugged him. "Thank you, Seth," she whispered.

He put his arms around her and hugged her back.

Wormhole. Here was his best friend's wife, thanking him for allowing her to run around naked in front of him.

Or he'd died and dropped into some weird mix of Heaven and Hell all swirled together—

kaden'sdying

Leah went to fix lunch. Seth put his things away and found Kaden in his study.

While he was being honest, might as well go all the way. Seth sat and looked at his friend. "What the fuck am I supposed to do without you around, man? You're my best friend."

Kaden leaned back in his chair. "You'll get through it. The two of you will have each other."

"Are you sure there's no alternative? Treatment? Clinical trial?" He'd gladly give up a future with Leah to have Kaden alive.

Kaden's face hardened. He glanced at the open doorway. Leah was in the kitchen, too far to hear his low tone. "If they'd caught it a year ago, I might have considered it. Then the five-year prognosis goes up. Two years ago, I definitely would have. I'm around stage three. They'd have to cut into me to tell for sure. I told them fuck that. Where the tumor is, it's not operable according to the tests and MRI. Treatment would buy me a couple of months at the cost of what I could otherwise be doing. I will not make myself sicker just to die a little more slowly. You remember my dad."

Seth nodded. "Okay," he softly said.

"I think she's still in denial right now," Kaden said. "I really do. She's praying for a miracle."

"She'll have to get in line behind me on that one."

Kaden returned to a normal tone. "I want to give you a lesson this weekend with the singletail. It's the hardest to learn."

Seth recoiled, horrorstruck. "I'm not using that on her yet! Especially not right now."

Kaden smiled. "Relax, I didn't mean on her. Target practice. You need to get the feel for it, and I want to teach you that now, before..." He didn't finish, but Seth figured he knew what he meant.

Before he got too sick to teach him.

Kaden changed the subject. "I'm flying to Atlanta in a couple of weeks, to the office up there. I need to put some things in order. I'll schedule it for after you're out of classes so you're home with her. She's already quit a lot of her activities even though I told her she didn't have to."

"You didn't order her not to?" Seth knew that came out sharper than he intended. Kaden smiled.

"Not for something like that. You'll see what it's like. I did insist she finish up that Christmas banquet fundraiser she does every year for Habitat. That's too important. Plus, she's going to need something to keep her mind off...stuff. Oh, almost forgot." He stood and walked to a closed armoire, opened it, and removed two books. "Reading material. Help give you an idea what's going on."

Seth read the back covers, both books on BDSM. "This is so whacked, dude."

"Yeah, but you're a lucky son of a bitch."

"How the fuck do you figure that?"

Kaden sadly smiled. "In the end, when all's said and done, you get the girl."

* * * *

Later that night Seth decided to go for a swim of his own. Leah and Kaden had retreated to their bedroom, and Seth didn't feel like holing up watching TV in his room. Maybe it was as good a time as any to start his own exercise regimen. Wearing himself out would help him work off the apple pie he'd had for dessert and allow him to get to sleep.

He'd been swimming a few minutes when he spotted Leah sitting on the edge of the pool, her feet dangling in the water.

He stopped in the shallow end, near her but not wanting to get too close. He hoped she didn't want to come in for a swim. At least she was still wearing a T-shirt.

"Couldn't sleep?" she asked.

He shook his head. "Fucking best bed I've slept in, and I can't sleep," he tried to joke.

She smiled. He'd turned on the pool light, creeped out by the total darkness otherwise. He loved the way the light shimmered and reflected on her from below. "Is it okay if I sit here and watch you for a little bit?"

He nodded. "Yeah." *Please don't ask to swim with me.*

He swam a fast pace for twenty laps, trying not to notice her sitting there. He stopped at the shallow end to catch his breath.

"I don't think you're fat," she said.

He laughed. "Hellooo, left field."

She smiled and looked at her hands. "I nearly slapped Jackie at that last Fourth of July cookout you brought her to," she quietly admitted.

This was news. "What?"

She nodded before meeting his gaze. "You and the guys were out back cooking the ribs. She was in the kitchen with me and Edina and Laura. She was on her third beer or something. The other two were talking about their husbands. She made this really bitchy remark about how you were getting fat and started making fun of you. I dropped a glass on the floor, pretended it was an accident."

Fat? Hell, he'd been five pounds lighter then than he was now. And now he was only pudgy around the midsection, not obese. But next to Kaden's trim body he looked huge. "Why?"

"To shut her up. If I didn't, I was going to slap her." She took a deep breath. "I wanted to tell her she wasn't good enough for you. That she didn't deserve you. That she didn't know how to treat a man right."

Thank God he was in the water, because he hardened. Hopefully she couldn't see. He didn't know what to say. "Oh."

"I hated her." Now it was out. Even after he filed for divorce from Jackie, Leah had never openly bad-mouthed her, although it was obvious she didn't like her. Leah's voice filled with emotion. "I didn't like Kelly or Paula either. At least Kelly seemed to care about you at the beginning. I despised

Jackie. I was so glad you divorced her."

"Yeah?"

"Yeah." Her voice dropped lower. "You spent more time with us when you weren't married. I know that's selfish of me but..." She finally shrugged.

Jackie hadn't been fond of Leah either. In fact, Seth had angrily defended Leah in a private argument while Kaden's house was being built. Jackie tossed out the accusation that Leah was trying to seduce him. "You should see the way she looks at you," Jackie had said. "Almost the way she looks at her husband. It's disgusting." He'd told Jackie she was drunk and imagining things.

What had been disgusting was his divorce, trying to ignore the stinging truth that he was only a meal ticket for her, the rumors of her catting around, and having to start over.

And now...

Kaden's voice startled him. "I told you she's always taken good care of you." He walked over and sat at the edge of the pool with Leah, brushed a stray hair out of her face. He kissed her forehead, and she closed her eyes and leaned against him.

What the fuck do you say in a case like this?

Seth didn't know, so he stayed silent.

"She spent more than one night in a gag after you left with one of those women, didn't you, sweetheart?"

Leah smiled and nodded.

"Gag?"

"She wouldn't shut up about how much she hated them, that they weren't good enough for you. On and on. There were a few nights I gagged her to shut her up."

Seth laughed despite the twisted knot in his stomach. "This is twenty kinds of übercreepy. You realize that, right?"

Kaden shrugged. "I told you, you've starred in her fantasies more times than I can count."

Okay, make that fifty kinds of übercreepy.

Leah blushed but she smiled again. "I've always thought that girl you guys shared that time was a lucky woman."

Now Seth blushed. Even in the cool water he knew he had to be beet red. "Dude, you told her about that?"

"Why not? It happened before I met her. She was curious."

Übercreepy was quickly giving way to whacked-out weird.

Kaden sensed Seth was at the end of his emotional rope again. He stood and gently tugged on Leah's hand. "Let's leave him alone, sweetheart. We've got a lot to do this weekend, and there's plenty of time to talk later."

She stood. "Good night, Seth."

He dumbly nodded, sinking further in the water, watched them return to their room through the sliders.

Lucky woman?

He wouldn't deny the fantasy had crossed his mind on more than one occasion about a three-way with Leah, but those were limited to his solo sessions when he needed a little extra umph over the hump, so to speak.

Never something he would have seriously contemplated.

He started swimming again, trying to drown Leah's words out of his head.

* * * *

A little after eight Saturday morning, Seth rolled out of bed. He stumbled into the shower and stood under the spray, trying to wake up. The week had taken a toll on him, and despite swimming for over an hour after Leah and Kaden went to bed, he'd still had a hard time getting to sleep.

He gave up fighting his morning boner and fisted his cock, let his mind drift to the fantasy of having Leah in his bed. *Why the fuck not? Might as well.*

He should have expected the tap on the bathroom door. He jumped, startled. "Yeah?"

The door opened. "Coffee."

"Thanks," he said, his voice choked.

"Are you okay?"

"Yeah. Fine." His cock didn't wilt. In fact the sound of her voice made him stiffer.

Fuck.

"Bacon or sausage? I've got links."

He pressed his forehead against the tile, his cock still throbbing in his hand and demanding attention. "Surprise me."

"Seth?"

"I'm okay. Just not awake yet."

"Okay."

He breathed a sigh of relief as he heard the door shut. He frantically pounded at his cock, closing his eyes a moment later as his climax took him.

He showered, shaved, and found she had once again made the bed.

* * * *

He beat Kaden to the kitchen. Leah refilled his coffee and studied him.

"I'm fine."

"You sounded weird. What was going on?"

He felt his face redden.

Leah's eyes widened. "Whoops. Sorry." Her playful smile told him she was anything but sorry.

He had a feeling she would now play some sort of "Catch Seth Jerking Off" game in the morning.

"I told you I'd help you with that."

He grabbed the newspaper and buried himself in the A section while she fixed his plate. Every time he glanced at her, he spotted her playful smile.

Terrific. That was all he needed.

Kaden appeared a few minutes later. Leah went to get fully dressed. She reappeared a few minutes later, wearing her silver necklace and a conservative short-sleeved shirt and shorts. An hour later, the three of them were browsing through furniture in Sarasota.

Seth felt guilty enough over what was going on. He didn't want them spending more money on him. He was smart enough however to not fight Leah. Kaden had apparently turned this task over to her. She was bound and determined to get something Seth liked.

Later that afternoon, the men had the pieces spread out on the living room floor with the instructions, trying to assemble everything. Once they were in place, Leah made the men leave Seth's boxes in his room, and she took over unpacking and arranging.

Kaden drew Seth back to the den and closed the door. "Let her do it. It distracts her. We'll have whip practice after dinner."

"Basic Carpentry in the afternoon, and Sadomasochism 101 in the evening. Terrific."

"You can't tell me she wasn't damn sexy the other night."

"What do you want to hear me say, man? 'Hell yeah, I'll do your wife.'"

Kaden grinned. "That's a start."

Seth shook his head. "Fucking whacked. Jesus H. Christ, you're fucking bonkers."

* * * *

They met on the lanai after dinner. Kaden had set up an archery target with some balloons taped to it. On the outside table lay several whips of various lengths and styles. Leah was dressed in jeans and an oversized heavy denim shirt Seth suspected was Kaden's. Kaden took a few minutes to explain some of the basics and differences of the various whips to Seth. When he finished he said, "I don't expect you to remember all that now, but do you have any questions?"

"Dude, why is she dressed like that?"

"Because I don't like hurting myself with the whip," Leah said.

Seth scrunched his eyes shut. "You're confusing me again. I thought that was the whole freaking point."

Kaden smiled. He was dressed in jeans and a T-shirt. "Explain it, honey."

"I'm not a pain slut. Depending on what's happening, I don't want to feel it anywhere but on my ass and thighs, and preferably only when in subspace. Trust me, getting nailed in the boob with a singletail would be like you getting nailed in the nuts with it."

He winced. "Ouch."

"Right."

She handed him a pair of protective goggles. Kaden was now wearing his glasses, Seth noticed.

"Why weren't you wearing them the other night?"

"I always wear eye gear for training." Leah also put on a pair. "You first, sweetheart," Kaden said.

"The family that flays together, stays together," Seth snarked, making his friends laugh.

She picked up one of the whips and expertly uncoiled it, flexing her shoulders and neck much the same way Kaden had.

Kaden pulled Seth back a few steps. She looked around as if judging her clearance. When she was satisfied, she sent the end of the whip at the target and took out one of the balloons on the first try.

"Shit!" Seth exclaimed.

Kaden proudly grinned. "You ain't seen nothing yet."

She proceeded to hit every balloon without missing. When she finished, she coiled the whip and smiled at the men. "Nothing to it."

"Bullshit," Seth said. "I'll end up taking off my own goddamned nose."

"Hopefully not. Maybe just an ear."

Leah was usually a bit of a gentle, playful ballbuster with him. It was nice to finally see that side of her personality again. If nothing else, Seth was willing to work with them to keep her pulled out of her emotional cesspool. She reset the target with more balloons while Kaden showed Seth the mechanics of throwing the whip. He then proceeded to take out all the targets without missing a single time.

Leah reset while Kaden practiced with Seth at the far end of the lanai. It didn't feel smooth and fluid the way both his friends had thrown it. In his hands it felt like a lethal weapon, able to kill without warning, and he felt terrified of it.

"You need to relax into it. If you're stiff you won't throw it right. Worse, you'll hurt yourself."

"Fuck, I'm going to hurt myself anyway."

Leah finished resetting the target and walked over to stand behind Seth. She wrapped her arms around him, gripped his hand, and showed him the movement without him holding the whip. He tried to focus on her words and not the feel of her body pressed against his. After a few minutes, she handed him the whip and slowly repeated it.

"Don't worry about force. Worry about accuracy at first. Force will come after you're accurate." Then she stepped back with Kaden, out of the way. "Go ahead."

Seth nervously stared at the target, did a few test flips with the whip to get a feel for it, and threw.

He missed the target, and on the return he threw up his arms and screamed as the end nearly wrapped around him.

Leah and Kaden both laughed. "See why we wear safety goggles for this?"

Seth glared at her but let her step in and tell him what he did wrong and work with him again for a minute. He tried again solo. That time it felt more controlled even though he didn't come close to hitting the target.

After twenty minutes he felt like his arm was going to fall off.

He handed the whip to Leah. "Can I take a break?"

"Not as easy as it looks, is it?"

"No. I'm going to be fucking sore tomorrow."

"Get used to it," Kaden said. "It takes a lot of practice. Lots of blisters, too. We need to get you some gloves." He picked up another whip and took out the balloons on the target. Seth had managed to strike the target a total of three times but never hit one of the balloons. With each hit, the whip cracked.

"Show-off."

"Think he's had enough for tonight, honey?" Kaden asked Leah.

As crazy as this was, Seth felt almost like his friends were back, before the news—

kaden'sdying

—drop-kicked his world on its ear.

Leah smiled. "I think he's had enough for his first lesson."

In addition to a sore arm, he'd worked up a hell of a sweat. Maybe a swim would do him good. He helped Kaden return the target to the storage shed and changed clothes. When he returned to the lanai they were gone, probably in their bedroom. Seth turned on the pool light and slowly lapped the pool.

He didn't bother counting, just took his time, his mind spinning. He rested for a few minutes at the shallow end, his eyes closed, head on his arms.

"How's the arm?" Leah's voice startled him.

"Jesus, hon, don't do that."

She sat near the steps, back in her T-shirt, feet in the water.

"Sorry."

He flexed his arm. "Going to hurt like a sonofabitch in the morning."

"Why don't you let me fire up the hot tub? You can soak and I'll rub it out for you."

Danger, Will Robinson!

"That's okay. I'll take a couple of Tylenol."

"Don't be silly. I've given you neck rubs before."

"Yeah but that was…"

Before.

His entire life would now be comprised of a series of benchmarks he'd rather not consider. Before and After Kaden told him he was dying.

Then Before and After Kaden died.

"Please?" She looked sad, nearly desperate.

He finally nodded. "You stay out of the hot tub though."

She smiled. "You don't trust me?"

"Oh, I trust you all right, to get my ass to a point where I can't back out." He dropped his voice. "I'm serious, Leah. I'm not ready to jump into this with both feet yet. I need more time to ease into this. I'll get there, but you gotta let me dip my toe in and get used to the water." *God, that sounded lame.*

"I'll go get it ready." She pulled the cover off and turned on the jets. She walked inside the house for a moment, and he quickly got out of the pool and transferred to the hot tub.

He sank into it, the perfect temperature for the warm night after the cool swim. Leah returned a moment later with a glass of water and two Tylenol. "Here."

"Thanks."

He relaxed as she sat on the edge of the hot tub and worked over his neck, arm, and shoulder, her skilled fingers knowing exactly how to soothe his muscles.

"God, that's good, babe."

"It's supposed to be."

"I guess you do this a lot, huh?"

She shrugged. "It won't hurt so bad tomorrow morning. If you'll not be stubborn, let me work on it for you when you get up."

"We'll see."

That was apparently good enough for her. He closed his eyes and let her massage his sore muscles. He didn't know how long she sat there with him when she gently patted his shoulder. "How's that?"

He'd nearly fallen asleep. "Real good," he mumbled.

She left her hand resting on his shoulder for a moment. Then he felt her place a tender, lingering kiss on the top of his head. "Thank you."

He reached up and patted her hand. "Why don't you go on to bed? I'll be fine. I'll turn the hot tub off when I get out."

He finally heard her leave. He didn't open his eyes until the sliders to their bedroom opened and shut. He didn't want to watch her walk into that room.

I'm such a fucking dumbass. How the hell did I let myself get talked into this?

He already knew the answer to that one.

Chapter Seven

Seth groaned when he rolled over. His arm and shoulder felt nearly dead. Between assembling and moving the shelving units, then the whip practice, he was in serious. Fucking. Pain.

It was nearly eight o'clock. Fortunately he hurt too bad to wake up horny. He suspected he couldn't have done anything about it anyway, unless he managed it southpaw.

He didn't bother closing the bathroom door all the way. Sure enough, Leah showed up a few minutes after he climbed under the hot spray.

"Is it safe?"

"You'd better have Tylenol with that coffee."

"I do."

When he realized she'd left, he stuck his head out of the shower. Yes, there were two capsules lying on the counter next to his mug.

Day-amn.

When he finished he heard her outside the bathroom again. "Is it safe?"

He wrapped a towel around his hips. "I guess."

She pushed the door all the way open. "Go lay down. Let me work on your shoulder."

He wasn't going to argue. She'd left the bedroom door open, which actually made him feel better.

Less like they were doing something they shouldn't be doing. Which was stupid, because they were doing exactly what Kaden wanted them to do.

It didn't make Seth feel any better.

Whatever she used to rub him with smelled like mint and burned like hell at first before warming up then cooling off. And it felt wonderful when combined with her talented fingers.

Fuck, there was his woody, making a late appearance.

At least he was lying on his stomach and she couldn't see it.

He heard Kaden in the doorway. "You alive in there?"

"Yeah, you're trying to kill me, all right."

He leaned against the doorway and laughed. "The more you practice, the less it hurts. You should work up to four or more times a week, about an hour each. At that point you'll be in good shape."

Leah finished and patted Seth between the shoulders. "All done. That'll help. Let me do it again at lunch. Between that and the Tylenol, it'll be okay. I'll get breakfast ready."

It did feel a little better.

He waited until he heard the door close to move. He was alone.

It was tempting to roll over and jerk off, but he didn't want to get caught in the act. He still had his dignity, at least.

* * * *

"Son of a *BITCH*!" Seth hopped around and rubbed his inner thigh where the whip had stung him, even through his jeans. Missed his balls by mere inches.

Leah sat off to the side. "You tensed on the swing."

He'd learned not only did he have to master throwing the damn thing but that there were different ways to throw it. In addition, depending on the type of whip and length, still more differences.

He glared at her and rubbed the sore place, then tried again. Every time he nailed himself with the fucking thing it made him tense even worse on the next throw. This time, however, he managed to hit the target, even though the throw was low and to the left.

"Can't I just shoot you in the ass with paintball pellets? Those fuckers hurt. I'm an expert marksman with firearms. I could turn your ass red, green, blue, whatever the fuck color you want."

She laughed. Not just a giggle, but a deep, pants-wetting, full-out belly laugh.

It made him smile. This was the old Leah. Once she recovered she giggled and shook her head. "You've had enough practice for tonight, I guess." They'd been at it for thirty minutes. That, for now, seemed to be his limit. Kaden had gone inside to take a nap after dinner, leaving Leah to help Seth.

Seth wasn't sure if Kaden really needed the nap, or was just being a sneaky fucking bastard.

He suspected the latter.

Later that night, Seth lay in bed and thought about Leah's laugh. If he could at least make her laugh like that every day, it would be worth most of this. Well, worth everything but losing Kaden in the process.

* * * *

As Seth suspected, Monday morning, Leah snuck in with his coffee after he'd started the shower. But he still stood, shaving and dressed in his boxers, at the counter.

She smiled and handed him the mug. "Dang."

Seth shook his head and laughed.

He almost had a normal day. The mental heartbeat—

kaden'sdying

—didn't drive him to his knees like it had been. Leah was a little upset when he admitted he would go through the Golden Arches for lunch. He consoled her by agreeing she could pack him lunch the next day.

Kaden went in to work. He returned home a little after Seth did late that afternoon, then called Seth into the study and closed the door.

"Why the confab?"

Kaden held up a folder of papers. Seth's stomach lurched.

"I don't want her overhearing. She seems to be doing better today. She knows this has to happen. I don't need to rub her face in it."

Seth felt a little sick signing the paperwork. Kaden tried to get Seth to read it all, and he waved him away. "Let's just sign them and get it over with, dude. Like you said, so we don't have to think about it."

"Ed'll come over later tonight and notarize them for us."

"How much does he know?"

"I told him about my cancer. He has to know."

"No." Seth nervously licked his lips. "About the other stuff?"

Kaden shrugged. "I told him most of the stuff. I was honest that I'm working to get you and Leah together. I want him to know that up front so he can help you out…after."

And there was that fucking word again.

Goddamn how he hated it.

* * * *

Tuesday was almost normal. Seth got up and walked straight out to the kitchen for his coffee before Leah could bring it in to him. She pursed her lips, then laughed.

"Cheater."

But she smiled. The new deep lines etched around her eyes saddened him. At least he could do this, make her laugh.

Wednesday she got the upper hand, sneaking in before he'd even got out of bed.

Either Leah or Kaden worked with him every night with the singletail. He was starting to get the hang of basic throws, but his aim still sucked and he had yet to make one pop loudly. He heard them in the playroom late Tuesday night, but the door was closed and he didn't feel he should intrude. Kaden had already said they were going to skip the club this week because of the private class they were teaching on Saturday at Tony's house.

Kaden and Seth started playing their guitars together every night, usually before dinner. Sometimes Leah would sit with them, with her head against Kaden's knee and either her hand or foot touching Seth's foot.

Thursday afternoon, when Seth returned home from his class, he rode with Leah to the doctor.

"Gee, Mom. You don't have to go in with me," he playfully groused.

She laughed.

That became his personal secret mission through all the crazy bullshit. To try to make her laugh, hard, at least once a day. He was even growing used to seeing her in the long T-shirt at home without springing a boner every time she walked into the room.

Leah went in with him anyway. She explained their situation to the doctor, who was also Kaden's primary physician.

It was strange to Seth that the doctor didn't bat an eye. When he left the room for a moment to get the nurse to come draw blood and other specimens, Leah seemed to read Seth's look.

"He's a friend," she said.

"Loan out a ladder kind of friend, or loan out a riding crop kind of friend?"

She laughed again.

Dang! Two in one day. Maybe he could go for a hat trick.

"The second."

For the more embarrassing part of the exam, Leah did turn around and not peek. He sensed her amusement though. After they were through and standing at the checkout desk, he poked her in the arm.

"You got entirely too much enjoyment out of that."

She smiled and winked. "Girl's gotta have fun where she can."

While the receptionist was running Leah's credit card, Seth leaned close and whispered in Leah's ear, "Just be thankful I'm not in full Dom mode yet, hon."

She gasped, blushed, and met his eyes. Spying his playful smile, she laughed again.

Ah, hat trick.

* * * *

Friday afternoon, Seth beat Kaden home. Leah spent some time with Seth, trying to explain to him what would happen at the class on Saturday.

"There's going to be a dozen students, all couples." She led Seth to the playroom. He nervously eyed the wall of implements as she tried to explain the basics and terminology.

"Why do I need to know all this for tomorrow? Can't I just follow along with the class and learn with them?"

Her eyes twinkled. It was the happiest he'd seen her look since this all started. "Because you're helping Kaden with the demonstration."

"What? No, Leah—"

"Please?" Her eyes went wide, big green jewels in the middle of her face.

"Aw, fuck, no puppy-dog eyes. You're not playing fair." Early on, years ago, she'd learned he was a sucker for "the look." She never hesitated to mercilessly skewer him with it to get her way.

"Please, Seth?"

"You're not fucking playing fair."

She added a pout and dropped her voice a little. "Please?"

He closed his eyes. "Fuck. That is so not fair."

"Thank you!" She continued the lesson. Thud versus sting, floggers versus cats, crops and quirts and bats, oh my! Singletails came in different flavors, from Australian to signal to snake whips and even more. Canes and birches, straps…he neared information overload. By the time Kaden got home, Seth knew much of the basics.

Whether he wanted to or not.

* * * *

Seth wasn't sure he wanted to go but knew he had to. He bypassed Leah's attempt to catch him in the shower by getting up early Saturday morning and rolling the lawn tractor out of the garage. He'd already put his foot down and insisted on doing those kinds of chores around the house. He was a third of the way through the front yard when she walked outside with a playful smile on her face and carrying a travel mug.

He pulled up to her and shut the tractor off. She wore a long T-shirt, the heavier collar, and a pair of sandals. Since the house couldn't be seen from the road there was little chance of anyone else catching sight of her.

"You're sneaky," she said.

He stuck his tongue out at her and accepted the mug of coffee. "Grass to mow and all that. I want to study a little bit for my finals before y'all put me through the wringer and fry my brain tonight."

She looked like she wanted to say something. He finally asked, "What?"

"Besides the obvious, are you happy here?"

His heart twisted. Or was it his gut? He'd managed to make it through most of the morning without thinking about after.

"Yeah. I wish it was under better circumstances though. Besides the obvious, are you happy to have me here? Honestly?"

She nodded and looked up at him, her voice soft. "Yes." She leaned in and kissed his cheek, then turned and hurried back to the house.

Fuck.

He started the tractor and went back to mowing the yard while he tried to sort out his conflicting swirl of emotions.

* * * *

Looks can be deceiving. Tony lived east of Sarasota on five acres, a few streets off of Bee Ridge Road, east of I-75. The community was comprised mostly of larger homes on several acres of land each, many with horses or cattle or both grazing in pastures.

They arrived an hour before class was to start. Tony invited them into his home. With Seth's nerves stretched to the limit, he mostly stayed silent and observed. Tony's house was tastefully decorated but nothing unusual to indicate a Dom lived there.

It was the large garage workshop where the differences became apparent.

He had his own personal dungeon, three times larger than the playroom at Kaden's home, with more equipment. Some of the items Seth wasn't sure he wanted to know their purpose, but he was relieved to learn the evening's class would be limited to basics. Leah jokingly referred to it as the Impact 101 class.

It also surprised him to learn Leah wouldn't be totally stripping for this class the way she had in the club or at home.

"Why is that?" he asked. It startled him to realize he was a little relieved. He knew she wasn't wearing underwear, because she'd taken great pains to flash him several times at the house. Somehow, the thought of people seeing more of her than they had to close up and personal in an intimate setting twisted his stomach in an unpleasant way.

"It's a class, not a scene." Seth mulled that over. "Confused you again, didn't I?"

He nodded.

Her smile faded with concentration as she tried to figure out how to explain it. She turned to face him and dropped her voice so the other two men couldn't hear. "This isn't a session for me, although frankly, I'll enjoy it. What we do when we scene, whether in private or public, it's different. It's for us. Us including you, too. It's not for anyone else, even though in public others see it happening. Does that make sense?"

"Not really."

She leaned so close he felt her breath against his cheek when she softly spoke. "I belong only to Master and Sir. No one else. I enjoy teaching others about the lifestyle. When Master and Sir scene with me in public, I'm only focused on what They tell me. No one else. No one else exists. This is different, because it's a class, and I will be participating and giving my input. I'll enjoy it, but I'm hoping later tonight that Sir will take what He learns here and practice in private with me." She stepped back, watching his eyes.

Seth's throat had gone dry. His cock stiffened, painfully throbbing in his jeans.

I belong only to Master and Sir.

Fuck.

* * * *

Before the first students arrived, Kaden sent Leah to the bathroom and turned to Seth. His eyes playfully gleamed. "What did she say to you earlier?"

"Huh?"

"She said something to you. While Tony and I were talking."

Admittedly, Seth was still in shock. "She explained why this is different from a scene."

"And?"

Seth reddened. Well, Kade wanted honesty, he'd get it. "She was telling me she belonged to Master and Sir, and hoped I'd practice with her later."

Kaden grinned. "Great! Well, not too great. She's getting pushy and borderline bratty. We need to have a talk with her about that."

"Huh?"

"That's almost topping from the bottom."

Seth closed his eyes and quietly swore. "I have no idea what the fuck you just said."

Kaden laughed and clapped him on the shoulder. "I'll explain later." He leaned in closer, his face momentarily sad. "But it's okay. This is good, buddy. Seriously. It's keeping her mind off...other things. Having you around has been really good for her. I knew you would be."

kaden'sdying

Seth didn't want to think about that tonight. He wasn't sure he'd enjoy what he was about to learn, but he damn sure knew it was a more pleasant subject than the alternative.

* * * *

Seth and Kaden wore black jeans and dark button-up shirts. Their students were dressed in a wide variety of attire, from vanilla street clothes to one guy who was sub to a Domme, and he wore nothing more than a leather harness around his crotch.

Helluva wedgie.

Kaden introduced himself, Leah, and Seth, and briefly explained ground rules for the class. Including that, while unlike in a normal scene, students were welcomed to gather close to watch, but they were not allowed to touch Leah. Also, that for the duration of the class, students were only allowed to touch the partner they were taking the class with.

There was also to be no body fluid exchanges, something Seth was still trying to wrap his head around. To learn that a group of activities he'd always thought were centered around sex were usually not sexual in nature still blew his mind. He thought that was the whole point.

He had a lot to learn.

Kaden had tried to explain it to him while Seth helped him pack equipment for the class. "There's a difference between getting someone off and getting it on with each other. There's a bunch of legal issues. I mean, you can't allow public sex. And most pro Dominants for hire won't perform sexual services."

"Dude, what do you call what you did to her at the club?"

"That's different. I couldn't, in a situation like that, drop my pants and fuck her. I mean, if we're at home or at a small private party somewhere, sure. But not in a public scene. Never. I mean, some people might do that but I won't. Most places don't allow it anyway."

"Well, isn't it sex if someone comes?"

Kaden smiled. "Not necessarily. That's incidental."

"You guys are fucking *killing* me."

Seth gave up trying to understand the technicalities. He could wrap his head around it on a health and safety basis, but he knew it would take a while to fully comprehend what Kaden tried to explain.

Seth nervously stood to the side while Kaden gave the first part of his lecture, explaining the different implements, why they differed from each other, how to use them, safety issues. Then he turned to Leah and nodded. She hiked her skirt up over her hips and lay down on what Seth now knew was called a spanking horse.

He'd softened a little during Kaden's talk. The site of her twin, pale cheeks exposed like that instantly hardened his cock again.

Fuck.

Kaden's smile took on a mischievous twist. He handed Seth a soft leather flogger. "Let's start with the easiest one first." He turned to the class. "Remember, you'll all develop your own style and routine. I personally like to go through a warm-up. It makes the experience, in our case, more satisfying."

Seth nervously stared at the flogger in his hand, then at Leah's ass. He didn't want to whip her—he wanted to fuck her.

Kaden looked at Seth again and nodded. "Go ahead, Seth."

Leah looked over her shoulder at him, a playful grin on her face. "Anytime, Seth."

Kaden had already warned Seth he wouldn't be putting Leah in formal mode for this, wanting her to stay mostly out of "subspace," another term Seth didn't quite understand yet.

Seth took a deep breath and swung. At least it was easier to use and not nearly as frightening as the singletail.

Leah didn't flinch.

Kaden nodded. "I'd say another nine, at least." He turned to the class and started talking to them, explaining why it was important to have some sort of warm-up routine and how it related to subspace.

Seth finished the set, feeling marginally more comfortable. But his cock throbbed in a nearly painful way.

"You okay, Leah?" he asked.

She winked at him. "Fine and dandy."

Next came a paddle. Kaden took the first two demonstration swats with it, scaring the crap out of Seth with how loudly it sounded when he smacked her.

Leah not only enjoyed it, she wiggled her hips at him.

Kaden handed the paddle off to Seth. "Finish with another eight."

Seth numbly nodded. After the first two, Leah looked back at him and dropped her voice so only Seth could hear.

"Swat me like you mean it, sweetie."

Fuck!

He added more force to his swing. By the time he finished, her ass was red and she squirmed on the bench.

Not counting the night at the club or the initial session he witnessed at the house that first night, it was the weirdest experience of Seth's life. When they left Tony's and headed for home a little after ten, Leah was happily stretched out in the backseat with a content smile on her face. Kade hadn't let her climax during the class. Seth had a feeling she would get a helluva good fucking when they got home.

Seth was also harder than he thought he'd ever been in his entire life.

Kade looked at him. "You okay?"

"Yeah."

"That was fun," Leah said from the backseat. "I can't wait to get home."

Kaden glanced at her in the rearview mirror. "Don't get pushy, love. You're treading into bratty territory."

Leah dropped her voice. "Sorry, Master."

But when Seth glanced over his shoulder, he noticed she wore a playful smirk.

Kaden spotted it, too. "You could easily spend the rest of the weekend tied to the bed with a vibrator up you and not a single orgasm in sight."

Seth swallowed hard.

Holy fuck!

Leah leaned forward between the seats, apparently genuinely sorry now. "I'll behave, Master. I promise." She looked at Seth. "Did you have fun?'

He dumbly nodded. What the hell else could he do or say?

"Is Master going to let Sir practice on me more tonight?"

Kaden looked at Seth, noticed his expression, and waved her back into her seat. "That's for Me and Sir to discuss, none of your business, love. Behave."

When they returned home, Kaden helped Leah out of the car and whispered something to her. She nodded and immediately disappeared into the house.

Kaden grabbed the duffel bag from the trunk. "Well?"

"Well, what?"

Kaden grinned. "Ready to help reward a good girl for her assistance tonight?"

Seth's cock screamed, "Fuck yes!" and tried to drag him into the house. However, his mind and conscience hadn't yet reconciled the situation.

Seth shook his head. "I don't think I'm ready for that yet," he hoarsely said.

Kaden hesitated before he closed the trunk. His face clouded. "She'll be disappointed."

"I know. Tell her I'm sorry."

Kaden waited for a moment before starting for the front door. "You coming in?"

"In a little while. I...need some air."

When he was alone he squatted in the driveway, head between his knees, and took deep breaths. *Fuck!*

Fuck fuck FUCK!

After twenty minutes he felt steady enough to walk again and went inside. Both the master bedroom and playroom doors were shut.

Where would they be?

He heard a sharp crack.

Playroom.

Part of him wanted to go join them, take pleasure in making her squirm and reddening her ass. It was something she enjoyed, something to, for a little while at least, take her mind off...after.

Yet he felt guilty. This should be Kaden's time with her. Time alone with her. He didn't have much time left.

Seth knew he could have his time...after.

He poured himself a stiff drink and took it into his bedroom. Then he turned on the TV and pulled the pillow over his head and tried to get the image of Leah's sweetly red and delightfully dancing ass out of his mind.

Chapter Eight

Seth awoke Sunday morning to bright daylight streaming through his window and hitting him in the face. He was surprised to see it was after eight. Leah hadn't brought his coffee in yet, even though he smelled it brewing.

His TV was still on, too.

He got out of bed, used the bathroom, and shut off the *TODAY* show while Lester Holt was in the middle of talking to someone about innovative pet accessories.

Sudden, irrational fear flooded him. He hoped Leah wasn't upset at him for not playing with them last night after class.

That's stupid. She's not yours to play with, dude. No matter what the two of them say. This should be Kade's time with her.

It still disturbed him.

He walked out to the kitchen and didn't look into the living room as he passed. He poured himself a mug of coffee, debated whether to shower or go jogging, finally opted for a shower. He could spend time swimming that afternoon. Frankly, it was probably too hot already for a good run. Dropping dead of heatstroke wouldn't help anyone.

He turned to walk down the hall and froze as he passed the living room doorway.

Kaden was stretched out on the couch, reading the Sunday paper and dressed in shorts and a T-shirt.

Leah was…

Holy fuck!

She was…

Fuck!

Kaden had bound her to the sturdy coffee table.

Not on.

To.

The rope harness formed intricate patterns around her torso. Her hands were bound behind her back, and she was trussed on her knees, ass in the air. Kaden had looped the rope around her legs in such a way that they were spread, leaving Seth staring at her open and defenseless shaved pussy. The rope was looped multiple times around her legs, forming another intricate pattern.

Seth's jaw gaped.

Kaden looked up and reached for his coffee mug. "Oh, good morning."

Seth stared.

Kaden took a sip of coffee, put his mug down, and went back to reading his paper.

Seth stared.

He didn't know how long he stared, only that not only was his morning boner back with a passion, it was probably standing straight out in his boxers. He couldn't bother looking. The sight of Leah tied to the table…

Holy fuck!

Seth slowly walked around the back of the couch. Kaden continued reading the paper, as if this was the most normal thing in the world. When Seth finally made it to the other end of the couch, where he could see Leah's head, he realized she had a pillow beneath her and she lay with her left cheek against it, staring at him and Kaden. She was also gagged. When she caught Seth's eye, she winked.

Holy freaking fuck!

Kaden read the paper.

Seth swallowed hard. "Um."

Kaden nodded. "Shibari. Also known as kinbaku, depending on who you talk to." He held up the rest of the paper, offered it to Seth, who numbly shook his head.

Kaden went back to reading the paper.

After more long, silent minutes, Seth managed to form vowels. "Is she…comfortable?"

Kaden didn't look up from the paper. "Are you comfortable, sweetheart?"

Well, they obviously weren't formal this morning.

She made a sign with her right hand. From this angle, Seth could also see the harness formed a sort of bra around her boobs, pushing them out in a way that didn't help things on his end.

Kaden glanced over the top of his glasses at her hands. "She's comfortable."

He went back to reading the paper.

Seth stared. He wasn't sure how long he stood there and stared. He was sure, however, that if Leah didn't have the ball gag in her mouth she'd be smiling. He knew that playful look in her eyes.

Seth walked around the couch and sat at the end, near Leah's head, staring at her. The knot work looked intricate, amazing.

That was when he noticed the paramedic scissors and Leatherman tool for the first time. Kaden had laid them on the table, near Leah's right knee.

"What are those for?" Seth hoarsely croaked.

Kaden looked to where Seth pointed. "Just in case. Never do rope bondage without them."

He went back to his paper.

"How long are you leaving her like that?"

Kaden glanced at the cable box. "Another ten minutes. Then her torture starts."

Seth thought Leah moaned, but it wasn't an "oh, shit" moan. It was an "oh, goodie" moan.

"Torture?"

"Yeah. For being a little on the pushy side yesterday. She's going to spend the day being tortured. Aren't you, love?"

She definitely moaned that time.

Seth stared, realized he still held his coffee mug and that his hands were trembling. He set it on the coffee table near Leah's head. Somehow that didn't feel right, so he picked it up and moved it to the end table.

"Do I want to know how you're going to torture her?"

"You should. You'll find this very effective." He lost himself in the paper again.

"Um, dude. Focus. What are you going to do to her?"

"Keep her on edge all day long, not let her come. Later tonight, if she's a good girl"—that comment he directed at Leah—"I might let her have an orgasm. If she's very good, I'll let her have two."

She moaned again.

Nope, definitely an "oh goodie" moan.

Seth could sympathize, because his dick throbbed in his pants.

"I didn't use a crotch rope this time because I knew she'd rub against it and try to get herself off." Instead of wrapping between her legs, he'd used a pattern that looped around her upper thighs. "That's why I've got her legs spread, so she can't squirm against the thigh ropes."

Seth swallowed hard. "Uh-huh."

Kaden finally folded the A section and laid it on top of the rest of the newspaper. "You've got to watch her very carefully. She's squirmy. She loves trying to get free. Part of what she really gets off on is not being able to get loose. And in the process of squirming, she'll rub herself into coming against the ropes. So unless you want her to be able to do that, you have to use a pattern like this." He pointed at the rope, showing Seth where he had looped it.

"Uh-huh."

Kaden glanced at the time again. "Watch her for me for a minute, please? Never leave her alone or turn your back on her when she's rope bound. Especially suspended. With cuffs, depending on the circumstances, if you're at home it's sometimes okay to leave her alone for a little while. Not leave the house, of course. But like in bed or over the spanking horse or something."

Seth nodded. "Okay," he whispered.

When Kaden left, Seth leaned close to Leah and whispered, "Are you really okay with this?"

She winked. The edges of her mouth definitely twitched in what he thought would be a smile if the ball gag wasn't in the way. And her eyes crinkled in a familiar look he recognized as amusement.

Kaden returned a moment later. He carried…

Holy fuck.

Seth sat back and stared, dumbfounded.

Definitely dropped through a wormhole. No other explanation.

Kaden held up a large butt plug. "Want to do the honors?"

Seth tried for words, had to swallow to form spit, and tried again. "No thanks. I'm good."

Kaden shrugged. "Suit yourself." He patted Leah on the ass. "Get ready, love." Apparently they'd dropped back into formal mode.

She closed her eyes and moaned.

He lubed the plug and carefully, gently slid it in. She immediately started squirming, and her skin flushed.

Kaden patted her ass again. "I know, this is especially mean of me, using that one on you. It'll really keep you hot all day, won't it?"

She moaned.

The other device...*good God almighty!* It was a large dildo with straps. Kaden reached between her legs and slipped two fingers inside her—Seth's cock painfully throbbed again—and Kaden smiled.

"Jesus, love, you're really wet. You must enjoy having Seth watch this."

Her eyes were still closed but she softly moaned.

Kaden pressed the large head of the dildo against her. "Here it comes. Get ready." He slowly slid it in while she struggled against the ropes.

Seth realized she was trying to fuck herself with it.

Kaden laughed. "No, you don't get off that easy. No pun intended." He seated it all the way inside her, then Seth saw what the straps were for. Kaden buckled it around her thighs and waist, holding not only it but the butt plug in place. When he was happy with how it was adjusted, he gently swatted her ass.

"Another twenty minutes like that." He reached into his pocket and pulled out a small silver...remote? Then he thumbed a button on it. Leah jumped against her tethers and moaned.

Seth heard a low buzzing sound and understood what it was. It wasn't just a dildo. It was a vibrating dildo.

He felt lightheaded, realized he'd been taking shallow gasps of air. Forcing a few deep breaths into his lungs, he watched as Kaden sat back down on the couch.

And started reading the funnies.

Seth stared. He realized the buzzing wasn't a steady constant. It alternated patterns, sometimes a steady hum, sometimes a start and stop rhythm, sometimes stopping altogether for a moment. When it did that, Leah would whine and squirm even harder until it started again.

As hard and painfully as his cock throbbed, Seth didn't dare move. He worried the very act of standing would trigger enough friction against his swollen member to make him come.

She was gorgeous, and as she knelt there a fine patina of sweat covered her skin.

"How do you know she's okay?" Seth whispered.

Kaden didn't look up from the paper. "Our code is two loud, long grunts, if she doesn't get my attention with hand signals. If she does that, it means the gag comes off immediately."

She was aware of them talking about her, because her eyes slowly opened. But they looked passion-glazed under heavy lids. As the vibrator cycled through another pattern, Leah closed her eyes again and softly moaned.

Kaden smiled, finally looking at her. "I don't dare spank her like this. She'll freaking explode. I mean, if she didn't have that gag in her mouth, she would totally scream her head off, buddy. Trust me. You work her up like this, it's absolutely amazing how hard she'll come. And she loves it."

Leah moaned her assent.

Kaden wasn't finished. "She really loves to be fucked like this. Perfect height on this table, too. Or in bed. She's totally helpless like this. You can play with her clit, lick her"—Leah moaned at that— "and do whatever you want to her. I love this position."

Seth's entire body resonated in time with the sound of the vibrator.

Kaden met Seth's eyes with a steady gaze. "Want to try her right now?"

He gasped for breath again and shook his head. Leah opened her eyes and moaned, this time in disappointment, at Seth's refusal.

As weird as this was, and as much as Seth wanted to take them up on the offer, he couldn't quite bring himself to take that step yet. Especially not with his best friend sitting right there.

But...

Day-amn.

Seth struggled for a gracious out. "I need a shower. And...and we don't have my test results back."

"I had her buy condoms."

Fuck.

Seth shook his head. "Um, maybe...later." He jumped up, grabbed his coffee, and hurried back to his bedroom, closing the door behind him. He started for the bathroom, then returned to his bedroom door and locked it.

Just to be safe.

He turned on the TV again—this time Lester was talking to some high-profile chef about raisins versus citrons—and turned on the shower.

It took three strokes on his cock to explode. And he didn't go soft. Almost frantically he continued stroking and a few minutes later he came again, the memory of Leah's ass in the air setting him off.

* * * *

When he finished his shower—after jerking off one more time—he wandered back out to the kitchen, relieved to see the living room empty.

And just a tad disappointed.

That was fucking hot, no denying it. Had he not been so absolutely shocked he would have enjoyed it.

Or might have forced himself to take them up on the offer.

It was nearly ten, and he was starving. What did that say about him that he felt a brief flash of irritation that Leah hadn't fixed his breakfast yet.

And where *were* they, anyway?

He looked down the hall, saw the playroom door standing open. Swallowing hard, Seth forced his feet to move.

Leah was now strapped to the spanking horse, her legs spread far apart and cuffed to the bench. She still had the butt plug and vibrator in. Her arms were also cuffed to the bench, and now she was blindfolded. She wore a smaller ball gag, though.

He heard the vibrator click on. Leah's hips jerked, frantically squirming against the bench. When the vibrator shut off she moaned, whimpering.

Kaden's soft voice in his ear nearly scared the crap out of him. "You know you want to."

"Fuck," he whispered.

Kaden handed him one of the riding crops. "Right now, before the vibrator comes back on, just one square across her ass. It's not enough to get her off."

Seth's dick led the way. He nervously lined up the blow as he'd been shown in class the night before.

Kaden crossed his arms and smiled, watching.

Fighting a twisting in his stomach, Seth swung. Leah jumped, whined, and wiggled her ass at him. He looked at Kaden. Kaden held up his hand, indicating wait.

Sure enough, the vibrator clicked on again. Leah moaned, squirming against the bench.

Kaden waved Seth out into the hall and whispered, "She doesn't know which of us did it, or when we'll do it again. It's driving her crazy."

"Are you really going to leave her like that all day?" The thought of that made Seth partly feel bad for her.

And partly excited him.

Kaden raised an eyebrow at him. "I wouldn't stop you if you want to give her some relief. You're entitled to."

Seth pointed down the hall to the living room. When they were safely out of Leah's hearing, Seth asked, "What if I can't be kinky enough for her all the time?"

"What do you mean?"

He wiped his mouth with his hand and wished for a drink. He knew he couldn't have one for that very reason. "I mean, geez, yeah, okay, right, it's fucking hot seeing her like that. But damn, you know, there's a lot of times I'll just want to cuddle or have straight sex and not all of…" He waved his arm down the hall. "That."

"What?"

"That!" He pointed again.

Kaden smiled. "She doesn't get off on the kink."

Seth took another step toward the hallway and waved his arm again. "Uh, duh! What the fuck is *THAT* then?"

Kaden sat on the couch and picked up the sports section. "She would be happy having vanilla sex for the rest of her life. That's not what this is about. It's hotter, sure, but that's just a bonus."

Seth's jaw dropped. "How about some fucking answers to my questions?" He stormed over to Kaden, grabbed the newspaper, and tossed it over the back of the couch. "What the fuck do you mean she doesn't get off on the kink?"

"The pain is to help her process emotions, especially painful emotions, when she's overstressed. If she gets off in the process, even better. They are totally different things, even though they're related sometimes. If you did nothing but missionary with her for the rest of your lives and spanked her with your hand over your lap when she needed it, she'd be perfectly happy with that, too."

"Then why do you do all of this other stuff?"

He shrugged. "We just sort of fell into it. As we got to know more people in the lifestyle and saw things, we decided to experiment a little. I told you, she's not a pain slut. You'll see people who put dozens of clothespins all over themselves, needles, hot wax, knife play, shit like that. She has no desire to do any of that. All she needs is the occasional grounding. That's what the spankings are about. She likes and enjoys the other stuff. It's fun. The shibari is nice for her—when done properly and she can't get loose—because it forces her to relax and just be for a little while. You know how they say you should swaddle babies?"

"Dude, I don't know nuthin' about swaddlin' no babies."

Kaden froze, then laughed, loud and hearty. It was good to hear that sound from him.

Seth struggled against the mental heartbeat, but it came back anyway.

kaden'sdying

When he could talk again, Kaden continued. "It's comforting. She'll have to get to the point where she trusts you to do it with her, and she will. She just..." He thought about it. "It's like she totally goes into subspace without laying a finger on her. She would literally allow me to keep her tied up twenty-four/seven if I found a position she'd be comfortable in without risk of her circulation being cut off. It's like she gives herself permission to totally relax and unwind."

Seth dropped to the couch and shook his head. "This is a lot to fucking learn."

Kaden nodded. "I'm trying to cram nearly twenty years of trial and error into...into a short amount of time. The good news is, I know what won't work and I can give you the benefit of my wisdom there, too." He leaned forward, elbows on his knees. "You saw how stern I was with her at the club?"

Seth nodded.

"That's a hard edge for her. You'll notice most of the time I don't talk to her like that. And you can only talk to her like that when you're dropping her into subspace or when she's fully there. However, as soon as the scene is over and you're giving her aftercare—and she must always have aftercare—then you need to be very gentle and tender with her. When the endorphin high starts to fade, you can amp it back up a little.

"I also never compare her to anyone else. Ever. And I don't ever use humiliation with her. I don't ever want her to feel like that. Frankly, I couldn't do that to her anyway. I have never threatened, even in play, to find a new sub or let a stranger use her. Ever."

"Okay. Explain what the fuck is subspace?"

"It's sort of like a trance. What this does to her, it releases a huge flood of endorphins into her system. It's like a natural drug for her. It medicates her, in a manner of speaking. That's why she swam herself to exhaustion in the pool the other night. Think of a runner's high. It's sort of the same thing. Sometimes she can do that for herself with swimming or even running. A lot of the time, especially when she's very stressed or upset, she can't. That's when you have to help her. Under normal circumstances it's more maintenance than anything."

Kaden took his glasses off, laid them on the coffee table. "Whether it freaks you out or not, having you here to teach has been a huge help for her. She's got something—someone—to distract her. An alternate focus. We'll deal with some major meltdowns with her as we go along. I have no doubt about that. For right now she's finding a basic center she can function within."

"What if...after. What if she slips too far away from me to bring her back?" Seth quietly asked. It was his greatest fear.

Kaden shook his head. "You won't let that happen. You love her too much to not find a way to keep her safe." He tipped his head toward the hall. "Why don't you go have some fun with her? Don't take the blindfold off. Just spend some time playing with her. She'll really love it."

"Does stuff like that put her in subspace?"

"A little. Not totally. The most intense is a public scene. Then private scenes like you saw that first night, only that was, like I told you, fairly tame. There's been times where even if we don't make the club, even just playing, literally slap and tickle in bed, it's enough to keep her grounded. If she's not totally stressed out or upset, it's very easy to maintain her mood without major scenes of any kind. That's why she enjoys the full-time slave lifestyle. It helps her give over some of her emotional baggage."

"You're telling me to go fuck your wife. That is *fucked* up, dude."

"Then don't do that right now if you don't want to. You've got hands." Kaden smiled. "Take the ball gag out and listen to her scream. Your cock will harden like concrete, buddy."

"Oh, *SO* not having this talk, Kade!" Seth stood and walked halfway down the hall. From there he could hear Leah whimpering in the playroom, obviously wanting relief.

Seth returned to the living room and jabbed his finger at Kaden. "*This* is fucked up."

Kaden sadly nodded. "Tell me about it."

But Seth's cock throbbed, wanting to return to the playroom for another look at her. Seth turned to Kaden. "I can't…with you watching…yet. Just stay out here, okay?"

Kaden grinned. "Should I turn the TV on?"

"Might not be a bad idea."

Kaden reached for the remote while Seth started down the hallway again. Seth heard *Meet the Press* come on in the living room. The vibrator was running. Leah trembled, squirming, trying to rub herself against the bench.

He took a deep breath and walked over, then sat down beside her. With trembling fingers he reached out with his left hand and gently caressed her ass.

Leah froze. For a second Seth worried she'd tell him to stop or grunt or something.

She moaned, furiously bucking her hips.

Her meaning was unmistakable—she wanted more.

Her skin felt cool and smooth beneath his hand. He'd be lying if he said he didn't want to rip the vibrator out and fuck her silly right there.

He leaned in and pressed his lips to her right hip. Then he closed his eyes and inhaled. Her bodywash and the musky scent of her arousal mixed together in an intoxicating way.

Leah moaned.

He laid his cheek against her. Closing his eyes, he stayed his hand, his palm warm against her flesh. When the vibrator shut off, she moaned in frustration again.

"Shhh," he whispered.

She quieted, waiting.

"Good girl," he whispered. He imagined she had to know it was him by now, even though she once joked that she had trouble telling his voice from

Kaden's over the phone without Caller ID.

The vibrator clicked on a few moments later, and she jerked, twisted, and whimpered.

Shifting position, Seth left his hand on her ass and reached under her with his other and found her clit.

Leah's whimpers changed tone, and she stilled her frantic squirming.

"Stay very still," he whispered, "and be a good girl, and I'll give you a reward."

Her high-pitched whine struck a deep chord of desire within him.

She froze, statue still.

He found her swollen nub and gently tweaked it, rolling it in his fingers in time with the vibrator's pulsation. He sensed the tension in her body, the urge to work her hips in time with his movements conflicting with her desire to do what she was ordered.

He pressed another kiss to her flesh and then whispered, "Do you want it, baby?"

A soft, keening whine in response.

"Give it to me." He gently pinched her clit. She exploded, screaming against the ball gag, her entire body tensing and straining against the cuffs. When she finished and collapsed, limp against the bench, Seth once again kissed her hip and gently patted her ass.

He went straight to his room, locked the door, and fell on his bed. With the sound of her cries still fresh in his head, he fisted his cock, and within a minute had come again.

Fuck.

He hadn't been this horny since high school.

* * * *

Despite knowing in his head—the one on top of his shoulders—that Kaden was copacetic with the situation, it took every last ounce of Seth's nerves to force himself out of his bedroom an hour later. The playroom door was closed, as was the master bedroom door, and the living room was silent.

Seth's stomach growled.

He silently walked out to the kitchen, no sign of life. He could see out the front windows and knew they had to be here somewhere, because the Lexus and Ridgeline were parked in the drive.

Trying not to make any noise, he opened the fridge and found a package of sliced turkey. He turned to lay it on the counter and nearly screamed. Leah stood there, smiling, in her collar and long T-shirt.

"Jesus Fucking H. Christ! You nearly gave me a heart attack!"

"Sorry. Want me to make you something? I'm sorry I didn't cook you breakfast this morning. You must be starving."

Seth waited for his heart to quit racing. "How'd you sneak up on me?"

"We're out in the garage. Kaden's up in the attic taking inventory of the Christmas lights and decorations. You know him. Even though it's still a few months away, he's got to outdo himself every year."

Danger! Danger!

Seth frantically struggled for something to say to wipe the impending storm clouds from her eyes. He knew she was thinking the same thing he was, that it was most likely Kaden's last Christmas. At the very least the last one he could actively participate in. Putting up lights was one of his passions. His displays were always a hit at their series of holiday parties and dinners they held every year.

Seth forced a growl he didn't feel. "You *should* make me something to eat. What kind of way is that to treat Sir?"

Her cheeks filled with color, and her lips slightly parted. Then a playful smile lit her face. "I'm sorry, Sir." She pushed him out of her way and practically dove into the refrigerator to get what she needed. He stepped to the side, silently relieved he'd distracted her.

Fuck.

Now he understood what Kaden meant.

He retook his usual place at the counter and watched Leah quickly put his lunch together. She turned and set the plate before him. Their eyes locked. He reached out and touched her hand, gently squeezed it.

"Thank you," she whispered.

"So he decided to let you out after all, huh?"

Another playful smile. *Thank God.*

"He said since I was apparently good enough to convince Sir to make me come, I must have been very well behaved and deserved time off for good behavior."

Seth's turn to howl with laughter. He stood and pulled her into his arms for a hug. "We're all crazy. You realize that, right?"

Leah pressed her face against his chest. "Yeah but it's a good kind of crazy."

"Got *that* right."

Chapter Nine

Seth somehow managed to pass his finals. Whip training continued, as did his education in other areas. Since he spent more time with Leah, she took over most of his shibari training. She worked with him on the basics while Kaden took over for the more advanced skills.

This would take a while.

Seth still wasn't comfortable being too intimate with Leah, even though he was constantly nudged in that direction by both his friends. Seth did allow them to demonstrate some of the various implements on him, including Kaden nailing him in the ass with a singletail—albeit while wearing jeans—so Seth could feel what Leah felt. One of Seth's persistent fears was that he would hurt her. After realizing most of the items weren't nearly as scary as they looked and sounded, especially considering Leah's years of experience, he did loosen up and take a more active role in her sessions.

Seth also took it upon himself to be their unofficial photographer, using any and all excuses to get as many candid photos of Kaden and Leah, especially together, that he could. The shibari lessons were an excellent excuse for this. Seth spent plenty of time taking pictures and video of Kaden tying her up on the pretense of needing them for his own use to master the techniques.

So far, he hadn't noticed much of an outward change in Kaden's appearance. Seth knew it was just a matter of time before his friend started losing weight. The Christmas lights and party plans continued full force. Kaden was only telling a select few people about his condition, swearing them to secrecy. He didn't want scores of people constantly coming up to Leah and telling them how sorry they were and dragging out her misery.

Not only did Seth agree with that, he thought it was pretty smart for Kaden to think about it.

Leah, for her part, did fairly well. A couple of times Seth awoke to hear them in the playroom in the middle of the night. One afternoon Seth had come home after class to find Leah crumpled in the middle of the living room floor, a wide-eyed look of despair on her face. She wouldn't—or couldn't—talk.

He scooped her up and took her to the playroom. Fortunately, Kaden was already on his way home. By the time he arrived to take over, Seth had warmed her up and gotten her into subspace, even though he didn't have the routine down pat yet and probably wasn't nearly as masterly as she would have liked. It took Kaden thirty minutes to get her to cry. When she did, she screamed her agony. Seth quietly slipped out of the room and left them alone.

He accompanied them to the club three more times. They saw Baxter on the second visit, but he didn't accost them.

On the third visit, Kaden called Seth over after he'd bound Leah to the bench not just with cuffs but with rope. He leaned in.

"Go sit by her head and talk to her, tell her to come for you."

"What?"

"Do it. It'll make it even hotter for her."

Seth dumbly nodded. Usually he just observed during public scenes. He'd never actively participated in one, even though he had at home. He walked over to the bench and knelt next to her, his cheek touching hers, his lips by her ear.

"Do you want to come for me?"

She whimpered around the ball gag. Kaden had already warmed her up with the flogger and paddle and was now standing behind her with one of the more flexible riding crops. It had a longer flapper on the end, and Seth knew when Kaden struck her just right with it, between her legs, it would quickly make her come.

Seth closed his eyes. "Come for me, sweetheart," he whispered.

She jumped and moaned as Kaden started swinging. Seth knew these kinds of swats weren't as hard as the ones he laid sideways across the fleshy part of her ass, but it still set off conflicting emotions inside him. Horror, that he was helping her get beaten.

And desire, wanting to make her explode.

To come for him.

He continued whispering to her. Within a few minutes, her body tensed as she screamed around the ball gag.

"Where are we, love?" Kaden asked.

She flashed an okay sign.

Kaden quickly worked to untie the ropes and undo her cuffs. When he was near her head, he leaned over and whispered in Seth's ear, "Take her off the bench, ungag her, and hold her."

Swallowing hard, he did. She curled in his arms, and he automatically cuddled her close to him, protectively, wanting to close out the world and do nothing but hold her like this.

Seth was vaguely aware of Kaden putting away their equipment and wiping down the bench.

Aftercare. He felt her need as she softly cried in his arms, like a violent earthquake had rocked her and now she was suffering through the aftershocks.

He pressed his lips to her temple. "You okay?"

She nodded but didn't move.

Once Kaden had put his shirt on, he knelt beside them and brushed the hair from her face. "How are we, love?" he softly asked.

"Green," she whispered.

"Very good love. Feel like getting dressed now?"

She nodded. Seth pressed a kiss to her forehead and helped her to her feet.

He could have sat there all night holding her like that. It wasn't even so much a sexual experience as it was an emotional one, like she'd been viscerally stripped bare and trusted him to keep her safe until she could function again.

Like he was protecting her.

It was that vision floating through his mind as he drifted to sleep later that night.

* * * *

Seth had lived with them for five weeks when Kaden informed him he had scheduled his Atlanta trip. The men were playing guitar in the den while Leah cooked dinner.

"You should probably sleep with her while I'm gone."

Seth groaned. "Dude, I told you—"

"I meant sleep sleep, not sex sleep. I don't think she'll do well sleeping alone. It'll be too much of a preview of...after."

Could he do that and not get himself in trouble?

Then again, was it "trouble" when that was the plan in the first place? "I'll figure something out. I'll keep an eye on her."

"I'll only be gone two nights. I'll leave Tony's number. If something really bad happens you can call him and he'll come help."

The thought of Tony touching Leah left a bad taste in Seth's mouth despite how much he liked the guy.

"Not to work with her personally," Kaden clarified, correctly interpreting Seth's expression. "To advise you on what to do. I already talked to him. He would come over only to talk you through things, be your safety net, so to speak."

That relieved him. That there would be backup a phone call away was reassuring. "I would still call you first."

"I would expect you to."

Kaden had a doctor's appointment before he left. He took Seth with him. Leah was at a meeting for one of her nonprofits.

The oncologist wasn't enthusiastic, just pragmatic. "You seem to be stable."

"How long?"

Seth sat in a chair in the corner and cringed. He didn't want to hear this.

The doctor shrugged. "You know I can't give you a definite. It could be two months, or it could be two years. Realistically I would safely estimate a year at this rate of progression. Possibly longer. It was caught early, all things considered."

Seth felt hopeful. "Did you say two years? You said two years!"

Kaden smirked. "And this is why I don't bring Leah. She would only hear the good stuff and not reality."

The doctor shrugged again. "You're refusing treatment. That would still buy you a few months."

Kaden firmly shook his head. "We're not having that discussion again."

"Okay."

Seth quietly rode home with Kaden. *Two years!* That would...well, it would still suck that they'd lose Kaden, but he wasn't taking a single day for granted.

As if sensing his friend's thoughts, Kaden said, "Don't you say a word to her about the appointment. Especially two years. If you tell her that and it happens next month, it'll kill her."

"I know. I won't." No, he wouldn't tell Leah.

But he'd hold on to his private, silent hope.

* * * *

The airport limo arrived early on Wednesday morning to drive Kaden up to Tampa International. The three of them took a few minutes hugging and saying good-bye. After Kaden hugged and kissed Leah, he hugged Seth. "Love you, man."

"Love you, too. Still not doing you."

Kaden laughed, which made Seth smile. "Still not doing you, either. Take care of our girl for me." He shook his finger at Leah and dropped his voice. "You behave yourself. You listen to Sir, love. Remember, make Me proud."

Her skin flushed, and she nodded. "Yes, Master," she whispered.

"Good girl, love. I'll be home day after tomorrow." He hugged and kissed her one more time before stepping into the waiting car. When it drove off, Seth followed Leah into the house.

Without classes to study for, Seth threw himself into his BDSM training. He had already read every book Kaden owned on the subject and spent hours practicing shibari with Leah. Later that afternoon they moved to the lanai for more whip training with the singletail.

His aim had improved, although he didn't trust himself with a live target yet, even one wearing protective clothing. He was still too erratic in his throwing style and worried about hurting someone. But he had worked up to forty-five minutes at a time with the thing.

They quietly ate dinner on the couch in front of the TV. Seth felt Leah's tension grow as the night wore on. Kaden called around nine, which helped her for a little while. Seth played guitar for her, sticking with more upbeat tunes he hoped would keep her out of her funk.

While he'd made her come several times as part of their sessions, an admittedly irrational mental justification allowed him to see that as part of something necessary for her. But to make love to her in a romantic, give-and-take way still lay beyond his mental and emotional ability to cope with no matter how okay his body apparently was with it. Hell, he was still trying cope with the fact that Kaden was dying when he looked so healthy.

They were just going to have to give him the time he needed to wrap his freaking head around it or he'd lose his mind.

Close to bedtime he sensed her disquiet. He pulled an ace out of his sleeve.

"Love"—it still felt strange to call her that—"I want you to sleep with me tonight. I'm very tired and just want to cuddle." He leaned close and dropped his voice to a firm growl. "But *only* sleep. If you don't behave, I'll have to tell Master you were not a good girl."

She smiled. "I'll behave."

He kissed her forehead. "Very good. I think I'd be more comfortable if you slept in my bed tonight. Go get ready."

"What should I wear to sleep in?"

While he'd let her run around naked more often, there was no way he could share a bed with her naked. "Long T-shirt." She started to look pouty, and he growled again. "Listen, I'm going to be sleeping with you. Remember, you're letting me ease into this. It's one step closer."

That lifted her spirits. She went to get ready, and he returned to his bedroom and left the door open.

He usually slept naked, but tonight he put on a pair of sleeping shorts. No way in hell would he risk it.

When they finally curled up together he spooned against her back and enjoyed the way his arm perfectly fit around her waist. Did she fit Kaden's body this well?

Oh, cut that shit out right *now.* That was not a healthy line of thought. Not a place he even wanted to think about going.

Surprisingly, even though he thought his cock might want to stiffen, he fell asleep. And he awoke from that sound sleep around two a.m., when he felt her shift in his arms and sit up.

"What's wrong?" he mumbled.

She didn't answer. His heart hammered in his chest, and he sat up, pulling her to him. "What's wrong?"

She still didn't answer but let him pull her closer. "I miss him," she finally whispered.

"I know, babe." He tried to relax. "It's okay."

He coaxed her into lying down next to him, but she wasn't settled by any stretch of the imagination. In a fit of inspiration, he told her to roll onto her stomach. She did.

He gently stroked her back and enjoyed the soft, pleasant sounds she made at his touch.

Now his cock tried to stiffen.

"Do you need to feel the bite?" he whispered.

"A little," she admitted.

He swatted her, bare-handed, across her ass. She jumped. He swatted her again, and he knew he didn't imagine it when she wiggled her hips against his hand and buried her face deeper into her pillow.

He spanked her as hard as he could, a total of twenty swats, leaving his hand stinging. When he finished she was breathing heavily, her body practically vibrating on the mattress next to him.

"Where are we, love?"

"Green, Sir," she said with a sigh.

He slid one hand between her legs and found her clit. She squirmed against the mattress, and in a few minutes she moaned into the pillow when she came.

It was almost like she melted into the bed from the sudden relaxation that swept over her.

He curled around her again, hoping she was too out of it to feel his stiff erection pressing against her backside.

After another hour, he finally fell asleep.

* * * *

When he awoke the next morning, he almost panicked when he realized she wasn't in bed with him. "Leah?"

"I'm getting coffee," she called from the kitchen.

Deep sigh of relief. If he fucked up and she did something while Kaden was gone, he'd never forgive himself. He got out of bed and used the bathroom. By the time he finished she was walking through the bedroom door with a beautiful smile on her face and his cup of morning goodness in her hands.

"Thank you, sweetie."

She paused, as if waiting for something else. He leaned in and kissed her forehead. He wanted to plant a deep one on her lips and knew that would lead to spending all day in bed with her.

Wait, why was he fighting?

Because she's still my best friend's wife, that's why.

"You're welcome, Sir."

Oh crap, formal.

"Are you okay, hon?"

She nodded and only a little cloud flitted through her eyes. "Is it okay if I'm formal?"

"Sure."

She relaxed. If it helped her, he'd do it. "Thank you, Sir."

"What's on the agenda for today?"

"Master said for me to work with You on the ropes and the singletail."

Seth also knew he needed to mow. It'd been nearly a week. In the wet Florida climate, the lawn was growing at a jungle-inducing rate. "I need to do some chores first."

"Will you go grocery shopping with me, Sir?"

Of course he would. He'd go to hell and back for her. Publix was easy. "Let me get my chores done first, and then we'll go."

She fixed his breakfast. Later, he noticed that she sat either on the front porch or back lanai and watched him mow. She reminded him of a lost child.

He was in the shower when Leah knocked on the bathroom door. "Sir?"

He'd grown comfortable with her coming into the bathroom when he was in the shower as long as she didn't try to open the shower door.

"Yeah, hon?"

"Master's on the phone. He said He has to talk to you right now."

"It can't wait until after I'm out of the shower?"

"No, Sir. I asked. He said it can't."

Argh. "Hold on." She only had her arm stuck through the bathroom door, anticipating he'd be naked.

At least she wasn't trying to push him too hard.

He stepped out of the shower, grabbed a towel and wrapped it around his hips, and then took the phone. She pulled the door closed.

"Dude, shower time. What is so fucking important it can't wait five minutes?"

"Is she all right? She doesn't sound right."

Seth shivered when he felt the AC kick on. "Yeah, she seems okay. Can't this wait?"

"No, it can't. She sounded out of it."

Seth dropped his voice, unsure if she stood on the other side of the door or not. "She had a little episode last night. Nothing major. I took care of it, didn't even have to take her to the playroom." It felt weird talking to Kaden about Leah like this.

"Why is she being formal?"

"She asked to."

"That's a warning sign right there."

Seth's gut curled in an unpleasant way. "Well, fuck, you could have told me that shit before you left! Is there anything else I need to know, genius?"

"Just keep a very close eye on her. Don't give her any more time by herself than you have to. Spend the whole day with her. Keep her busy."

"I'm going to the store with her in a little while."

"Good. You might want to get her to the playroom before you go to bed."

His stomach curled again. "Why do it if it's not necessary?"

"Blow off some pressure before it builds up. Use training as an excuse. It'll help."

He hated using the harder implements on her even though he knew it was relatively safe. Swatting her on the ass with his hand, he could dig that. Frankly, it was kind of hot the way she squirmed and enjoyed it, and he knew he couldn't hurt her. "Can I just play it by ear?"

"Don't leave her alone today. Seriously."

"All right. Fine. Let me get back in the shower. I'm fucking freezing."

He hung up and peeked out the bathroom door. Leah was nowhere to be seen. Hopefully she hadn't listened in. "Leah?" he called.

She appeared in the bedroom doorway a moment later. "Yes, Sir?"

He held out the phone. "Thank you."

"You're welcome, Sir."

He climbed back into the shower, turning the water hotter to get rid of his chills. While he had been planning on blowing off a little of his own tension, the worry now pulsing through his mind killed his boner.

* * * *

With Kaden's words echoing through his brain, Seth kept close tabs on Leah. If she was slipping into a deeper sadness, she was doing a damn good job of hiding it from him. He drove Kaden's truck and talked Leah into taking a few side trips before hitting the grocery store, getting parts he really didn't need for the mower and items he did need to add some external electrical circuits to accommodate Kaden's amped-up plans for his biggest light display ever.

It apparently worked. By the time they returned home late that afternoon and he helped her unload the groceries from the back of the Ridgeline, Leah seemed fine.

He was out in the garage when the sound of shattering glass and Leah's strangled cry scared the living crap out of him. He ran inside and found her clutching her arm, red splattered all over the kitchen floor. He slid to a stop at the edge of the kitchen, only marginally relieved to see the red covering the tile floor was red glass from a shattered pitcher.

"I'm sorry! I'm sorry!" Leah cried. She looked panicked. He spotted a trickle of blood between her fingers where she had her right hand clamped around her left forearm, just below her elbow. "It was an accident, Sir! I was trying to get the pitcher down so I could make your sangria!"

"It's okay, hon." He forced his voice to stay calm and steady. "I know it was an accident. I can see that. Don't move." She was in bare feet, and he had already kicked his shoes off. The kitchen floor was a minefield of red glass. The stepstool and open top cabinet door were more proof of her intentions. "Stay right there. Do *not* move." Seth raced to the front door, yanked on his sneakers, then carefully stepped into the kitchen.

Glass crunched under his feet. Now she trembled, and he worried about her going into shock. "How bad is your arm?"

"I'm scared to look. It hurts really bad. I didn't mean to do it, I swear! I lost my balance when I was stepping down. I guess I hit the pitcher on the counter." The slate counters looked totally stunning but were fucking murder on anything breakable. He'd already broken two glasses and a plate himself. A few pieces of glass on the counter also supported her story.

The sight of her blood turned his stomach. He tried for a masterly tone. "Calm down, love. You're okay. It was just an accident."

She nodded, her eyes tearing up.

He grabbed a dish towel off the counter. She lifted her fingers enough he could slip it around her arm. From the amount of blood, he suspected she'd need stitches.

Fuck. Great. Kaden goes off for two fucking days, and I have to take her to the ER. Fuck!

"Hold that there. Don't let go."

She nodded.

He carefully scooped her into his arms and stopped at the doorway so he could kick his shoes off. He didn't want to track glass through the house. Seth carried her down to the master bathroom and set her on the counter. First things first, he checked her feet for glass so she could walk. She had two scratches along the tops of her feet, probably from bouncing glass, and one small shard still embedded in the side of her foot. She told him where the tweezers were, and he removed the glass from her foot.

Next, her arm. Yes, it was deep, fortunately not into a vein, from the looks of it. He put the dish towel back and clamped her hand over it.

"Okay. Listen to me. You have to get stitches." Her eyes welled with tears, and he shook his head. "This was an accident, love. Stop worrying. Master will not be mad at you. If anything, he'll be pissed at me because I'd asked you to make the damn sangria in the first place."

At that she smiled a little.

"We've got to get you dressed. And that"—he pointed at her collar— "has to come off." While it was the thin leather collar, and her long hair hid the locking buckle in the back so she could wear it in casual situations in public without worry, there was no way in hell he could take her to the ER wearing it.

She blanched, vigorously shaking her head. "No! Master put it on me. I can't take it off!"

Fuck.

"Leah," he sternly said, "Master told you I'm in charge and you listen to me, right?"

She finally nodded, her eyes wide and brimming with tears.

He kept his voice firm and stern. "It has to come off. I take you to the hospital wearing that, they'll call in the cops to ask how the fuck you got hurt and accuse me of doing it. Where's the key?"

She finally answered him. "On a silver chain, in the top left dresser drawer. My day collar is there, too." The locking silver necklace looked completely harmless in vanilla situations.

"I'll make you a deal. I'll put your day collar on you. Okay?"

She relaxed a little. He needed to speed this up because blood had started seeping through the dish towel. He had to drive her to the emergency room and get her taken care of. He rushed into the bedroom, found the key and her silver necklace, and made the switch. Then he guided her into the bedroom and helped her get dressed. He had to change the sodden dish towel out and grabbed a bath towel for her to hold around her arm.

"Where's your purse?"

"Living room."

He found it and carried her out to the Lexus, ran back inside to grab his cell phone and lock the house. Now the adrenaline crash hit him and he had to focus to keep his hands from shaking as he got into the car and started it.

Leah looked pale. "Talk to me, love," he said.

"It hurts."

"I know it does, love."

"I have to call Master and tell Him. I have to tell Him immediately when something happens."

"Hey, kiddo, I was right there. Remember, I'm in charge. It's okay. I'll call him once we get you taken care of."

She nodded and rested her head against the seat.

He gently slapped her thigh. "Don't close your eyes." They were ten minutes from the closest hospital. He didn't know if she'd go into shock over something like this, but he wasn't taking any chances. "Stay awake. Don't go to sleep."

She nodded again, but he didn't like her pale skin tone.

At the hospital he parked, then carried Leah into the ER. The triage nurse took one look at her arm and immediately directed them back to a bed. Within five minutes Leah was being examined and sutured. At least she'd kept enough of her wits about her to drop the formal act.

Seth handled registration and insurance for her while she was being treated. Kaden had set up medical power of attorney paperwork already, but Seth never imagined he'd need it for Leah. When asked his relation to the patient, Seth took a nervous breath.

"Family caretaker," he answered, handing over folded copies of the paperwork from his wallet. It was a term Kaden had come up with, thinking it would cause them the least amount of grief and raise the fewest eyebrows over the next several months.

Apparently, it was more than good enough for the administrator. She made copies and returned them to him without further questions. By the time he returned to Leah's side the doctor was almost finished suturing her. She'd gouged a deep, four-inch-long gash along the meaty part of her inner arm. With a shot of pain meds to calm her, Seth asked her for more details.

"It happened so fast. I was stepping down, and I lost my balance. I was holding the pitcher in my right hand, by the handle. When it broke I still had the chunk of handle in my hand, and I think that's what got me. Glass was bouncing all over the place."

That made sense. "I'll call Kaden in a few minutes. You relax. That's an order."

She closed her eyes and nodded.

They wanted to keep an eye on her for a little while. While her blood pressure had stabilized, it had been on the low side when he brought her in. He agreed with that and stepped outside to make the call he didn't want to make. By this time it was after six. He knew Kaden would be out of his meetings.

"Hey, what's up?"

Seth closed his eyes. "Do *not* freak out on me."

"What?"

"I'm serious, dude. Do *not* freak out on me."

"You're freaking me out now, goddamn it! Is Leah okay?"

"She's fine. There was an accident. It was just an accident."

"Oh my God! What happened?"

Seth related the incident. Kaden sounded shaky. "I'll try to get a flight home tonight."

"No, she's okay. Seriously. She's fine. Once they release her I'll get her home and put her to bed. They've given her pain meds. I've got a fucking mess to clean up in the kitchen."

Kaden hesitated. "Are you sure it was an accident?"

"Yeah. I know it sounds coincidental, but if you'd seen the way she was freaking out—"

Kaden breathed a deep sigh of relief Seth heard on his end. "Okay. If she was upset then it probably was an accident. If it's not an accident, if she does something on purpose, she tries to hide it and blow it off. At least, she used to."

"No, dude, I'll swear it was an accident. I'd asked her to mix a pitcher of sangria."

"Aw, it was the red pitcher she broke?"

He expected a lot of comments but not that. "Yeah. How'd you know?"

"She always uses that one to make your sangria. She likes the way the orange slices look inside it. It's one of her favorites. Damn, I'll have to see if I can find her another one."

Seth sat on the curb, his own stress catching up with him. "She panicked when I told her I had to take her collar off."

"Poor thing. As soon as you can, I want to talk to her. Tell her I'm not mad at her."

"Let me get back in there and check on her."

She was dozing but opened her eyes when he took her hand. "Did you talk to Master?" she whispered.

He nodded. "He's not upset. He told me to tell you he's not mad." She closed her eyes again, and a tear rolled down her cheek, scaring Seth. "Hey, what's wrong?"

"I'm so sorry."

"It was an accident, Leah. Accidents happen."

"But now He's worried. He shouldn't be stressed in His condition."

Danger!

"Love"—Seth made sure to use a low, firm voice—"calm down. He's not stressed. He was worried until I told him the whole story. He knows it was an accident."

"Really?"

"Yeah. I mean, he's not happy you got hurt, but he's not stressed like that. He's okay. Shit happens."

She nodded.

She was released a half hour later. Once they were in the car, Seth dialed

Kaden and handed Leah his phone.

He watched as she closed her eyes and talked with Kade. Her left arm was bandaged, and she needed to get it checked in a couple of days. He had two prescriptions to fill for her, an antibiotic and pain meds. He pulled into a pharmacy and left Leah in the car, still talking to Kaden on the phone while he was inside waiting for the medicine.

Back home. He'd finally stopped feeling weird calling it home. It was home. It felt like home. Maybe he wasn't at the point where he could think about it as his in terms of owning it, but he certainly felt comfortable there, like he was part of the family.

He carried her inside and laid her on the couch. "I'll make you some dinner after I get the kitchen cleaned up," he said.

She started to protest. He cut her off. "No. You get taken care of tonight."

"But that's my job!"

He whipped out his cell phone and called Kaden, then put him on the phone with her while he went to clean up the glass and heat her some leftovers. By the time he returned with her food, Kaden had apparently mollified her.

She handed Seth the phone. "Master wants to talk with You, Sir."

"Thanks, love." He took it to his bedroom and shut the door. "Don't fucking tell me to give her a session tonight. I won't do it. I don't care what you say."

He laughed. "No, I wasn't going to tell you that. Pain meds zonk her out. She hates taking them. She'll be sound asleep in an hour, I bet. Probably sleep until noon tomorrow."

Relief! "Thank God."

"You did good."

"Promise me this gets easier."

"Just follow your heart. We'll talk more tomorrow after I get home."

Seth returned to the kitchen, nuked himself a plate of food, and sat next to Leah on the couch. She'd picked at her food but hadn't made much headway.

"You'd better eat."

"I'm so sleepy."

"I know, babe. It's the meds they gave you."

He finished his dinner and made her lay down with her head in his lap while they watched TV. Before long, she'd developed an unfocused stare he knew was due to the pain meds taking hold in her system.

"What are we going to do without him?" she whispered.

Oh, fuck. He did not want to have this talk with her right now.

"We'll be okay. It'll take some time, but we'll be okay."

"Really?"

"Yeah."

She was quiet for a while. He'd hoped she'd fallen asleep. Then she spoke again. "I'm going to miss him so much." Large tears rolled down her face.

"Me too, babe." He felt his own tears close to the surface and tried to push them away.

"How long do we have?"

"Babe, we don't need to talk about this."

"How long?" Her voice sounded soft but firm. Her quiet tears unnerved him. Maybe being zonked out on pain meds was helping her safely process things.

"I don't know. Every day is a gift. He's still strong. He's got a lot of life in him. I can't give you a time frame."

"You went with him to the oncologist."

Shit. She hadn't acted like she knew about Kaden's appointment. "The doctors don't know."

She turned her head and looked him in the eye. "I know he made you promise not to tell me. That's something he'd do. But I need to know, Seth. I need an idea."

He shrugged. "They don't know. At least several months if there's no drastic decline."

"After Christmas?"

He nodded. "Hopefully. At this rate, most likely well after Christmas."

She nodded and wiped her face with her good hand. "Okay. That's good enough for me for now." She fell silent again for a few minutes. "Thank you for taking pictures. I appreciate that."

"I didn't know you were paying attention."

She smiled. "I see more than you think I do." Her smile faded. "I keep trying not to think about it. That it's probably his last Christmas. But it's hard not to."

"I know."

"He wants you to go to the club alone with me before we get crazy with the holiday stuff."

That was news to Seth. He fought a brief moment of panic. "What?"

"You're ready."

"Like hell I am."

"He didn't tell me exactly why, but I know." She took a deep breath, more tears flowing. "He wants it to happen so he can help us work on it more if we need him. Before he starts to get really sick. He said it was because of the parties and lights and stuff, but he's not fooling me. I know he's trying to take it easy on me."

"Does that bother you?"

"No. It doesn't hurt so much to think about it tonight because I'm in a lot of pain already."

Ahh. That explained it. "The drugs help, too, I'm sure."

She weakly smiled. "A little."

"Listen, I catch you trying to doctor shop to get scripts, I'll freaking tie you up and not let you come for a month."

Her eyes widened, then she laughed, long and hard.

Well, he'd finally managed to make her laugh for the day.

She was still crying, but at least she smiled. "Thank you, Seth."

She finally fell asleep. Once she was softly snoring in his lap, he carried her to his bedroom and gently tucked her into his bed. He cleaned up their dinner dishes and turned out all the lights. Turning on his TV, he set the sleep timer, then curled around her and gently kissed her forehead.

"I promise, I'll take care of you. We'll get through it, babe."

It took him a long time to finally get to sleep, the memory of her tears fresh in his mind.

* * * *

She was still sound asleep at seven the next morning. He carefully extricated himself from her arms. In sleep she had rolled over and cuddled tightly against him, practically clinging to his side. He started coffee and checked his cell phone, no calls from Kade. He knew Kade's flight was at eleven and his friend would already be awake.

"She still asleep?" Kaden asked.

"Yep. Dead to the world."

"Good. The irony is, perhaps it's for the best she did this."

"I told you, it was a freaking accident."

"I know. I believe it was, too. I'm not saying I'm happy she got hurt. In the grand scheme of things, it'll probably help her."

Seth didn't know if he wanted to fess up about their conversation. That could wait until Kade returned. "How do I convince her to just sit and chill out today and let me take care of her?"

"Sit and talk. Play your guitar for her. Tell her what would make you happy for today is to spoil her rotten."

Well, that *was* the truth. She already took damn good care of him. It didn't matter that both Kade and Leah thought they owed Seth for doing this. Seth felt he owed them.

He scrambled himself some eggs and frequently walked down the hall to look in on Leah. Still zonked. He suspected it probably wasn't just the meds but the accumulated stress and grief taking its toll. It was good she could rest.

Now with Kaden's trip out of the way, he would spend most of his time at the house. Still some work to clear up, he'd explained, but what he had left, he could mostly do from home.

A little before eleven Seth grabbed his laptop and started back to the bedroom to sit with Leah when the house phone rang.

"Shit." He raced for it, hoping it wouldn't wake Leah.

"Kaden?" the woman asked.

Aw, fuck. He knew that voice. Kaden's younger sister.

"No, Denise, it's Seth." He wished he'd let it go to voicemail.

The frost in her voice would have comfortably air-conditioned the entire house, even with every last freaking window open. "What are *you* doing answering their phone?"

Denise had never liked Seth, even as kids. The feeling was mutual. Kaden hadn't broken the news to his family yet about him dying, hadn't told them about Seth living there either. He wanted to wait until after the holidays, if possible.

"Kaden's out of town. He's coming back tonight." The less said, the better.

"I tried his cell and he didn't answer. Leah's not answering hers, either."

"She's asleep." He realized as soon as the words left his mouth that it was the wrong thing to say.

"What do you mean she's asleep? How would you know?"

He might as well have waved a red flag in front of a bull. "She had a small accident yesterday, cut her arm, just a few stitches, no big deal. The pain meds knocked her out."

"Well, I'll come over and stay with her until he gets home. You said he's coming home tonight. You can go do whatever you do." First the suspicion, now the condescension.

Fan-fucking-tastic. "No, Denise, that's not necessary. It's under control."

"*You* can't stay with her."

"I'm studying to be a nurse, and I've had medic training. I'd say I'm a better person to stay with her than you are."

"If she's hurt she should have family with her."

I am family.

Instead, he said, "Kaden asked me to stay with her. You have a problem with that, you can take it up with your brother tomorrow. You will not come in here and start your shit."

"How *dare* you!"

If he didn't get off the fucking phone with her and fast, he would blow his top. Leah didn't like Denise either. It confused the hell out of him why Denise was suddenly so insistent on taking care of her sister-in-law when they rarely spoke anyway. He glanced at the time and knew it was too late to call Kaden. He'd be on the plane already.

"Good-bye, Denise. When Kaden gets home, I'll tell him you called." He hung up before she could argue, then he turned the ringer off.

He was sitting in bed with his laptop propped in his lap and MSNBC turned on low when Leah finally awoke around noon.

"Hey, babe. How you feel?"

She winced, trying not to move her arm. "It hurts."

He helped her sit up and got her another pain pill. "Master's orders, you let me take care of you today. Got it, love?"

She weakly smiled. "Believe it or not, I won't argue with you. It really hurts."

"Not the good pain, huh?"

She laughed, wincing. "No, not even close to the good pain." At least he'd gotten his laugh for the day out of her. He made sure she could stand without falling and helped her to her room. She promised to yell if she had problems. He left her bedroom door open so he could hear her.

In a little while she emerged, and he brought her breakfast out to the couch. They watched TV, talked, and she dozed while he caught up on his e-mail. When the doorbell rang a little after one, Seth carefully extricated himself from where Leah was using him as a pillow.

Denise glared at him and pushed her way inside. "Where is she? I want to talk to her."

Leah sat up. "Denise?"

"Oh, you poor thing! What happened to you?" The fake syrupy concern dripping from Denise's voice could have put an elephant into a sugar coma.

Leah nervously glanced at Seth. "It's nothing. What are you doing here?"

Denise glared at Seth. "Well, this so-called friend of yours tried to keep me away. He was very rude. I told him I'd come over to take care of you until Kaden comes home."

Seth walked to the back of the couch and stood behind Leah. "I told you, Denise, no. Your presence isn't required or desired."

"How *dare* you!" Denise looked at Leah and grabbed her right hand. "Listen, my friend, Brianna, she overheard Kaden and Ed talking the other day at a Rotary meeting. What's going on? Why haven't you two told us he's sick?"

Aw, fuck. "Okay, Denise, that's enough." Seth walked around the couch. "Out you go."

"You have no right to run me out of here!"

"Yes, I do, because it's my house. I live here now."

He could have dropped his pants and taken a shit on the coffee table, and it wouldn't have shocked her as much as that revelation. "What?"

"He doesn't want anyone to know about his personal life, so keep your fucking mouth shut." Now it made sense. The greedy bitch wanted to worm her way into Kaden's good graces and hopefully get her hands on some of his money. She was always in debt, and her lazy-assed husband spent more time getting fired than he did working.

Denise looked at Leah. "Tell him he can't order me out. I'm your sister-in-law."

Leah's blank stare scared the crap out of Seth. "He told you to get out. I'm telling you to get out. I'm also telling you to keep your fucking mouth shut. Kaden doesn't want anyone to know his private business. If he wants you to know what goes on in our lives, he'll tell you."

Had she yelled it, it would have relieved Seth. But Leah's soft, nearly passive whisper made his balls draw up tight against his belly in fear.

Fuck.

Denise sat back, briefly stunned into momentary silence. "You don't mean that."

"She meant it. Now do you leave, or do I call the cops and have your ass hauled out of here in handcuffs?"

Denise glared at them both before finally storming out of the house. She made sure to slam the door behind her. He'd have to see about getting their front gate code changed. He'd forgotten she knew it.

Whew. Now for Leah. He turned and dropped to his knees in front of her, grabbed her hands. "Babe, talk to me."

She closed her eyes and cried. It started quietly, building into anguished screams similar to what happened after a particularly intense session.

He sat next to Leah on the couch and carefully folded her into his arms as she sobbed herself to sleep. She was still asleep when Kaden rushed in a little after four. "Is she okay?"

Seth carefully extricated himself from Leah, grabbed Kaden's arm and dragged him back to the playroom, shutting the door behind them.

"Call your fucking sister right now and ban her from the goddamned house."

"What?"

Seth related the events. Kaden looked like he would explode. "Okay. I wondered why she was calling me all of a sudden." He pulled out his cell phone, and Seth returned to the living room after closing the playroom door behind him. A few times he thought he heard Kaden's enraged voice screaming from the back of the house. Fifteen minutes later, his face red, Kaden made a beeline through the living room and straight to the kitchen.

Seth followed him and found Kaden pouring himself a drink. "Want one?" Kaden asked.

Seth shook his head. He was trying not to drink. He was never an alcoholic, but he certainly didn't need to be overimbibing at a time like this. He'd been limiting himself to just a few beers or glasses of wine a week, usually one after dinner, if even that.

"Well?"

Kaden took a drink. "God only knows how many people the bitch has told by now, even though she doesn't know anything. Looking for sympathy. Fuck." He set his jaw. "This is what I did *not* want to happen. I had no idea anyone could hear us talking. Fucking nosy eavesdropping bitch." He took another drink.

"What did you tell her?"

"I told her our personal life was none of her fucking business, and if I caught wind of her spreading stories about me, that I would tell everyone how I had to bail her husband out of jail on solicitation charges a couple of years ago."

Seth froze, then laughed. "You never told me that! Fuck."

"If you were married to Denise, wouldn't you want to see a hooker?"

Seth laughed, long and hard, enjoying the slight smile that finally crept across Kaden's face. "Well, I guess you're right there." Seth rubbed his face. "Go sit with her. She'll be happy you're home when she wakes up. I'll fix dinner."

Kaden drained his drink and turned to Seth. When he finally spoke, his voice sounded thick with emotion. "Thank you. I mean it. For everything. Especially for taking care of Leah. I meant it when I said I love you."

"Yeah, well, I love you too, dude. But like I said—"

"I'm still not doing you," Kaden finished.

They grinned and laughed. This time Kaden's broad smile made him look a couple of years younger.

Chapter Ten

Leah's arm healed nicely and probably wouldn't leave too much of a scar. Three weeks after the incident, life settled back into normalcy.

Normal for them, anyways.

Kaden was having a blast with his plans for the light display. Seth even had to admit he was getting into the holiday spirit. Leah split her time between preparing for the huge charity Christmas banquet and helping plan the dinners and parties they'd hold at the house throughout the season.

Seth had worked up to nearly an hour at a time with the singletail. His aim was slowly improving, but he had a ways to go. An hour working with the whip left him...well, whipped. Between his nearly-numb arm and blistered palm, even when using gloves, he was beat. He changed into his swimsuit and climbed into the hot tub. He was too fucking tired to go for a swim.

He didn't know how long he lay there when Leah's voice startled him. "Want me to rub your arm?"

He nodded. He wasn't going to fight her anymore on this. She wanted to do it, it felt good when she did it, Kaden wanted her to do it, so why the fuck not? "Please."

"You know," she said, her voice soft, "it'd be easier if you'd let me get in the hot tub with you."

He didn't open his eyes, too tired to argue. "Okay."

The soft *whisp* of fabric against flesh, then he felt her sit next to him in the water. Her hands felt good, he wouldn't deny it. One day...

Hopefully far in the future. He still prayed for a miracle and knew part of his reluctance stemmed from that. If he held off, didn't push forward as hard as Kaden wanted him to, maybe there wouldn't be an after to mourn through. Maybe he could stave off the inevitable.

Then he wouldn't feel guilty about sleeping with his best friend's wife when it wasn't necessary after all. Kaden still looked good, didn't look sick.

Maybe it wouldn't happen.

Seth didn't mind taking a dip in the River Denial.

His body succumbed to her touch, relaxing as she slowly worked his muscles. It felt better than good. Who the fuck was he kidding? It felt great.

He'd nearly gone to sleep when he was aware of her changing position, straddling his legs, her hands going to his—

Seth's eyes popped open and he grabbed her hands as they tried to tug at his waistband. Leah had sunk into the water, visible only from the shoulders up.

"What are you doing?" he hoarsely asked. "That's not what's sore."

She smiled. "I bet it's stiff."

Yeah, she wasn't kidding there. Despite his shock, he was stiff, all right. Like fucking concrete. Just as Kade said.

Stalemate. She didn't try to pull away, simply let him hold her there.

"Babe, I'm not ready to make love to yet. It's not that I don't want to. It's just too soon for me."

"You don't have to do anything but lie back and enjoy it."

What the fuck!

"What?"

"Just enjoy it. Let me take care of you. Please?"

"What about Kaden?" he hoarsely whispered.

"He's okay with this. You know that. He's okay with whatever you want to do with me."

Fuck, he knew that. He was stalling for time and running out of excuses.

"I don't have any protection." Even he thought that sounded lame.

"The doctor said you don't have cooties. It's not an issue for me anyway. Even if it was, I don't think any woman has ever gotten pregnant giving a hand job."

Stalemate. Again.

Her eyes focused on his, steady, calm. He wouldn't deny he wanted it. The proof was standing straight up in his swimsuit, screaming at him that he was a stupid motherfucker for refusing in the first place.

She pulled out the secret weapon. Her eyes brimmed with uncried tears, melting his heart. "Please, Seth? Let me do this for you. I want to. You're not forcing me. I know Kaden told you about me. This isn't the same."

"I feel like it is."

"He asked me when he told me about... He asked me that night he first talked to you. He did ask me if I wanted him to go through with it or if I wanted him to find someone else." Her voice choked, breaking his heart. "You were the first one I thought of, Seth. If he's not here, I can't imagine being with anyone but you. Not just to be my master. I don't *want* to be with anyone but you. Please?"

Seth pulled her into his arms, holding her for a long moment. His desire to adhere to Kaden's wishes and to keep Leah safe and sane battled with his heart and body and conscience.

It would have to happen sometime.

"I'm not ready to... I'm not ready to take that next step yet. And it doesn't seem fair to you to be one-sided about this. I mean, this isn't the same as doing something to you during a session."

She turned in his lap so she could face him. Whether it was intentional or not, she ground against his stiff cock. "This isn't one-sided. You're doing something for me that no one else can do. I understand if you need more time for some things. Let me at least take care of you. Please?"

"I could play the Dom card and order you back to your bedroom right now."

She nodded. "And I would go."

"You wouldn't be happy if I did that."

She shook her head.

He took a deep breath. "We're not, like, going to be talking about this at breakfast tomorrow or anything, are we?"

She finally smiled. "No."

"Because that would push me over the fucking edge, man."

Leah caressed his cheek. "No. We don't have to talk about things."

"It's bad enough... I feel bad enough as it is. My weird-o-meter would shoot off the scale if I had to talk to Kaden about this kind of stuff."

She nodded. "I'll tell him that. But it'll make him happy that you're finally letting me take care of you like this."

"I *so* cannot get my head around that."

"That's okay. He understands."

After another long moment, he brought her hands up to his lips and kissed them. "All right. I'm not comfortable with... Let's take this one step at a time. Okay? If I let you…" He silently swore. "Just hand jobs. For now. Okay? Don't try to push me to take the next step yet. I mean hey, you got to sleep in bed with me, right? I'll get there, but I need time to get used to this and try to get over feeling fucking guilty about it. Promise?"

She nodded.

He released her hands after a final, gentle squeeze. "Magic fingers, do your stuff."

He'd kill for the bright smile she gave him. His heart melted. This was so fucked up on so many levels, but it was worth it to see her smile.

Seth recalled he was approximately the same size as Kade. So unless his friend had suddenly mutated, that was, at least, one less metaphorical shoe for him to fill. He didn't want to disappoint Leah.

She turned, straddling his legs again. He lifted his hips so she could pull his trunks down and off him. He closed his eyes and heard the wet *splat* as she dropped his trunks out of the hot tub and onto the lanai. He laid his head back against the edge of the hot tub and tried not to moan too loudly as her fingers gently wrapped around his shaft.

It was amazing. With one hand cupping and milking his sac, her other slowly massaging his cock, he knew it wouldn't take her long to get him off.

Hell, her hand job was better than any fucking blow job he'd ever gotten in his life! She took her time, drawing it out, caressing him in a way…

In a way no one had ever touched him before.

The right fucking woman. How had he never had the right woman before?

Before Leah.

It built deep in his balls. When he tensed, Leah seemed to anticipate his release. She tightened her grip and squeezed what felt like every last drop out of him, leaving him spent and trembling in the water.

Damn.

It never felt that good when he did it himself.

Reading his body, Leah stilled her hands without releasing him. He eventually opened his eyes.

Her smile lit every inch of her face, for once erasing a few of the grief lines slowly attempting to take over. "Thank you," she said.

He laughed. "No, thank you."

She leaned forward. He thought she might kiss him, but she simply touched her forehead to his. "You have a very nice cock, Sir."

"Don't harsh the mellow, girl."

She giggled and gently squeezed him. He didn't think he'd be up for more and was extremely surprised to feel himself stiffen in her hands.

"Ooh!" she cooed. "Seconds."

He laughed and closed his eyes again. He lasted longer this time, due in no small part to her talented skills in bringing him close and letting him cool off. When he exploded the second time he grabbed her and pulled her into his lap, holding her tightly, his face buried in her hair.

He didn't think it was his imagination that she seemed more relaxed now.

Seth released her with a deep sigh and a kiss to her temple. "Thank you, darlin'. That was wonderful."

"Not going to fight me on this anymore?"

"I guess not. As long as you don't try to push me too fast and you're really okay with it. And," he added, leveling his gaze at her, "you don't do it in front of Kaden. I don't think I can handle that yet."

"It's not cheating."

"It feels like it to me."

"It's not cheating when he's okay with it."

"He wouldn't be okay with it if the circumstances were different."

She spoke so quietly he almost thought he'd misheard her. "He was going to ask you to move in anyway, before this happened. We've talked about it for years. We wanted to wait until your divorce was final."

He grabbed her arms again and made her sit up so he could look at her. "What?"

Now she looked uncomfortable. "We were going to ask you to move in and maybe see what happened from there."

"Leah, what the fuck?"

"I didn't want you to meet someone else and get stuck with a shitty woman again," she quickly said, the words spilling from her. "I was so sick of these women not treating you right. None of them were good enough for you, Seth. Face it, they weren't. I thought maybe if you were here, where I could take care of you…maybe you'd let me do that for you."

Sometimes he was terminally slow on the uptake. Many of her previous comments from the past weeks and even from several years earlier slammed home. "How long have you been in love with me?" he whispered.

"Always."

Stunned, he released her. "Go to bed, sweetie," he numbly muttered.

She quickly climbed out of the hot tub, grabbed her shirt, and returned to her bedroom.

Seth sat there in emotional shock, trying to absorb this information. He needed time alone to process this. How much did Kaden know? How much had she told him?

How much had Kaden *not* told him yet?

Chapter Eleven

After a restless night, Seth awoke early the next morning, a little before dawn. His plan had been to go jogging and try to quiet his mind. When he started the coffee Kaden must have heard him and walked out to the kitchen.

Seth looked at him. Despite what he'd told Leah the night before about not wanting to talk about it, he needed to talk about it. "Dude. What. The. Fuck?"

Kaden's sneaky smile told him a lot. "What?"

"Don't bullshit me. I know you two talked last night after…you know."

"Know what?"

"Quit busting my balls. Don't make me fucking say it."

Kaden leaned against the counter and crossed his arms. "What do you want me to say?"

"I want—" Seth realized his voice had risen. He dropped it, speaking low. "I want you to tell me. What. The. Fuck?"

The men heard the door to the master bedroom open. Kaden looked at the floor. "Go back to bed, love," he called out. "You don't need to get up yet."

There was the briefest of pauses, then Leah's slightly puzzled-sounding, "Yes, Master."

They heard the door close.

Kaden looked at Seth and dropped his voice. "She's always been in love with you."

"She's. Your. Wife!"

"I know."

Speechless, Seth stood there, trying to sort out his emotions. "How can you even stand to fucking look at me?"

"I'm looking at the man I love even more than a brother, a man I know would gladly switch places with me in a heartbeat to save my life if he thought he could. A man who will love and cherish the woman I love as much as I do."

"How long have you been planning this? And why the fuck did you lie to me? What was all that adjusting your thinking and being honest bullshit you talked about?"

"It wasn't bullshit. I just sort of fudged the timeframe. We've been wanting to approach you for years. You kept meeting those asshole women before we could talk to you. And we didn't want to mess up your divorces once you'd left them. I was waiting this time until you told us you were legally free again." He studied his hands. "I was going to ask you...before."

That fucking word again.

Kaden continued. "We weren't going to tell you about the BDSM stuff at first. We were going to talk you into moving in with us and then go from there, kind of ease you into it. I didn't want to shock you too much at first. I didn't want to freak you out," Kaden calmly said.

"Well, um, congratulations, you freaked me out anyway."

"I know. I'm sorry."

Seth studied him. "How can you say you want to share your wife with me?"

"Because I love you."

"Dude, I am sooo not doing you! I thought we settled that."

"We did. I already told you I don't swing that way. I don't mean that kind of love. I knew I needed another person I could trust to help take care of her. What the fuck would happen, for example, if some drunk driver hit me on the way home? It'd fucking kill her." He took a deep breath. "I didn't seriously think it was something I'd have to worry about for years. I thought I had all the time in the world. I trust you with her, man. I wasn't bullshitting you when I told you that. Look at how good you took care of her while I was in Atlanta."

"How can you stand there and tell me you're really okay sharing her with me?"

"Compersion."

Seth did a double-take. "What the fuck?"

"It's a term the poly community uses. It's basically the opposite of jealousy, although it's more complex than that. If she'd loved anyone else, it'd fucking kill me. But it's you. And as weird as it sounds—and yes, I'll be the first to admit it sounds weird—I'm not jealous of you."

"Poly? Polyester?" Seth didn't know polyester had its own community. "What the fuck does that have to do with what we're talking about?"

Kaden laughed, long and hard. "Polyamorous," he finally managed.

"I am *so* not becoming a fucking Mormon." He thought Kade was raised Methodist, even though he and Leah didn't go to church.

Kaden rolled his eyes. "Not polygamy. Jesus Christ, we're not talking *Big Love* here, dude."

"What about all that crap you said about being angry and jealous?"

His eyes grew sad. "I am angry. And I'm jealous. But not about you being with her. I've never felt that. I'm angry and jealous I don't get to be there with the two of you. You will get all these years with her that I won't have. It's not fair."

Seth studied him for a long time before speaking again. "So what was your original plan? To freaking share her?"

"Yes. Once I realized she loved you I talked to her about it. Not about specifically training you to be her Master. Just about moving you in and seeing what happened."

"You're a bigger fucking man than I am."

He shrugged. "I love to make her happy. It's not like she begged me to do it, but she loved the idea when I brought it up. We figured if nature took its course and things worked out, then I could talk to you about the BDSM stuff and see if you'd be interested in learning that."

"How were you planning on keeping that secret?"

"We weren't. We were just going to tone it way down around you so you didn't know the full extent of what we were doing, that's all."

"Last night she sounded like this plan was a surprise to her. About the making me her master shit."

He shrugged. "You've seen how she is. I don't like to tell her more than I have to. If I'd told her my worries, she would have panicked and thought something was wrong with me. I was going to ease you into the Dom training with her and figured after a year or two it would be an automatic assumption on her part. She would have naturally accepted you as her Dom, so if anything did happen to me, you could simply pick up from that point and move on with her." He picked at his fingernails. "I never figured on having to give you a crash course like this."

Seth remained quiet, trying to absorb this new information.

Kaden eventually spoke again. "If you're going to back out on us, I need to know. Right now. As in *right* now. Because I have to make plans for her. Can I count on you?"

"You said honesty was the most important thing. What else haven't you told me?"

"That's it. I'm sorry. I was trying not to dump everything on you at once. It was shitty enough circumstances to begin with."

Seth leaned against the counter and closed his eyes.

kaden'sdying

There had been times, stretches of hours, where he didn't hear that mental heartbeat. Could almost kid himself that it wouldn't happen.

Kaden's voice dropped to nearly a whisper. "I need you, Seth. She needs you. You can doubt yourself all you want, but I know you. I know you would rather die than let her down."

"I still can't get over you wanting to share her."

"She's not your average woman. You and I are it for her. Imagine how hard it was on her all those years watching you with those women. It killed her. I wasn't kidding when I said there were nights I had to gag her to shut her up. Not just that, give her sessions in the playroom to take her mind off of things. Lots of distraction. She hated your wives. I told her she couldn't dump her feelings on you, because while I could understand why she felt that way, I knew it would freak you out."

"Such an understatement, you have no clue."

"The right woman, Seth. We're not the only people in the world who live in a poly triad. At least, for a little while, we can make her happy, make her dream come true." He looked sad again. "Not as many years as I had hoped."

"I can't share her with someone else, dude. I mean, yeah, you. Okay. She's your wife. What if she falls in love with someone else in the future? I can't do that."

"She would never make you do that. In nearly twenty years, she's never expressed an interest in anyone else but you. Ever. She would have sat back until the day she died and never told you how she felt if I'd had a problem with it. She didn't want to admit it to me, but I saw her. I saw how she tried to take care of you. I've never seen her react to someone the way she reacts to you. She's always been naturally submissive to you. I've seen her take on old farts on the boards at some of those nonprofits, and she's a fucking ballbuster. She normally doesn't take shit from people. You know that. She trusts you. She's always trusted you."

Despite his new flurry of conflicting emotions, Seth had to admit he'd always felt a connection with Leah. Something he'd never had with his ex-wives or girlfriends.

Something he'd always wished he had.

"Admit it," Kaden whispered. "You've always loved her, too."

Seth studied the Italian tile floor. He remembered the day he went with Leah to help her pick it out, how she'd deferred to him, asked him the pros and cons of this versus different ones.

How she'd trusted him.

His eyes lifted to the cabinets. The day she picked out the style and finish, Kaden had sat in the showroom, a subtle smile on his face, while Leah asked Seth for his opinions.

The house was full of memories of helping Leah make decisions about it. Kaden had never, not once, spoken his opinion. He'd told Seth that whatever Leah wanted, Leah got.

At the time, Seth assumed it was simply the words of a loving husband with a pretty fat bank account.

Now he saw it in a new light, illuminated from a different point of view.

Leah calling him, sometimes fifteen or twenty times a day while the house was being built, asking for his opinion on something. When he asked Kaden about it, nervous it might be construed the wrong way, Kaden shrugged. "If it doesn't bother me, it shouldn't bother you. If she's bugging you, tell her. She'll try not to."

No, it hadn't bugged him, although it pissed his ex off every time she saw Leah's number show up on his phone.

In fact, he wouldn't deny he'd dragged his feet on a few things, trying to prolong the experience.

He'd really missed talking to Leah when the house was done.

Leah asking him, almost a hopeful look in her eye, if he liked something she'd picked.

Not Kaden.

Him.

The paint and carpet and furniture. The landscaping.

Taking him with them when she shopped for mattresses for the guest rooms, making him lie down and try them all out, picking the one he'd liked the best...

Fuck.

He met Kaden's eyes again. His friend watched him from across the kitchen. "Can I count on you?" he quietly asked again.

Seth nodded. "I won't let her down. Or you."

Kaden nodded, sighing. "I know you're weirded out and don't want to discuss details. I understand that. Just know that whenever you're ready..." He smiled. "We've got a big fucking bed, dude."

Seth laughed and closed his eyes. "I'm sooo not ready to have this conversation, Kade."

"She's going to be upset she didn't get to wake you up this morning." Seth didn't miss the playful gleam in his friend's eye.

Seth patted his stomach. He'd managed to lose ten pounds over the past several weeks despite Leah's great and plentiful cooking. "Yeah, well, I need to go jogging. I've got to get in shape. If I'm going to do this, I need to get my ass in gear and get my body back in condition. I look like a fucking slob compared to you."

Kaden laughed and left the kitchen. Seth decided to forgo the coffee until after his run, sure that Leah, once released by Kaden, would come looking for him and he might not get out of the house once she got her hands on him.

Literally.

While muggy, the morning hadn't turned obnoxiously hot yet. Seth set a fast pace, pushing himself, trying to remember his Army PT crap that he'd spent too many months and years trying to forget. He needed to get into shape. That wasn't bullshit on his part.

He needed to get in shape because he promised Kade he'd help. Leah needed him.

And as much as he despised exercise, he would do it for them.

For Leah.

* * * *

Sure enough, a few minutes after Seth returned from his run and stepped into the shower, Leah tapped on his bathroom door.

"Yeah?"

She stepped in and closed the door behind her. She was naked, except for the collar. When she opened the shower door he didn't stop her.

"Want me to scrub your back?"

"That's not the part of me you want to scrub, and you damn well know it."

She smiled. "I never said I didn't want to scrub other parts of you too."

He motioned her inside. She stood behind him and wrapped her arms around him, pressing her body against his.

Damn, she felt good.

She slid her hands down his abs and found his cock. Just the sight of her stepping into the shower had made him hard again. As Seth rested his forehead against the shower wall, Leah worked her fingers up and down his shaft and around his balls. Not just her hands but the feel of her arms around him, her body pressed against his…

It would be easy to turn around and pin her against the wall and fuck her silly. He bet she was wanting him to do just that, probably wet and ready to go for him.

Fuck.

He pressed his palms flat against the cool tile and closed his eyes. She felt damn good. The only thing stopping him was a realization he'd had on his jog. Maybe Kaden could feel compersion or whatever the fuck it was called. Maybe Kade was a bigger man than him, able to share his wife.

But when all was said and done, Seth wasn't sure he could share those feelings. He wasn't sure he could share Leah with Kaden.

If he didn't take that one final step, it wasn't so painful for him to watch her walk through that bedroom door every night and close it and know she was curled up with his best friend.

Guilt wouldn't eat him alive over the jealousy he felt.

Because if he didn't take that last step, she was still just Kaden's wife, and his personal guilt over getting involved with her was limited in scope. He felt he had no right to stake a claim to her if he didn't claim her in the first place.

If he didn't claim her, maybe Kaden wouldn't die.

Conscious thought escaped him as she brought him close and finally gave him release. He bucked his hips in time with her hands, softly moaning as he shot off all over her fingers.

He felt her kiss his back, between his shoulder blades.

"How was that?" she whispered.

"Good," he said, his voice ragged. He couldn't face her. He gently patted her arm. "Thank you. Let me finish up, and I'll be out in a little bit for breakfast."

"Okay."

He didn't move until he heard her leave the bathroom. Then he leaned against the wall, laid his forehead against his arm, and silently cried.

* * * *

Kaden was working in his study when Seth emerged from his bedroom a little while later. If Leah noticed his red eyes, she said nothing. She was once again dressed in a long T-shirt.

"Here's your breakfast."

He tried not to look her in the eye. "Thank you, hon."

She left him alone, perhaps sensing his disquiet. She was always good about that. Like she clued in and seemed to know when to hover and when to clear out.

Maybe that was one of the things that made her a good slave.

God, he couldn't get used to using that word when referring to Leah.

He didn't want to face Kaden yet. He *really* didn't want to feel the force of Leah's eyes on him either. He retrieved a six-foot singletail and took it out to the backyard, started practicing on a tree. Kaden had told him if he could start taking the tips off of leaves without knocking the leaf off the tree, he'd be on his way to mastering it.

Seth would be happy if he could just hit the freaking tree.

He worked for over an hour, taking his time, trying for accuracy instead of power. When his arm had reached its limit for throwing the whip, Seth sat in the shade under one of the large live oaks toward the back of the property, his back against the trunk, facing the woods. Their property bordered a large state park, a nature reserve. It wasn't unusual to see deer early in the morning or late in the evening.

What the fuck was he doing? Why was he holding out? Part of him called himself a fucking dumbass. That part was located immediately north of his testicles and south of his navel.

Kaden wanted him to do it. Leah wanted him to do it. His own body wanted him to do it.

His heart and mind and conscience wouldn't let him do it.

Seth closed his eyes. What they were asking him to do went against every grain of his being. Yes, some of the BDSM stuff was easier to deal with now. He imagined making love to Leah was yet another milestone he'd have to deal with. He spent his life in mediocrity and he damn well knew it. He hadn't gone to college, had joined the Army to try to figure out what to do with his life. Kaden was always the smart one, the one with his shit together. And while Seth knew he wasn't a stellar success in his life, he'd tried to always deal honestly and honorably. He'd never cheated on his wives or girlfriends—ever. He'd never knowingly gone out with a woman who was already involved with someone else.

Fucking his best friend's wife was *not* honorable.

No matter how much all three of them wanted it.

He couldn't put it off much longer.

He sat there for over an hour when he heard footsteps in the grass. He knew from the sound it was Kaden.

"Can I join you?"

Seth nodded.

Kaden stretched out in the shade. "What's on your mind?"

He shrugged. "Lots of stuff. Just trying to make a bunch of freaking square pegs fit in round holes."

"BFH."

Seth laughed. "Yeah. Bigger fucking hammer time, all right." He was quiet for a moment. "I know you probably think I'm a chickenshit."

"I don't think that about you. I never have. I never will, either."

"Come on, Kade. You're the successful big-shot attorney. I'm the fuckup. Let's face it, even when we were kids, everyone thought of me as your mercy friend. I still don't know why you liked me all these years."

"Because you're my friend. Because you didn't give a shit that I was a big-shot attorney. You were always willing to volunteer to help me with projects or just come over and hang out, and you never asked me for anything."

"Bullshit! I've asked you for tons of stuff over the years."

Kaden rolled over onto his back and stared up at the branches. "I don't give a shit about favors and stuff. You never asked me for anything you couldn't give back in return. You never tried to use me. You never tried to ask me for money. You never tried to get free legal advice from me. When you got divorced, you never asked me to handle your cases or even for a referral. I had to practically force you to take Mike's name and number. I've always been 'just Kaden' to you."

"Yeah, well who the hell else would you be?"

"That's my point." He leveled his grey eyes at Seth. "I don't trust my own brother and sister the way I trust you. I sure as hell don't like them the way I love you."

Seth was quiet for a moment. He smirked. "Still not doing you."

Kaden laughed. "Me either." They sat there for several long, quiet minutes while two squirrels chattered and chased each other in the branches overhead. "What's really going on?" Kaden quietly asked. "It's more than feeling guilty."

Seth shrugged.

"This has to—absolutely must—happen…before. You know that."

Seth shrugged again. "I know."

"You didn't have a problem with it that one time."

"Uh, yeah, thanks to the freaking tequila. Oh, and, by the way, she wasn't your wife."

"It's more than that." Kaden sat up. "You can't put off the inevitable on my end by putting off the inevitable on yours. This is for her. I want to see her happy. I meant it when I said she's fantasized about you plenty of nights. Let's make her dream come true while we still can."

"Be a little more fucking eager to pimp your wife out, why dontcha?"

"Damn it, it's not the same thing and you know it!"

Seth stewed. He did. He also didn't want to admit the truth.

"This week, you're taking Leah to the club. Alone. Tony will be there if you have questions."

Seth's jaw clenched. "I don't think I'm ready."

"Yes, you are. You're a damn sight more ready than most of the asshole wannabes that show up. Leah trusts you to take her. Just go, play an easy scene, and come home. That's all you have to do."

Seth didn't respond.

"You need that alone time with her."

"Fuck, Kade, that's taking you away from her. She doesn't have much time left with you!"

"Is that what this is about?" he quietly asked. "That you feel guilty you're spending time with her and it's taking time away from me?"

Seth didn't answer. That was part of it, but not all.

"I already told you, we've got a big bed. Feel free to sleep in it with us every night."

"I don't know," Seth whispered, "if I can handle seeing her..." He couldn't finish.

Kaden studied him. Then, after a long moment, he spoke. "You don't know if you can handle seeing her make love to me."

Seth closed his eyes, took a deep breath, and nodded.

The laughter surprised Seth enough he opened his eyes. Kaden was howling, loud and hearty.

"I don't see what's so fucking funny." And it sort of pissed him off.

Kaden shook his head and laughed harder. When he finally could speak, he said, "Dude, that's great!"

"I think you're getting off on fucking with my mind."

"No! Don't you see?" He sat up again and looked at Seth. "You're jealous—of me!"

"You sure you don't have brain cancer, because you're acting like you've got no brains left."

"You love her, asshole! That's what I've been trying to get through your thick goddamned skull! It's what I want to happen, because the more you love her, the less likely you are to divorce her at the end of the first year!"

Seth wasn't yet ready to admit that he didn't give a shit about the time limit. If Leah would have him forever, he'd keep her forever.

Kaden still tried to reason with him. "Would you do anything to make her happy?"

Seth nodded. Of course he would. He'd do anything, including trade places with Kaden so she didn't lose him.

"Having you and me, together, would make her the happiest woman on the face of the planet. Maybe so goddamned happy that, for a little while at least, she wouldn't be thinking of the thing that's going to make her pretty miserable for a long time. Is it worth it to you to make her happy?"

As whacked as it was, he couldn't deny Kade's logic was valid.

Whacked, but valid.

Kaden leaned in a little and dropped his voice. "Here's what I feel. When I think about her being alone with you, yes, I feel a little jealous. Not because I don't want her with you, but because I'm not there with her. When I watch you make her come while we're having a session, I stand back and I enjoy how she's enjoying it. It's what I don't see and I'm not a part of that rips me up. Being there and seeing and hearing her enjoy herself...it's great. Think about it."

Seth did. He had to admit in retrospect that, yeah, it was always a lot easier to watch Kade work with her than it was to lie alone in bed and wonder what they were doing behind closed doors.

"Okay. I can wrap my head around that," Seth admitted.

They sat in silence for a few more minutes. "Does she ever take charge?" Seth asked.

Kaden laughed. "Oh yeah. Buddy, there's been times she's hopped on and rode me like a fucking pony. All I could do was just lie back and let her have fun."

Kaden left him alone. After another few minutes, Seth returned to the house.

Leah had dinner in the oven, and it smelled great. He let her hug him. Admittedly, putting his arms around her felt right. Kaden's words hung in his brain. Yes, it was the unseen he hated. When his imagination ran wild and he couldn't be part of what was happening.

But to see her enjoy herself...

She was beautiful.

Chapter Twelve

After dinner, Kaden returned to his study to finish a few things. Seth sat on one end of the couch and watched TV while trying to quiet the swirl of emotions in his brain. *Why am I fighting this?* Was a blow job so much different from a hand job? And was having sex much more than that? Honestly?

Leah finished the dishes and softly padded into the living room. She wore her heavier collar and a long T-shirt. When she started to sit down, he stopped her.

"Wait."

She looked puzzled but complied. After a moment, he softly said, "Take off your shirt, please."

Her skin flushed, but she immediately pulled the shirt over her head and dropped it to the floor.

She looked beautiful. Sweet, soft, rounded curves that felt right when pressed against his body.

Leah stood, waiting. He knew he could keep her standing there all night and she wouldn't move, wouldn't complain.

Seth did something he'd never done before—he made the hand gesture he'd seen Kaden make countless times during sessions or around the house.

Leah's eyes widened, but she dropped to her knees in front of him.

His heart raced. Was he really going to do this with her?

He leaned forward and whispered, "Leah, answer me a few questions. Honestly."

She met his eyes and nodded.

"Do you really love me?"

"Yes."

"Are you honestly doing this willingly? I mean, besides the obvious reasons, because you *want* to do this with me, not because you think you have to?"

"I want to do this with you, Sir."

He sat back again and spread his knees, then crooked his finger at her. "Do you want to do something else? Something…more?"

She eagerly nodded. His cock throbbed in response to the hopeful look on her face.

"Would you like to go down on me?"

Another eager nod.

Point of no return. "Okay."

She slid forward, between his legs, and helped him open his shorts and pull them down his hips. Then came her gentle, tentative touch as she carefully caressed his shaft and sac.

He moaned.

When her warm tongue flicked the head of his cock, he closed his eyes and gently fisted his hands in her hair. He had a feeling he could sit here all night with her going down on him and maybe glimpse what heaven felt like. Her lips softly closed around the sensitive ridge at the base of the head, massaging him.

He gasped.

It was a struggle not to shoot off, and she seemed to sense it. She slowly worked her way down his throbbing cock, her lips and tongue laving every inch of flesh.

The right woman.

He'd finally found the right woman, and she was married to his best friend.

He shoved that thought back into its cage and threw away the key.

He knew Kaden could and probably would walk out at any time and find them there like that. Seth figured it was time he got himself used to the situation. Obviously Kaden was okay with it.

And deep inside him, he was surprised to find it thrilled him just a little, too.

Five minutes later, he heard Kaden walk into the living room. His low, growling voice made Leah moan. "Beautiful," he said.

Seth opened his eyes. Kaden knelt behind her and caressed her ass. She moaned again, setting off a pleasant flurry of sensations in Seth's cock.

"How far do you want to go tonight?" Kaden quietly asked him.

Seth shook his head. "Not all the way."

Kaden nodded. "But you're willing…"

"At least a little more than before."

Kaden caressed her ass again, his hand following the curve of her hip down her thigh and between her legs. He slipped two fingers into her, triggering yet another moan from her, vibrating her mouth around Seth's cock.

Just that sensation alone would make Seth come if she kept it up.

Seth closed his eyes and threw his head back. That way he could pretend he was alone with her.

He heard the soft sound of a zipper, then Leah paused for a moment before going back to the delicious attention she was paying him. He dared crack an eyelid and watched Kaden fuck her from behind, his eyes closed, hands gripping her hips.

She moaned.

He tangled his fingers in her soft hair. Why had he waited?

Right. Best friend's wife.

Goddamn it.

He pushed the thought away again.

Unable to help himself, Seth watched. Now Kaden had an arm around her waist, and presumably his fingers between her legs from the way she was moaning and bucking her hips against him.

Fuck.

That was…

The sexiest thing he'd ever seen in his life.

It was easy to hold his release back as he breathlessly watched her surge toward her own. He listened to the sounds she made, as they climbed the register in octave and grew shorter in duration. Then she screamed around his cock, her hands sliding behind his hips and holding on as she literally engulfed him, deep-throating him.

The sudden change in sensation finished him. He moaned as he came and shot down her throat. It felt like he came harder and longer than he ever had in his entire life, and she swallowed every drop.

Damn! None of his exes ever did that!

Kaden took several hard deep thrusts into her with his eyes closed. Then he groaned and fell still.

She held Seth's cock in her mouth, gently sucking. Within a minute, he was already stiff again.

Day-amn.

Kaden's voice sounded hoarse as he withdrew and moved to the couch. "Come here, baby." He had her lie facedown across his lap, with her face in Seth's lap. She immediately went back to sucking Seth.

Seth gently cupped the back of her head.

"Let's show Seth another of your fantasies, sweetheart."

She moaned her assent around Seth's cock.

Kaden tenderly stroked her ass, massaging it, caressing it. She wiggled her hips at him, trying to entice him.

He hauled off and spanked her once, hard.

She jumped but moaned loudly and took Seth a bit deeper into her mouth.

"You like that, baby?" Kaden asked her.

It sounded like she mumbled *mmm-hmm* around Seth's cock.

Kaden smacked her ass again. Then he slipped two fingers into her, drawing another flurry of moans from her.

Fuck!

Seth checked to make sure he wasn't drooling.

She frantically wiggled her hips. Kaden withdrew his fingers and spanked her several times in quick succession, and it sounded like she was close to coming just from that. He stopped and gently caressed her red cheeks.

"This has been one of her favorite fantasies," Kaden softly said. Seth was a little surprised to see Kade smiling. "She's going to have a lot of fun living out her fantasies. Aren't you, baby?"

"Mmm-hmm!"

Kade tenderly stroked her back, then slipped his fingers between her legs again. "Just wait until you're ready to go all the way, Seth. She's got some doozies that will blow your mind."

Seth was aware his fingers had tightened on her scalp, and he loosened his grip a little.

Fuck!

Kaden fucked her with his fingers as she eagerly devoured Seth's member. "Some nights we used toys and she pretended it was you, and she screamed when she came. She's wanted this for a long time."

"It doesn't bother you?" Seth gasped. That was probably close to the weirdest question he could have asked under the circumstances, but he needed it answered.

"She loves me." Leah moaned her agreement and wiggled her hips against Kaden. "I know she loves me. Like I told you, if it was anyone but you, it'd piss me off. And yes, I was the first one surprised that I could feel this way."

He spanked her a few times, drawing more eager, hungry moans from her, then went back to finger fucking her. "You're the only one she's ever fantasized about. No one else." He laughed. "Well, she went through a James Spader phase after we saw *Secretary* for the first time but that's different. I don't think that counts."

Seth brushed the hair away from her face and carefully pulled it back, holding it out of her way. She looked up at him and winked.

His heart flipped inside his chest.

I love you.

He wanted to say it to her. He couldn't bring himself to say it. Not with Kaden sitting right there. Maybe he had to share her for now, maybe he'd even quickly grow to enjoy sharing her. But damn it, he wanted one thing to be his alone, one milestone in their relationship where he didn't have to share her with anyone and could have a guilt-free moment with her.

I love you, Leah.

Kaden alternated spanking her and finger fucking her. In a few minutes, her moans changed tempo and sound again. She laved Seth's cock even more eagerly. He quit trying to hold back. She wanted it…she got it. He closed his eyes and stroked her hair, rocking his hips in time with her mouth. He moaned when he came, and Kaden picked up the tempo of her spanking. She screamed around him, finally releasing his limp cock from her mouth as she climaxed.

When she finished, Kaden grabbed her, sat her up in his lap with her back to him, and quickly fucked her. He must have been rock hard with her squirming against him all that time. It only took a few strokes for him to finish.

She relaxed against him, her eyes closed and a satisfied smile on her face. Kaden's arms circled her waist and he kissed her shoulder.

"Are you okay?" he asked her.

She nodded.

Seth realized he was still sitting there watching them with his dick hanging out. He reddened and started fumbling his shorts. Leah leaned over and kissed him, hard.

"Thank you," she whispered.

"Um. Yeah. Thank you, too." He went to his bedroom and closed the door behind him, leaning against it for a moment to catch his breath.

Day-amn.

* * * *

Seth didn't emerge from his bedroom again that night. Early the next morning, he arose at dawn and slipped out of the house to go running. He'd spent a restless night dreaming about the feel of Leah's lips around him and imagining how it would feel sliding his cock into her.

Daylight crept up on him. The light changed from deep shadowy purple to grey, then finally the reds and oranges of a fiery Florida sunrise, dappled golden patches of warmth striking him between the shoulders as he ran.

He punished himself, a blistering pace that finally forced him to stop on the other end of the development to catch his breath. He stretched, did some push-ups, and walked in circles to cool down.

The sound of Leah as she came with his cock in her mouth.

Fuck.

He was an evil asshole for wanting her all to himself, wasn't he? Especially when it seemed to make his two friends happy every time he gave another inch in this debate.

Especially when—

kaden'sdying

There were no fucking manuals for shit like this.

He circled the entire development three times but avoided passing the house. By the time he couldn't run anymore he knew he'd gone at least eight miles. The sun was fully up, probably closing in on nine o'clock. Heat had started filtering through the trees and displacing the cooler oases of shadows under the live oaks.

His body drenched in sweat, he quietly let himself in through the front door and returned to his room. He didn't hear or see them.

He debated locking his bedroom door, then hesitated. It would hurt Leah's feelings if he did. He sensed that.

What if she *didn't* come in?

That would hurt *his* feelings.

Fuck.

If he locked his door, he wouldn't know if she tried to come in.

He turned and looked at his bed. It was already made. At some point she had come in. What had she thought when she found he wasn't there?

He left it unlocked.

He stood under the spray and tried to quiet his mind. That was when he heard the bathroom door open and quietly shut.

Seth didn't open his eyes. His heart hammered in his chest.

He sensed more than heard the shower door open. He felt a brief draft of cool air as Leah stepped inside with him.

Then her hesitant touch, her arms sliding around his waist from behind.

Seth turned and enveloped her in his arms, pressing his lips to the top of her head. He stood with her like that for several long moments, neither of them speaking.

Kaden's words reverberated in his brain. It was for her, to make her happy.

He wanted to make her happy.

He looked into her face and kissed her forehead. Then he gently pushed her away and gave her the signal.

She dropped to her knees and eagerly swallowed his cock. He cupped the back of her head with one hand and braced himself against the shower wall with the other as she worked him over with her mouth and hands. When he came she grabbed his ass and held his hips tight against her face until she knew she'd sucked every last drop from him. She finally released him and rested her face against his abs.

Seth sank to his knees and held her again, hiding his quiet tears from her by keeping his face buried in her hair.

Sensing something was wrong, she wrapped her arms tightly around him and held him.

He hated that he was so fucking weak, to lose it like this, especially in front of her. How was he going to be strong enough for her when she really needed him?

After?

"It's okay, Seth," she whispered, changing position so she could hold him. She pressed his face against her chest and stroked his hair.

He hated himself but didn't move. "Forty goddamned years," he whispered. "Since we were fucking babies."

"I know."

Who was he kidding? Kaden wasn't his oldest friend—he was his only true friend. His best friend. He had acquaintances and drinking buddies and guys he kept in touch with that he'd served with in Iraq and Germany. He had professional associates from when he was a contractor.

Then he had Kaden.

Okay, that wasn't true. He had Kaden and Leah. When he came home from overseas and met her, it was like she completed their friendship. He'd never felt like the odd man out with them.

He talked to Kaden not every day but several times a week at least, before all this happened. Whether he called Kade or Kade called him, just to chat.

Or to ask his advice on something.

To share good news.

To commiserate about the bad.

Or just to say hi.

He usually ate at their house at least one night a week, sometimes more. If he was in the neighborhood he could stop by, and if Leah was home they sat and chatted or she insisted on making him lunch if he hadn't eaten. He and Kade always had their night out alone every week.

His friend.

And he was dying.

She gently rocked him, stroked his hair. "You have to let it out," she whispered. "You can't hold it in. It'll eat you alive from the inside out. It's okay. I want you to lean on me right now. I know you two are trying to make this as easy on me as you can, but right now, I'm strong enough to be there for you. Let me do this for you while I can. I won't always be able to."

He sobbed. He didn't know if he cried five minutes or an hour, but she wrapped her arms around him, murmured soothing words to him, held him tightly against her. He wanted to curl up and die.

kaden'sdyingkaden'sdyingkaden'sdying

Every step he took toward fulfilling her dream made his nightmare that much more real.

When one of the redneck assholes in their junior class tried to jump Seth at a football game one night, Kaden helped nail the fucker. Kaden always watched Seth's back.

Kaden helped him study for finals, helped tutor him in his weaker subjects.

Kaden never teased him in a mean way. Seth could always confide in him when he had a problem, and he knew if Kaden didn't have any advice to offer that at least he would quietly listen and provide an ear.

A safe harbor.

When Seth's own parents died, when fucking bitch wife number two was less than comforting after she found out there wasn't any money to inherit, it was Kaden who stepped in and quietly took over making the arrangements, making sure everything was taken care of, gently guiding Seth through the process with Leah always there to listen and help.

He finally pulled himself together. "I'm sorry," he said hoarsely, unable to look her in the eyes.

"Why are you apologizing?"

"Because I'm supposed to be strong for you and I'm fucking bawling like a goddamned baby."

She gently grabbed his face and made him look at her. "I would be very upset if you didn't cry. If you didn't show any emotion, it would worry me."

"Why?"

"Because I know how close you are, and let's face it, you've loved him longer than I have. I'm his wife, yeah. But you're his friend. You're closer to him than family. You've been through hell and back with each other over the years. You've seen a side of him I'll never get to see, share things with him that I never have and never will. If this didn't affect you, I'd seriously think about giving you a session in the playroom." She smiled.

As her words sunk in, he laughed. He pulled her to him. "Oh, damn it, I'm such a fucking loser and you still want me. I think you're delusional."

"Honesty, Seth. Part of being honest is showing your emotions when you need to. This isn't a one-sided relationship. He wasn't kidding when he said that what we have isn't about doing this all the time. Plenty of times it's just…normal."

"Naked normal."

"Oh come on. You know you love it."

He coarsely laughed again. "Yeah, I have to admit that part is nice."

"Will you please take me to the club tomorrow night? It would make me happy. I know it will make him happy."

He sighed. "Yeah. Okay."

"You feel a little better?"

He nodded.

She brushed her lips against his and sat back so he could stand. He helped her to her feet. "I need to finish my shower before the hot water runs out."

"French toast or pancakes?"

He smiled. "Surprise me."

* * * *

That night after dinner, Leah popped in a DVD and sat on the couch between the men.

Seth had never seen *Secretary* before. In some ways, it could have been Leah's biography. Even though the story wasn't exactly the same, it gave him yet another perspective into her mindset and helped him understand why this lifestyle was so important to her.

Halfway through the movie she slipped her hand into Seth's lap and started rubbing his cock through his shorts. It didn't take much to get him fully stiff. Within a few minutes they were repeating the encounter from the night before. Hot didn't begin to describe it.

When he finally went to bed, he thought about their impending trip to the club.

He was a little surprised to find part of him eagerly anticipated it.

Anticipated being alone with Leah.

* * * *

Seth spent a restless night alone. The memory of the feel of Leah's mouth on him kept him hard for hours despite jerking off twice.

Moron. Go sleep with her.

He tried to roll over and go to sleep. By the time he stumbled out of bed the next morning, he didn't feel like a run. He barely felt like getting out of bed, but the thought that he'd be taking Leah alone to the club that night made further sleep impossible.

He stepped into the shower after he shaved. Sure enough, a few minutes later, she joined him.

"What is *that*?" He pointed to the can of shaving gel and disposable razor in her hand.

"I'm going to shave you." Her matter-of-fact tone possessed more than a little "Duh!" factor.

"Um, sweetie, I appreciate that, but already done. See?" He tapped his stubble-free chin.

She rolled her eyes. "No, Sir. I'm going to shave your body."

"What?" He stepped back, bumping against the cool tile wall.

"Don't you want to look your best tonight?"

"Okay, Leah. Time out, or red light, or stop sign, or what the fuck! Huh?"

She looked at him as if explaining to a child. "We're going to the club tonight. You need to look your best." She stepped forward. "I shave Master all the time."

Well, come to think of it, he had noticed Kaden was a little lacking in the body hair department from the hips up, but he hadn't really put much thought into that, or what lay below Kaden's belt. It wasn't exactly on Seth's top-ten list of fantasy thoughts, that was for sure.

"Why?"

"Because it looks nicer." She reached down with her free hand and trailed her fingers along his shaft, which immediately responded, dang traitor. "And, if you use a cock ring, it won't get caught in your hair—"

"Whoa!" He grabbed her hand and tried to shift his hips away from her. "Holy fucking shit, you're going to *shave* my *balls*?"

"Yes. Besides, it's better for me. I don't have to keep spitting out hair."

Wormhole. He was back to the wormhole theory. "Honey, I don't mean to hurt your feelings, but I'm not sure—"

"Please, Sir?" She turned the puppy-dog eyes on him.

"Aw, fuck no. Leah, babe, come on. Cut me some slack."

She pressed her naked body against him. "Please, Sir? I just want you to look your best."

He wouldn't be looking his best. That was still probably a month or two away at least, provided he kept up a workout schedule of some sort. He still looked like a pig next to Kaden. Although, compared to many of the people who were regulars at the club, he was stick-thin.

Those freaking lethal green eyes of hers. She'd figured out how to twist him around her finger years ago, nearly from the first moment they met.

She damn well knew it, too. Now she used them to her full advantage.

He closed his eyes and fought the nausea churning in his gut. "You aren't shaving my legs, right? That's just freaking creepy."

She laughed. "No, silly." She gently pulled him away from the wall. "Just stand here and spread your legs a little. I'll do everything."

He refused to open his eyes. "You know, I've already been circumcised. Don't go taking any more off me."

She laughed again. "Master will tell you I do a very good job."

"This isn't exactly a conversation two guys have over coffee. 'Hey, dude, how well does your wife shave your balls?'"

She laughed, loud and hard.

Okay, well at least got that daily mission out of the way.

When she quit laughing she started on his back, which only took a minute. Not that he'd ever paid much attention, but he must not have been very hairy back there. He stood quietly while she lathered his chest and shaved him, working her way south.

He nervously gulped but still stiffened as she slowly took her time and shaved his groin and sac. He barely dared to breathe. She apparently had total confidence in her skills.

When she finished she rinsed him off, then dropped to her knees again and ran her tongue and lips over his throbbing shaft.

Okay, this made it worth it. No doubt about it. He leaned against the wall and gently fisted her hair as she went down on him. The feel of her fingers over his now nekkid balls felt different, and not in a bad way.

One more adjustment he'd get used to. If she could keep her pussy shaved—and apparently, that was exactly what she did—he supposed he could let her do this.

He'd had more almost-sex in the past few days than he'd had real sex in the past few years. And the best sex—almost or not—of his life, to boot.

How pitiful does that make me?

His best friend's wife.

She gripped his hips and wouldn't let go as he came, taking every last drop until he finally had to gently tap her on top of the head.

"Okay," he hoarsely whispered.

She sat back on her heels and smiled up at him. "Now, wasn't that nice?"

He laughed and rolled his eyes. "I don't know why I bother even trying to stand up to you." He helped her to her feet. "You're going to drag out the secret weapon every time." He pulled her into his arms.

"No, Sir. Not every time."

It felt so...weirdly right holding her. Like she fit his body. How would it feel to have his cock buried in her?

He kissed the top of her head. "Okay, out you go. I'm sure Master wants breakfast. Don't keep him waiting. I'll be out in a few." What he needed was a few minutes alone to settle his brain.

"Okay." She kissed him before stepping out of the shower. When he was alone in the bathroom again, Seth turned the water as hot as he could stand it, let it practically scorch him, then turned it cold and forced himself to stand there for a minute before shutting it off.

It was going to be a long. Fucking. Day.

Chapter Thirteen

Seth kept his eyes on the road and not on Leah's short skirt. Fuck, this was the world's longest, weirdest, and simultaneously the best and worst dream possible. This couldn't be his new life, could it?

When they pulled up outside the club, Seth threw the Lexus into park and stared at the sign. He felt Leah's eyes on him as he took a deep breath. He needed to do this. He'd promised.

God, please don't let me fuck this up.

He shut the car off and stepped out. He walked around, grabbed the duffel bag from the trunk, then opened the car door for her. She didn't move at first. He realized what he'd done.

Fuck, I'm screwing up already.

He held out his hand to her. She took it, pressing her lips to the back of his hand and casting her eyes down.

"Thank you, Sir."

It felt creepy and weird and good all at the same time, hearing her talk to him like that.

He'd promised. He had to do this for them. "Let's go, Leah."

She held his hand and walked close at his side but let him lead the way.

Inside the foyer, Seth nervously scanned the people there, looking for Tony. He spotted him talking with someone in a corner and held up his hand in greeting.

Tony nodded, finished his conversation, and walked over. He shook Seth's hand. "Hey, Kaden called me." He looked at Leah. "How are you?"

Leah glanced up at Seth. For a second, he wondered what the hell was going on. *Fuck.* His second screwup.

He nodded.

She smiled at Tony. "I'm okay. Thank you for asking." She was a good liar. He almost believed her, would have if he didn't know how much this was ripping her up inside.

He gently stroked the back of her hand with his thumb, trying to comfort her. He wanted to pull her into his arms and hold her and let her cry on his shoulder, but that wasn't something she could probably ever do.

If he wanted to help her, he needed to do what Kaden told him to do.

What she needed him to do.

Tony guided him through check-in and helped him sign up for a turn at the bench. In his mind, Seth tried to run through everything Kaden had taught him, the list he'd memorized. The rules.

He looked at Leah. "Do you need to go to the bathroom?"

She nodded.

He led her to the doorway, waited for her just outside.

Never take your eyes off her unless she has to go to the bathroom.

Never leave her alone.

Never turn your back on her when she's bound. Always keep your eyes on her.

Never let anyone else touch her unless it's an emergency and they're trying to help you get her free.

He patted his back pockets again, felt the Leatherman tool and the paramedic scissors. He'd clip them to his belt when they started playing.

Leah emerged from the bathroom, and this time he remembered to extend his hand to her. She took it without hesitation, pressing her lips to his flesh.

"Thank you, Sir," she softly said.

He led her back to Tony to talk. In a few minutes, it was their turn.

Kaden had told Seth he wouldn't make him memorize all the lines, that he would eventually learn them over time and come up with his own routine for her.

But Seth wanted to do this for her as well as he could. He wanted this to be as right for her as he could make it. Not that he ever imagined he'd be as good at it as Kaden.

They stepped to their designated play area. Seth dropped the duffel bag at his feet while Tony stood nearby, silently watching. Seth made the hand gesture and Leah dropped to her knees in front of him, waiting.

The dungeon monitor walked over and talked to Tony, then to Seth. "Safe words?"

Seth nodded. "Leah, tell him."

She didn't look up. "Green, yellow, red."

Kaden went easy on Seth tonight. He told Leah no ball gag, so she could verbally reassure Seth throughout the scene.

The DM nodded and stepped back. "Have fun. You have one hour." He set up a timer that was on a nearby table for sixty minutes. It started counting down.

Seth glanced at Tony. Tony nodded, stepped back, his arms crossed, watching.

Seth looked down at Leah. "Tell me what you want, love," he said, hoping his voice sounded strong enough.

"I want to serve my Master, Sir."

"And how do you wish to do that?"

"However my Master thinks is best, Sir."

He *so* could not get used to her talking to him like this but supposed he'd better.

"Do you want to feel the bite?"

Her skin flushed, the same way it did when she played with Kade.

"Yes, Sir. I need to feel the bite."

Ah, fuck. He'd screwed up again. But she seemed to be okay with it. "Prepare for me." He knew his tone wasn't as firm and stern as Kaden's, but he couldn't make himself talk like that to her. Not yet, at least.

She stood and walked to the bench, undressed, neatly folded her clothes, and laid them nearby, as if stripping naked in front of a room full of strangers was an everyday occurrence. Then again it was, in a way, for her.

Seth fumbled the buttons of his shirt because his fingers trembled.

Fuck.

He finally got it off and dropped it on a nearby chair. Somehow, he didn't think he looked nearly as imposing as Kade did despite his larger frame. Kaden radiated a quiet, calm confidence and strength.

Seth felt scared to death.

He rummaged through the bag, feeling slow and stupid when he couldn't find the fourth cuff. He finally located it and tipped his head to Tony, motioning him over for this part.

Without speaking, Tony pointed, indicating the connection points. Seth secured her legs and arms to the bench, leaving her ass an open and prime target. Next, the rope.

Kaden had drilled the pattern into Seth's brain. He quickly secured her legs, from knee to ankle, with the wrapping pattern. When he finished, Tony looked, examined Seth's work, and nodded. Seth spoke to Leah.

"How does that feel, love?"

"Green, Sir."

Tony nodded to Seth and stepped out of the way, to the edge of the play area.

Seth nervously studied her, noticed her breathing had quickened, her entire body now flushed. She wiggled a little on the bench as if trying to rub herself.

He knelt beside her head and dropped his voice, trying not to fuck this up. "Are you ready to feel the bite?"

Her eyes were squeezed shut, and she nodded, almost eagerly, squirming against her bindings now.

"Show me your hands."

As much as she could, she lifted her hands, made several fists, and wiggled her fingers. He knew it wasn't as important now, because he only had her in wrist cuffs, not arm ropes, but he needed to get a handle on this routine.

He held her hands. "Squeeze."

She squeezed, hard.

"Very good. Your feet."

He was more worried about her circulation down there because of the ropes. She wiggled her feet and toes, flexing them. He felt them, and they weren't any cooler than the rest of her body.

He stepped back to the bag and dug out the flogger. "Fifteen, love." It felt strange calling her that, but it was part of their game and he was determined to get this as right as possible for her.

For Kaden.

"Fifteen, Sir," she repeated.

"Count." He swung, admittedly not very hard the first time. She didn't even flinch.

"One, Sir."

Around the fifth swing he finally found his stride. He took his time, frequently glancing at Tony, who nodded but remained silent and out of the way. Leah counted every stroke, her voice deepening, tinged with arousal as the count rose. By the time he reached fifteen she was squirming on the bench—and he was ashamed to realize he had a raging hard-on.

He took a deep, steadying breath. "What is the count, love?"

"That was fifteen, Sir," she gasped. "Thank you."

"Where are we?"

"Green, Sir," she immediately replied.

He checked her feet and hands, relieved to see she seemed okay. He stepped back. "Fifteen more, love."

"Fifteen, Sir."

"Count."

He saw the obvious effect this had on her, wished he could drop his pants and fuck her silly right there. He paused between the tenth and eleventh strokes, took a swig of water from one of the bottles they'd brought. Her ass looked pink. This flogger was one of the mildest in Kade's collection, would barely bruise a tomato. He knew that was more for his peace of mind and to build his confidence than Leah's safety.

When Seth felt he'd regained control he glanced at Tony, who nodded. Seth continued the set.

At the end he repeated the check-in. She was doing okay, a damn sight better than he was, from the looks of it.

He dropped the flogger into the bag and took out the mild crop. Tony held up a finger. Seth stepped away from Leah and nodded.

Tony stepped over, leaned in close to his ear. "They need a hand upstairs for a minute. Will you be okay until I get back?"

Seth nodded.

"You can ask the DM to come get me if you need me. Don't hesitate to call the scene if you feel uncomfortable. She'll understand. Kade's trained her well."

Seth nodded and waited until Tony left. There weren't many people watching them right now, maybe a dozen or so at a discreet distance. He tried to tune them out and return to the scene.

Stepping back to Leah, he caressed her ass, heard her responding sigh of pleasure. "Where are we, love?"

"Green, Sir," she breathlessly replied.

He nervously positioned himself, took a couple of practice swings that didn't make contact so he could adjust his aim.

"Five, love."

"Five, Sir."

"Count." He knew he pulled his first stroke. He couldn't help it. This went against the very core fiber of his being.

She almost sounded disappointed. "One, Sir."

Grow a set, he thought. *You have to do this right for them.*

He landed the second much harder, making her jump against the restraints.

"Two, Sir." But she sounded relieved.

He drew the set out, checking her at the end. Light red welts appeared in a few places, and her shaved pussy looked red and swollen.

He dug into the bag and found the vibrator, slipped it into her and quickly hooked up the straps. With the remote in his left hand, he firmly grasped the crop in his right. "Set of ten, love."

"Ten, Sir."

"Count."

He nearly moaned at the sight of her hips jerking against each impact from the crop. His dick painfully throbbed as he heard the vibrator pulsing inside her. He was doing this to her.

She kept count, barely, her voice moaning by the end of the set.

He shut off the vibrator but left it inside her. He knew she hadn't come yet and was probably as horny as he was at this point.

He bent over the bag to go for the next implement when he heard the man's voice. "You need a little help there?"

He looked up. Baxter.

Seth glanced at Leah, noticed she'd tensed, and not in a good way. "No, we're okay. Thanks."

Baxter walked over, standing entirely too close to Leah. "She needs a lot more than this, you know. Kaden's usually gone thirty on her with a singletail by this point. I could help you out. I'd love a chance to play with her."

Seth stepped between him and Leah. "I said, no thanks."

"She needs a firm hand. You're barely making contact. I paddled my kids harder than you've used her."

Seth fought his barely constrained rage. "Back. Off." This guy had reproduced? *Yech.*

Baxter quickly stepped around him and leaned in to speak to Leah. *Where the fuck is the DM?*

"Leah, do you want a real Dom to take care of you—"

"Enough!" an enraged voice ordered.

Whose voice was that? *Oh, man, that's me*, Seth thought.

"Get. The *fuck*. Away from My slave."

Baxter looked at him. "She's not your anything. She's Kaden's wife."

Seth touched the end of the crop to Baxter's chest and shoved him away from Leah, who silently watched the drama unfold. Seth was barely aware of raised voices and someone calling for the DM to get their ass back there.

"She is *My* slave," Seth growled. He looked at her. "Leah, who is your Master?" he barked.

Stunned, she whispered, "You are, Sir."

"Who do you obey?" he demanded.

Her voice gained strength, but she still looked wide-eyed. "I obey only You tonight, Sir," she answered.

Baxter started to say something else when Tony and the DM returned. "What's going on?" Tony demanded.

Seth pointed the crop at Baxter. "Keep that asshole the fuck away from My slave and out of My way." He heard the capital letters in his voice.

Two other DMs showed up and escorted Baxter out of the building. Tony looked at Leah, then Seth. Seth knelt by Leah's head.

"Look at me."

She did.

"Where are we, love?"

She didn't hesitate. "Green, Sir."

She *was* his slave. He felt it in his core.

He understood.

He knew something had changed inside him. Even he could hear it in his voice. "Do you need to feel the bite?" he asked. He knew his voice sounded deeper, stronger, even though he wasn't quite sure how or why.

She nodded. Eagerly. "Yes, Sir. I need to feel the bite."

His intention had been to switch to the strap next. Loud, but not any more severe than the mild crop.

He rummaged through the bag, keeping an eye on her while Tony and others silently watched from the sidelines.

At the bottom of the bag, in the storage tube holding another crop, Seth found the mild, springy switch, not quite a cane. Far from the most severe in Kade's collection but more severe than the strap or first crop he'd used. He'd planned on finishing everything out with a set of five from it after spending more time with the other implements.

Something told him they both needed it now.

Seth stepped back to her and lined up his strokes. "Set of ten, love."

She wiggled her ass. "Ten, Sir."

"Count them off." He didn't pull back and she gasped as the switch left a red stripe across her flesh.

"One, Sir," she breathlessly whispered.

He left the vibrator off and knew she desperately wanted to feel it buzzing. He also knew Kade was helping him out a lot by including it in the night's play. He'd seen Leah climax from play with Kade, but Kade had no problem going after her more tender areas with the whips and crops. Seth knew he was nowhere near that level of skill or confidence yet.

Maybe one day.

The thought that they would be playing like this long enough for there to be a "one day" made his dick throb even harder.

He striped her ass and thighs, her desperate squirming setting something on fire deep within him. What the hell kind of sick freak was he? Here he was, whipping his terminally ill best friend's wife and wanting to fuck her brains out.

And he'd been told it was okay to do it!

And he *wanted* to do it.

At the end of the set, Leah writhed against her bonds, wiggling her nicely red ass in the air. Seth caressed her flesh, marveling at the long, striped welts, the texture and heat of them on her skin.

"Where are we, love?" he hoarsely asked.

"Green, Sir."

He glanced at the timer—they had twenty minutes left.

He checked her hands and feet again and knelt by her head.

"Leah, look at me."

Her eyes looked glazed under heavy lids.

"Do you need to feel the bite?"

She nodded, her eyes locked on his. "I need to feel the bite, Sir."

"I want you to come for me, love. Do you want to come for me?"

She eagerly nodded. "I want to come for You, Sir."

He couldn't help it, knew it wasn't part of their routine, but he leaned in and gently kissed her lips. "You will come for me, love."

He returned to the end of the bench. "Set of fifty, love."

She shuddered, but in the way he knew meant she was close to the edge. "Set of fifty, Sir."

"Count." He backed off the force of his swing, not enough to do more than add a mild sting. As the first stroke touched her flesh, Seth thumbed the button on the remote control, turning on the vibrator.

Her body shook, but she maintained the count.

By the time he hit ten he knew she was almost there. He stepped up the force behind his strokes, alternating his angle, covering her flesh with a fine mesh pattern of stripes, careful not to break the skin.

She came at thirteen. She came again at twenty-seven.

Then one last climax at forty-five.

Breathing heavy, he turned off the vibrator, returned the switch to the tube they carried them in, then took the vibrator out of her.

She lay, spent and limp, across the bench.

He knelt beside her and caressed her face, laying his palm along her cheek. She'd cried at some point, probably numerous times, but a slight smile caressed her face as she kissed his hand.

"How are we, love?" he whispered.

"Green, Sir," she murmured.

He carefully untied her, gently rubbing her legs and arms. Seth held her tucked against him in his lap for a few minutes while she recovered. He kissed the top of her head, stroked his fingers down her spine, murmured soothing words to her. Then he offered her a bottle of water and told her to get dressed. He quickly put away their accessories in the duffel bag and, with instruction from the DM, wiped down the bench. As Leah dressed, Tony stepped in and nodded to Seth.

"You okay?" Tony asked.

Seth slowly buttoned his shirt. He felt drained, hornier than hell, and...

He couldn't identify the mystery emotion now bouncing through him. It damn sure hadn't been there when they started.

"Yeah. I'm okay."

Leah finished dressing and knelt in front of Seth. "Thank you, Sir," she said, picking up the game again.

He held out his hand and she took it, kissing it. He pulled her to her feet and kissed her.

She froze for a second but then returned it with urgency. When he broke the kiss their eyes met and he couldn't help but say it.

"I love you, Leah."

The brightest of smiles curled her lips. He thought his heart would implode. "I love you, too, Seth."

Chapter Fourteen

Seth wanted to bend Leah over the hood of the car and fuck her right there in the club parking lot. Somehow, he managed to get her into the passenger seat before he slid behind the wheel.

He looked at her. Then he leaned in and kissed her, his hand fisting her hair, deeply tasting her.

His slave.

His.

He closed his eyes and gasped for air as he pressed his forehead to hers. "I love you so much."

"I love you, too."

"I don't want to do this all the time. I'll do it for you, and yeah, okay, it's fun. But sometimes I'm going to need to just be…normal."

"I know. That's okay. I'd like that, too."

"Will that be enough for you?"

"Yes."

He kissed her again, softly moaning as her tongue pressed against his lips. They parted under her touch, and before long he knew if he didn't get her home he was going to fuck her right there.

His hands shook. It took him three tries to get the key in the ignition to start the damn car.

They held hands on their silent ride home. When they pulled into the yard, Leah waited for him to walk around the car and help her out. He kissed her again and didn't try to hide his rock-hard erection. She ground her hips against him.

"You were great tonight," she whispered.

"I wanted to kill that bastard."

Her sly smile made his cock throb even harder. "You felt it, didn't you?"

"What?"

She kissed him, then whispered in his ear, "I'm Your slave. I belong to both of You, but You finally want to claim me, don't You, Sir?"

He nodded. "Yeah."

"I think Sir should take what's rightfully His to have."

He closed his eyes and forced air into his lungs. "What are some of these other fantasies Kaden was talking about?"

She stepped away from him and seductively smiled. "Why don't you let us show you? We'll leave the bedroom door open. Feel free to join us."

He watched her walk into the house, her hips swaying in a mouth-watering way.

Fuck.

He wiped his mouth with his hand, certain he was drooling. After he caught his breath he carried the duffel bag inside.

Kaden sat on the couch. He looked up from his newspaper and glanced at Seth over his glasses. "Well?"

Seth rolled his eyes at his friend's knowing smile. "Well, what?"

Kade dropped the paper and laid his glasses on the coffee table. "Come on. You nearly decked Baxter. Tony called me after you guys left the club." He leaned back and crossed his arms. "Felt good, didn't it?"

Seth dropped the duffel bag on the couch and nodded. "Yeah," he softly said.

Kaden stood. "I think our girl has some plans of her own for how the night will end. You're more than welcome to join us. And I mean that. It would make her very happy." Kaden walked down the hall, and Seth stared after him.

Was he really ready to do this? He had been an hour or so ago.

With leaden feet he walked down the hall, hesitating at his bedroom door.

Was he ready to do this?

Would he *ever* be ready to do this?

kaden'sdying

Nothing short of a miracle would change the course of their future. Certainly not his reluctance.

With a deep breath, Seth forced his feet forward, stopping in their bedroom doorway.

Kaden had unbuttoned his shirt but not taken it off yet. Leah had kicked off her shoes, but was still dressed. She spotted him in the doorway, and the brilliant smile that lit her face drew him inside their room.

She rushed to him and put her arms around him. "Kiss me."

He did.

As she ground her hips into him, he skimmed his hands down her back and cupped her ass, then pulled her tightly against him so she could feel how hard he was.

She softly moaned.

Kaden walked over. He'd shed his shirt but still had his shorts on. He pulled her hair away from her neck and brushed his lips against her nape, making her shiver in Seth's arms.

"Are you ready to get fucked, love?" Kaden softly spoke in her ear.

She practically melted against Seth as she moaned.

Kaden wasn't finished. His voice dropped to a low growl. "We're going to make your fantasies come true, love. We're going to fuck you all night long. You're going to have two hard cocks to service from now on, and you're going to be a very busy girl."

Seth's cock painfully throbbed in his jeans, but he didn't break their kiss.

Leah mewled, squirming between them, obviously excited.

"Tell Sir what your biggest fantasy is," Kaden growled.

Her head lolled back against Kaden's shoulder. Her eyes looked glazed with passion. "I want Master and Sir to fuck me at the same time," she whispered. "I want to feel both of your cocks in me."

Kaden's hands cupped her breasts, squeezing her nipples through the fabric of her shirt. "Be more specific. Tell him exactly what you've told me."

"I want one of you to fuck my pussy while one of you fucks my ass. I want you both to come inside me at the same time. I want you both to claim me. I want both my masters to use their slave hard tonight."

Seth's mouth dried up.

"Tell him another one."

Her eyes fell closed as Kaden pinched her nipples. "I want Sir to fuck me while I suck Master's cock."

Kaden nipped the side of her neck. "Another."

She was squirming between them now. Seth suspected if he slipped his fingers inside her that she'd be drenched.

"I want to take turns sucking my masters' cocks while one of them licks my pussy. I want my masters to tie me up and use me all day long and fuck and suck me. I want to run around naked all the time, and whenever Master or Sir wants, they fuck their little slave, whether it's inside or outside, or they make me suck them. I only want to please my masters."

Seth took a ragged breath. "Okay," he hoarsely whispered. If she kept talking like that, he would come in his jeans.

"Go get in bed, love," Kaden softly ordered.

Seth released her. She frantically ripped off her clothes and threw herself onto the bed.

Seth stared. Kaden looked at him. "Well?"

"Well what?"

Kaden laughed. "Let's go fuck our slave."

Seth's fingers felt numb as he unbuttoned his shirt. Kaden turned off the lamps. Soft light spilled in from the bathroom, making it more intimate and still giving them enough to see.

Kaden finished undressing and lay down next to Leah. She kissed him as he slipped a hand between her legs. She spread them wide and moaned as he pushed a finger inside her.

The sight broke through Seth's mental paralysis. He finished stripping and lay down on her other side. She turned and kissed him as he cupped her left breast. He brushed his thumb over her nipple, and it immediately hardened in response.

He wanted to fuck her all night long.

But first he wanted to make her come.

Seth slid down the bed and pushed her legs further apart. She turned her face to Kaden and kissed him as Seth wrapped his hands around her thighs.

"Tell me what you want," Seth hoarsely asked.

She broke her kiss with Kaden. "I want to feel your lips on my clit."

Seth groaned with need. He could easily squirm against the bed and make himself come at this rate. He lowered his mouth to her sex and gently traced every curve and fold with his tongue.

Leah loudly moaned.

Kaden played with her nipples, alternating between them, rolling them between his fingers. "Let him hear how much you enjoy it," he ordered.

"So good," she gasped. "Feels so good."

Seth took his time, flicking her clit with his tongue, then alternating long, firm strokes, laving it.

He had to fuck her. Now.

He wrapped his lips around her clit and gently bit down, setting off a thermonuclear explosion inside her body. She cried out, her body tensing on the bed. Seth firmly clamped his hands around her thighs and kept her coming, refusing to let go until she was trembling and whimpering in Kaden's arms.

With one last swipe of his tongue along her clit, he lifted his head. "How was that?"

Her eyes were still closed but she nodded.

Seth sat up and grabbed her hips, pausing with his cock at her ready entrance. "Look at me," he whispered.

She opened her eyes.

"Do you want me to fuck you, baby?"

She nodded.

"Ask for it."

"Please fuck me!"

He sank his cock into her and paused, enjoying the feel of her hot, slick muscles. Seth closed his eyes and waited before slowly thrusting. He would explode if he went too fast.

Leah tried to thrust against him and he held her hips. "No, just lay there and let me feel you," he said hoarsely.

She fell still. Kaden kissed her and played with her nipples.

She felt incredible. It was easy to lose himself in the sensation and forget about the future with his cock buried balls-deep inside her.

Kaden broke their kiss and nibbled on her ear. "He's going to fuck you good. But we're not going to let you come again yet. After he comes, you're going to get him nice and hard again, and then we'll both fuck you, love."

She softly moaned.

"If you're a good girl, we'll make you come while we're both fucking you."

Seth stopped thrusting. He was near the point of climax as it was, and the thought of feeling her come with his dick buried inside her was almost enough to send him over the edge.

After a few deep breaths he started thrusting again, and this time he gave in to the wave. With a final stroke he came deep inside her, then collapsed on top of her. She wrapped her arms and legs around him, holding him hostage in her embrace until he recovered enough to push up off of her.

"I love you," he whispered, kissing her.

She smiled. "I love you, too."

He was suddenly aware of Kaden lying right there. He looked at his friend.

Kaden smiled. "Still not doing you."

Seth laughed, long and hearty, dropping his head to Leah's chest while it rolled out of him.

When he finally recovered he looked at Kaden again. "We're okay?"

Kaden nodded. "Yep. We're okay."

"Seriously?"

"Seriously."

Seth looked at Leah and noted her pleased smile. "You realize," he said, "that you've just created a monster. You're gonna get fucked so much you'll be walking bow-legged."

She smiled. "Master and Sir can fuck me anytime, anywhere They wish."

"Holy fuck," he whispered.

He rolled over, pulling Leah on top of him. He knew he was stiffening again. "Get down there and do what Master told you to do, love."

It felt right calling her that.

She *was* his love.

She grinned and crawled down his body, not even hesitating when she sucked his cock into her mouth.

Seth closed his eyes and enjoyed the sensation. He was aware of Kaden getting up because he felt the mattress move. When he looked he saw him standing behind Leah with a bottle of lube in his hand.

Kaden patted her ass. "Hurry up. I want my cock buried in you."

Seth had never tried anal sex before and was glad Kaden was taking the lead on this. He wouldn't deny it was something he wanted to try…just not tonight.

Leah did something delicious with her fingers around Seth's sac, and he felt himself fully harden in response. She released his cock from her mouth with an audible pop and then straddled him. He grabbed her hips and pulled her on top of him, impaling her.

He knew he could last longer this time, and enjoyed it as she squirmed around on his cock.

Kaden pushed her down onto Seth's chest. "Relax, love. You've been wanting this for years."

She rested her head on Seth's shoulder and kissed him. "Thank you," she whispered. "Thank you so much."

His hands still rested on her hips but she reached behind her and guided his hands to her ass and had him spread her cheeks.

Kaden drew in a sharp breath. "Fuck that's sexy!"

She wiggled against Seth's cock. "Please fuck me, Master!"

"Damn straight."

Seth looked over her shoulder and watched Kaden prepare her, lubing her and him. He pressed his cockhead against her rim. "You ready for me to fuck you, love?"

"Please fuck me!"

He pressed forward and she moaned, shifting her hips against them. Seth thought his eyes might have rolled back in his head. She felt so tight and hot, and when Kaden had fully seated himself inside her, he pulled her up against his chest.

"How are we, love?"

Her eyes were closed. "Green," she whispered.

He cupped her breasts, rolling her nipples in his fingers. "Make Your slave come, Seth."

Seth wasn't sure he was capable of coherent thought, much less any activity requiring fine motor skills or dexterity, but he finally brought his trembling hands under control and stroked her swollen clit with his thumb.

She moaned.

"How's it feel, love?" Kaden asked.

"Oh...it's sooo good!"

"Maybe we should fuck you like this every night. Would you like that?"

Seth wasn't capable of speech at this point and happily let Kaden take the lead.

Leah shivered. "Yes!"

Kaden nipped her earlobe. "Yes, what?"

"Yes, Master! I want Master and Sir to fuck me like this every night!"

Kaden took a couple of strokes inside her ass and the feeling…

Seth realized he was wrong about lasting longer this time. It felt amazing. He would come soon if she didn't come first.

"Maybe we should tie you up every night, get your ass nice and warmed up with a flogger, then take turns fucking you in the playroom," Kaden said.

She shivered in his arms. "Oh…yes!"

"Or we'll leave your ball gag out and one of us can fuck you while you suck the other off. Maybe we'll keep you full of cock at both ends all night long."

She shivered again, her skin flushed. "Please!"

"Please what?" Kaden gruffly demanded.

"Please keep me full of your cocks all night long!"

Seth rolled her clit between his fingers, triggering her climax. And not a moment too soon, because he was right on the edge. As her muscles milked his cock he exploded inside her. He moaned, grabbed her hips, and thrust.

Kaden pushed her down on top of Seth again and grabbed her hips, fucking her hard, adding his release to theirs. They collapsed in a panting, sweaty heap with Seth buried at the bottom.

After a few minutes, Kaden sat up and carefully withdrew. "Are you okay, sweetheart?"

She didn't open her eyes, just nodded against Seth's shoulder. Her hair clung to her damp forehead.

Kaden walked into the bathroom, and Seth heard water running. A moment later, Kaden turned off the bathroom light and returned with a wet washcloth and carefully cleaned her up.

Seth rolled to his side, still inside her, and cradled her in his arms. Kaden curled up behind her, his arm slipping around her waist. Seth didn't even mind the incidental contact.

Kaden kissed the back of her neck. "Ready to call it a night, sweetheart?"

She nodded and made a soft, mumbling sound.

Seth suspected she was already falling asleep. He knew he was.

"I love you," Kaden whispered to her.

She mumbled something back that sounded like, "I love you, too."

Seth remained silent, not wanting to interrupt them. He would have years to say it to her. He didn't want to take a second away from Kaden if he didn't have to.

He closed his eyes and let exhaustion carry him into darkness.

* * * *

Seth awoke early the next morning, feeling disoriented. The night came back to him. He realized he was still curled around Leah, although at some point she'd rolled over to face Kaden. The light outside still looked purple, and he considered going for a morning run. As much as he hated exercise, he was determined to get and stay in shape for her.

Then she shifted, pressing against him. The cleft of her ass rubbed perfectly along his shaft. He stifled a soft moan as he stiffened in response.

When she did it again, he realized she was awake.

He reached around and tweaked one of her nipples. "Good morning," he whispered.

Kaden was still asleep. She covered Seth's hand with hers and squeezed, then tipped her head back.

"Good morning," she whispered. Her gorgeous smile made up his mind for him. Fuck the run. He'd swim later.

"What do you want for breakfast?" she asked.

He rocked his hips against her ass, his cock nicely sliding along her cleft. "You."

"Make mine double," Kaden mumbled.

Seth laughed. "I thought you were asleep."

Kaden stretched, then kissed Leah. "I think we're going to be spending a lot of time in bed over the next few days."

Leah softly moaned.

Kaden kissed her again, urged her to sit up. "Why don't you give Sir a nice wake up while I get my morning helping?"

Leah knelt over Seth and wrapped her lips and fingers around his shaft. He closed his eyes and enjoyed it, vaguely aware of Kaden moving into position behind her. Kaden fucked her, hard, as she sucked Seth's cock deep into her mouth. Seth tangled his fingers in her hair, and she moaned a little as he thrust his hips against her.

She loved it.

Kaden slowed his strokes. "I don't think I'm going to let you come this morning, love. I think we're going to make you wear the butterfly this morning, and then, if you're very good, at lunchtime maybe we'll think about giving you some relief."

She moaned, loudly, around Seth's cock.

Seth couldn't stand it. "Butterfly?" he gasped

Kaden smiled and took long, deep strokes into her. "It's a devious little vibrator I strap onto her. It's also got a remote control. But it's not a large dildo like the other one. Drives her crazy because she gets this teasing sensation but not enough to get off on."

"Fuck!"

"After a few hours of that, she's begging to do anything to come."

She moaned again. Seth gave up trying to hold back. It felt too damn good. He grabbed her head and worked his hips in time with her mouth, moaning as she firmly stroked him with her tongue and lips. He closed his eyes and rode his climax until he collapsed, spent, on the bed.

She lifted her head and smiled at him. Kaden started fucking her, hard, moaning as his release hit.

When Kaden caught his breath, he patted her on the ass. "Go get cleaned up, love."

She went into the bathroom while Kaden walked out of the bedroom. He returned a moment later carrying something.

Seth realized it was the aforementioned butterfly.

When Leah returned, Kaden had her climb up on the bed on her hands and knees, and he hooked her up to the vibrator. He turned it on and she dropped her head to the mattress and moaned.

Kaden slapped her ass. "Go show Sir how a proper slave acts in the morning. Make Me proud."

She jumped off the bed and ran down the hallway.

Seth shook his head. "*Twilight Zone.* I'm expecting Rod Serling to jump out of the closet at any minute." He looked at Kaden and laughed. "You really gonna torture her all day?"

Kaden nodded and climbed back in bed. He grabbed the remote and turned on the TV. "At least until lunch."

Seth and Kaden watched TV until she returned with their coffee a few minutes later. Kaden used the vibrator's remote to switch it off.

"Good girl," Kaden cooed as he accepted his mug. "Now go make us breakfast."

"Yes, Master." She leaned in and deeply kissed him. Then she walked around the bed and kissed Seth.

Seth watched her walk out of the bedroom again. Kaden laughed.

"You're going to wish you'd done this a long time ago."

Seth's guilt returned. "Man, do we have to talk about this?"

"Suit yourself." Kaden had pulled the sheet up to his waist. "I'm just saying, a man can quickly grow used to a sweet, naked love slave serving him breakfast in bed every morning."

"Is this what you used to do—"

beforekaden'sdying

"—before I was living here?"

"Not every morning. Usually just weekends. A lot of the time I was moving too fast in the morning to spend time playing. Trying to get out the door to the office." He looked at Seth. "I know you want to get your degree, and that's fine. What I'm saying is, if you wanted to spend your whole life at home, you could. There's other shit to do, you know. I've got the commercial properties that have to be managed. You could take over doing that, and then you wouldn't have to pay Ed to do it. Set your own hours. Spend more time with her. Work from home."

Seth knew Kaden owned quite a few properties, but Seth had never discussed Kaden's business with him before. He'd never thought it was any of his business and didn't want to be nosy.

Seth sensed Kaden's sadness. "I want to work."

"I know you do. You've always been a hard worker, not like that asshole brother-in-law of mine. If I have one regret, it's that I spent so much time working and not more time with her. You could avoid that mistake. This house is paid for, cars are paid for. There will be life insurance and income from the properties and the trust I've set up, the retirement accounts, too. You could spend your life playing with her."

Seth didn't want to have this conversation. "Dude, I'm not cut out to be like that."

"That's why you're perfect for her."

"You're harshing the mellow," he tried to joke.

Kaden smiled. "Give it some serious thought. If you go to work though, keep in mind that there's more to life than work. Don't ever forget that."

Seth nodded.

The smell of bacon wafted down the hallway. A few minutes later, Leah appeared, a smile on her face and two plates in her hands. Kaden hit the button on the vibrator control, and she moaned a little when it kicked on but didn't drop the plates.

He grinned and handed the remote to Seth. "Have some fun."

* * * *

They did torture Leah most of the morning. By lunch she was rubbing herself against Seth's leg like a hump-happy terrier anytime he stood still long enough for her to latch on to him.

Kaden laughed. "She knows I won't let her do that to me. Too much risk of her getting off that way."

"Ah." Seth gently pushed Leah away despite her pouty look. "Quit being sneaky." He slapped her on the ass. She moaned in disappointment, but her eyes twinkled.

After lunch, Kaden appeared in the living room with some rope and a knowing smile. "On the table, love. Now we can really show Seth the ropes."

She groaned at the pun but smiled and complied.

Kaden removed the vibrator and quickly lashed her to the table. Seth took plenty of pictures and worked the video camera. He had to admit he enjoyed the view.

When she was firmly bound, Kaden stood behind her and gently stroked her ass. "This is a game I like to call 'Torture the Slave.'" He leaned over and gently flicked her clit with his tongue. She jumped, moaned, and wiggled her ass as much as she could against the ropes.

Kaden smiled. "I think we can invent a new version of 'Beat the Clock.' Seth, why don't you sit on the edge of the couch?" Kaden pushed the table across the floor so Leah's mouth was perfectly positioned. Seth immediately caught on. He dropped his shorts before sitting in front of her.

Without any prompting, she opened her mouth, trying to reach his now stiff member.

Kaden laughed and swatted her ass again. "Not so fast, love. You need to hear the rules first. You need to put your best effort into making Sir come. If he comes before you do, I stop what I'm doing. So if you want to come, you'd damn well better do it. Then, Sir and I will switch positions. And again, you'd better not hold back. If you still don't come before I do, you'll have to sit here for a little while with the vibrator in and think about why you're being such a stubborn thing. If you can come before one of us does, and you only have to come once, not for each of us, I'll let you up."

Seth struggled, and failed, to contain his laughter. "That doesn't sound much like punishment."

Kaden swatted her ass again. "It's not. She wins either way, don't you?"

She wiggled her ass at him. "Yes, Master!"

"Wait a minute," Seth said. "What if she holds back?"

"You haven't seen all the toys yet," Kaden said. He leaned over her. "If you hold back, you will get strapped down in bed, and I'll put not only the biggest butt plug in your ass but I'll also put the big blue vibrator in you. And you won't be allowed up until you've given us at least ten. Even if you have to lie there all night."

Seth thought back to his first trip with them to the club and the woman he'd seen strapped to the frame. He'd since learned that was called "forced orgasm" torture. Well, torture depending on how you were looking at it.

Leah moaned and shivered. He strongly suspected it wasn't from fear.

"Again, dude, I mean, I know I don't know as much as you do, but that doesn't sound like torture to me."

Kaden winked. "Just because she enjoys it doesn't mean it's not torture. All right, let's begin." He sat at the end of the table and licked her clit.

She moaned and eagerly swallowed Seth's cock.

No, she wasn't holding back. If she was, he didn't care. It was damn good. Seth suspected Kaden was holding back, however, because a few times she moaned in frustration as he stopped or slowed what he was doing.

It only took her ten minutes to get Seth off. When he recovered he carefully moved out of the way and swapped places with Kaden.

Kaden kissed her, then got into position. "Make Me proud, love."

She went down on him. For a minute, Seth almost forgot what he was supposed to be doing on his end as he watched.

He was closer to understanding now. It was the sexiest thing in the world, watching her do that.

Seth took his time, enjoying the sounds she made as he flicked his tongue across her clit. Taking his cue from Kaden, he backed off several times, not quite bringing her release.

He lifted his head to look down her back at Kaden. When their eyes met, Kaden nodded.

Seth gently sucked on her clit, and she moaned. Her hips twisted as far as they could against the ropes, and Kaden closed his eyes.

"That's it, sweetheart," he murmured. "You know what to do."

When Seth sensed she'd had enough he sat back and gently caressed her hips and thighs, ran his lips up and down her flesh.

Kaden grunted as he came, and they all sat there quietly for a moment. "Very good," Kaden whispered, stroking her hair. "That was wonderful."

Seth helped Kaden free her, and she curled up on the couch with them, her head in Kaden's lap, her feet in Seth's. In a few minutes, she'd fallen asleep.

Seth smiled. "We wore her out," he whispered.

Kaden nodded. "Yep." He looked sad as he stroked her hair. "I was hoping to."

"Why?"

He shrugged but didn't look at Seth. "She needs to relax, keep her mind off things."

Kaden didn't need to specify what "things" he meant.

* * * *

Seth eventually extricated himself and put up the "toys" they'd used for their activities. He went outside to work on the electrical system. He'd sat down with Kaden and figured out, based on his friend's design and newly added lights and accessories, what he'd need to add to the existing circuits.

Kaden wanted a complete walk-through winter wonderland, including a setup for the backyard, where they'd hold some of their dinners and parties if the weather was good enough. Some of the areas would be run off extension cords, but some would require buried wiring and dedicated GFI outlets because of their distance from the house.

A few hours later, Seth was outside marking off sections with stakes and string when Leah walked outside, a glass of iced tea in hand. She wore a long T-shirt.

Seth gratefully accepted the tea. "Thanks, sweetie."

He couldn't quite interpret the look on her face. "What's going on?" he asked.

She shook her head, then a smile broke through and she hugged him. "Thank you."

He kissed the top of her head and left his free arm around her shoulders as he surveyed his progress. "I should be thanking you, babe."

"No. I mean...everything." She took a deep breath as her smile faded. "I'll understand if at the end of a year you'll want to—"

"Oh, no you don't. You think you're getting away from me that easy, think again."

Her smile returned. "Really?"

He nodded. "Yeah. Really."

She hugged him, surprising him with her strength. "Thank you," she whispered. "I love you."

"I love you, too, babe." He closed his eyes and inhaled her scent. She'd taken a shower not too long before, and her damp hair smelled freshly shampooed. "Just don't be upset if I don't say it a lot in front of him, okay?" he softly said. "I'm not comfortable with that."

"Okay."

"And don't be upset when I don't spend every night with you two. I'm not going anywhere, but it doesn't feel right taking time away from him. I want you to focus on him. I'm all right with that."

"Okay."

He kissed her again and gently patted her behind. "All right, let me get back to work. Clark Griswold in there has really planned a doozy for this year, and I need to make sure I've calculated everything right so we're not blowing breakers all the time."

She returned to the house. Seth tried to focus and couldn't. He'd managed to put before, after, and the mental heartbeat—

kaden's dying

—out of his mind for a while.

And now it was all back.

He sat in the shade and looked over the yard. He knew, no matter what, he would set up the display again next year. Hopefully in honor of Kaden but most likely in memory of him. And every year after that.

How much longer did they have?

Thanksgiving was just a few weeks away. Was this the last? The last Halloween? Would the three of them celebrate Easter together and watch Fourth of July fireworks in Lemon Bay?

Seth had thought, one day, he might have kids. If he found the right woman. Thankfully he hadn't had any with the ex-hell-bitches. He could only imagine that shit storm over this latest development.

And Kaden and Leah couldn't have any.

He would never ask her, as Kaden hadn't, to go through hell just to have a baby.

But now, the thought that the choice had been made for him, without a chance to try, saddened him in some ways. Or maybe it was his crushing melancholy over his other thoughts, trying to force the phrase "last Christmas" from pounding through his mind.

It felt *wrong* to step into Kaden's life, to take over, almost seamlessly, and carry on. He'd spent much of his life wishing he was Kaden, had Kaden's life and family and money…and yes, his girl. And now, at this most critical of times, he desperately wished he could take Kaden's place.

So Kaden could live.

It wasn't fair.

Why couldn't he, the fuckup, be the one dying? Not the good guy with everything to live for.

The sound of tires on the shell rock driveway caught Seth's attention. He craned his neck to look. Ed's car. He didn't know Ed was coming over today. That explained why Leah wasn't running around totally nekkid outside.

Well, unless Kaden needed him for something, he'd prefer not to hang around and listen to their conversations. It sucked to be him, but he knew it really had to suck to be Ed, responsible for helping Kaden make the legal arrangements.

Seth had gone back to work when Leah returned a few minutes later. She wore a different T-shirt, tucked into her denim shorts.

"What's up, babe?" Seth asked.

"I was sent to help you."

Seth's gut twisted. That meant Kaden didn't want her overhearing, confirming his suspicions. "Sure." He handed her a spool of string. "Follow me and you can help me mark the paths."

* * * *

An hour later Ed left, waving as he drove down the driveway. Seth and Leah returned the gesture. Kaden soon joined them outside.

He acted normal, not letting anything slip. "When's dinner, sweetie?"

"Whenever my guys want it."

Seth's heart flipped at her statement. She wasn't just his. He was hers, too.

It felt good.

"How about in an hour?"

"Okay. I'll go get it started."

As she walked away, Seth sat in the grass. "Well? Want to spill it now or keep me in knots all night?"

Kaden laughed and sat with him. "Naw, it's okay. Just more paperwork."

"I figured you were trying to get rid of her to talk to me. Like you got rid of her to talk to Ed."

"Think she noticed?"

"Duh. She's not stupid, dude."

Kaden shredded a blade of grass in his long fingers. "Just more preparations. I want everything I can get handled now done before the first of December."

Seth's heart froze. "Why?"

Kaden noticed his look and laughed. "No, dork. No bad news I haven't shared already. I want to kick back and totally relax. Enjoy. I want to be able to spend time with you two. Besides, you still have a lot to learn."

"What about Denise?" Kaden's sister had called and left Kaden a message on his voice mail the day before.

Kaden shrugged. "That was one of the things I was taking care of today. I redid my will and totally cut her out."

Seth laughed. "That's going to piss her off."

"Yeah, well, I won't be around to deal with it. I'm sure you can handle her." He met Seth's gaze and laughed.

"Thanks, buddy."

Chapter Fifteen

Two weeks before Thanksgiving, Seth and Kaden had half of the light display up. Seth was in a great mood. He'd accompanied Kaden to the doctor two days earlier. Apparently Leah's rabid insistence on vitamins, supplements, and a healthy diet were paying off. Kaden was still dying, nothing had changed there, but his test results hadn't declined from the last visit.

The oncologist was still noncommittal concerning a time frame, other than to offer a guesstimate of at least six months, probably longer, and two years wasn't looking impossible at this rate.

Two years! Seth knew it was stupid to latch on to that, but he did anyway.

He spent several nights a week in their bed. Sometimes Leah came to his room and spent a little alone time with him before going to spend the night with Kaden. As weird as it was, Seth now understood Kaden's point of view. He rarely felt jealous, and subdued his sometimes envious pangs with the thought that it was only right and fair she spend time alone with Kaden. Sometimes he found himself insisting she spend the time alone with Kade.

Making love to her was beyond description. And even when it was the three of them together, there were plenty of nights it was vanilla—as vanilla as it could be in a ménage.

Leah also seemed to need fewer trips to the playroom, something that greatly relieved Kaden.

Although Seth had to admit he was growing more comfortable taking the leading role in their private scenes. He'd taken Leah to the club twice more, and two more times the three of them went.

Seth was outside with Kaden, trying to set up another set of lighted animals, when Leah walked out with two glasses of iced tea. The men gratefully took a break, sitting in the shade. Even for a Florida November, the day was unusually hot, and they'd quickly shed their shirts as the heat built.

Kaden noticed her look first. "What?"

"Hmm?"

"I know that look, babe. What's on your mind?"

Leah plopped down in the grass in front of them. She reached out and traced Kaden's tattoo with her finger. "I was thinking."

After a minute he shook his head. "Seth, I think we'll need the singletail to get this out of her."

She laughed. "No. Okay. Fine." She took a deep breath and dropped her gaze to the ground. "It'd be nice if you both had one." Then she lifted her eyes to Seth.

He wasn't following her. "Huh?"

"I know you said you didn't want me to get you anything for Christmas, but…" She didn't finish.

Kaden looked at Seth and laughed. "Ah. I see. She wants a matching set."

Seth had worried that was what she meant. "Oh."

"I mean," she quickly said, "if you don't want to, I understand. It's okay. I shouldn't have mentioned it. I'm sorry." She'd started to stand, but he grabbed her hand.

"I hate needles."

She looked at him. "I know," she softly said. "It's okay if you don't want to."

Seth studied her green eyes, finally nodded. "You guys might have to carry me out of there if I faint, but okay. I'll do it, babe."

* * * *

That was how, two days later, Seth found himself seated in a tattoo parlor in Sarasota. It was the same place Leah and Kaden had gotten theirs.

He hoped they kept a barf bucket close by.

Kaden smiled. "I can't believe you were in the Army and never got a tattoo."

"I can't believe you're an attorney and you aren't a slimy asshole."

Leah laughed. "Touché."

Seth gripped her hand a little tighter as the tattoo artist began inking the design. Seth had learned the circular motif was called a "triskelion" and was the unofficial symbol of BDSM practitioners.

"I do appreciate this, Seth," Leah whispered.

"Make sure you show me," he managed through gritted teeth.

"Man up," Kaden teased. "Don't be a pussy."

"Fuck you."

"Not in your wildest dreams, dude."

Seth tried not to watch what the tattoo artist did. It hurt like a sonofabitch. He admitted it—while he was good with pain, he sucked with needles, which was why he never got inked before.

Kaden, a smile on his face, sat near the end of the table. "Just be thankful I didn't let her talk me into the other one she wanted me to have."

"I don't want to know."

He grinned. "No, you don't."

Leah pouted. "It would have looked so neat."

"Hey, I never made you get your clit pierced, so don't go playing the pouty card on me, little girl."

Seth tried not to shudder. "You guys are gonna make me faint. If I don't puke first."

Kaden used his foot to nudge the garbage can a little closer to Seth.

Several hours later, he had a design identical to Kaden's. After getting instructions on how to properly care for it while it healed, he turned to Leah. "I wouldn't have done this for anyone but you."

She smiled and stood up on her toes and kissed him. "I know. And I love you for it."

Well, damn. That was more than enough to make the pain worth it.

"Now I have another request," she said.

Kaden turned. "What's that, sweetheart?"

"Can I get my masters' names added to my design?"

Seth couldn't read Kaden's expression. After a long moment, his friend nodded. "It's all right with me." He looked at Seth.

Seth shrugged. "Okay."

She told the tattoo artist what she wanted and lay down on the table while he traced a design on her lower back with a pen. She looked at it in the mirror and nodded. "Perfect."

Seth closed his eyes and didn't watch. He sat next to Kaden, each of them holding one of her hands. When it was done, she jumped up to look at it in the mirror. Kaden's name gracefully curved over the top of the triskelion, and Seth's below it.

"Thank you!" She kissed Kaden, then Seth. She drew them both close and dropped her voice. "Now there will never be a question who my masters are," she whispered to them.

Despite his queasy stomach, Seth nodded. "All right. Can we go now? Before I barf all over the place?"

"Wuss," Kaden chided.

"Yeah, and proud of it."

After the bandage came off later, Leah was after Seth every couple of hours with the moisturizer lotion recommended by the tattoo parlor.

"Gee, Mom. I'm a big boy now," he playfully groused.

"Shut up. You don't want to have problems with it."

He wouldn't deny she took damn good care of him. He sat on the end of his bed while she finished applying yet another round. He pulled her into his lap. "I meant it when I said I wouldn't have done this for anyone but you."

She put her arms around him. "I know."

He kissed her, enjoying the feel of her body against him. "So the right woman was under my nose all this time, hmm?"

"Yeah." She ran her fingers through his hair, smoothing it. "I prayed you'd eventually figure it out."

He captured her hand in his and brought it to his lips. "Seriously." He took a deep breath. "I can't share you with anyone else but Kaden. I mean that. You know that, right?"

Her smile broadened. "I know. And I'm not sharing you with anyone."

"You're okay with that?"

"I'm really okay with that." Her face saddened a little, but he recognized it as a newer expression she'd worn lately, one that meant she was dealing okay with her emotions and didn't need a trip to the playroom. "I just wish the three of us could have a lot more time together."

"I'm sorry I was an idiot for so long."

That brought her back. She smiled again. "But you're mine now, and I love you."

Chapter Sixteen

"I hope we don't get FPL climbing up our asses over this," Seth groused as he looked over the sketches and worked on his final calculations. "We might need to rent a generator."

Kaden shrugged. "Whatever we need to do."

"I think it's safe to say you've outdone yourself this year."

"That was the plan, man." Kaden's satisfied smile couldn't be denied a reply.

Thanksgiving was in five days. The first of Kaden and Leah's dinners would be held the evening after next, a small, private dinner for some of Kaden's closest staff at his office. Seth had thought about going to his brother's house to leave them alone. Leah nearly burst into tears when he broached the subject.

"You can't go!"

"Honey, you don't need me in the way."

"I need you here!"

He hugged her, calming her. "Okay, I'll stay. Calm down." His brother and sister-in-law were coming to the house for Thanksgiving dinner, along with some other family and close friends. The three of them had finally broken the full news to them, as well as Kaden's brother, about why Seth was living with them. Not in total detail, leaving out the BDSM stuff, of course. Seth was surprised they took it as well as they did.

Helen was especially sympathetic. At one point she pulled Seth aside when they were alone. "Don't forget that if you need a shoulder, I'm here for you."

Seth nodded, wiping his eyes. "Yeah, thanks."

"I know it's unusual, but in the grand scheme of things, if it brings them both comfort to have you in their lives, then don't worry what anyone else thinks."

He'd always liked Helen. Not the way he liked Leah, more like a true sister. "I wish everyone was as understanding as you."

It was one less stress on Seth's plate. He didn't give a shit what people he barely knew thought about him. He did care what his brother thought. He didn't want them thinking any less of Leah for what would happen…after.

Kaden had told a few people close to him what was going on and what would happen. They were sworn to secrecy and to not shower Leah with well-meaning condolences before his death. Everyone was to go on as normal.

As normally as they could.

Seth walked the entire setup one more time, checking connections and outlet placements. They'd done limited zone tests as each section was set up but not the entire thing at once. As dusk drew close, Seth put away the sketches. "Okay, I guess we're as ready as we'll ever be."

Kaden called Leah from the house. They gathered around the breaker box. Seth had wired in separate sub-boxes to handle the new circuits.

"Okay, gang. If I get electrocuted, call 911," he joked.

He threw the switch.

The entire property lit up. Inflatables started inflating, moveable animals started moving, and the lights drove back the falling dark.

Kaden's face lit as brightly as the yard. "Wow!" he whispered, awestruck.

Seth hung back as Kaden walked out to the driveway and surveyed the front yard area. "This is amazing!" he exclaimed. "I mean, seeing it all at once like this… You did a great job! It's fantastic!" He enveloped Seth in a bear hug. Seth didn't feel at all uncomfortable returning it.

"Thanks, man. It was your design."

Kaden clapped him on the back and released him, then turned back to the display. He wiped his eyes. "It's great, man!" He pulled Leah to him and hugged her. "What do you think?"

"I think it's gorgeous."

Seth hung back while Leah and Kaden walked the paths through the displays. He felt glad he could do this for them despite the sadness threatening again.

Seth walked back to the house and fired up the grill for Leah, wanting to leave them alone for a while. When they finally made it around to the back side of the house, Kaden laughed and hugged Seth again.

"It's great, man. This is awesome. Everyone's going to love it."

"It's the least I can do."

The men relaxed on the lanai while Leah cooked dinner. "I wish we could have been doing this years ago," Kaden softly said so Leah couldn't hear.

Seth shrugged. "Don't harsh the mellow, dude," he tried to joke.

"How are *you* doing?"

Seth shrugged again. He really didn't want to have this conversation now. Especially not with Leah nearby. He'd been doing pretty well. A few times he went over and cried on Helen's shoulder to get it out of his system, trying not to burden his friends with his grief. "I just want to sit back and enjoy our hard work."

"*Your* hard work."

"You were out there with me, dude."

"I never could have pulled this off without you, Seth. Quit the modesty bullshit. You've made me really happy."

"Then let's just sit and ponder the miracle of outdoor illumination, bro. God bless Thomas Edison and his freaking lightbulb."

Kaden laughed and shook his head. "Okay. I'll leave you alone."

"Greatly appreciated."

* * * *

Normally, Leah didn't put up their Christmas tree until Thanksgiving weekend. This year she wanted it up in time for all their dinners.

Seth didn't have to read between the lines to understand why.

The men helped her assemble the massive thing, nearly twelve feet tall. Once the lights were on, Leah took over the decorations. By later that evening she was almost finished. Seth had helped her put the star on and climbed up the ladder to put some ornaments toward the top.

Kaden walked in, his hands behind his back. "Looks beautiful."

"You think so?" she asked. She hugged him. "What's that?"

He motioned Seth over and produced a small, wrapped box. "This is for the two of you."

Leah took the box but looked puzzled. "For me and Seth?"

Kaden nodded. "Yep. Well, open it."

She exchanged a curious glance with Seth. He shrugged. "I don't know, babe. He didn't tell me."

She opened it. Her hand flew to her mouth as she looked inside. "Oh, Kade!"

"Go ahead."

"What is it?" Seth asked.

She handed the box to him and threw her arms around Kaden. She cried. "Thank you! It's beautiful!"

He hugged her, stroked her back. "Hey, it's only right, sweetie." He kissed her forehead. "You two should have something. I want you to have this. I wanted to be the one to give it to you."

Seth carefully lifted out the delicate, porcelain star.

In the center, in gold: *Our First Christmas, Seth and Leah*, followed by the year.

Seth felt himself tear up. "Thanks, man."

Kaden gently patted Leah on the back. "Well? Go ahead and hang it."

Seth wanted to position it toward the back of the tree. Leah wouldn't hear of it. She positioned it near the "First Christmas" ornament she had with Kaden, and the "Our New House" ornament Seth had given them their first year in this house.

She stepped back and wiped her eyes. "There. It's perfect."

Seth wasn't so sure it should be where everyone could easily see it. "Maybe we should—"

"Leave it where she wants it," Kaden firmly said. He clapped Seth on the back and left his hand on his friend's shoulder. "She's right. It looks perfect there."

Leah beamed.

Chapter Seventeen

Seth awoke Thanksgiving morning to Leah kissing him. "Here's your coffee." She set it on his bedside table. He'd slept alone the past couple of nights, claiming exhaustion—partly right—and because he felt guilty about all the time he was spending with Leah and Kaden in their bed.

"Thanks, babe." He started to roll over. "What time is it?"

"Six. You said you'd help me with the turkeys."

"Yes, I did." Two were being traditionally roasted. A third would be deep-fried later, closer to dinnertime, since it wouldn't take as long to cook.

"Where's Kade?"

"I'm letting him sleep in." A shadowy frown flitted across her face.

"Is he okay?"

"I think he's really tired and he's trying to hide it."

Seth damn well knew he was trying to hide it, because he'd seen the exhaustion in his friend's face the night before. Yet another reason he'd opted to sleep alone, hopefully allowing Kade some well-needed rest.

Leah sat on the edge of the bed and kissed him again, this time long and lingering and stirring more than a little interest on Seth's part. "Why don't I take a shower with you this morning after we get the birds cooking?"

Seth smiled. "Sounds like a good plan to me."

He met her out in the kitchen a few minutes later. Within an hour, they had the birds stuffed and in one of the large double ovens. Leah checked on Kaden, found him still asleep, and then joined Seth in his bathroom.

"Let's make this one quick, sweetie," Seth said, hugging her to him. "I don't want him waking up alone and ignored." As much as his member was now throbbing, he knew it wouldn't take much to set him off.

"Okay."

Seth slid down her body, kneeling before her. She leaned against the shower wall as he gripped her hips and licked her slit. She moaned, tangling her fingers in his hair.

He loved doing this for her, bringing her pleasure without an ounce of pain involved. Before long she cried out and ground her hips against him. When he knew she was finished he stood, pinned her against the wall, and easily slid his cock inside her.

"How was that," he whispered, taking a hard stroke.

"Good," she whimpered as she wrapped her arms around him.

Leah worked her hips in time with his. It didn't take him long. He cupped her ass and held her as he took several last strokes, then came deep inside her.

He dropped his head to her shoulder. "I love you, babe." He kissed her. "I love you so much."

Leah's smile lit his heart. "I love you, too. Will you spend tonight with us?"

"Let's see how he feels. If he's worn out I don't want to disturb him. He needs his rest. Maybe a little playtime if he feels up to it."

"Okay." She closed her eyes and relaxed in Seth's arms under the warm spray. "Let me catch my breath, and I'll scrub your back for you before I go check on him."

Seth tried not to feel a guilty pang for enjoying this time alone with her. He should be past that now. He knew, ironically, if it wasn't for the fact—

kaden'sdying

—that the future was hanging over their heads, he wouldn't feel guilty.

As guilty, anyway.

When he was alone in the shower a few minutes later, he rested his head against the tile and let the tears flow. This was his alone time, something he desperately needed. It was the only way to release his crushing grief without his friends seeing. He didn't care if Leah wanted him to lean on her. If he really did that she would collapse under the weight of his emotions. Hell, it was barely all he could do to keep a lid on it.

He made it out to the kitchen twenty minutes later. Leah wasn't there. He hoped that meant she was spending private time with Kade.

And he smiled as he realized he wasn't the least bit jealous at that thought.

Progress.

He hummed to himself as he spooned out a bowlful of stuffing left over from the batch they'd made for the turkeys, then he walked out to the couch to eat and watch the news. The first guests wouldn't start arriving until nearly noon, so he wasn't worried about someone catching him half-dressed except Leah and Kaden. And since they'd seen him nekkid more times than he could count, they didn't count.

Kaden walked out a few minutes later, bleary-eyed and yawning. "Morning."

"Morning." He studied Kaden. "Where's Leah?"

He smiled. "She'll be out in a minute. Oh, here." He tossed Seth something. Seth quickly realized it was the remote control for the butterfly.

"What's this for?"

Kaden had made it to the kitchen. "She got a little pushy with me this morning," he called out. "Was trying to tell me to stay in bed. So I decided she needed a little reminder who's in charge." He returned with his mug. "She has to wear it until one."

Seth snorted in amusement. "One?"

Kaden nodded and started back toward the bedroom. "Under her clothes."

Seth shook his head and looked at the remote before slipping it into the pocket of his shorts. "This should be interesting," he muttered.

Leah appeared a few minutes later, fully dressed in a blouse and jeans, wearing her silver day collar and looking a tad...uncomfortable. He barely heard the faint humming of the butterfly.

"So you got a little pushy, hmm?"

She blushed. "I wasn't trying to be. I just wanted him to rest."

He stood and walked over to her, then handed her his empty bowl. Brushing the hair back from her neck he whispered, "He gave me the remote. When the guests arrive, I'll turn it off. But you still have to wear it as long as he says."

She breathed a deep sigh of relief. "Thank you!" She kissed him and went to the kitchen.

Seth wasn't an idiot. He was well aware Kaden knew Seth wouldn't fully torment her with vanilla people around.

Kaden, however, was more than devious enough to do it. And Kade probably realized the temptation to torture her would be too great if he held the remote.

Seth finished dressing and helped Leah and Kade in the kitchen. He loved surprising her with the vibrator, usually just as she was reaching for something. Around eleven thirty, and no guests had arrived yet as she helped him outside in the backyard. He had to pre-measure how much oil he'd need for the turkey by using water in the pot to find the level. Leah was holding the bird for him while he filled the pot.

"Okay, set it in there."

She did. Once her hands were empty, he stepped behind her and wrapped his arms around her waist. Then he slid one hand between her legs and firmly pressed the butterfly tight against her. He felt it buzzing through the denim.

He nibbled on her neck behind her ear. "You being a good girl, now?"

"Yes!" she gasped.

He pressed a little more firmly, giving her enough contact with the device to really feel it. "If you can come for me right now, I'll turn it off and leave it off, but you still have to wear it until Master told you."

She nodded and threw her head back against his shoulder. He gently rubbed his hand in circles between her legs and she moaned. She was so close.

He used his other hand to gently pinch her nipples, rolling them through the fabric of her shirt, alternating from one to the other.

"Come for me, babe," he whispered. "Come hard for me."

She ground her hips against his hand. He knew she was close. Just when he thought he might have to stop, she let out a soft cry and tensed in his arms. "That's it, babe. Come for me." He was there to hold her as her post-climax weakness hit, and he lowered her to the grass and sat behind her.

"How was that?"

She nodded, her head still resting against his shoulder. He reached into his pocket and shut off the vibrator. "Okay, sweetie. A deal's a deal."

She turned her head and kissed him. A playful smile filled her face. "You're finally getting into the spirit of this, aren't you?"

He shrugged. "Maybe when I hit my stride I can find some things to do for you in my own way."

She closed her eyes and snuggled against him, her face buried in the crook of his neck. "I'm sure you will."

"Okay, enough loafing. Master will come looking for us and might find other ways to torture you if he thinks you're goofing off." He stood, then helped her to her feet.

* * * *

It was easy for Seth to stay distracted once the guests started arriving. He knew, at least in passing, most of the people invited. He noticed Kaden leaned in to Leah around one o'clock and whispered something. She hurried down the hall to their bedroom.

Ah. He'd finally let her loose.

Kaden looked over at him from across the room and winked. Seth smiled and winked back. He had to admit it was fun having this private game with them.

Seth knew most of the people in attendance weren't aware of Kade's secret. He planned on telling them today, individually, as the day progressed. Seth had tried to talk him into just doing one announcement and getting it over with, but it was Kaden's call.

It was, after all, his party.

Seth sat outside later while the third turkey deep-fried. He'd spent much of the afternoon shooting video of the festivities but needed this alone time to emotionally recharge. Leah brought him a glass of tea and sat next to him.

"You okay?"

Seth nodded. People had drifted in and out of the house all afternoon to talk with Seth, some in obvious shock at Kaden's news. Right now, it was just him and Leah.

Leah touched his hand and he met her eyes. "I'm okay," she said. "I've been preparing for this. I'll be okay today."

"You sure?"

"Yeah. I don't like that we have to do it, but it's a relief to have it out there." Seth knew Kaden was only telling people he'd asked Seth to move in to help and care for him and Leah. Seth also knew the way Kaden was telling it left it more than open to interpretation that Kaden was fine with whatever happened…after, between Seth and Leah. Even putting out the comment that he hoped they would find happiness together.

He had to hand it to Kaden, the man was a thorough planner. One good thing about him being a control freak. He didn't want people thinking badly of Leah any more than Seth did.

She patted him on the hand again and stood, then walked away as one of Kaden's cousins, Tom, walked over with his wife to shoot the shit for a little while. Seth had grown up with Tom even though he was a couple of years younger than Kaden and Seth.

"This really sucks. Man, I'd never thought it. He looks so good."

Seth nodded and tried to focus his gaze on the flame from the propane burner under the turkey pot. He did not want to have this conversation. Most people had left it as a simple, "I'm sorry, let me know if I can do anything for you guys," generic bullshit comment.

Tom shook his head. "I can't believe it."

"Join the club."

The three of them sat in silence for a moment before Tom spoke again, his voice nearly a whisper. "Is Leah going to be okay?" Seth knew Kaden had revealed a little of Leah's past to his cousin but not about their lifestyle choices.

Seth nodded. "I think so. That's why Kaden asked me to move in now." Well, that was close enough to the truth to count, he supposed.

"Yeah. I think she'll be okay eventually if you're there for her." He kept shaking his head. Seth wanted to pound it down between his shoulder blades to make him stop. "She always seems very relaxed around you, sort of like she is with Kaden. You'll be good for her."

Seth didn't want to have this conversation. At all. He couldn't leave the turkey while it was cooking, and he couldn't tell Tom to get the hell away from him.

He hunkered down. "We'll all get through it."

* * * *

When they gathered around the tables outside to eat around five o'clock, Kaden stood and proposed the toast. He had Leah sitting on his right and insisted on Seth sitting on his left even though Seth had tried to move to a different table to not call attention to himself.

By this time, Seth knew everyone had been told the news. A few of the women looked a little red-eyed and weepy, as did Kaden's brother.

Denise had specifically not been invited.

"I want to propose a toast. To all my family and friends who have gathered to eat with us today, thank you for joining us. I want this day to be fun, and I have a surprise for you all once it gets dark enough." Kaden had been eagerly talking up the light display all afternoon.

He paused, gathering his thoughts. "This is a great day, and it's the kind of day our lives should be filled with. I want you all to remember that for me. I feel blessed to have my beautiful wife and my best friend beside me. I love all of you, but these two people are my strength and my closest comfort." He raised his glass. "To family, to friends, and to life. Cheers."

Everyone joined him. Seth fought to control his rolling stomach. He'd noticed that lately, little jagged bursts of grief threatened to spill out sometimes when he could least afford to lose control.

Once everyone was up and taking turns going through the buffet line, Seth snuck inside the house to his room for a moment. He thought he'd gone unnoticed when he heard the tap at his door a few minutes later.

"Yeah?"

Kaden stepped inside and closed the door behind him. "You okay?" he softly asked.

Seth started to nod when it hit him. He hated himself for it, but he sat on the end of his bed and cried.

Kaden sat next to him and silently put his arm around his friend's shoulders. When Seth composed himself a few minutes later, he apologized. "I'm sorry, dude. I shouldn't be dumping this on you. I just... I couldn't hold it back. I don't know how you're dealing as well as you are, man."

Kaden smiled but it looked sad. "Who says I am? I've had twenty years of practicing putting on a poker face as a Dom. Plus I'm an attorney. We're all good liars. It's genetic."

His comment had the desired effect—it made Seth laugh. Then they hugged, long and hard. Kaden patted him on the back. "Having you here makes it easier, believe it or not. I can see how good she is with you, and it's one less worry. I really mean it when I say I love you."

"Love you too, dude. Still not doing you."

Kaden laughed and sat back, brushed his hands across his eyes. "Not doing you either, buddy."

The men sat and looked at each other. "Happy Thanksgiving, Kaden. I'm glad we've still got you here. I hope you're here next year."

Kaden smiled. "That makes two of us."

Chapter Eighteen

The week after Thanksgiving, Seth methodically worked at the oak tree with the singletail. It was one of Kaden's favorite whips, a sixteen-plait six-foot bullwhip made of kangaroo hide, with a well-balanced handle. Seth seemed to have the most accuracy and control with it and worked to master it first before tackling some of the others. He'd gotten good enough he could nail all the balloons on the target without missing and now worked to fine-tune his control and aim with both hands, not just his right. He had also progressed enough that he was equally good in the three main throwing styles, overhand, reverse and forward crack.

Kaden lounged in the shade of another nearby tree. There were no Christmas lights or decorations this far back on the property, so Seth didn't have to worry about accidentally snagging any wiring with the whip.

"Time for you to tackle a different target. That tree never did shit to you, buddy."

Seth looked at him. "And what would you suggest? You told me when I could take the tips off leaves, I'd be ready."

"I'd say you're ready. You keep that up, I won't have a goddamned leaf left on that thing." He stood, then walked back to the house.

Seth continued practicing. A few minutes later, Kaden returned with Leah, who was now dressed in jeans, a heavy leather jacket, heavy leather gloves, and sneakers. Kaden carried another heavy leather jacket and a bottle of talcum powder.

As realization dawned, Seth felt his balls crawl up tight inside him. "Oh, *hell* no. I'm not using this on her yet!"

"Why not?" Kaden asked. "You're good enough."

"What if I hurt her!"

Leah smiled. "That's sort of the point."

Seth glared. "You know damn well what I mean!"

"You won't hurt her through her jeans. That fall and popper can't cut through denim. Not the way you're throwing, at least. And that's why I brought this." He held up the jacket. "I'll lay it over her ass while you practice. Once you're sure on your distance, we'll take it away and you can hit her on denim."

Seth vigorously shook his head, nausea threatening. "No! I'm not ready to do that."

Leah walked over and looked up into his face. Her eyes went wide. "Please?"

"Oh, no. Not the fucking puppy-dog eyes. Stop it!"

"Please, Seth?"

He clenched his jaw. "This isn't fair. I'm not ready!"

She gently grabbed his collar and stood on tiptoe so she could kiss him. "Please, Sir? For me?" Her huge, green eyes melted him.

He closed his eyes and swore. "All right. But it's your ass."

"Thank you!"

Kaden laughed and handed Leah the jacket. She walked a short distance away and knelt on the ground, her rear facing them. She draped the jacket across her hips.

Kaden leaned into Seth. "You are so fucked, buddy. You know that? She's got you wrapped around her little finger."

"Look who's talking."

Kaden smiled. "Yeah, I know. Who's really in charge, right? We've both got it bad."

Kaden dumped some talc into his palm and laid the tip of the whip in it. "This'll help you see where you're hitting."

Seth nervously gauged his distance before he threw, hitting her a little lower than he intended but on her right ass cheek. The faint white mark from the talc showed the strike.

Kaden nodded. "Excellent." He grabbed the end of the whip, applied more talc. "Do it again."

Kaden worked with Seth for fifteen minutes. Then Kaden removed the jacket from her ass and brushed the powder off. "Now, hit her like that."

Seth's nerves returned. "Man, I don't know about this."

"It's okay. Go ahead."

Leah looked like she was in heaven, the thuddy and not at all uncomfortable impact through the multiple layers of clothing nearly putting her in subspace despite the lack of an ongoing scene and relatively minor discomfort. She wiggled her ass at Seth. "Please, Sir."

He took a deep breath. "All right." On his first throw he choked and pulled at the last second, sending it wide and to the left.

"Stop." Kaden walked over to him. "Don't hesitate. That's when you will hurt her. Or yourself. You changed at the last second. Just picture where you want it to strike and don't hesitate. If you're going to hesitate, it's better to wait and not throw than it is to throw badly."

"All right." Seth tried again, this time hitting her exactly where he intended, on her left cheek.

Leah wiggled her ass at him and made a content sound.

"You okay?" Seth asked her.

"Ohhh yeah."

Kaden leaned against another tree, out of the whip's range. "She's going to jump us once we're finished, so you might as well nail her good now."

After a few throws, Seth didn't need the talc anymore. He slowly gained confidence as he took his time, carefully placing each strike to hit as close to the fleshy center of her ass cheeks as he could.

Kaden could easily go after her bare flesh. Seth knew it would take him some time—and a hell of a lot of practice—to reach that degree of confidence in his abilities.

After twenty minutes, Seth's arm and nerves had reached their limit. He coiled the whip. "I'm done. I need a break."

Leah sat up and pouted. "I didn't get any sting out of that at all."

Kaden laughed. He pushed away from the tree, handed the jacket to Seth, and took the whip from him. "Then get your ass bare for me and I'll take care of that, love."

Like a flash she was on her feet. She kicked off her shoes, jeans, and panties, then knelt on the ground again. "Thank you, Master!"

Kaden uncoiled the whip and took a moment to stretch his neck and roll his shoulders. As weird as it was, Seth never tired of watching Kade work with a whip. He was truly a master at it. Seth knew he needed to get plenty of video footage of them together, not just still pictures. Pictures couldn't capture the confidence, the fluidity of Kade's movements, the surety of his aim.

A true Dom.

"How are we, love?" Kade asked.

"Green, Master."

"Set of twenty."

"Twenty, Master."

"Count." He struck, nailing her square on the right ass cheek.

Leah sighed and said, "One, Master…"

Now she'd fully dropped into subspace. Even Seth could tell from the way her eyes looked glazed and the almost dreamy quality of her voice. Even when she didn't need a session she still enjoyed them.

Kaden worked her through the full set, and she begged for another. After the second twenty he walked over to her and she curled in his arms, sated and content. She hadn't climaxed from the session, and since she'd started it in a good frame of mind emotionally, she simply closed her eyes and cuddled with him.

Seth walked back to the house and left them alone. A few moments later, Leah, still naked from the waist down, ran into the kitchen and threw herself at Seth. He was forced to catch her, and she wrapped her arms and legs around him as she kissed him.

He turned, setting her on the counter before he managed to come up for air. "Whoa, hey. Hello to you, too."

Kaden walked in. "Our girl needs some relief. I warned you she'd be jumping us." He held up her clothes. "Go take these to the bedroom and wait for us there."

She jumped off the counter, grabbed the clothes from Kaden, and ran to do it.

Kaden laughed and started unbuttoning his shirt. "Well? You can't say you don't want a nooner with her, can you?"

Seth rolled his eyes. "No, can't say that." He followed his friend to the bedroom.

* * * *

Leah spent nearly two hours turning her men every which way but loose. When she finally fell asleep, contentedly tucked between them, Kaden fumbled for and found his glasses and the television remote. Seth needed a nap. He dozed next to Leah while Kaden watched TV.

It felt right. He wouldn't deny it. With the initial weirdness out of the way, and except for his sometimes guilt, it felt right sharing her.

The woman they loved.

The right woman.

* * * *

A few days later, Seth had conquered the worst of his hesitation over using the whip on Leah's denim-clad rear end. Each time he did she always jumped the two men, who were more than willing to allow her to lead them to bed.

Seth was eating breakfast when Leah sidled up to him and wrapped her arms around him. "I know what I want for my birthday."

He had a feeling it was a present he couldn't buy. His friends had insisted on giving him an allowance when he refused to let them pay him for being there. He didn't have to spend any of it and kept it in the joint account he now shared with Leah—yet another of Kaden's careful plans. Seth was also a cosigner on their other bank accounts, but he didn't want to have anything to do with those yet if he didn't have to.

"What would that be?" He slipped his arms around her bare waist.

"I want you to use the singletail on me."

He frowned. "How's that a present?"

"On my bare ass."

"Oh, no you don't. That's not fair!"

She broke out the puppy-dog eyes. "Please?"

"Why can't I just buy you something?"

"This is what I really want. Please?"

"Stop the puppy-dog eyes."

"Please?"

He groaned. "You're killing me here, babe. Why are you asking me to do this?"

Kaden rounded the corner with his morning cup of coffee in hand. "What's she prying out of you now?" he teased.

"I told Seth what I want for my birthday," she said with a fake pouty lip, "and he won't agree to it."

Kaden took one look at her and burst out laughing. "You are too much, little girl." He leaned in and kissed her. "And what are you trying to sucker Seth into now?"

"Using a singletail on my bare ass."

Kaden's spit take looked genuine. His rolling laughter certainly was. "Holy shit! She's really got you this time."

"How about a little backup here, dude?"

Kaden grabbed some paper towels to wipe up his spewed coffee. "No, I'm not getting between the two of you on this one." He pointed at Seth. "You've got to man up and learn to stand up to her."

"She used the eyes!"

Kaden laughed again. "I know. They're lethal. That's one thing I can't teach you, buddy. You're on your own there."

Leah wore nothing but her heavy collar because they weren't expecting any company that day. She pressed her body against Seth and squirmed. "Please?"

Kaden's laughter didn't help Seth any. "Dude, stand up to her."

He looked at Kaden over her shoulder. "You put her up to this, didn't you?"

Kaden leaned against the counter with his fresh mug of coffee and shrugged. "I might have suggested a course of action to her that would most likely get her the desired result." He took a sip.

"Fucking traitor."

"Fucking pussy. You're her Dom. Stand up to her."

She widened her eyes and pouted her lip. "Please?"

Seth closed his eyes and groaned. "I'm so fucking screwed."

"Yep," Kaden agreed.

* * * *

That was how Seth found himself nervously staring at Leah's bare ass a few hours later out in the backyard. The six-footer was too big to use in the playroom. With the Christmas tree in the living room, there wasn't enough room there, either. With the lights on the lanai, in addition to the tables, it was easier to take her out back. Neighbors couldn't see them anyway because of the woods.

"Your birthday isn't for a couple of weeks yet. Why can't we wait? Let me practice a little more?"

She wiggled her bare ass at him. She had donned a leather jacket and gloves at his insistence and Kaden's agreement that it might be a good idea. "Please, Sir? I really want it."

"What if I hurt you? Don't be a smart-ass, either. I mean, what if I hit you in the wrong place?"

"You're good. I've watched you. You won't hurt me."

Kaden sat with his back propped against an oak tree. "Pussy," he taunted.

Seth turned and pointed the whip at him. "Don't you fucking start on me. I'll practice on you."

He smiled and shrugged.

Seth took a deep breath. "All right. Just…hold still, okay? Don't move." He carefully lined up his throw, choked and stopped, walked in a circle, repositioned himself. "Hold still."

He took another deep breath, closed his eyes for a moment to settle his nerves, then took aim and threw.

The hit landed squarely in the middle of her left ass cheek, leaving a pink welt behind.

Leah moaned. Not in pain, but in a "oooh, someone's getting fucked soon and I hope it's me" way.

"You okay, babe?"

She wiggled her ass at him. Her voice sounded deep and husky. "Don't stop!"

Kaden laughed. "Go ahead. That was perfect. Could have stepped into it just a hair more. You barely touched her."

"That was my intention." He lined up another one. "Don't move a fucking muscle." He threw, landing the hit in the middle of her right cheek.

She moaned again. "Yes!" she hissed.

Kaden nodded. "Good. Now loosen up a bit. You're too tense. You're going to hurt yourself throwing like that."

Seth took a moment to roll his neck and shoulders and another deep breath. "Okay, you ready?"

"Yes!"

He threw, then another one immediately after, both hitting their intended target.

"Okay, honey, please. I'm a wreck. Can I stop now?"

"Two more. Please?"

Kaden stood and motioned for the whip. Seth stepped out of the way and swapped him the whip for the video camera Kaden had been filming the practice with. "You'll get more than that," Seth said.

Kaden took over. "Where are we, love?"

She immediately slipped deep into subspace. Seth had suspected she was close but not that close. "Green, Master."

"Set of thirty, love."

"Thirty, Master."

"Count."

Seth filmed them, in awe of Kaden's skill. Would he ever be that good, that sure of himself? Kaden told Seth he'd started with the bullwhips fifteen years earlier, after Leah had seen a demonstration and nearly came in her pants at the thought of Kaden using one on her.

Kaden also assured him that, despite his calm, outward demeanor, he'd been just as terrified of using one on her bare flesh as Seth now was.

Leah was in heaven. After the set, Kaden handed the whip back to Seth and walked over to her. She curled in his arms as he softly whispered to her.

Seth almost shut off the video, then decided maybe he should film it. She might want video of them together like that. How he felt filming it should be immaterial.

After a few minutes, Kaden kissed her forehead and she got to her feet. Seth stopped filming. She walked over to him and kissed him, long and deep. "Thank you, Sir. That was wonderful."

"Hey, Kade did the worst of it."

"But I knew you could do it."

"Yeah. Just don't ask me to do long sets yet."

"Okay." She headed to the house. The pink and red welts crisscrossing her ass were clearly visible.

Kaden stopped beside Seth. "She's something else."

"How did you not lose your fucking mind while learning all this shit?"

Kaden shrugged. "I had a woman who loved and needed me. I was going to do everything in my power to give her whatever she needed to make her happy. She didn't want me to buy her things. We'd be living in a crappy apartment in Tampa still if it wasn't for me insisting on moving someplace nicer. You know she drove that goddamned piece-of-crap junker car for years. A friend of mine sabotaged it for me one night so it caught fire. She had to let me buy her a new one."

Seth remembered Kaden e-mailing him about it while he was still in Iraq. "No shit? I thought that was an accident."

"So does she. Let's keep that our secret, okay?"

Seth smirked. "Yeah."

They started walking to the house. "Seth, I know this is all a mind fuck. She's not a complicated person. She wants to feel safe, to trust, to feel secure. She gets that from me, and now from you, too. If she has that, she's happy. The rest she doesn't care about."

"The pain."

He shrugged. "That's a coping mechanism. It's a necessity. Some women need shoes. She needs whips."

"I couldn't have learned as much as I have without you. I never could have...after." He stopped and turned to Kade. "I understand. If you'd left me a fucking note or something, I never could have done this."

Kaden sadly smiled. "I know. Neither could she. I told you, I knew I had to make this happen. I had to show you. It was the only way. You can't begin to explain shit like this and have it make any sense whatsoever." He clapped Seth on the shoulder. "Now quit harshing my mellow, dude."

Seth laughed but they continued to the house. "That's my line."

* * * *

Two days later, Seth was outside alone with Leah, practicing in the backyard. He was about to take his third throw when a wasp dive-bombed him. Without thinking, he stepped to the side as he threw in an attempt to avoid the bug.

Leah yelped, a sound he'd never heard her make before. The pained sound sent Seth's heart through his feet.

He dropped the whip and ran over to her. "Oh my God! Babe, are you okay?"

"Yeah, what happened?" She'd rolled over, sitting up, and had her hand clamped to her inner thigh.

"A goddamned wasp almost nailed me. Let me look." Seth's heart raced, and he was terrified he'd wounded her.

"I'm okay. It's okay."

"No, let me look!" He finally pried her hand away and saw the blood. "Oh…shit! Oh, honey, damn it! I'm sorry! I'm so sorry!"

She clamped her hand over it again. "Seth, it's okay."

"You're fucking bleeding! It's *not* okay! Goddamn it, I'm so sorry!"

Kaden apparently heard the commotion and raced down from the house. "What's wrong? What happened?"

Leah proudly smiled and showed him. "My first mark from Sir."

Kaden examined it and laughed. "Very good, love."

"This isn't funny!" Seth screamed, trying to get a better look at her leg. Leah kept pushing his hands away.

Kaden shook his head. "I guarantee you it hurts you worse than it hurts her."

"This isn't funny!" Seth screamed again. "Goddamn it, Leah. Move your fucking hand." He finally got a good look at it, relieved to see it was only a minor cut. "It's not fucking funny! If I'd hit your artery or something—"

She grabbed his chin. "Stop." Her voice dropped, firmer than he ever remembered hearing it. "I'm okay, Seth. *Sir*, I'm fine." She pulled him in and kissed him. "Master put far worse and deeper ones on me while He was learning. Trust me, this is nothing. I consider this a badge of honor to finally wear Your mark." She kissed him again, then let him help her to her feet. "I'll go wash it off and put some ointment on it. It'll be fine. It's all right."

Seth watched her walk to the house, his entire body trembling from nerves. He shook his head and looked at Kaden. "I can't do this, man. I can't fucking do this! I can't hurt her like that! Goddamned wasp came out of fucking nowhere—"

"Stop." Kaden's firm tone startled Seth. "It was an accident. I meant it when I said it'll hurt you a lot worse than it hurts her. The pain's already fading for her. You'll be stinging every time you see the scar." His face darkened. "Trust me on that."

Seth swallowed hard. "I can't stand hurting her like that, man."

"I know. It sucks. The first time I cut her with a whip I nearly bawled like a baby. You saw how she reacted. She did the same thing to me. She's strong when she needs to be, when she can be, in the ways she can be strong. Don't ever forget that." He looked at Seth. "There are times, like this, when you have to trust her. Remember, pain is nothing to her when she's in subspace."

"She was in fucking pain that day she sliced her arm open. I thought she would go into shock on me."

"That was different. She wasn't in subspace when it happened. She wasn't trying to hurt herself. When she's in subspace, you could probably pull out every one of her goddamned fingernails and she'd beg for more. There's a huge difference. If you hadn't wigged out on her, she'd be begging for more right now, I guarantee you."

Seth eventually sighed. "I probably harshed her mellow by freaking out, didn't I?"

"Dude. You did." Kaden smiled. "But that's okay. You can make it up to her later, I'm sure."

* * * *

Later that night after dinner, Seth willingly gave in to Leah's request to not just join them but to spend the night. He spent a long time loving her while Kaden held her in his arms. He gently ran his lips over the welt on her leg, hating himself.

Leah sensed his inner turmoil. She kept her fingers tangled in his hair, or her fingers laced through his, and constantly murmured to him.

When they all fell asleep later, she had her back tightly nestled against Kaden, with his arm around her waist. But she had Seth tucked against her chest, cradled in her arms as he cried himself to sleep while Leah whispered to him.

* * * *

The next morning, Seth still felt like shit. The wound would heal cleanly, but the ugly purple bruise surrounding it would take days to fade.

Leah started to get up to make coffee, but he grabbed her hand. "No, babe, I'll go do it. You stay in bed."

She tried to protest. Then, one of the few times Kaden ever overruled

Seth.

"Love, go make our coffee. We'll be out for it shortly."

Leah quickly kissed them both and jumped out of bed. She left the bedroom.

Once Kaden was sure she was out of earshot, he turned on Seth. "Stop it. You can't do that."

"I fucking hurt her, man! I feel horrible!"

"She's already over it. She was over it minutes after it happened. She humored you last night because she felt bad that you were so upset, but fucking stop it. Enough's enough."

Seth felt shocked. "You cold-hearted bastard! That's your goddamned wife! How can you sit there and tell me enough's enough?"

He leaned in. "Because that's the way she wants it. Remember how she freaked out over the laundry when you first moved in? I'm not kidding when I say she needs you to man up now." He dropped his voice even lower. "I've been busting your balls about her leading you around by the short hairs, but I'm also telling you it's got to stop. Now."

A haze of rage clouded Seth's mind. "What the *fuck* is wrong with you?"

Kaden frowned. "You have *got* to get a handle on this. It's okay while I'm still around, because she's got me. But quit this fucking bullshit once and for all before I'm gone! She needs to know you're strong and steady and will take care of her. I'm not talking about grieving. She expects that from you. I'm talking you cannot let her get her way all the time. She needs to feel you're her Master. Right now, you're acting like a fucking pussy!"

Seth opened his mouth to argue, then snapped it closed. He wanted to deck Kaden. Never in his life had he ever felt that before.

Kaden met his angry gaze. "You know I'm right. You've seen her long enough now to understand what I mean."

"*You* let her get her way."

"When *I* decide to. In things that don't fucking matter. *This* matters. This is an issue of strength. This is a time when you have to put on your goddamn big-boy britches and just suck it the fuck up. It's done. It's over with. She knows it was an accident. Believe me, she understands you're upset about it. It's over, it's done, move on."

He got out of bed, leaving Seth sitting there stewing. Kaden walked into the bathroom. Seth finally got his wits about him and went to his own room.

He started for his bathroom, then turned and locked his bedroom door.

Fuck it.

He used the bathroom before pulling on some running clothes. He listened at his bedroom door for a moment, heard Leah and Kaden talking in the kitchen, and quietly walked down the hall and let himself out the front door.

The morning felt cool, but even though it was December the highs were predicted to be in the upper seventies. Seth didn't bother stretching. He hurried down the driveway at a quick, loping pace, wanting to put distance between himself and the house and the sound of Kaden's accusation ringing in his ears.

How could he not feel badly about what he did? *Fuck!* He'd hate himself every time he saw the mark. Maybe it wouldn't leave one. Still, he'd feel horrible about it.

The sound of her pained yelp as the whip cut her.

Christ, he'd never get that out of his brain.

He picked up the pace, running faster, harder, until he was pushing himself at a blistering sprint. When he finally ran out of wind he was on the other side of the development.

At least this whole thing had forced him to get back in shape. He'd almost returned to his Army weight, and most of the flab around his belly had melted away. He looked decent, had regained most of his stamina. In the small park he stopped, did fifty push-ups, fifty sit-ups, and started running again.

He didn't want to return home.

Home. Funny, it *was* home. Kaden said he needed to see it as his home. Despite hating the circumstances, Seth begrudgingly admitted yeah, it was home.

His home.

His woman.

Maybe he was still missing a key point in understanding this crazy mess. When he thought of Kaden being angry, Seth still wanted to punch his lights out.

He'd *hurt* Leah. How could Kaden be okay with that?

He purposely avoided the house. He didn't know what time it was. He guessed he'd been gone for over an hour by the way the sun had moved.

He stopped at the park again, took a sip of water from the drinking fountain, then stood in the shade to stretch. He lay back in the grass and clasped his hands behind his head. Above him, soft clouds scudded across a bright, blue December sky.

His first year in the Army, he'd been stuck in Germany. What a fucking miserable place that had been for a native Florida boy. After he was sent to Iraq he missed the cold Berlin nights while he was sweating his ass off inside a Humvee under thirty pounds of body armor and another thirty of gear while trying not to get shot at.

He closed his eyes and tried to clear his mind. Every time he did, the sound of Leah's pained yelp pierced through his soul.

Well, imagine that. Something to finally take the mental heartbeat—

kaden'sdying

—away. I'll be damned.

What a fucking suck way to do it.

After a while he stretched, did more sit-ups and push-ups, and slowly lapped the development again. Back to the park.

School was still in session, so he had the place to himself.

He lay back in the grass and stared at the sky. This was too much. *Too. Fucking. Much.* He'd finally fried his brain.

He didn't pay any attention to the sound of the car pulling into the park. He heard a door open and close and someone walking on the sidewalk toward him.

When the shadow fell across him, he realized it was Leah.

"Is this a private pity party, or can anyone join?"

He rolled into a sitting position. "How can you fucking stand to look at me?"

She sat close, cross-legged, in front of him on the grass. She'd put on a T-shirt and shorts that covered the bruise.

"It was an accident. Accidents are going to happen. I meant it when I said Kaden nailed me a lot worse than that over the years. You will too. It's going to happen. It's just an occupational hazard."

"That's not funny."

"If this isn't bothering me, why is it bothering you? What's really going on?"

He clenched his jaw. "I can't understand why Kaden was pissed at me this morning for being upset that I hurt you." *Might as well get it all out there.* They'd told him they wanted honesty. "I fucking hate myself, and he's calling me a pussy for feeling bad that I hurt you."

She grabbed his hand and wouldn't let him pull away. When he finally met her gaze, she softly spoke. "You love me. And I know that. You were doing what I asked you to do. You didn't punch me or stab me. If I was helping you work on the car, for example? What if I was helping you do that, and in the process you accidentally hurt me? Would you feel like this then?"

"That wouldn't be deliberate. It's not the same fucking thing."

"It *is* the same thing." She squeezed his hand. "It would be an accident. No different. The first time Kade drew blood on me I thought he was going to barf and cry, and I was praying oh, God, please don't let him pass out because we were alone and I was tied to the bench. I love you, Seth. Trust me, everything you're feeling, he's felt. Only it's taken him twenty years and we're trying to cram it all into you in a few months. This makes me love you more, that you're doing something so obviously unnatural for you because of your love for me. How could I hate you when you're my life?"

"You love Kaden."

"And I love you." Her eyes brimmed with tears, but she looked away for a minute and composed herself. "When you went in for your hernia operation, who was there waiting for you in recovery?"

"You."

"Who took care of you?"

"You."

"If you'd come to Kaden and told him the news he'd knocked you and me over with, I would still be taking care of you. I love you. I love you as much as I love him. Yes, I have a longer history with him, have shared things with him that…" Her voice choked, and she held up a hand to make him stay silent while she recovered.

"I'm going to miss him like hell when he's gone," she eventually continued. "It's going to rip half my soul out. If you weren't here for me, I would fucking give up and die the minute he quit breathing. I'm still not sure how I'm going to keep going. All I know is you won't let me die."

Her voice dropped to a whisper. "We don't have time for you to learn every single thing he's learned about me in twenty years. You have to trust us when we tell you things. I'm telling you, this is okay. This is *not* a big deal. You've come so far and learned so much in the past few months, it's amazing. It's breathtaking. I've loved him as his wife for years. But from the moment I met you, I knew you completed me. I couldn't tell you, and it killed me for so long."

She looked away again, but he spotted her tears. "For all three of your weddings, Kaden made me promise not to say anything when they asked if there were objections. He almost forced me to stay home for the third one."

It would have been impossible for Kaden to miss them—he was always Seth's best man.

Seth felt his heart roll again. "I'm sorry. I didn't know."

"It's okay." She looked at him. "It's done. We can't get that time back." She leaned in closer. "We have *now*. Right now. He's still strong, and he's still in decent health. Please don't let guilt over something you don't need to keep feeling guilty over ruin what time he's got left with us. He needs to feel sure that when he goes, we'll be okay."

She laid her palm against his cheek. "I love you. I have to focus on him, I know. But it helps knowing I have you there to catch me when I get to the point where I don't think I'll be able to go on. You're my safety net. And while it fucking hurts like hell to think of a future without him in it, I know that somehow, you'll get me through to the other side and we'll start healing together."

"He said I need to learn to stand up to you."

"Well, that's easy for him to say. He's had twenty years. But he's right. I do tend to push your buttons more because I know I can. There are times I wish you'd stand up to me more."

"Really?"

She nodded. "Yeah."

"Not about this whipping crap."

She wiped her eyes and laughed. "No, I was ready to play even dirtier to make that happen." She laced her fingers through both his hands. "Come back with me. Please? Let's take a shower and start the day over. There will be times you accidentally hurt me. I trust you, Seth. I know you don't take this stuff lightly. I know you do everything in your power to make it as safe as possible. I trust you with the ropes even, because I've seen how closely you pay attention to what he tells and shows you. I can turn around and get out there right now and let you take a turn at me with the singletail, without hesitation. I know the risks. I know there is always a chance of injury. I also trust you will do everything in your power to be as safe as you can."

"He's right. I am a fucking pussy."

"No, you're a guy in a tough situation. You grew up with Kaden. He didn't go from being nice guy to Master and Dom in a couple of months. I'll never forget the look on his face that first night." He knew from her expression that she was recalling the past. "He was so angry at me for hurting myself. But even more, he was scared. I remember I screamed at him that he didn't know shit about me and he was fucking mean to make me promise not to do it and I don't know what all I said. I couldn't tell you if I tried.

"Then he grabbed me and spanked me. And when I looked up at him, he was just…well, sort of like you looked when you were trying to see how bad I was hurt. Horrified. I knew immediately he didn't mean to do it. I knew he didn't enjoy doing it." She shook her head. "I think maybe that's why I wanted him to keep doing it. Why I was able to promise him and keep it that time, mostly."

Her voice dropped to a whisper. "He was the first person in my life who hurt me but he didn't enjoy it. Do you think he just jumped into this with both feet? You *know* him. The only reason he did it was for me. Not because he enjoyed it. Don't let him fool you. He was just as scared as you are now. Probably even more."

"He sure doesn't look like it."

"That's twenty years of experience."

Seth took a deep breath, trying to buy himself time. "I meant it when I said I'm going to need time to just be vanilla."

"I already told you, that's fine. I'll be honest if I need a session or spanking."

He studied her. "How can you be so certain I'm capable of doing this?"

"Because I love you. I have more trust in you from nearly twenty years of friendship than I do in Tony's twenty-plus years of being a Dom. He's a great guy, and I consider him a friend, but he didn't walk through hell and back with me."

"I haven't."

"You are right now, aren't you?"

Yeah, she was right about that.

She stood and offered her hand. "Please?"

After a long moment he stood, took her hand, and followed her to the car.

* * * *

Later that afternoon, Leah made Seth go to the backyard with her. "You have to do this. Just two strikes, that's all I'll make you do. If you don't do it, you'll never want to do it."

"Get back on the fucking horse, huh?"

"Well, spanking horse." She grinned.

"Oh, fuck me. You are too much, girl." He finally took the whip. "Okay, but it's your ass."

She turned, winked. "No, actually, it's Your ass, Sir."

He couldn't help it. He hardened in his jeans. Fuck, that was one button he didn't mind her being able to push.

She knelt on the ground while Seth tried to shake the tension out of his arms. After he couldn't put it off any longer, he threw.

He nailed her perfectly, right in the middle of her ass.

He struck again, another perfect hit.

She sat up and turned, looked at him. "You okay?"

He nodded. "Yeah." He hesitated. "Do you want a few more?"

She smiled and wiggled her ass. "I thought you'd never ask."

He went a total of ten before his nerves gave out. "I'm done. I'm sorry."

She stood, walked over to him. She put her arms around him and kissed him. "See? That was perfect."

He knew what she was up to. She wore nothing but the heavy leather jacket, and the way she was bumping and grinding against him made him even harder.

"You keep that up, you're getting fucked."

"Really?" She grinned.

He dropped the whip and pushed her to the ground. He shoved her legs apart and unfastened his jeans. "Yeah, really."

He plunged into her wet heat, grabbed her hips, and fucked her hard. She held on and met each thrust. When he came he collapsed on top of her.

"Feel better?" she purred.

"No."

He heard her puzzled tone. "Why not?"

"Because you need a good spanking before I let you come, that's why. I want to get every inch of that sweet ass red. If you behave, I might talk to Master about us both fucking you tonight."

She made a small, surprised sound. "Really?" she gasped.

"Yeah, but only if your ass is waiting for me on the spanking horse when I get up there."

She practically pushed him off her and ran for the house.

Seth shook his head and laughed. Okay, so maybe some of this he *could* get into.

Kaden looked up from his newspaper when Seth walked through a moment later. "What's going on?"

"I've got me a slave to spank and molest, buddy. Care to join me?"

He threw the paper down and stood to follow him. "Duh."

Chapter Nineteen

Leah hated spending time away from "her boys," but both men were in agreement she needed something to keep her busy. Seth wondered if Kaden shared his worry that once the fundraising banquet was over she would need something else to distract her.

Not only did Leah coordinate all those arrangements, she still dealt with the parties and dinners they would have at the house. Seth helped out as much as he could, as much as Leah would let him.

She'd worked herself half to death, nearly to the point of exhaustion, Seth opined, but he followed Kaden's lead and let her do what she needed to do.

As the night of the banquet drew near, Seth was surprised to find he'd be going. Not only that but sitting at the table with her and Kaden.

"Um, sweetie, not a good idea."

"Why not?"

He couldn't think of a legitimate reason. Most of Kaden and Leah's closest friends and family already knew of Kaden's "hopes" that Leah and Seth would get together after his death. Seth was surprised to find that most supported them. The ones that mattered, at least.

"You sure you want me there?"

"I already got your tux. You have to go."

He didn't force the issue. He'd also hoped to stay home and have a long evening alone so he could cry himself to sleep. And give them a special evening alone together, one Leah could remember and enjoy.

That plan, shot to hell.

Seth had a thought and made a couple of phone calls. Kaden would be surprised, but he wouldn't let Leah balk and spoil Seth's fun.

The night of the banquet, Seth finalized his plans and rode with them in Leah's Lexus to Sarasota. As the organizer, Leah introduced the keynote speaker, a county commissioner. Then she returned to sit between her two men. Under the table, she reached out a hand to each and held them.

Seth worried everyone watched them. No one did, of course. No one could even see.

At one point after the food was served, Seth slipped out to the car to take care of his plans. He smiled, knowing that while Leah might be a little irritated at him at first, she would thank him later.

He knew Kaden would.

After dinner there was dancing. Seth hated to dance. He sat back and watched as Kaden and Leah gracefully moved around the floor with other couples. They looked so perfect together. Seth knew Kaden had lost a pound or two, but his skin color still looked normal. The typical jaundice hadn't set in yet, might not for a while. A few times he'd caught Kaden looking a little queasy. Kaden had sworn him to secrecy on those incidents.

Still, at the last doctor visit he was doing well, all things considered.

Seth slipped outside for some air. He stood and stared at the well-decorated atrium. In some ways, this Christmas was the best and worst of his life. Best because he felt like, for the first time since he'd left home, that he was part of a family again. Not even with his exes had he felt like that. Was that a fault on his part, or theirs, or both? And the worst…

Well, obviously.

Thank God Kaden wouldn't die this Christmas. Not with Leah's birthday so close to the day. That would push her over the edge.

When he felt a hand on his shoulder, he turned and looked into Leah's green eyes.

"Hey, why are you out here?"

He shrugged and offered up a wan smile. "Just needed some air."

"Will you come dance with me? Please?"

"I think you should go dance with Kaden. I'm a sucky dancer." The music drifted out to them through the doorway.

"One dance?" Her green eyes melted him.

"One. Right here." He opened his arms and enfolded her. He rested his cheek against the top of her head and slowly swayed in time with the music. He'd give her this much tonight, because he wanted her happy. But he wanted her focus to be on Kaden.

At the end of the song he kissed the top of her head and gently patted her ass. "Go back inside. I'll be there in a minute."

She went.

He took a deep, ragged breath. It would be lonely this weekend without them at home, but it was for the best. He'd have, hopefully, a lifetime with her.

After.

Kaden wouldn't.

When he knew he could maintain his façade, he finally walked inside.

* * * *

While Leah consulted with the caterer about some last-minute dessert logistics, Seth moved to sit next to Kaden. "Hey. Need to talk to you."

"What?"

"When it's time to leave, the two of you go on without me, okay?"

He frowned. "What?"

"Don't ask questions, dude." He glanced around to make sure they weren't being overheard. "It's my birthday present to Leah, and my Christmas present to both of you. Don't let her call me either. You'll find a note in the car explaining it. I want you both to have fun. Don't you dare let her spoil this for me."

Kaden nodded and leaned in to hug him. "Thanks." He clapped him on the back. "How will you get home?"

"Already under control. Just keep her on a leash." Seth laughed. "Well, you know what I mean. I'll see you guys sometime late Sunday."

"Okay. I appreciate it."

Kaden would laugh when he saw the extras Seth had packed for them. Not just clothes—mostly clothes for Kaden, because Leah wouldn't need many—but a few of the less extreme toys.

More than enough for them to have some creative fun over the weekend.

They would spend the weekend at a beachside resort on Longboat Key. There would be a chilled bottle of champagne waiting for them. And hopefully a sweet weekend of memories for Leah.

Seth waited until Leah had disappeared again to handle something to make his exit. He'd already programmed the taxi company's number into his cell so he'd have it. Within fifteen minutes, he was riding south.

Toward home.

Seth loosened his tie and stared out the window at the passing landscape. *Home alone.*

"So'd you have a little too much to drink tonight, buddy?" the driver asked to make conversation.

Seth shook his head. "Nope. Not nearly enough, I'm afraid."

"Car break down?"

He sat back in the seat and closed his eyes. "Nope. I was odd man out. Wanted to give my friends some time alone. You know how that goes."

"Ah."

Fortunately the driver fell silent, opting to listen to stale Christmas songs on a local station. When they reached the gate, Seth leaned forward and paid the fare. "I'll get out here and walk. I need the air. It's not far."

"You sure?"

"Yeah. I know the way home."

He got out and punched in the code, waited for the gate to open enough he could slip through, and walked back to the house.

The holiday lights, now set on a timer system, welcomed him as he reached their drive. He spent a few minutes walking through the displays, trying to put off the inevitable.

They would be heading to the resort.

Inside, the hollow sound of his dress shoes on the tile floor echoed back at him. He turned on the Christmas tree lights and living room TV before walking to his room. He turned his TV on, too, and kicked off his shoes. He started to drop the tux on the bed, thought better of it. Just because Leah wasn't around was no reason for him to be a slob. He'd had plenty of years' experience picking up after himself.

He neatly hung the tux in the closet. She'd take care of it Monday, he knew. Get it to the cleaners. Not that he'd ever use it again, probably.

Then again, he might. Knowing Leah, she'd drag him to any banquet she could.

And he'd go.

He slipped on a pair of sleeping shorts and padded out to the kitchen. It was tempting to make himself a drink, but he opted for fixing a mug of the herbal tea Leah was making Kaden drink by the gallon. He damn sure didn't need to be drunk tonight, alone, when it would be hard enough to keep the bad and depressing thoughts at bay. And he damn sure didn't need the extra calories. He was almost pleased when he looked in the mirror, his old Army body finally visible without years of accumulated flab in the way.

He didn't want to lose the progress.

It was nearly midnight when he settled on the couch in front of the TV and surfed until he found a stupid holiday horror movie. An axe murderer dressed as Santa, terrorizing some sorority sisters.

Tits, ass, terror, and tinsel. What a combo.

He settled in for a long night alone.

* * * *

He awoke the next morning on the couch with a crick in his neck.

Well, won't have to make my own bed, at least.

He started a pot of coffee before going to take a shower. Then he poured himself a mug and walked down to the end of the driveway to get the paper.

He turned the living room TV to one of the digital music stations, a classic rock channel. He turned the volume up loud so it blared through the stereo speakers and made the subwoofer throb.

Very loud.

Loud enough he couldn't hear the empty house.

Leaving the sliders open so he could hear the music, he took the singletail outside and practiced for two hours with both arms, until his palms and arms were sore.

Then he swam for nearly an hour.

He silently screamed the music lyrics in his mind, trying to drone out all other thoughts. For the few songs he didn't know he focused on the bass line and tried to chant that.

He used a rolled-up blanket to practice ropework for an hour.

Another swim.

Repeat.

Seth realized around four that he'd forgotten to eat both breakfast and lunch.

Fuck.

Maybe that was why he felt sick to his stomach.

He fixed a bowl of cereal before walking over to the TV. He turned it off.

The sudden silence sent chills down his spine. He nearly threw up.

TV on. Oh boy. Definitely *on.*

He turned the volume down and found a college football game on the Deuce. He didn't give a shit about either team, knew nothing about them. But he cheered each play regardless of who came out ahead.

By seven, he was pacing the house.

kaden'sdyingkaden'sdying

Finally, he forced himself to sit on the couch.

He turned off the TV.

Seth heard the tick of the coffee pot in the kitchen—*fuck, forgot to turn that off*—the sound of the air handler in the hall as it ran, the pool pump chugging outside on the lanai.

He screamed.

Seth closed his eyes and let out a deep, long, gut-twisting primal cry of rage and grief and hopelessness—

kaden'sdyingkaden'sdyingKADEN'SDYINGGODDAMMITIT'S NOTFUCKINGFAIRKADEN'SDYINGANDI'MNOT

—until he fell over on his side and sobbed himself to sleep on the couch.

* * * *

Around two a.m., Seth awoke and realized he was still lying on the couch. He walked to the kitchen, shut off the coffee pot. Thank God he hadn't burned down the fucking house.

My house.

He squeezed his eyes shut as the mental heartbeat threatened to return but apparently his mini-meltdown had helped.

Seth switched the TV on and found another stupid B-movie marathon on one of the premium channels.

He grabbed a pillow from his bed, curled up on the couch, then fell asleep again.

* * * *

Sunday morning he awoke around dawn. The TV droned on despite his inattention.

Seth felt dead inside.

He sincerely hoped they were having a good time. In his note to Kaden, he'd specifically requested they not call to check in. He claimed it was because he wanted them to have a good time and focus on each other.

In reality, he knew damn well it would fuck his mind if they did. He'd suspected he would feel achingly lonely without Kaden and Leah around. Hearing them talk about how good a time they were having wouldn't help him any. He didn't want them to feel guilty if he couldn't sound convincingly cheerful enough.

Seth didn't predict, however, how bad he'd feel. How dead inside.

Not just without Leah, but without Kaden.

It had become so natural to chat over breakfast every morning, then around dinner every night. Playing guitars and singing together. Working with the two of them during sessions or learning from them.

The three of them making love.

And this preview of what his life was about to become…

Yes, Leah would be there.

But Kaden wouldn't.

Fuck.

He needed to get his shit together and get his fucking head on straight before they got home. Leah would be all over him like white on rice if she suspected he'd been upset while they were gone.

Their checkout time was three. He'd requested Kaden stay and use the full time. Whether they would was another matter entirely.

At least an hour to drive home.

If they stopped to eat on the way, more time.

His day progressed much as Saturday had, trying to keep himself busy and distracted. When three o'clock rolled around, Seth found himself pacing again.

A little after five, he heard the sound of tires in the drive and looked.

A huge sigh of relief. They were back.

Leah's beaming smile as she jumped out of the car and ran to hug him on the front porch warmed his heart.

He swung her around and buried his face in her hair.

"Thank you," she whispered. "Thank you so much!"

"Did you have fun?"

"Yeah. A lot of fun. But I missed you."

He gave her one final squeeze before releasing her. "I missed you too, babe. Both of you."

"Did you eat?"

And so it started. He laughed. "I did manage to take care of myself while you were gone, yes. No wild parties, and no messes." He walked down to help Kaden with the bags.

Kaden's face looked a little younger than on Friday. He also hugged Seth. "Thanks, buddy."

"Hey, least I could do." Seth grabbed a bag.

When Leah walked inside, Kaden grabbed Seth's arm. "You really okay?"

Seth didn't meet his friend's eyes. "Yeah. I'm okay."

Kaden refused to let go.

Seth finally took a deep breath and shrugged. "Preview of coming attractions, that's all. I'm fine now that you two are home. I needed a little alone time to blow off some steam."

That seemed good enough for Kaden. He let him go, and they walked into the house.

* * * *

Three more dinners and parties. On Christmas morning, Leah burst through Seth's bedroom door and flung herself at the bed. She landed squarely on top of him and barely missed nailing him in the nuts with her knee.

"Good morning!"

In a fit of Christmas spirit, Kaden had equipped her with a red and green holiday collar, complete with several jingle bells.

Their own little pornographic elf.

Seth blearily looked at her. "What time is it?"

"It's seven!" She kissed him and sat up, straddling him, bouncing on top of him. "We need to open presents!"'

He groaned and pulled a pillow over his head. "Babe, dinner isn't until eight tonight. Couldn't you let me sleep in a little?" Guests weren't expected to arrive until at least five.

She yanked the pillow out of his hands and smacked him with it. "No. Come on, you have to get up. Now." She climbed off him and started tugging on his arm.

He grabbed her, dragged her back into bed with him and kissed her. Her protests weakened and stopped as he slipped a hand between her legs and found her clit.

"Why don't we elf around a little?" he joked as he nipped the side of her neck.

She started to squirm in his arms, giving in. Then, she stiffened and pushed him away. "No. Come on! Presents!" She rolled off the other side of the bed, out of his reach.

"Where's my fucking coffee?" he grumbled. Now he really had a morning woody, and her teasing him hadn't helped the situation any.

"It's brewing," she said from the doorway.

He rolled over and closed his eyes. A moment later, Leah startled him by slamming the back of his head with a pillow.

"Get. Up!"

"I was, you fucking tease, but you got out of bed."

She giggled and kissed the back of his neck. "After presents, you two can unwrap me."

"You're already nekkid."

"You know what I mean. Get up. Now."

When she was like this, even Kaden wouldn't argue with her. Seth blearily rolled out of bed. He used the bathroom, then pulled on a pair of shorts and stumbled out into the kitchen.

Kaden, looking equally bleary, stared at him from his place at the counter. "Morning."

They'd had a fairly late night of play. Seth had opted to sleep in his room afterward. Kaden looked as sleepy as he felt.

"Mornin'. What the hell's up with her?"

Leah pranced into the kitchen and poured the men their coffee. Now she was wearing a leopard print Santa hat and a long red T-shirt that said "Naughty and Proud of It" in addition to the elf collar.

"Come on! Why are you in here? Go to the living room!"

The sounds of carols drifted to them. Apparently she'd tuned the TV to the holiday music channel.

Seth sipped his coffee. "Can we get conscious first? What the fuck did you put in your coffee this mornin', speed?"

She grinned. "It's Christmas morning! Come on!"

Seth and Kaden rolled their eyes at each other and followed her into the living room. Apparently their little elf had been a very busy girl. A huge pile of presents was stacked under the tree. Seth had tucked a few small things under there the night before, after he left Leah and Kaden. Most of the other stuff hadn't been there.

"Oh, wait!" Leah had set up the video camera on a tripod in the corner. She checked it, then flashed a thumbs-up. "Okay. Time for presents!" She started handing out gifts to the men. "Go on. Open them!"

Kaden grabbed her arm and hauled her down to the couch between them. "Calm down, babe. Relax."

Seth started on the first present she'd plopped in his lap. Inside lay a beautifully made kangaroo-hide bullwhip.

"It's a BDSM Christmas," he joked.

"You like it?"

He smiled. "Of course I do. Thank you." He leaned over and kissed her.

She'd gotten them a wide variety of gifts from practical shirts, to the playful end of the scale, from novelties and remote-controlled cars, to…well, whips.

"These are more a gift for you," Kaden joked.

She grinned. "Well, yeah. Duh."

Kaden had bought her a gorgeous ring. Seth had gotten her matching earrings.

"Oh! They're beautiful!" Her eyes teared up as she hugged the guys.

For her men Leah had gone all-out. She'd even snagged a Wii game system for Kaden. The men wasted no time getting that hooked up.

Once all the presents were opened, Leah still wore a playful smile. "What's going on?" Kaden asked from the floor where he was working with Seth to hook up the game console.

"I've got one more." She looked at Seth. "For Sir." She handed him a small, brightly wrapped box.

Seth opened it, a puzzled look on his face. He pulled out a set of keys.

They weren't car keys. "What's this?"

"Why don't you come look?" She grabbed the camera from the tripod and waved him to the front door.

If he didn't know any better… The keys looked familiar. He'd once owned a set of keys similar to these. When he'd had a…

He opened the front door. In the driveway, with a big red bow on the handles, sat a Harley Roadster.

He'd had a Harley once, years earlier, but his first ex made him sell it because she claimed she was terrified of them. Seth remembered how, at the time, Leah begged him not to sell it. She loved it when he rode her around on it.

His jaw dropped. He turned to Kaden. "Did you know about this?"

He shook his head as he smiled. "No. I suspected though, when she asked to spend the money. I was sworn to secrecy even though I didn't know what I was swearing to."

Leah handed the video camera off to Kaden and grabbed Seth's arm. "I had them deliver it early this morning."

"So that's why you're wired to the gills," Seth joked.

He walked around the bike, then pulled her to him for a big hug. "I guess I know what you want this afternoon."

"At least one time around the development."

"It's great, babe. Thank you."

"The helmets are in the garage. I got you a bike jacket and stuff, too."

"That was going to be my next question." Seth loved motorcycles but wasn't an idiot. He never rode without a helmet or gear. He'd suspected his ex's fears had been more about how much Leah enjoyed the short rides and the fact that he'd bought Leah her own helmet and jacket than any worry about his own safety. When the four of them would go out to eat, Kaden and Leah would stop by their place. Kelly would ride in the car with Kaden while Leah rode on the bike with him.

He recalled Leah nearly cried when he'd told them he was selling the bike. She'd begged and pleaded with him not to.

Now he saw that in a different light.

He pulled her tight against his side. "You were mad because you were losing time alone with me."

She nodded. "Yeah."

"You barely spoke two words to Kelly after that."

Leah shrugged. "Let's just say I wasn't happy with her for making you sell it."

* * * *

Leah got her short ride that day, before they had to prepare for their guests.

Seth tried to relax during the afternoon. Leah convinced Seth and Kaden to play their guitars for everyone, and they had a cheerful session of singing Christmas carols…some with risqué, made-up lyrics.

When the last person left a little after eleven, all three were exhausted. Seth gave in to Leah's request to sleep with them, even though all they did was go to sleep.

As Seth drifted, he thought about the day. It was a good day. He'd taken lots of video and hundreds of pictures.

He closed his eyes and tried to go to sleep without thinking the phrase "last Christmas."

Chapter Twenty

December thirtieth dawned cold and rainy, perfectly matching Seth's mood. While the day quickly cleared, his mind did not.

Leah seemed to sense his need for space and didn't hover.

He pulled on sweats and went for a run, his sneakers squishing on the wet asphalt as he tried to run his foul mood out of his mind.

Tomorrow night they'd have the last party of the season, fifty guests expected to show up.

Seth felt tired. He wanted it over with so he could relax and quit worrying about whether or not his fake smile looked right. He was tired of watching friends and family force smiles. He was sick of their private comments to him, how sorry they were, and that they were there for him if he needed anything.

Bullshit.

All words. Well-meaning words, but when the time finally came, Seth knew it would be up to him and Leah to shoulder the burden while others uncomfortably withdrew with their worthless platitudes.

He didn't want to lose Kaden. He wanted to lose the world and spend the time they had left together, alone with his friends.

He'd also realized he loved Kaden. Not in a "hey, you've got a cute ass" kind of way, but more than friend or brother.

And looking into the barely masked faces of their friends and family didn't help Seth handle things any better.

Leah quietly fixed him breakfast. Later that afternoon, he settled on the couch and played Wii Bowling with Kaden.

They curled together in bed later that night. While tired, Seth was content to lie back and watch Kaden make love to Leah. Seth held her, softly whispering to her while Kaden made her climax.

* * * *

Last party. Kaden wanted to keep the lights and displays up until the first weekend in January, which was fine with Seth. It would take him a week or more to dismantle everything. He'd already laminated the sketches so he could have them for next Christmas.

In case.

Leah had bought him several dozen large plastic tubs. He would carefully store and label everything to make it easier to find next November.

Especially since he suspected he'd be putting it up alone.

Seth resisted the urge to drink, saving it for the midnight champagne toast. As they counted down, Leah dragged Seth and Kaden into the kitchen and kept a firm grip around their waists. When midnight arrived, she kissed Kaden, then Seth, and hugged them tightly to her.

"I love you both," she whispered. "My boys."

Kaden nuzzled her ear. "I love you, too, babe."

Seth kissed her other cheek. "Me too."

Once all the guests had left, Seth and Kaden talked Leah into going to bed and leaving cleanup for morning. With all three of them exhausted, it wasn't hard to talk her into going to sleep, cuddled together.

* * * *

Seth gave up trying to sleep in his own room. Leah rarely allowed it. Sometimes she would settle for him staying out in the living room late, giving Kaden private time with her. When Seth tried to talk to Kaden about it, reason with him, his friend shrugged.

"She wants us both with her. If it doesn't bother me, why should it bother you? You're not feeling guilty again, are you?"

Yes.

"No."

"Liar." Kaden smiled. "It's okay. If it bothered me, I'd tell you guys. Seriously. Have I ever hesitated to ask for alone time with her before?"

Seth shook his head. No, he hadn't. Although Seth hadn't asked for alone time with her, Leah seemed to make sure he always got a little, at least once or twice a week, usually in the morning.

In Seth's brain, an invisible calendar ticked down. Not with dates and days and neatly marked squares, but more of a gauge, like a fuel tank. Right now, the level still floated in the lower end of the green region even though it had dropped somewhat over the past few months. The needle now dangerously hovered near yellow. Next would be orange, followed by red, each zone progressively narrower than the last. Then...

Black.

Seth knew damn well two years wasn't realistic, even though he prayed for it. If Kaden was still here next Christmas...it would be a miracle.

Kaden kept Leah away from his appointments. While Seth didn't want to lie to her, he knew he couldn't keep rebuffing her attempts to get all the details.

Kaden focused more on the ropework than he did on the whips now that Seth had regained most of his confidence. Seth started working with the four-footer but wouldn't use it on Leah yet. He needed to fine-tune his control with it first. Less forgiving if he nailed her with it, less room for error despite its shorter length.

* * * *

For Valentine's Day, Seth again presented them with a weekend alone. This time he took off, rode the bike up to Pensacola to spend the weekend with a former Army buddy who was in town for a family reunion. When he returned late Sunday night, Leah raced outside to greet him when she heard the rumble of the bike.

She nearly tackled him before he could get the kickstand down. "I missed you!" She threw her arms around him and hugged him as soon as he stepped off.

"I missed you, too, babe. How was the weekend?"

He didn't miss the sad cloud behind her eyes. "It was good. We had fun."

From the look on her face, Seth suspected she'd spent a lot of time in the playroom working through her growing grief.

Kaden read the newspaper on the couch. When Seth walked in, Kaden put the paper down and took off his glasses. "Hey. How was the ride?"

Seth dropped his bag on the floor behind the couch so he could pull off his jacket. Before he could say anything, Leah had grabbed it and carried it back to his room. "It was fine. How are you feeling?"

Kaden shrugged. "Same ole."

"She okay?"

"Probably better with you back."

Kaden gave them all a belated present. He'd had three matching bands made, two for the men and one for Leah, to wear on their right hands. An intricate, twining vine like the one in the tattoos, with a tiny triskelion engraved on it. Kaden slipped Leah's ring on her hand, then the other ring on Seth's.

"Still not doing you," Kaden said with a grin.

Seth hugged him. "Ditto, buddy."

But he looked at the ring and it...felt right. Like the three of them belonged together in an unofficially official way.

* * * *

Time ticked on. While Leah was out grocery shopping one day, Seth walked into the den and caught Kaden with a pained look on his face, bent over in his chair. He rushed to his friend's side.

"What's wrong?"

Kaden shook his head. "Just a little pang, that's all. Feels better if I lean forward."

"Do you want me to call the doctor?"

"What is he going to do? He'll tell me to try chemo or dope me up to the gills. It'll pass in a little while. It always does."

Seth's heart chilled. "How long have you had this pain?"

"Off and on for a few weeks. It goes away if I lean forward for a while." He looked at Seth. "Don't say a word."

Seth swallowed hard but nodded.

* * * *

The men's birthdays were just a couple of weeks apart, Kaden's first. Seth told Leah he would sleep by himself that night after they had a small cake following a meal of Kaden's favorites, allowing Kaden alone time with her. The next morning she slipped into Seth's room and brought his coffee, then snuggled into bed next to him.

"Good morning," he said.

She kissed him. "Good morning."

"How'd you sleep?"

"Not nearly as good as I do when you're both there." She rolled over and rested her chin on his chest. "I want a night alone with you for your birthday."

"That's not necessary." When her face clouded, he sighed. "All right. Quit pouting. Your face will fucking freeze like that."

She laughed. "Thank you."

"Like I can say no to you."

* * * *

For Seth's birthday she cooked all his favorites and fixed apple pie for dessert. Seth tried not to feel guilty when later, as they were sitting on the couch watching TV, Kaden leaned over and kissed Leah good night.

"See you two in the morning," he said with a smile, winking at Seth.

Leah snuggled tightly against Seth's side. "Well?"

"Well what?"

Her hand settled in his lap. "What now?"

He kissed her, slowly brushing his lips across hers. "We've done things your way. Tonight, we do them mine."

Seth wouldn't let her rush him. He took his time teasing her, tasting her, gently flicking his tongue against hers.

She tried to squirm, and he held her tightly until she relaxed against him. Eventually he pulled her across his lap, curled in his arms, still kissing her.

"I love you, babe," he whispered against her throat as he slowly worked his lips south. "I love you so much."

Her fingers tangled in his hair. "I love you, too."

He made her look at him. "I'll let you keep your collar on tonight, but it's just you and me and no protocols or titles or anything. Okay?"

"Okay," she softly agreed.

He stood, carrying her to his bedroom. He used his foot to push the door closed behind them and then gently laid her on his bed. If he was supposed to enjoy this night guilt-free, he would take full advantage of it in a way he usually didn't push for.

Seth took his time, carefully exploring her body with his lips and hands, forcing reality out of his brain. He could pretend she was his without a looming cloud of grief to taint his emotions.

He made love to her, taking his time, the way he always wished he could. Gently, tenderly, easing her through two climaxes before he finally entered her and slowly stroked.

"Look at me, babe," he whispered.

She opened her eyes.

"I love you."

She smiled. "I love you, too."

He felt his release build. "There will be a lot of nights I need this and not the other stuff," he said.

She nodded. "I know."

"I'm going to have to be enough for you."

"You are."

"I promise I'll take care of you and love you, babe. Forever." He grabbed her hips, thrusting.

"I know." He leaned forward and her hands slid down his hips, around his ass, her fingers brushing against his balls.

"I'll do nearly anything you need done, but I've got to be enough for you."

Her nails gently raked against his sac, sending a pleasant shiver through him. "You are. Now shut up and fuck me good, baby," she whispered in his ear.

That finished him. He cried out when he came. Leah wrapped her arms and legs around him, tightly holding him. When he caught his breath he rolled them over, still inside her, Leah on top.

He thought she'd fallen asleep when she spoke. "What do I have to do to convince you?"

"What?"

She lifted her head. "You and him and no one else. Ever. You guys are like twins."

Seth snorted. "Not even fucking close."

She nodded. "Yes, you are. Maybe you don't see it, but I do." She laid her palm along his cheek. "I want you to believe me."

It was still hard for him to believe she wanted him in the first place, not when she had Kaden. If Kaden wasn't enough for her, how the hell was he supposed to do it all?

He kissed her palm and rolled to his side with her still nestled in his arms. "Let's go to sleep, babe."

It felt so good, so right holding her. Good enough to keep the mental heartbeat away that night.

* * * *

They still went to the club on occasion. Seth preferred not going alone with Leah, even though he would if Kaden asked it of him. Seth realized he didn't enjoy the public sessions as much as he did their private ones.

"Why is that?" Kaden asked one morning when they were discussing it out of Leah's earshot in the den.

Seth shrugged. "I don't know. I guess I feel self-conscious for one thing. And I don't like her being naked." With things open between the three of them, it was fun incorporating sex into their private play.

Hottest sex of his life.

Kaden leaned back in his chair. "You need to find what works for you. She'll understand. What she gets from a scene is different than what you get from a scene. You can tailor things to work for you and for her. You can save the more intense stuff for at home."

"She won't mind?"

"No," Kaden said. "I mean…" He laughed. "Between you and me, I don't like her being naked either. She saw it once with someone else, asked if we could do it." He took his glasses off and looked at Seth. "*That* one took me a while to get used to."

"I bet."

"I mean, I don't mind her being naked with you, obviously. That's different."

* * * *

Later that afternoon, Seth ran out to the grocery store and left Leah at home with Kaden. Seth tried to limit Kaden's exposure to crowds as much as possible. He didn't want him getting a cold or something that, with his already compromised immune system, could put him at risk for worse problems than he already had.

No sense in speeding up the inevitable if they could avoid it.

When he returned over an hour later, they were on the couch, Leah naked and straddling Kaden's lap. While Seth didn't look over the back of the couch, he guessed what was going on.

"Whoa, sorry, guys. Didn't mean to interrupt," Seth joked on his way to the kitchen.

Kaden laughed. "You're not. Why don't you hurry up and get that stuff put away and come join us?"

"Don't have to ask me twice."

The irony struck him that now, the better part of a year since this crazy mess started, he didn't have to be asked twice.

He put the cold stuff away and walked out to the living room. Seth suspected it was a bad day for his friend, easier on Kaden to sit up, less uncomfortable than lying down. Not that Seth would say anything about it and spoil the mood.

Leah rested her head on Kade's shoulder, her eyes closed, her hips moving in a slow, seductive grind against his lap.

Seth detoured to the bedroom and grabbed the bottle of lube. He'd finally popped his cherry, so to speak, in that department. Now that he knew it wouldn't hurt her, he had no qualms about taking her from behind.

And she sure loved it.

He stepped behind her and stripped, dropping his clothes to the floor. He'd started going commando because it was easier logistically considering how often Leah jumped him or vice versa.

Seth stroked her back, drawing a soft, pleasant moan from her. He kissed the nape of her neck. "I think I know what you want, don't I, baby?"

"Mmm-hmm."

She stopped moving as he lubed her and himself, then carefully nudged his cock against her puckered ring. Kade reached around her and gently spread her cheeks.

"Tell me what you want, babe," Seth said, grabbing her hips.

"I want Master and Sir to fuck my brains out."

Both men groaned. Seth slowly slid home.

Kaden pushed her up. Seth wrapped his arms around her and played with her nipples while Kaden stroked her clit.

"Are you going to come for us, love?" Kaden asked.

Her head lolled against Seth's shoulder. "Yesssss," she sighed.

This was one thing Seth knew he would miss…after. Leah loved having them both together. He still couldn't claim to understand how Kaden felt compersion, but as the odd man out, Seth no longer questioned it. He couldn't honestly say if their positions were reversed that he could be so magnanimous.

He also knew damn well that…after, there would be no more sharing.

Seth cupped her breasts in his palms, tweaking her pebbled nipples between his fingers. He gently nipped her neck and she shivered. "Don't be stubborn," he coaxed. "Give it to us, baby."

Her body responded to their touch, tensing, her muscles throbbing around them as their combined efforts drove her toward release. She reached behind her with one arm and slipped it around Seth's waist. With her other, she grabbed Kaden's free hand. She cried out, and both men felt her muscles clenching around them as her orgasm hit.

When they knew she'd finished, Seth lowered her into Kaden's arms and thrust inside her as Kaden drove into her from underneath. It didn't take them long to finish. As Seth's release took him he braced himself on the back of the sofa so he didn't fall on them.

Breathing heavy, he kissed her shoulder and carefully withdrew. "You okay?"

She nodded against Kaden's shoulder, her eyes closed and forehead damp with sweat.

Seth went to clean up and brought her back a wet washcloth. Then he sat next to them on the couch, and Leah shifted position so she was curled up with both of them. Something else he'd miss, the quiet cuddling together after they were all spent. Something he'd never felt before this all happened.

Something he'd never felt with his exes, or anyone else for that matter, except for that one time years ago, together with Kaden and that girl…

Seth closed his eyes. Occasionally he'd lie in bed in the mornings when he woke up and pray he'd open his eyes and find himself in his bed in his brother's house, the past several months a strangely twisted dream.

That wasn't happening.

How could it have taken so long to find this peace? And now that it was within his grasp it was also slipping away, day by day, before his very eyes.

* * * *

Two weeks later, Kaden surprised them. "We're going to Disney!" he announced.

Seth looked up from the morning paper. "What?"

"I made the reservations. It's been years since I've been. I want to go."

Seth hoped the "we" meant Kaden and Leah. He was definitely not in a Mickey Mouse mood. "I'm sure you'll have a blast."

Kaden laughed. "Oh, no you don't. You're going with us."

Crap. He should have known he wouldn't get off that easily.

Like most residents of places where there's some sort of major attraction, Seth rarely ventured to Orlando. When he did, it wasn't to visit Rat World. But three days later, Seth was loading the trunk of Leah's Lexus with their bags. When the three of them were together, she rode in the backseat and let the men ride up front. Seth always volunteered to drive now, mostly because he saw Kaden's increasing discomfort, even though it wasn't all the time. If a spell hit him in the car, it was easier for him to hide it from Leah when he wasn't driving.

Seth suspected there were things she actively chose to overlook. If it helped her cope, he was fine with that.

When they spotted the large, mouse ear-shaped electrical pole next to I-4, Kaden guided Seth to the right exit. They'd stay at the Animal Kingdom Lodge, visiting that park first over three days. Then he'd planned two days at the Magic Kingdom, followed by three at Epcot.

He'd gone whole hog, in typical Kaden fashion. A suite with a king-size bed—answering Seth's question about sleeping arrangements—with a Savanna view. They could look out their windows and see the animals.

There was also the "safari" trip package, where a private guide drove them in a vehicle out onto the grounds to see the animals close up and personal in a way most park guests usually didn't.

Leah was in heaven. Kaden indulged her, spending as much time shopping for souvenirs as they did touring the parks. No photo op went wasted, either. Leah made sure Seth was in most of them, the park employees always helpful and offering to take pictures. She also took quite a few of her two men together.

While they did make love a few times, most nights they were too tired to do anything but curl up in the luxurious bed with Leah happily nestled between them. Seth worried Kaden was wearing himself out, but Seth wouldn't put the kibosh on their activities. All he could do was slow his own pace, forcing Leah and Kaden to take it a little easier.

Seth wasn't sure on the first day how to handle being together with them in public. This wasn't the club, where he discovered poly relationships weren't even a blip on the oddity scale. A person had to be a true freak, like having three testicles or six nipples, to raise those sometimes heavily pierced eyebrows.

When he tried to trail behind and look like he wasn't part of a "couple," Leah would grab his hand and force him to stay by her side while she walked hand in hand with Kaden.

At first, Seth imagined every eye was on them. After a few hours he realized it was all in his head. Families were too busy keeping track of squealing children. Couples were too busy looking at the attractions or each other.

As they stood in the queue for the Kilimanjaro Safaris ride later that afternoon, Kaden leaned in to Seth. "Relax and have fun. Enjoy being here with her."

Leah hadn't heard, too busy taking pictures of everything around them.

"Easy for you to say, dude."

"We're strangers here, buddy. Who gives a shit what the hell they think?"

It finally slammed home for Seth that this was yet another of Kaden's carefully executed plans.

"You didn't just want to come to Disney, did you?"

He shrugged, but from Kaden's sly smile, Seth knew his suspicion was on the mark. "She should have a chance to be happy with us and not worry about being self-conscious. It's a small world, after all, and we kind of just blend in here."

Seth groaned at the bad pun. "Aw, *fuck* me, dude."

Kaden laughed. "Still not doing you."

Seth loosened up. Leah especially enjoyed being able to dote on both her men. Kaden responded to her joy. And Seth enjoyed seeing them happy.

What was supposed to be their last morning there, Kaden left the room for a little while and returned with a satisfied smile.

"What did you do?" Seth asked.

"Got us three more days," he replied.

Leah squealed with delight.

Seth pretended to groan. Inwardly, he smiled. If it made Leah happy, he'd gladly do it.

It certainly seemed to make Kaden happy. Seth had to admit it was nice not giving a flying fuck what anyone thought of the three of them going somewhere together.

They walked the parks hand-in-hand, Leah between them. This was the most relaxed she'd been in months. Their entire time there, they'd only engaged in a little playful spanking one night before making love to her.

She'd really needed this.

Seth would never deny her a chance to have these memories, or this time to decompress. God knew they had some damn dark times ahead of them.

Chapter Twenty-One

Kaden and Leah's wedding anniversary was July nineteenth. The three of them celebrated together at a beach resort in St. Pete at Kaden's request. Seth tried to gracefully suggest he stay home or get a separate room, but Kaden wouldn't hear of it.

"I want you there, man," he'd quietly insisted one morning while they were discussing it without Leah.

"But that's for you guys to celebrate." In Seth's mind the phrase "last anniversary" had to be pounded back into its dark hole with a mental sledgehammer before it started him crying.

"You're a part of us. I want you there."

Seth studied him. "Why?"

Kaden wouldn't answer at first. Finally, "Please don't make me say it."

Seth closed his eyes. "Okay," he softly said.

It was a good weekend. Seth did his best to take as many pictures of the two of them together as he could. Leah did let Seth get his way once. He sent them out for a sunset walk together, alone, after taking pictures of them on the beach. The next night, Seth gave in and joined them, the three of them walking hand in hand in the white sand as the sun disappeared beyond the horizon into the Gulf.

Seth did his best to take pictures in a way that wouldn't accentuate Kaden's weight loss.

* * * *

In early October, an unwelcomed late-season guest by the name of Hurricane Mabel formed in the Caribbean Sea and worked her way north. Seth kept a close eye on it. By the time it drew south of Cuba, he knew he needed to prepare.

The corrugated metal window shutters were neatly stacked in the corner of the garage. He sent Leah out for supplies and several gallons of diesel for the backup generator he'd installed that spring. Kaden walked outside as Seth started moving the shutters to place them by their respective windows.

"What can I do?" he asked. He'd lost more weight, and his skin tone didn't look good. The jaundice had started.

Seth shook his head. "You can chill out and keep me company. You get hurt, Leah will have my nuts in a sling."

Kaden frowned. "Come on, I'm not fragile. Let me help."

"No. The last thing I need you doing is stressing yourself out. You want to help? Go move anything you can off the lanai into the dining room."

"I'm not a fucking invalid!"

The anger in Kaden's voice made Seth turn.

"Dude, I'm not saying you are. I don't need you wearing yourself out. Leah needs you. Anything you do that stresses you or tires you out, that cuts down on the time." It was a cheap shot, Seth knew it. But he also didn't want Kaden getting hurt. His strength and balance had deteriorated over the past month. "Seriously, if you can clear out the lanai, that will help me. And walk around the property, make sure there's nothing that can blow around, make room for Leah's car and the bike in the garage. That's stuff you can do and I won't have to. It'll save me time, seriously."

Kaden scrubbed his face with his hands. "I'm sorry."

"No, don't apologize." He sensed an imminent meltdown. Better now than if Leah was home.

Sure enough. Kaden closed his eyes. Seth cringed when he saw his friend's tears. "I just feel fucking useless."

Seth put his arms around his friend, held him, tried not to think about how he could feel nearly every rib and vertebrae through Kaden's shirt. "You're not useless, buddy," he gently said. He felt Kaden crying, didn't acknowledge it, didn't try to comfort him the way he comforted Leah. Kade didn't want that. He just needed to vent. "You don't make my job any easier if you wear yourself out and make yourself sicker faster."

Kaden eventually nodded and stepped away, turned, wiped his face. "Thanks, man. Sometimes I just…" He faced Seth. "Sometimes I just wish it was over. And then I feel fucking selfish."

Seth shook his head. "No, don't feel like that. I know you're in pain."

He knew Leah had to see it, but she didn't talk about it.

* * * *

Two days later, they sat in the living room and played Monopoly while the storm howled outside. They'd lost cable an hour earlier. The lights flickered several times, but they hadn't lost power yet. Leah sat on the couch with Kaden while Seth sat on the floor.

He'd noticed, especially over the past few weeks, that Kaden had stepped back in many ways. Seth suspected it was a combination of having his hands full dealing with his illness, he felt like shit, and that he was trying to get both Seth and Leah used to Seth's new role.

Seth also noticed he was now the hard-ass, the one who had to stand up to Leah and discipline her when she needed it. Kaden would let her get away with anything and everything.

He wasn't sure if that was intentional on Kaden's part or not. But now Seth led every session, took the lead in keeping her focused and calm.

He tried not to think about it. It was hard enough doing it. Especially when she turned the full force of her eyes on him.

He'd creatively used the blindfold on her one day when she tried to sucker him into getting her way, made her stay blindfolded for over an hour while she went about her daily business, blindly groping her way around the house. Kaden had laughed and deferred to Seth and his creative use of corrective measures.

At least it worked.

Later, when the men were alone, Kaden had smiled. "You're getting the hang of it, buddy."

The power finally went out. When the lights didn't come back on, Seth grabbed the battery-powered lantern he'd kept at his side. "I'll go check the genny."

Fortunately, the generator breaker panel was inside. For some reason the genny main had tripped, probably because of the frequent power surges. When he flipped it, it rumbled to life outside and the lights came on. When the power was restored, it would automatically trigger the genny to shut down.

He returned to the living room. "I suggest shutting off anything we don't need." He'd already unplugged the stereo system and TV in the living room to protect them from surges.

They tuned their radio to a local station simulcasting a Sarasota TV station and listened as the weatherman gave them a play-by-play of Mabel's torturously slow landfall on the Florida peninsula.

By seven o'clock it was pitch black outside, and Kaden suggested going to bed early. It was either that or sit and listen to the wind howl outside and the eerie sound of things thumping against the house.

The next morning they still had no power, but the worst of the storm was over even though gusts of wind and trailing rain bands still swept through their area.

Seth went outside and did a quick check of the yard. Kaden's truck and his own car, parked by the house, were undamaged, just covered with leaves plastered on by wind and rain. Some small limbs down throughout the yard, one on top of the house but it didn't look like any tiles were damaged. He couldn't tell from the ground, and it was too windy to get a ladder out to go up and look. No rain had leaked through as far as he could tell from checking the ceilings inside. Until he could get into the attic for closer inspection, he wouldn't know for sure. He'd have to replace some of the screens on the lanai, which was to be expected and something he could do himself.

Kaden stepped outside. "Well?"

"I think we're okay. I'll start taking the shutters down tomorrow. Too windy to do it today."

"With both of us doing it, it won't take long."

Seth didn't reply, pretended he was studying the power lines running along the edge of the property. They looked intact.

"I said, with both of us doing it—"

"I heard you."

"You were ignoring me."

Seth turned to him and dropped his voice. "Let me do it. Come on, it's *my* job, okay? This kind of shit is what I can do. Let me do it."

Kaden's face hardened. For a moment, Seth thought he was in for another confrontation.

Then Kade laughed. "You're not going to melt down on me like Leah over your laundry, are you?"

"I just might if you don't let me do my job."

Kaden looked up at the gunmetal grey sky and took a deep breath, blew it out. "Okay. I still feel useless."

"No, you need to change your thinking like you've done all along. I feel like a fucking freeloader. This kind of shit, I can do it and I do it well. At least one thing I don't totally fuck up. Let *me* have *my* pride, dude."

Kaden met his gaze. "Sure you don't want to go into psychology instead of nursing?"

"Fuck you." But Seth smiled. *Crisis averted.*

"You wish. Not in your wildest dreams, buddy."

Chapter Twenty-Two

Kaden didn't feel up to going out to shop for Christmas gifts. That relieved Seth, because he worried about Kaden picking up a cold. Seth helped him shop online or made mall runs for him, conversing over the phone to coordinate his purchases for Leah.

Seth put up the holiday lights and outdoor decorations, adding even more blow-ups and menagerie animals to the displays than the previous year.

Kaden helped with some of it, sometimes simply sitting in a lawn chair and untangling and testing lights for Seth. He didn't push the issue, didn't try to wear himself out. Many times Leah would join them, helping Seth or just sitting on a blanket by Kaden's feet, her head resting against his leg.

None of them spoke the obvious, that it was Kaden's last Christmas. They also didn't make references to "next" Christmas.

It was too painful.

When Seth flipped the switch on the lights the night before Thanksgiving, Kaden's face lit as brightly as the display, one of the few times Seth witnessed true joy in his friend in the past month. Seth knew the pain had to be miserable, but Kaden rarely complained.

Leah and Kaden slowly walked through the displays, her arm around his waist to steady him as he looked at everything. Seth grabbed the video camera and filmed them. In the dark, against the soft glow of the colored lights, Kade's skin tone looked nearly normal if you could ignore the deep hollows forming in his cheeks and under his eyes.

And he looked happy.

She would want these memories. Seth knew he did.

They put up the Christmas tree. Seth teared up when Leah hung their "First Christmas" ornament prominently at the front of the tree, next to her one with Kaden.

Where did the fucking year go? Too fast. *Way* too fast.

Thanksgiving was very quiet and subdued. Just Tony, Ed, Kaden's brother and sister-in-law, and Ben and Helen joined them. Leah had made no mention of holiday parties, one worry off Seth's plate. If she had he would have been forced to put his foot down. It was too close to the end for him to try to pretend to be okay in front of people he barely knew, and Kaden didn't want others seeing him like this.

* * * *

Seth was taking Kaden's blood pressure one morning while Leah was in the shower. Kaden grabbed his wrist. "Thank you."

Seth briefly met his friend's gaze and nodded, focusing on what he was doing. It hurt to look into Kaden's grey eyes and see them yellowed by jaundice.

It was two days before Leah's birthday. Kaden could still keep water, clear fluids, and some starches like rice and mashed potatoes down. They'd have to stop the Ensure soon. That was starting to upset his stomach. It wouldn't be long before he was down to water and broth, and then…

Seth had quit weighing him the first of December. It was too hard emotionally to document the decline. By now he knew Kaden had to be under one thirty. It was stupid and pointless to continue.

When they needed groceries, Seth usually forced Leah to go alone, leaving Kaden time to talk with Seth about things that needed discussing outside her hearing. Seth didn't want her to know his biggest fear, that Kaden might die while she was alone with him, and Seth didn't want her alone with him when it happened. His second greatest fear was Kaden's weakened condition, that he might fall and not be able to get up and Leah wouldn't be able to help him.

It kept her mind focused, got her out of the house for a little while. Even though Kaden got out of bed and walked around and was still continent, he spent most of his time either in bed or on the couch in the living room.

On the morning of Leah's birthday, Kaden produced a tiny box and handed it to her. Seth knew its contents because he'd wrapped it for Kaden.

She smiled as she fingered the small silver tags, with both Kaden and Seth's initials engraved on them. Then she leaned over and gently hugged him. "Thank you, Master."

Seth's present was an intricately braided silver locking choker necklace, similar to her other day collar. It already bore a matching engraved tag.

She hugged him, hard. He heard her barely choked back sob as she pressed her face against his chest. "Thank you, Sir," she whispered.

"Well, let's put it on you and see how it looks," Kaden said.

She leaned in and held her hair up while Kaden made the switch.

"It's beautiful, love," he said with a smile. "Now you've got another collar in your collection. Sir picked this one out for you."

Kaden wasn't fooling Seth. He probably wasn't fooling Leah, either, unless she was really burying her head in the sand. Seth knew damn well why Kaden insisted on Seth ordering the necklace. He wanted Leah to get used to the fact that she'd be wearing other collars in her life, not just the ones he'd bought for her. The dual-engraved tags were yet another tactic, helping ease her through the transition as gently as possible under the circumstances. Kaden hadn't pushed the issue sooner and knew he couldn't put it off any longer.

* * * *

Christmas morning, Seth awoke and held his breath as he watched Kaden's face. Kaden's chest rose as he took a breath.

Seth closed his eyes and breathed a sigh of relief. *Thank you, Jesus.*

Any day but today. They'd made it through Leah's birthday. If they could at least make it until December twenty-sixth that was fine with him. After that...

After that, every day was numbered. Kaden refused doctor-recommended IV fluids and nutrients that would keep him going a little longer. He was down to water, broth, and pediatric electrolyte solution. The lever had dropped to the lower end on Seth's mental gauge. Nearly pegged out at E.

Black.

He silently prayed for any time after January first and suspected that might be pushing their luck. It would be far easier on Leah emotionally to handle Kaden's death on a date at the beginning of the year rather than at the end.

She was in the kitchen fixing Seth's coffee the morning of December twenty-eighth when Kaden turned in bed and looked at him. "You know where all the paperwork is, right?"

Seth nodded. "Yeah."

"DNR?"

Seth nodded.

"Okay." He reached for the remote and turned on the TV. "I think you'll be making the call pretty soon."

Seth's heart chilled. "Not yet. Please."

Kaden's wan smile didn't reassure him. "I know. I'm trying to hang on until after New Year's."

"That's fucking spooky, dude. Reading my mind again."

"It's logical. I don't want to ruin this time of year for her or you. That would suck."

"You're a piece of work, you know that?"

Kaden smiled a little broader, reached over and patted Seth's arm. "You say that now. But brother, you ain't seen nothing yet."

Seth didn't know if he even wanted to ponder what was in store.

Chapter Twenty-Three

Another prayer answered—Kaden quietly celebrated New Year's with him and Leah alone at home, although they all drank white grape juice and not champagne at Leah's insistence.

Kaden, of course, smiled and let her have her way.

But he barely sipped his. Seth took the glasses away before Leah could see Kaden hadn't really drank any.

On January third, Seth closed the door to Kaden's study before making the phone call he dreaded. Everything had been arranged in advance. Starting tomorrow, the hospice nursing staff would be on hand to help.

Kaden called Tony and asked him to stop by. When he arrived, Kaden asked for some private time to talk with him. Seth took Leah out to the backyard and held her as they sat under an oak tree.

She couldn't cry.

Twenty minutes later, Tony walked out to them. "How are you two doing?"

Seth nodded. "Hanging in there."

Tony crouched down and started to reach out to Leah. She sat with her eyes closed and her head tucked against Seth's shoulder. Tony met Seth's gaze. Seth finally realized what he wanted. He nodded.

Tony gently touched her arm. "If you guys need anything, no matter what, and I'm talking not even…the other stuff. Anything I can do, please don't hesitate to call me, day or night. Okay?" Tony was one of the few people Seth knew really meant it, not just spouting meaningless bullshit he had no intention following through on.

She nodded without opening her eyes. "Thank you," she whispered.

Seth felt it, the dulling down Kaden had warned him of. Beyond exhaustion and grief, something more, something deeper, like a hard shell forming around her.

After Tony left, Seth helped Leah to her feet. He kept an arm around her waist, afraid she might fall.

Kaden was sitting up in bed. He had his glasses on and watched TV. Leah immediately curled up in bed beside him, tucking her head against his side, where she spent most of her time now.

Kaden reached over and stroked her hair. "Hey, beautiful."

"Hi, handsome."

Seth leaned in the doorway. "Honey, can I make you any dinner?"

She shook her head.

The strength in Kaden's voice surprised Seth. "Leah, you will eat a bowl of soup or I will send you out to the kitchen."

Eventually, she nodded. "Thank you, Sir," she whispered. "I'll take a bowl of soup, please."

Kaden stroked her hair again. "Good girl, love."

Seth fixed her a bowl of soup and brought it to her. He sat on her other side and watched her eat it, making sure she finished every drop.

When she finished she immediately curled against Kaden's side again. He looked tired, haggard. The weight loss was especially hard to witness, and why Seth suspected Kaden always insisted on wearing loose T-shirts now. The sight of his bones pressing against his flesh was almost painful to look at.

No matter what, Kaden still tried to make this easy on them. Forever a control freak.

Kaden carefully rolled to his side and curled his arm around her. "Love, you need a session tonight with Sir."

She shook her head and clutched his T-shirt in her fingers. "No. I want to stay here with You."

"You can come back to Me after you have a session, love."

"Please don't make me go right now."

He nuzzled the top of her head. "No, not right now. Later. All right?"

"All right."

Seth couldn't guess how much longer they had. The fact that it was nearly impossible for Kaden to keep down anything, including water, wasn't a good sign.

* * * *

Ed had been another call to make. He stopped by the house every morning and evening. Seth fully appreciated Kaden's planning now. He would have a hard enough time functioning, plus keeping Leah safe, without trying to deal with everything else.

Thank God for that.

The hospice nursing staff was excellent. Having been fully briefed ahead of time by Ed and Kaden, no explanations for Seth's relationship was necessary.

Seth and Leah rarely left Kaden's side. Seth timed her sessions to coincide with the nursing shift changes. They were quick and with very little ritual. Just enough to keep her with them.

Just enough to keep her crying.

Every time Seth woke up, his first action was to look at Kaden. Seth was unable to sleep more than an hour or so at a time, the slightest sound or movement from either Leah or Kaden jolting him awake and aware.

They were down to waiting.

Seth realized that with the den door closed, the nurse couldn't hear if he used the crop on Leah. He started carrying her into the den, giving her a superquick session, and immediately forcing her to eat something while she was still responsive enough to not fight him. All usually in the space of ten minutes, then she was back in bed with her fingers laced through Kaden's.

How much longer could he hold on?

How much longer could Leah hold on?

While the previous months seemed to fly by too fast, the minutes now crawled, every tick of the clock an agony. He didn't want Kaden to die. He didn't want to lose his friend. He wanted to put off the inevitable as long as possible.

But he also couldn't stand seeing his friend's obvious pain. How he'd made it all this time without using anything but minimal pain meds toward the very end. Seth couldn't believe it.

Then again, that was Kaden, the ultimate control freak. Why should his death be any different than his life?

* * * *

On the eighth afternoon after hospice started, Seth sensed the change in Kaden's breathing, knew the nurse did but wasn't sure if Leah understood. He touched Kaden's arm.

His friend opened his eyes and sadly nodded. He licked his cracked lips. "Can the three of us be alone for a minute?" he whispered.

The nurse kindly smiled and left the room.

Leah sat up and held his hand. "Can I get you anything, Master?"

He nodded. "You need to do something for Me, love."

"What?"

Kaden removed his wedding band and held it up. He looked at Seth. "Give me your left hand."

Confused, Seth did.

"Slave, take his hand," Kaden ordered.

Leah choked back a sob, but did as he commanded.

Kaden looked at Seth and nodded, then slipped his wedding band onto Seth's left ring finger. He took the engraved band off his right hand and put it on Seth's right hand, on the same finger as the other one.

They were the only pieces of jewelry Kaden ever wore.

He curled his fingers around their clasped hands and gently squeezed. "Slave, behold your Master. I swear to you, He will protect you, He will care for you, and He will never lie to you."

Seth nodded. "I promise."

Kaden looked at her. "Slave, you will obey your Master. You will take what I have taught you, and you will make Me proud. Your behavior still reflects upon Me and what I have taught you. This is what I order you to do."

She nodded, large tears running down her face. "I promise," she whispered.

"Love each other."

They nodded.

"I love you, Leah. I will always love you, babe. You've been a wonderful slave, and you've been the best wife I could have ever prayed for. I've been the luckiest guy on the planet."

She nodded and touched her forehead to his. "I love you so much," she whispered. "I'm always going to love you."

"I know. But you need to love Seth now."

She nodded. "I will."

He looked at Seth. "I love you, man."

"I love you, too…"

"But I'm still not doing you," Kaden completed.

That finished Seth. He sobbed. He leaned forward and kissed his friend. "I wish I was you right now."

"I know. It's okay."

Kaden motioned Leah to lie with him. He kissed her and let out a sigh. "I love you, babe. I wish I could keep saying it to you. It doesn't seem like enough."

"I know you love me. I love you. I love you so much."

He patted the bed beside him. "I won't think you're trying to do me if you lie here with me, buddy."

Seth harshly laughed. He carefully curled up next to Kaden, trying to ignore how fragile and bony his friend's body felt against his.

Kaden closed his eyes and pulled Seth and Leah's arms around him so he was holding their hands. "I love you, buddy. And I love you, babe. I think I'm going to go to sleep now. I'm really, really tired." Seth heard how weak Kaden sounded, knew it was time.

Leah continued whispering to him, over and over, that she loved him. Seth saw his weak smile. "It's okay, babe. I love you, too. Both of you. Never forget how much I love you." Kaden whispered.

She kissed Kaden again.

Seth counted the seconds between each breath. They grew longer, weaker.

Eventually, Kaden drew in a breath, let it out.

Seth held his breath, waiting.

He felt the tension relax in Kaden's body.

Seth closed his eyes and pressed his lips to Kaden's forehead. "Go in peace, man," he whispered.

The nurse appeared in the doorway a moment later and caught Seth's eye. He nodded.

She silently walked in around the bed, to Seth's side.

Leah's eyes were closed, her lips silently moving.

The nurse leaned in and touched her fingers to Kaden's neck for a long moment since Leah still gripped his wrists. She took out her stethoscope and listened.

She nodded, noted the time on her notepad, then left without comment to make her call.

Seth wasn't sure how long he should let Leah stay there. He had to call Ed, get that ball rolling, as Kaden had said. The undertakers would come to take Kaden's body…

He clamped his jaw shut and forced the sob back.

To take Kaden away.

Kaden's orders, what he did reveal to Seth ahead of time, was that no one else, besides them and the nurse and undertakers and Ed and possibly Tony were to see him after he died. He'd already told his brother he didn't want to be seen like that, said his good-byes so there weren't any hard feelings later.

He didn't give a shit what Denise felt or thought.

After thirty minutes, Seth carefully got out of bed and walked to the doorway. The nurse stood just outside, watching. He leaned in close.

"How long should I let her stay with him?"

She smiled kindly. "As long as you think she needs."

He motioned for her pad and wrote Ed's name and number. "Can you please call him for me? Tell him."

She nodded and went to do it.

Seth walked back to the bed and curled around Leah. Kaden looked peaceful, out of pain.

Leah's body felt rigid. She still silently moved her lips, something he'd never seen her do before.

Ed arrived twenty minutes later and stood in the doorway, waiting until Seth turned to him.

Seth got out of bed again and went to talk to him.

"How long ago?" Ed asked.

Seth looked at the nurse. "Nearly an hour," she answered.

"His orders were to not let her stay longer than ninety minutes. If the funeral home arrives sooner, try to get her out sooner. Try not to let her see them."

Seth nodded and returned to Leah, his grief sliding to the back of his mind.

Kaden's orders.

He would follow them to the letter.

Seth wrapped his arms around her from behind, and she still felt like a board against him. She held Kaden's hands, stared at him, wouldn't let go, her fingers stroking his.

Still silently talking to him.

"Babe, I'm so sorry," he whispered.

Leah moaned. She closed her eyes and a deep, gut-wrenching moan escaped her. He worried she might start screaming, but that was the only sound she made, like a howling wind over a rolling hillside. Over and over she moaned while Seth gently rocked her in his arms. Her body eventually relaxed a little against him while the moaning continued.

His heart broke for her. Was this a glimpse of the woman Kaden saw that afternoon when she finally confessed her past to him? The raw anguish?

It wasn't fair. She had to go through so much shit in her life, and now this on top of everything. Losing the man who saved her life.

How could he ever hope to measure up to Kaden in her heart?

Eventually her moans dissolved into silent, hitching gasps. She kissed Kaden's hands and face.

Seth was aware of Ed and the nurse quickly moving away from the doorway. Seth sensed he needed to get Leah out of there, and soon.

"Babe, it's time."

"Nooooooooooo!"

He closed his eyes and strengthened his grip around her. "Love, Master has given us orders to follow. Remember your promise."

She sobbed and went limp in Seth's arms. She kissed Kaden's lips one last time, stroked his hair. "I love you," she whispered.

Then she let Seth carry her to the den.

Ed followed them and stood in the doorway. Seth was aware of the nurse letting someone into the house, followed by two low, unfamiliar male voices. A metallic rattle, like a stretcher being rolled through the front door and across the tile floor.

Leah trembled in his arms, curled nearly in a fetal position, but her tears had stopped.

That frightened him.

Seth pressed his lips to her ear. "Love, do you need to feel the bite?"

She nodded but didn't speak.

He shifted position on the sofa, his back to the doorway. He slipped one hand up the outside of her leg, under her shorts.

"Count," he whispered. He pinched her, as hard as he could, on the inside of her thigh. Leaving a bruise was the least of his concerns, but he knew he couldn't take her to the playroom right then.

After a long moment, she whispered, "One."

"Very good, love. Again." He pinched her again.

"Two."

He did it a total of ten times until, finally, tears slid down her face. She buried her face against his shoulder and sobbed.

"Do you want to see him one last time?" Seth asked.

"What did Master want?" she whispered.

Seth looked at Ed.

Ed shook his head.

"Okay. We'll sit here for a while longer, love," Seth said. "Let's just sit here and wait for a while."

Leah clung to Seth. "Thank you, Master," she whispered.

Seth held her tightly against him, his face buried in her hair, and cried his own silent tears.

Chapter Twenty-Four

Ed's orders were to stay all night with them and, if necessary, help Seth take Leah to the hospital to have her forcibly sedated. It would be Seth's call if they had to go that far. If so, Seth was to use his power of attorney to do it. Kaden had already talked with their family doctor to assist Seth if it was the course of action needed.

Seth didn't think it was necessary—yet—but he was glad Kaden had thought that far ahead.

Ed waited until Leah cried herself to sleep in Seth's arms to hand him an index card with Kaden's writing on it.

1 - Day Of

Keep her crying. Your only job for the next twenty-four hours is to feed her, keep fluids in her, hold her, and keep her crying if she's awake and starts to dull down. To take care of her. Do not leave her alone, do not let her out of your sight, not even for her to go to the bathroom. When you have to go, make sure Ed or Tony stands watch over her. Ed will take care of getting the arrangements in order, make the phone calls, and guide you through the process. Tony will come by to stand watch while you sleep in case she gets up without waking you. You've got to be fucking exhausted by now. I'm so sorry, brother. Thank you for staying with me until the end.

I have already talked to Ed and Tony, and they know what to do. What little sleep you can get while they're there, take it.

I love you, dude. And tell her I love her, too.

Seth closed his eyes, nodded, and handed the card back to Ed.

Ed leaned in close and whispered into his ear, "I have a lot to give you, some a little at a time, some at certain stages. I'm to save everything for you to have after, if you want to keep it. He really did plan everything."

Seth nodded.

* * * *

Seth was aware of the sound of low voices, the stretcher rolling across the tile again, the front door opening and shutting. A few moments later, the sound of a vehicle leaving. The nurse stopped in the doorway and whispered something to Ed. Ed nodded and walked over to Seth and leaned in close to whisper in his ear.

"She asked where the sheets are. She said she'd change the bed for you, if you'd like."

Seth started to tell him, then stopped. "No, I'll do it. Tell her thank you, though."

Ed nodded. He walked out of the room with her for a few minutes. Seth heard her leave a little while later.

Seth didn't know if Leah was asleep or catatonic, but he knew she needed a little while to decompress before he gave her a full session.

He hoped Ed brought ear plugs.

He eventually untangled himself from Leah. She stirred and looked at him.

"Love, we need to take care of a couple of things. Can you help me?"

She numbly nodded.

He helped her to her feet and, with an arm around her waist, led her to the linen closet. "Let's change my sheets for Ed." He hadn't spent a full night in his own bed in months, but he had slept there in the past week during the day, napping when he knew Leah was asleep with Kaden, the hospice nurses having strict orders to wake him if Leah even so much as coughed in her sleep.

Leah helped him change the sheets, and she gathered the dirty ones to take them out to the garage.

Next, the harder one. Seth helped her walk down the hall to their bedroom. She stopped in the doorway and sobbed, but let him lead her inside.

He'd changed the sheets earlier that morning. The nurse had tossed the disposable pads they'd used on top of the sheets. Frankly, it didn't need changing.

Leah climbed into bed, grabbed Kaden's pillow, and deeply inhaled.

Seth didn't have the heart to move her.

Ed watched from the hallway, and Seth walked over to him. "Just keep your door open in case I need you," Seth whispered.

Ed nodded and went to get his bag from his car.

Seth slipped into bed with her and wrapped his arms around her. She rocked herself, the pillow in her arms, her eyes squeezed shut. Maybe this wasn't a good idea.

She rocked herself for an hour, Seth trying to hold onto her. She didn't speak, didn't make any noise other than to sniffle and weep.

She finally fell still, and he thought maybe she'd cried herself to sleep. When she spoke, her flat, dead voice startled him.

"Please let me die," she said.

"What?"

"I want to die. I can't do this. It hurts too much. I thought I could, but I can't. Please."

He held her tighter, scared. "No."

"Please, Master. Let me die."

He tried not to sob. "No, babe, I can't do that. I won't let you do that. I need you."

She squeezed the pillow to her. "It hurts. It hurts so bad. I knew it would hurt, but it hurts so much."

"I know, babe. I hurt too. I can't let you die. I promised. You promised him. We promised him."

She sobbed, cried for hours. Seth lost track of time. Tony arrived and Ed let him in. He brought water to them. Seth had to force her to drink. When Seth got up to go to the bathroom, Tony sat with Leah.

Time blurred for Seth. He didn't even know what time Kaden had died, just that it had been late afternoon, and now it was after three in the morning.

Seth dozed, vaguely aware of Tony quietly sitting in the chair in the corner and reading a book. Seth didn't dare let Leah out of his arms, afraid she would hurt herself before he could stop her. The slightest movement, even a subtle change in her breathing, woke him.

In the morning, Seth realized he'd dozed off. Ed sat, reading, in the chair. Leah was asleep. Seth smelled coffee and eggs cooking.

Moving slowly and carefully, Seth got out of bed, used the bathroom, and left Ed watching Leah while he walked to the kitchen.

Tony was cooking breakfast.

Seth poured himself a cup of coffee and sat at the counter. "Thank you," he hoarsely said.

Tony nodded, scooped some eggs and bacon onto a plate, and put it in front of Seth. "I know you don't feel like eating, but force it down anyway. You'll need it."

Seth nodded and complied without question. He felt alternately numb and like he wanted to curl up and die.

Kaden's dead.

The mental heartbeat had reached its inevitable end.

He finished, quickly showered in his old room, then went to relieve Ed. Leah awoke a little after nine. The only indication Seth had was her sudden, sharp intake of breath, followed by a deep, sad sigh.

She didn't open her eyes, hadn't moved, still clutched the pillow.

He waited twenty minutes before gently stroking her cheek. "Honey, you need to get up, go to the bathroom."

She vigorously shook her head.

Okay, then.

He scooped her up. She wouldn't let go of the pillow, so he let her hold it. He carried her into the bathroom and set her on her feet, forced her to stand. Forget modesty. He pulled her shorts and underwear down, made her sit on the toilet.

She looked like a dead woman walking. The utter lack of emotion on her face scared him. He knew she needed a session. He just didn't know if he could bring himself to do it.

Eventually he heard her go. When he figured she was finished he pulled her to her feet, cleaned her up, and carried her into the bedroom. Tony waited by the door.

"She okay?"

Seth shook his head. "Playroom code is 1218. Can you bring me a crop, please?"

"Moderate or severe?"

"Moderate."

Tony left. Seth didn't have time or energy to consider how truly freaky that conversation was.

Tony returned a moment later with a suitable crop. Leah was curled on her side, still clutching Kaden's pillow. Seth didn't even care that Tony could see her naked from the waist down. Seth knelt next to her. "Love, do you need to feel the bite?" he whispered.

She didn't respond, just closed her eyes.

He looked at Tony, who nodded.

Seth took a deep breath. "Love," he said sternly, "do you need to feel the bite?"

After a long moment, she nodded.

Seth didn't have a good angle and carefully lined up his strokes. A paddle would be easier to manage under the circumstances, but Seth didn't think he could stand the sound.

The crop was quieter. And harsher.

He kept one hand on her waist and laid a stroke across her ass. She didn't flinch.

Seth continued, a set of ten as hard as he could manage. At the end he curled around her. "Love, we need to do this. Where are we?"

An agonizingly long moment later she whispered, "Green, Master."

He breathed a sigh of relief. "Set of twenty, love."

"Twenty, Master."

He closed his eyes and swallowed his sob. He got back onto his knees on the bed. "Count." He put as much force behind the swing as he could, then waited.

After nearly a minute she whispered, "One, Master."

"Very good, love."

It took them twenty minutes to get through the set. But she was talking.

And she cried.

If you could call screaming at the top of your lungs and begging to die crying.

Even Ed and Tony looked near tears.

After an hour she settled down again, glassy-eyed and staring. Ed motioned to Seth, calling him into the hallway.

"Why don't I call her doctor?"

Seth shook his head. "No. Not yet. She has to deal with it now or later. If we dope her up, she'll still have to deal with it. I don't want to resort to that unless she tries to hurt herself."

"Are you sure?"

"Yeah." He stared through the doorway to the bed. She wouldn't let go of Kaden's pillow, hadn't released it.

* * * *

By that night, he'd managed to get her to go to the bathroom without assistance, although he stood next to her. He took a shower with her, shaved her legs for her, got her to swallow some lukewarm chicken broth and Ensure along with some water.

Tony and Ed both spent the night again and took turns standing watch so Seth could sleep.

The next morning, Seth panicked when he awoke and Leah wasn't in bed with him. Neither Ed nor Tony were in the chair in the corner.

He heard voices in the kitchen and raced out there. Leah sat at the counter, the glassy stare on her face. Ed stood behind her while Tony cooked. She had a cup of coffee on the counter in front of her, but it didn't look like she'd drank any.

Seth touched her arm. "Sweetie, are you okay?"

Eventually she slowly swiveled her head to look at him. Huge tears rolled down her cheeks. "He's gone," she whispered. "I got up to look for him and he's gone."

He pulled her into his arms. "I know, babe. I'm so sorry."

"He's gone, Seth. I couldn't find him."

He looked over her head at Ed.

"She got up an hour ago," he whispered. "We didn't want to wake you. I woke Tony up, and we followed her around the house. She went outside, wandered around, then came back inside and just walked around for a while. She finally sat down here and wouldn't talk to us. We figured we should let you sleep."

"Can I go with him?" she asked. "Please, Seth, I want to be with him." The dead tone of her whisper filled him with fear.

He held her tighter, glancing over to the counter. Tony or Ed had apparently hidden the knives from the butcher's block. "We promised Kade, love. You can't leave me. You promised him."

She shuddered. He scooped her into his arms and carried her to the bedroom. He gave her a set of twenty and held her while she sobbed against him.

After she went back to sleep, Ed quietly walked in and handed him another index card.

2 - Aftermath

Keep her crying. Keep her breathing. Don't let her out of your sight, and don't let her get dehydrated. If she asks to kill herself, remind her of her promise. I know I don't need to tell you not to let her do it. Use whatever you can to keep her with you. Even if you have to play dirty and make shit up, whatever. Tell her I'm ordering her to stay with you and serve you. I have faith in you. You are the only one who can keep her safe, buddy. I know you don't want to dope her up, but if you have to, I understand. You are there and I'm not, and I know you'll do whatever she needs.

Seth cried as he handed the card back to Ed. He handed Seth another one.

3 - Arrangements

Ed will take care of everything. All you need to do is, when he tells you, get her dressed in the outfit in the closet, the one in the garment bag. I already put it together for you. Shoes, everything. Let her keep her formal collar on, the neckline on the shirt will hide it. She'll feel better. It will be held five days after I'm gone, so you've got that much time to get her vertical again. I imagine we're on day two at this point. When you get a moment, when she's sound asleep, let Tony watch her, and Ed has something he needs to let you see.

Seth returned the card and studied her. Sound asleep. He nodded and carefully got out of bed. Tony, carrying a book, walked in and settled in the chair again.

Ed led Seth to the study and quietly closed the door. Kaden's computer was on, and the DVD program was up.

Before he clicked the mouse he looked at Seth. "I'm warning you now, he's left quite a few. For you to watch. He has a couple for her, but most of them are for you."

Seth nodded.

Ed hit *play* before stepping out of the room and closing the door behind him.

Kaden had obviously recorded this early on, because he looked good, healthy.

"Hey, buddy." Kaden smiled. It looked like he'd filmed it with his webcam here at the desk, in this chair. "I know, this sucks. I'm sorry I'm dumping this on you. Up front, I love you, man. I know you love me. I know she loves me, and believe me, I love her…"

Twenty minutes later, Seth opened the door. He'd cried buckets of tears but felt a little better. While watching Kaden waste away over the past several months had been horrible, and his twinge of relief at his friend's release from his pain filled him with guilt, his overwhelming grief and loss had been at the forefront of his mind.

But Kaden was still there taking care of them in many ways. He had, in typical Kaden control freak fashion, literally arranged every last detail.

Seth felt even more guilt that he didn't have to do anything but take care of Leah. Kaden had assured him on the DVD that it was supposed to be his only task right now, but that didn't assuage him. Shouldn't he be in charge and taking care of things?

As it was, he had all he could do to keep from agreeing with Leah that dying looked like a damn good option.

Kaden had even anticipated that in his message to him.

Damn, he was spooky.

He gave Seth several suggestions on how to keep her focused, how to keep her feeling, subtle things Seth could do to keep her alive.

Seth returned to Leah's side and napped until late afternoon.

* * * *

The phone calls started that evening as people learned of Kaden's passing. The phone ringer was turned down low, and Helen came over to answer it, giving Tony and Ed a respite. By day four, Leah would speak in short, simple sentences. She'd also stopped asking Seth to let her die.

Ed came in the fifth morning and motioned to Seth. He joined him in the hall. Leah was still asleep.

"The limo will be here at four to pick us up. I suggest getting some solid food in her this morning so she doesn't collapse on us this afternoon. It'll last until about seven or so."

"I can't leave her side."

"You're not supposed to."

"How do I explain who and why—"

"Seth. You don't."

He studied Ed. "Let me guess."

Ed nodded. "He's got it planned. Don't worry about it. You don't worry about appearances or anything else. Just her. Those are his orders." Ed looked through the bedroom doorway at Leah's sleeping form and sadly shook his head. "You know, I honestly thought he was overreacting. You know how he is...was. I was just humoring him. I had no idea..." He sighed. "Thank God he thought this through. He made it all easy for me, really."

You're not the only one.

* * * *

Seth got her into the shower a little after nine. She docilely stood while he washed her hair, shaved her legs, everything. He carefully towel dried her and slipped a large T-shirt over her head before leading her to the kitchen.

Between him and Tony, they coaxed a half a bowl of oatmeal and two scrambled eggs down her. Good thing, because Seth estimated she'd lost about ten pounds in the past week simply from not eating. He hoped her stomach would kick in and demand more food once it got its teeth into that.

He gave her a session in the playroom, taking the four-foot whip to her, got her to cry. She was actually speaking in coherent sentences by two o'clock when he led her back to the kitchen and coaxed her into eating a bowl of clam chowder.

He dressed her, left her sitting on the couch with Tony sitting on the coffee table in front of her, whispering to her, trying to keep her distracted while Seth got dressed.

The four of them rode in the limo. Seth was vaguely aware of people talking to them at the memorial service, but he kept his arm firmly around Leah's waist the entire time during visitation. Tony stood on her other side, ready to help catch her if she collapsed. Leah rarely spoke, mostly nodded and said thank you.

At least she appeared to be functional, even if she wasn't.

Because of the cremation, there was no casket. Kaden instead had picked a picture of the three of them from their Disney trip, taken in front of the Tree of Life at Animal Kingdom, all three of them wearing Mickey Mouse hats, smiling, having fun.

There were over five hundred people there. Seth didn't know most of them, but apparently they'd known Kaden. The funeral director started a DVD, and Seth both cringed and laughed throughout it.

Kaden the control freak strikes again.

The message was, again, recorded in the early days, when Kaden was still healthy and looked good. How he would have wanted people to remember him. When it finished, a few people gave eulogies. Seth watched but didn't really listen. His entire focus was on Leah, listening to her breathing, keeping her pulled tight against his side to keep her from collapsing.

Keeping himself from collapsing under the weight of his crushing grief.

* * * *

Time blurred.

* * * *

Three mornings later, Leah rolled over in bed and looked at Seth.

"Good morning, sweetie," he said.

She nuzzled her face against his shoulder, and he cuddled her close. "Good morning, Master," she whispered.

Tony and Ed were now switching off days. Kaden had left a bunch more cards. So far, Leah was acting nearly exactly as he'd predicted.

Damn, he was good.

Seth wondered if he'd ever know Leah that well.

"Can I get you some breakfast, babe?" He held his breath. Normally she would shake her head, and it would take him twenty minutes to wheedle and beg her into eating something.

She nodded.

He stroked her hair and prayed he didn't cry with relief. "Scrambled eggs?"

She nodded again.

He hugged her, relieved. Maybe they had finally turned the corner.

* * * *

Ed stopped by even though it was Tony's day. "I need to drive you two to the clerk's office up in Venice this afternoon."

Leah was napping. "Why?"

He handed Seth another card.

32 - Moving On

Time for you to take the next step. Ed will take you to the clerk's office and help you get the marriage license. Even if he doesn't have a death certificate back yet, there shouldn't be a problem. Congratulations! Ha-ha! No, you're not getting married today. That's in a few days. Ed has to arrange the other part for me.

Horrified, Seth stared at the card. "You can't be fucking serious!" Kade had talked about it, but Seth didn't honestly think he meant this soon.

Ed nodded, held up another card. "I have to give this to her."

Seth reached for it but Ed pulled it away. "No, I have to give it to her. You can read it after she does."

Leah stirred when Seth woke her. Once she was awake, Ed handed her the card. She slowly took it, then closed her eyes and took a deep, shuddering breath before opening them again and reading.

She took a long time. Seth resisted the urge to read over her shoulder. When she finished the card she was crying, but she nodded and wiped her eyes and handed the card to Seth.

He read it.

Seth looked at the ceiling and silently swore.

Kade, if you were here, buddy, I wouldn't know whether to kiss you or kick your ass. But thank you for arranging everything. At least I can blame you if it doesn't work out.

Chapter Twenty-Five

Ed drove them to the clerk's office and helped them get the marriage license. Leah and Seth signed where the clerk indicated.

"So when's the big day?" Seth snarked.

Ed smiled. "Should be this weekend. I have to get everything put together."

* * * *

Kaden had left a DVD for Leah to watch. It was the only time Seth was told to leave her side. Ed had to stay with her while she watched it.

When she emerged from the study, she looked stunned but…

Seth couldn't put his finger on it.

He'd been sitting on the couch, and she slowly walked over to him and curled up in his lap. He automatically wrapped his arms around her. "Are you okay?"

She nodded and closed her eyes as she curled tightly against him. "You can watch it now, if you want."

He wasn't sure he wanted to. "What did he say?"

"He wanted to explain why he set it up like this. I mean, I knew why, but he wanted to make sure I understood."

"Are you really okay with this, hon?" Seth wasn't sure *he* was okay with it. Marry Leah, hell yeah, that was a no-brainer. But this soon? Wasn't that sort of tacky, even if it was the dead husband setting it up? "I mean, seriously, if you're not, it's all right. We don't have to do this right now. We can wait."

"Yeah, I'm okay with it. He's right. He wants you to have the full legal ability to take care of me and to be able to access everything. The sooner we're married, the better."

"That's not what I mean."

She opened her eyes and looked at him. "I want to be your wife. I love you."

Seth nodded and kissed her forehead. "Okay." He snorted in wry amusement. "Will you marry me?" Seemed a little moot, considering he was already wearing Kaden's wedding band—like hell he'd ever take that off—as well as the other band.

He'd never take that one off either, despite already wearing one just like it on the same finger.

Leah made a small sound he realized was a laugh. "Yes, I'll marry you. I don't want to be anywhere but right here with you."

He breathed a silent sigh of relief. "Okay."

* * * *

Ed arranged everything. All Seth had to do was pack according to a list Kaden had prepared on another card Ed gave him.

He did this while Leah slept one afternoon. Kaden's instructions to Seth, what little he let on, were to not tell her what was packed.

Late Saturday, a limousine arrived at the house to pick them up. Leah looked beautiful in a simple black dress Kaden had apparently bought months earlier, before he became housebound, and tucked in a garment bag in the back of Seth's closet. Loose, flowing, with long, full sleeves, it fell just above her knees.

Kaden had instructed her to put her hair up, to wear the collar she'd had on—still the same one from the day he died—and to put just a little makeup on, tasteful and subdued.

She curled in Seth's arms during the limo ride, nestled in his lap with her head resting on his shoulder. Kaden the control freak had picked his outfit as well, only he hadn't needed to shop for his friend. Jeans and loafers, and a dark charcoal button-up shirt.

Seth wasn't sure about their final destination, only that from what was packed, it would hopefully be warm.

Either that, or the two of them would freeze their asses off because Kaden figured he'd die in the summer.

Somehow, Seth didn't think that was the answer.

The limo headed north on I-75. It was with no surprise the limo driver turned off at Bee Ridge and headed east.

Toward Tony's.

Whatever was in store, Seth suspected Kaden had planned this part of the freaky festivities with Tony's assistance.

Sure enough, there were several cars parked at Tony's. Ed and Tony met them as the limo pulled up to the house. Seth helped Leah out. He'd given her a hard session at home just before helping her get dressed. She seemed to be handling things okay so far.

With her arm hooked through his for support, Seth led her inside.

There were a few people Seth knew from the club, people Kaden and Leah had known for years. Candles set an intimate tone. Seth cringed when he saw the large TV and DVD player.

Oh boy.

Ed introduced another man. "Seth, this is Judge Donnelly."

Oh, crap.

Leah managed a wan smile. "Hello, Pat. Nice to see you again."

Seth breathed a sigh of relief. Kaden's instructions were to allow her to freely speak to people while they were at this gathering.

Apparently this guy was one of their "loan a whip" kind of friends.

He nodded. "I'm sorry I was out of town the other day and couldn't make it to the service."

"That's okay."

Folding chairs had been set up in a semicircle around the TV. Ed directed everyone to be seated, Leah and Seth at the front.

Ed consulted with Tony, turned on the TV, and hit *play* on the DVD remote.

Another of Kaden's early recordings, again made in his study at his computer, most likely over a year earlier from how healthy he looked. Seth waited for Leah to react, but she held it together.

She was doing better than he was, apparently. Maybe he should let her whale on him for a while with the whips.

"Well, guys, I know this is weird and strange," Kaden said with a smile, "but you know me. I'm a control freak."

Leah and Seth both laughed. That apparently gave the rest of the people, fifteen in all, permission to laugh, too.

Kaden continued. "Everyone here knows Seth and Leah. And you guys know me. You were invited here tonight because you are, other than my brother and Seth's brother, the people I want here. For obvious reasons, I'm not involving them in tonight's activities.

"Seth, Leah, I love the two of you. You know that. I've got something for you. Ed and Tony will give it to you here in a minute. I wanted people as witnesses to this who would understand, who wouldn't judge. No offense, Pat." More nervous laughter from those gathered. "I wanted people who would support you and make this day as easy as possible on you."

Kaden addressed everyone. "For everyone's information, I've left Seth and Leah a very explicit set of instructions to follow. They've been following them—I hope—and tonight is part of that. I know I don't have to explain to you all why it's important Leah not be without a Master. I don't have to justify myself, and Leah and Seth don't owe you all any explanations. I know all of you gathered here will understand and accept and support them. That's what I wanted. Maybe later they might want to have a public ceremony down the road, but I'm leaving that up to them. Most people won't even know what's going on until much later, so that will help them out.

"I don't want people badmouthing Seth or Leah over this. I'm a lucky bastard that these two people loved me enough to stand by my side when I needed them the most. And I want them to be happy."

Kaden took his glasses off and wiped his eyes. "Ed, go ahead and take a moment to get them up here and arranged."

Ed hit pause on a remote control and consulted another index card. "Leah, Seth, I need you up here." He motioned them up front, near the TV but not blocking it from everyone else's view.

"Pat, you can stand here." The judge stood near them.

Ed grabbed a small, rolled-up rug, shook it out, and laid it on the floor between Seth and Leah. Then he consulted his card again, patted his pocket, and motioned to Tony. He leaned in, said something in low tones to him, then handed him something.

Tony and Ed moved into position, flanking Pat. Then Ed hit *play* again.

"Okay," Kaden continued. "Let's begin. Pat's here more for window dressing than anything."

Pat laughed.

Kaden smiled. "Sorry, buddy, but you know why."

That made Pat laugh again, and he shook his head.

Leah even managed a slight smile.

Seth tried not to think about how weird this was.

Kaden continued, his voice turning Master-firm. "Leah, kneel."

She automatically dropped to her knees in front of Seth and looked up at him.

So that explains the carpet.

"Leah," Kaden said, "behold your Master. The man who I give you to, in front of these witnesses, the man who will take my place. Take his hands."

Seth didn't try to fight back his tears, didn't care who saw him cry at this point. Fuck, it's not like it could get too much weirder. Unless Kaden asked him to fuck her in front of people.

He froze. *No, Kade wouldn't do that.*

Would he?

Oh, God. Please, no.

Leah reached up to him. He took her hands in his.

"Too bad we can't call Guinness about this," Kaden quipped. "How many people can say their husband married them off?" His smile set off another light round of soft, amused laughter from the audience. "Leah, repeat after me. This slave gives herself to You, Master. Completely. Mind, body, heart, and soul. To love and serve You in any way You decide."

She looked into Seth's eyes and repeated the vows.

After a moment, Kaden continued. "Seth, repeat after me. As your Master, I vow to love, protect, and care for you, always."

Seth did.

Kaden wasn't done. "Tony, the rings. Seth first."

Tony stepped forward and handed Seth a wedding band.

"Seth," Kaden said, "place this ring upon the finger of your slave so she never forgets who she belongs to. It's up to You if You want to keep the other rings on or not."

With trembling fingers, Seth slipped the ring on Leah's left ring finger, leaving Kaden's engagement ring and wedding band on her hand. "I want them both," he softly told her.

She nodded. "Okay."

"Now Leah." Tony handed Leah a ring.

"Leah, place this ring upon the finger of your Master as a symbol of you giving yourself, fully, completely, and forever to Him."

She did.

"Okay, guys," Kaden said. "Leah, stand and join hands with Seth."

Seth helped her to her feet.

"Do you both swear to love, honor, and cherish each other?"

"We do," they answered.

"Never lie, always be honest. Find a path that works for the two of you. I'm hoping at the end of the year the two of you won't want to separate." Kaden wiped his eyes again. "Master, behold Your slave. Slave, serve your Master well. Remember, your actions still reflect upon how I have trained you."

They nodded.

"Seth, do you take Leah to be your lawfully wedded wife?"

He gently squeezed her hands. "I do."

"Leah, do you take Seth to be your lawfully wedded husband?"

She nodded. "I do."

"Okay, Pat. Call it. Make 'em legal."

Everyone in the room laughed. Pat wiped his eyes. "By the power invested in me by the State of Florida, I now pronounce you husband and wife."

A moment later, as if he knew how long it would take, Kaden piped up. "And I now pronounce you Master and slave. Go ahead and kiss her. She's all yours, buddy." He smiled.

Seth gently held her, kissing her. It felt different than all the times they'd kissed before.

The right woman.

And she was all his.

Of course, Kaden wasn't quite finished.

"I want you two to be happy. We've talked about this. Seriously. I know you both need time to heal, and that's fine. Try to enjoy life. Find some simple pleasures to start with. Ed's got some more—surprise—instructions for you. My orders for both of you are to enjoy what's next and try to focus only on each other for the next couple of days. It's been a long haul. I know you two are worn out. Don't feel guilty about taking this time together, okay? Please? I need the two of you starting out on the right foot. It would really harsh my mellow if you didn't."

At that, Leah and Seth both laughed.

"Fucking ballbuster," Seth muttered.

"I love you, Leah," Kaden said. "And I love you, too, Seth."

"I love you, too, dude," he said. "But I'm still not doing you."

"I'm still not doing you either, buddy."

Seth froze, then laughed loud and heartily as Leah tightly hugged him. The DVD ended.

* * * *

Kaden knew Seth and Leah wouldn't be in much of a mood to socialize. He'd instructed Ed to offer some very light refreshments, just enough to be polite, before the celebration broke up. Leah and Seth signed the marriage certificate, as did the judge, Tony, and Ed.

"I'll save the DVD for you with the others," Ed said.

"So when do you tell us what's next?"

"There's an envelope in the limo. You don't open it until you're on the road again. The driver knows where to take you."

They said good-bye to everyone, hugged Tony, Ed, and Pat, and then Seth helped Leah into the limo.

The sealed manila envelope lay on the seat.

Leah cuddled tightly against Seth's side as he took a deep breath and slipped his finger under the flap.

On top, another card in Kaden's handwriting.

Congratulations! This is your honeymoon. Now don't get freaked out, for chrissake. You two need a fucking vacation after what you've been through with me, admit it. A few days away that I know you normally wouldn't take. I meant it when I said I want you two starting out on the right foot.

The two of you have never had a chance to just be alone and just be together. I want that for you. That's my wedding present to you. No guilt allowed, and try not to rehash what's happened. Just try to enjoy each other, go for some quiet walks, hold each other, talk. Hell, watch TV if that's what you want to do. Recharge. I'm not saying I think the two of you can just drop your emotions and party, but I want you to try to relax, kick back. Just...be for a few days.

Inside were plane tickets, their passports, reservation information for a small resort in the Bahamas. A five-day stay. A handwritten note, from Ed, detailing their itinerary.

The limo took them to Tampa International Airport where they caught a short flight to Miami. From there, another flight to the Bahamas. A man waited for them at arrivals with Seth's name on a sign. He helped them with their bags and drove them to a small, secluded resort.

Too tired to do anything else, they fell asleep almost immediately after check-in, tightly curled together.

* * * *

The next morning, Seth awoke with a start. Leah wasn't in bed with him.

He sat up, heart racing.

"I'm here," she softly said.

He turned and saw her standing at the open window. A sweet, salty breeze blew in.

He walked to her and put his arms around her. They had a gorgeous view of the ocean. The sun rose from behind them, painting the turquoise water with a golden glow.

Seth kissed the back of her neck. "Are you okay?"

She hugged his arms tightly around her. "Yeah," she said. "Just...sad. Not about you," she quickly added.

"I know. I understand." Now he understood why Kaden hadn't included any "toys" in the packing list. Would have been hard to explain some of those to the TSA and customs agents. "Do you feel like breakfast?"

She nodded.

He ordered room service for them. Seth had to admit Kaden was fucking smart to do this, to totally get them out of their usual setting, away from reminders and normal routines, to jar them out of their funk.

But how the fuck had he lived all those months, well over a year from the looks of him on the videos, knowing damn well what he'd done for them? The videos he'd made, the messages he'd left?

Seth realized Kaden was telling the truth when he said he could share her. In Kaden's world, he'd already married her off to Seth and said his final good-byes to them.

Seth and Leah just didn't know it.

An almost lost feeling filled him. Today Leah seemed…peaceful. He suspected the worst of his worries over her safety were over, but he still worried about her health. The months of accumulated stress on both of them wouldn't just magically disappear.

Without Kaden to care for, without a vigil to stand over Leah, Seth was left wondering what was next for them both.

After they ate they took a long, warm bath in the huge sunken tub. They didn't speak, just lay there soaking in the water. Seth had finally taken a good look at the new bands. Matching, of course. Intricately engraved with a vine pattern. Not quite like the other bands but similar.

Leah twined her fingers through his. "Thank you," she whispered.

He kissed the top of her head. "For what?"

"For everything. For being there for him, and for me."

He tightly hugged her. "Babe, I love you. This was a no-brainer."

She took a deep breath. "I meant it when I said if you really want out at the end of the year—"

"Stop." He turned her to face him. "Let's get this straight right now. I said it before, and I meant it. If you want out, you can tell me. As far as I'm concerned, this is for life, babe. I wouldn't have married you if I didn't mean it for life. I don't care what Kade planned. I'm not leaving you unless you tell me you don't want me anymore."

She threw her arms around him, tightly holding him.

Then her tears.

It relieved him that she could cry without help. He settled back in the water and soothed her, consoled her.

When she relaxed in his arms she looked into his eyes. "Can we stay in the room for today?"

"Sure. Whatever you want."

She caressed his face. "Please make love to me."

It'd been over a month for them. Even though Kaden had encouraged them to make love, neither Seth nor Leah had been in the mood to do so. They'd opted for power cuddling together, the three of them in bed, Leah firmly sandwiched between them.

Seth drained the tub, dried her off, and carried her to bed. He knew what Kaden wanted them to do—spend their time bonding in a way they really couldn't before when it was the three of them.

He brought her hand to his mouth and feathered his lips along her knuckles. "Are you okay, babe?"

She nodded.

"Do you need to feel the bite?"

She shook her head. "Not now. I think I'm cried out in the good way for now. At least for a day or so."

He kissed her, taking his time, savoring her. He was intimately acquainted with every centimeter of her body already. But this was different.

She was all his.

Seth took his time, slowly working his way south. There would be no spankings, no whips or vibrators or cuffs or safe words this time. Just the woman he loved and his love for her.

He prayed that was enough to satisfy her, at least for now. Because it was all he wanted.

Her nipples peaked as he circled them with his tongue, teasing them, alternating between them. Her soft sigh of pleasure stirred him, stiffening his cock.

"You like that?" he whispered against her flesh.

Leah tangled her fingers in his hair. "Yesss."

They could never be "normal" with a picket fence and two-point-three kids in the yard. There would always be the dark corners of her soul requiring regular cleaning to keep her sane. But for this moment in time, with the sound of the ocean outside their window and a salty breeze to stir the air, she was fully there with him. He felt it. Her mind, her heart, her soul…

Her love.

He traced meaningless patterns across her belly with his lips and resisted her attempts to nudge him down where she wanted him.

When he finally let her coax him into settling between her legs, he peeked up at her. She looked beautiful, with her skin flushed and hair mussed, and her lower lip clamped under her teeth.

His wife.

He was a lucky bastard.

"Tell me what you want, babe," he gently teased as he kissed her inner thigh.

She opened her eyes, and the full force of her green eyes hit him. "I want my husband to make love to me. I want you to make me come, baby."

The word flipped his heart inside out in a good way.

Husband.

Who was he trying to kid? Maybe he helped keep her sane, but he'd do whatever, anything she wanted.

He lowered his lips to her mound and slowly traced her clit with his tongue. A soft, replying moan rewarded him.

Gripping her thighs, he teased her, not trying to make her come, just to keep her hovering, floating in a state of mind he knew she could safely enjoy without any sad or painful thoughts intruding.

Leah softly whimpered but didn't beg, didn't plead.

Didn't slip into slavespeak.

He closed his eyes and pretended this was the first time he'd ever touched her, truly his wedding night—well, morning—spent long, slow, delicious minutes exploring her. Making love to her without guilt or melancholy or the sad ache in his heart that she wasn't really his.

He didn't let her come. He sat up and pulled her into his lap, settling her onto his shaft. She kissed him and wrapped her arms and legs around him as he rocked his hips against hers.

Seth slid his hands down to her hips and cupped her rounded curves. "I want to make love to you forever," he said.

Leah rested her forehead against his. "Please. This feels so good."

Caressing her back, he kissed her jaw, down her neck and across to her shoulder where he gently nipped her. She shivered with pleasure and squirmed against him.

She felt different today. *He* felt different. He didn't want to drift into sad thoughts. Those would return soon enough when reality called them back to Florida.

To their home.

He slipped a hand between their bodies and found her swollen nub, gently stroked it. She moaned and rested her head against his shoulder. He kissed her neck and nibbled on her earlobe. "Come for me, sweetheart."

Rocking her hips in time with his, he felt her body struggling to make it. Her breathing grew quick and shallow as a fine sheen of sweat covered her.

Seth forced himself to maintain his rhythm, knowing she was close. He didn't want to break her concentration.

When she gasped he felt her muscles contracting around him and knew he had her. "That's it," he murmured. "Give it to me, baby."

She cried out, sobbing as she clutched at him. When he suspected she'd finished, he gently lowered her to the bed and kissed her face, brushing her tears away.

"Are you okay?" he asked.

She nodded and weakly smiled. "Yeah." Her fingers found his, laced together, and she kissed his hand. "I'm okay. I love you."

"I love you, too, babe." He shifted position to hold her. Even though he was still horny, more important to him was holding her.

His wife.

He suspected she was drifting to sleep again. "What about you?" she mumbled.

He smiled and kissed her forehead. "We've got a lot of time to worry about that."

* * * *

He awoke an hour later to the delicious feel of her lips wrapped around his cock. He lifted his head and looked at her. She winked, then went back to what she was doing.

Fuck it. She was obviously feeling a little okay, at least. He closed his eyes and dropped his head onto his pillow. His fingers tangled in her hair.

He was close when she sat up and straddled him, hovering, not impaling herself. "How are you feeling?" she playfully asked.

"I'd be feeling a lot better if you'd quit teasing me, girl."

She rocked her hips along his shaft, letting it glide along her slick cleft but not letting him penetrate. "Teasing?"

He smiled. "Teasing." He cocked one eye open and glimpsed the ghost of a smile. She was beautiful. "You keep that up," he warned, "and you're gonna get fucked."

"Isn't that the point?"

He surprised her, flipping her over onto her back and sliding home. He held still for a moment. "Is that what you wanted?"

She nodded. "Yeah." She tried to kiss him, but he raised his mouth out of her reach. With her arms gently pinned over her head, he slowly stroked into her.

"You're a tease, babe."

"Is that a problem?"

He smiled. "No." Then he stopped and nuzzled her nose with his. "As long as you're only a tease for me."

"Only for you," she echoed, kissing him.

Something surged deep inside him, nearly overwhelming. He took several deep thrusts and came inside her, releasing her arms and rolling over with her clutched tightly against his chest.

He cried.

* * * *

They ate dinner at a nearby restaurant recommended by the resort. Then they walked along the beach, hand in hand, and silently watched the glow of the waves as they softly lapped against the shore in the moonlight.

He made love to her until well past midnight, silently and gently branding her flesh with his lips and hands. It felt so much different now. She seemed to feel it, too.

The third morning they curled up together in bed and watched a rainstorm blow in off the Atlantic. She lightly trailed her fingers down his chest, across his abs, to his shaft, gently played with him, stirring his interest.

"This feels right," she whispered.

He nodded. "Yeah."

She was quiet for a long time. "I miss him."

"It's okay, babe. I miss him, too. We're going to miss him for a long time. Probably forever." He didn't panic, knew he could take care of her if she needed help.

Another comfortable silence. "I told you it's not always whips and stuff."

When he processed what she'd said he laughed and rolled over on top of her. "Yeah, you were right. Is this the point where I start yes-dearing you all the time?" He kissed her.

She brushed the hair away from his forehead and smiled. "No."

"Do you…need anything?"

She shook her head. "I'm okay for now."

He didn't feel a dulling down from her, just a quiet melancholy that echoed his own mood. Her eyes still looked sad, without the humor and joy that used to light them from within.

"Do you want anything?"

She nodded. "Yeah."

"What?"

She wiggled her hips under him, pinning his cock between her legs in an erotically wonderful way. "This."

* * * *

Another limo picked them up at the airport in Tampa and drove them home. Ed had brought in their newspapers and mail while they were gone.

Seth somewhat dreaded this even though he longed to be home. He knew a pile of condolence cards would await them. He didn't want to be away from Kaden's memory but worried Leah's mood might slip upon their return.

The driver unloaded their bags from the trunk for them. At the front door, Leah unlocked it and started to step inside when Seth had a thought and grabbed her arm.

"Wait."

"What?"

He scooped her into his arms. "Humor me."

She wrapped her arms around his neck as a faint smile caressed her lips. "Okay, handsome."

His heart twisted in a hot and pleasant way as he kissed her and carried her over the threshold.

Chapter Twenty-Six

Was it only a month since they lost him? Seth watched Leah sleeping one morning. He knew she struggled with depression despite the good days of mental and emotional decompression they'd had in the Bahamas. Perhaps it was time to take her to the doctor. Every morning she sluggishly awoke and started her day, more a rote routine than with genuine enthusiasm.

They spent their days talking, quietly watching TV, and he played his guitar for her, soothing her to sleep.

The worst of her tears hadn't returned, although it wasn't uncommon for him to find her crying in the middle of the day sometimes.

She hadn't mentioned killing herself anymore either.

Thank God.

He hesitated to drug her, afraid she might come to rely on it instead of dealing with things.

She rolled over and cuddled up to him. How long until he saw the light in her eyes again?

Would he ever see it?

It didn't matter what she claimed. Would she ever truly come to love him as much as she loved Kaden? Easy enough for her to swear before they lost him, but with the truth in front of her, perhaps she couldn't.

She opened her eyes. "Good morning," he said.

Leah offered up a sad smile. "Good morning, Master."

Crap. It would be a bad day for her. She was going formal right off the bat. He stroked her cheek. "Do you feel like making coffee this morning?"

She nodded, then slowly climbed out of bed to do it. He watched her walk, naked, through the bedroom door.

Their bedroom.

He could almost feel Kaden's presence with them, an empty longing for his friend. And yet he couldn't bear to change a single thing in the house.

Leah had told him if he wanted to, she was okay with it.

He didn't want to.

Maybe that wasn't healthy, but he didn't care. It was a connection, a tangible link to his friend.

He suspected never again in his life would he ever have a friend like Kaden.

* * * *

Ed stopped by a little after lunch. Leah was taking a nap. Seth walked outside to greet him when he heard his car pull up.

"I have something to give you," Ed said, walking around to his trunk.

Inside was filled with boxes. He reached in and handed one to Seth, grabbed another.

"What's this?"

"They're all for you. They're Kaden's old journals."

Seth stopped short and nearly dropped the box. "What?"

Ed nodded. "You'll want them in the study. Lock them in the closet until you've read them all. I'll give you the card here in a minute. All of these boxes are yours. He printed out the newer ones on the computer, saved them on CD for backup, too."

Numb, Seth helped him unload them all. Then he noticed the boxes were neatly labeled in Kaden's handwriting, from one to seven. He looked inside one box and saw every journal was labeled with a number.

Ed handed him the index card. Seth sat to read it. It had been over two weeks since the last card. He'd both missed and dreaded them.

139 – Me Again

Hey. Yeah, I know. Surprise! Heh, heh, heh. Listen, I didn't tell you about these before because I didn't want you trying to read them all and learn stuff at the same time. And some of the stuff... Well, you'll see. I wanted Ed to wait to give them to you to give you time to process everything. Please start at the first one and read through them in order. They're numbered for you. Don't cheat and skip to the last one. I mean, you know how the story ends. Ha-ha. Sorry. Anyway, enjoy, buddy. If Leah wants to read them, don't let her do it until after you've read them all first, and only if you think she's

strong enough. There's some stuff in there for her, but I never let her read
them when I was alive. I love you, man. Love and kisses to our girl for me.

Seth sat back and fought his tears. Just when he thought he had a handle
on his grief, Kaden popped out of the woodwork again and it poured out of
him anew.

"You okay?" Ed asked.

Seth nodded. It took him a few minutes to speak without choking up.
"Yeah. How much other stuff is there?"

"I'm not supposed to tell you. Nothing like this. This was the biggest
bombshell. Mostly cards and a few more DVDs."

Seth nodded. "Okay. I'm guessing there's one for the anniversary?" Just
so he'd know what to expect.

Ed nodded. "I can tell you that much." He scratched his chin. "I'm not
supposed to tell you there are ones for his birthday, yours, hers, their
wedding anniversary, your first anniversary with her, Thanksgiving,
Christmas, things like that."

"Okay." Seth took a deep breath.

* * * *

He started reading that evening after Leah went to sleep. The first
journal started when they were in junior high. He didn't write every day.
Usually a couple of times a week on average. Seth was startled to read
Kaden's entries.

Seth and I went out fishing today. Man that was a blast! If it hadn't been
for him, I would have lost the first one I landed...

Seth came over today for help with his math. If I could just get stupid
Denise to leave us alone. I wanted to brain my bratty sister. He helped me
fix my bike...

That stupid asshole in our sixth period English class, David, he got
pissed because I wouldn't let him cheat off me. He said he was going to
pound me. Thank God Seth walked up when he did. I think Seth's going to be

taller than me...

He sat back, stunned. No, not every entry was about him. But shit he didn't even remember happening, here it was in black and white.

And he'd played a starring role in much of it.

He never dreamed... He always saw Kaden as his strong and steady rock. He never imagined he was the same for Kade.

* * * *

Three days later he'd worked up to Kaden's college days and his friend's take on the threesome.

Man, that was fucking INTENSE! I will never, till my dying day, forget that. I never could or would have done that with anyone but Seth, but MAN...

Seth choked up as he worked his way through the journal.

I took Seth out for lunch today. He leaves for basic training tomorrow. What the hell am I going to do without my best friend? God, I'm not much into prayer, but please let my buddy come home safe when he's done with all of this...

Weeks later, Kaden wrote:

Seth's coming back from basic tomorrow! He'll only be home for a week before he ships out, but damn it I'm going to be so glad to see him!

Seth checked to make sure Leah was still asleep. She still spent most afternoons napping, although her naps were slowly growing shorter in duration.

He returned to the study, locked the door, and cried.

The next day he read about when Kaden first met Leah.

She's so beautiful! But she looks so scared, like that rabbit I raised for

4H that time. Like the slightest thing would send her running...

Only three days, I know she's the one! I've never felt about anyone like this before. I can't wait for Seth to meet her...

A short time later, Kade wrote,

She broke up with me. I don't know what I did wrong, but I can't lose her. It's like the thought of being without her rips my heart right out of my chest. I've got to do something, convince her that I love her. Damn it I wish I could call Seth and talk to him, ask him for advice, for his help. She scared the shit out of me when I caught her with that knife. Then I wanted to take it and kill her father myself after she finally confessed what she's been through. Fuck. I can't let her get away. God help that bastard if he ever gets out of prison and tries to contact her. I'll kill him with my bare hands. Hell, Seth can help me hide the body...

He laughed at that. How many times over the years had they joked that "friends help you move, and real friends help you move bodies"? They'd always claimed they were "body-moving friends."

Kade's entry the day after the first spanking.

I felt like total shit, man. I have never, EVER, hit a woman. But I'll do whatever I have to do to make her happy and keep her from hurting herself. Even if I hate myself every time I do it...

It took Seth another three weeks to work his way through to the day Kaden first found out.

I went to the doc today. I'm going to get a second opinion. This can't be right. What am I going to do?

Kaden journaled even more frequently in his last months, leaving Seth a detailed blueprint of things he might not have covered well enough in person.

The final entry, dated the day before Seth called hospice.

It's close. I can feel it. I wake up every morning first surprised I'm even here, and then mad I won't be there for them. And then grateful that Leah has stood by my side for this journey, and beyond grateful that Seth has joined us and is here for me and then will be there for her. We finally get our happily ever after, and I can't be here longer for it. Fuck. Seth, man, I love you, brother. You know that. I'm so sorry to bail on you like this. I feel like I'm letting you down. I'd hoped it would be the three of us forever. I know there's no miracle, and I know these journals aren't a substitute for the real thing. I hope reading them helps you understand why. Helps you understand her, and how I could share her with you. I don't expect you to share her with anyone. Frankly, I hope you don't. No one understands our girl as well as you do now. I've told Ed to wait a month before giving these to you if Leah seems to be hanging in there. If not, I told him to wait a little longer because I don't want you stressing, and I want your focus to be totally on her if she needs you.

I don't seriously think I have any worries after a year, do I? Really? Let's face it, you love her as much as I do. I knew it from the first time you guys met, I think. I never admitted that to you or her before. It didn't matter. In a way I was glad, because I knew then I'd met a girl good enough for you, buddy. I wish I'd been brave enough to talk to you sooner, years ago. This would have all been so much easier with you here from the start, from before my life got ripped apart.

I always had this weird thought, even years ago, when we were kids, that I wished we could marry the same girl and all be together. I had no idea what that meant back then, only that the thought of not seeing or talking to you every day ripped me up from the inside out. I thought I was weird or freaky. I didn't know then what I know now, duh. I hated it when you were gone overseas. I worried about you every day, fucking missed you like crazy.

How much of our lives, any of us humans, do we live spent in fear of some sort? I was always worried you'd think I was gay or something, and that was never it at all. I just...wanted you there. With me. I had no frame of reference to explain it before. And I couldn't tell you how much I hated your wives. Not because of them (well, okay, a little) but because they cut into how much time I could spend with you.

I was so happy when I knew Leah loved you. Fuck, I wanted to jump up and down and scream it! You have no idea. I'm sorry I didn't admit that to you sooner. I should have, but again, you had so much on your plate to deal with. Why one more worry? I knew you'd understand later, as you lived with us. As you felt it yourself.

The right woman. I'm sorry I can't be here longer with you and her to enjoy...

Seth closed the journal and took a deep breath. He needed time to compose himself. Twenty minutes later, he started reading again.

...and her to enjoy our life together. Please make sure she understands how sorry I am about that. And you too. I never would have shared her with anyone else. I know you don't want to share her with anyone else. And I think maybe she sensed how much I loved you. Maybe that's why she was able to feel the way I did about you, even though I never admitted everything to her. Tell her I'm sorry about that, too.

If she reads this, then babe, please understand, I didn't know how to tell you. You know how much Seth's meant to me all these years. He's been my rock. He was the one person I knew—besides you—would always be there for me, who would be honest with me and didn't give a shit who or what I was. I could have been a bum somewhere, and Seth would still be my friend. I always wished he'd been my brother. I always wanted to spend the nights at his house when we were kids, loved his mom and dad even more than my own, I think. They were fantastic.

Well, I can't write forever, can I? Ha-ha. I've given Ed, as you've already seen by now, lots of instructions, lots of things to give both of you. Hopefully to keep the two of you going. I'm sorry I've got to leave you sort of flying blind. I've never been through something like this before, but I have every faith in you, Seth, that you will keep her safe and keep her wanting to live. Or get her back to wanting to live. She loves you. She'll respond to you if nothing else.

Find your own path with her. Don't worry about trying to do everything exactly the way I did it. That won't work for you, and it'll leave her confused and angry. She'll understand and adapt better if you start trying to do things your own way. I don't expect you to change things overnight, but do what feels right for you. Don't worry about if I'd approve. If you keep your promise to me and her, that's all I care about. The details of how you do that don't matter to me. I know you love her and will do everything in your power to keep her safe and loved.

Take care, and go in peace, brother. I love you, Seth. I love you, Leah. You have both made me so proud.

Seth sobbed. That Kaden's words were so much his own at the end…it sent a shiver up his spine. And that last piece clicked into place.

He understood. Finally.

Completely, utterly.

When he was a kid, maybe six, around that age, he remembered going to one of his cousin's weddings. Thinking how cool it'd be if his best friend and him could be together, Seth had asked his mom if two guys could marry the same girl. She'd gotten this horrified look on her face and said, "Don't be ridiculous!"

He'd never dared, ever, to ask about it again.

He never dreamed Kaden had thought the same thing. But then again, didn't it fit? They were like twins in many ways, born only weeks apart. Their mothers had drifted apart as close friends over the years before their respective deaths, but their own friendship had never faltered, never wavered. It had grown stronger, deeper.

He carried the papers—Kaden had put the later journals into three-ring binders for him—into the bedroom.

Leah awoke as he climbed into bed with her. When she saw his face, sleep left her system.

"What's the matter?"

He held her close and read Kaden's final journal entry to her. This one time, he knew she should see it out of order. By the time he finished, she was sobbing, too, clinging to him.

Then he told her. He admitted what he'd never told anyone else.

Admitted what he'd wished he'd told Kaden years ago.

She finally sat up and looked at him, wiped his tears away, and kissed him. "I love you, and I don't want anyone else. Ever. I've lost Kaden, but I still have you."

"I won't share you. I'm telling you that right now."

She smiled. It was the first time he'd seen a smile actually reach her eyes since Kaden's death. "I hope to hell you don't. It'd really piss me off."

Chapter Twenty-Seven

I'd spent the better part of the past two months out of town, both on vanilla business and teaching classes. It was good to be home. I'd almost decided not to go to the club, then thought it might not be a bad thing, get caught up with the latest chatter, chill out a little. I was currently without sub or girlfriend, and the club always needed volunteer DMs.

I was standing in the foyer talking to Becca, one of the registration volunteers, when I heard the bike outside. No mistaking that sound. They walked in a moment later, and it took me a minute to process the sight.

I hadn't seen them in a couple of months even though I talked to them on the phone once a week on average, e-mails even more frequently. Seth walked over, smiled, and shook my hand. "Hey, Tony. When did you get back?"

"Yesterday. Still unpacking. I was going to call you tomorrow."

Leah looked good, a world better than a year ago, even better than the last time I'd seen her although I suspected she'd always wear her deep grief like an invisible veil. She had her bike helmet tucked under her arm, black jeans, and her black bike jacket was unzipped over her heavy leather bustier that—barely—covered her breasts and kept her street-legally dressed. Her custom-tooled, locked black leather collar looked good. The little silver tags caught the dim light. She glanced at her Master. He gave her a quick nod.

"Hi Tony," she said, leaning in for a quick hug.

"You two doing okay?" I knew the anniversary had been two weeks earlier.

She smiled and it looked genuine, unlike the horrifically awful mask she forced in the early days and weeks after Kaden's death. I preferred to witness her honest private grief than the façade she'd tried to portray to the rest of the world.

"We're good. We still have rough days sometimes. We deal with them together." She glanced at Seth.

Lucky bastard.

He signed them in, and as they walked through the door to the back, I noticed his demeanor changed. He seemed to grow in height as his arm curled protectively around her shoulders. She leaned into him, her steps perfectly synced with his. I hadn't watched them scene in many months, knew from our talks that they had shifted into a different style. Their private time together, what she needed, they did at home. What they did in front of others was strictly for play unless they were teaching.

I followed them, wondering what toys he had in the duffel bag slung over his other shoulder. Didn't look like he had any canes or crops from the way it hung.

They walked to the St. Andrew's Cross, which I thought was curious. Kaden had rarely played with her on that in public, although they had one at home that received a lot of use. I stopped at a discreet distance and watched as she stood in front of her Master and kissed him, then dropped to her knees with a beautiful look on her face.

Lucky bastard.

"What do you want to do?" he asked.

"I want to please You, Master."

"Be a little more specific, girl."

Her eyes lit up. That was encouraging. She'd seemed so dead at first, I wasn't sure if he'd be able to pull her through. Frankly, I'd had doubts about his state of mind. I'd warned Ed that if Seth lost her, he might as well plan Seth's funeral, too, because I knew she kept him alive every bit as much as he kept her going.

"Master, I want to feel the bite."

He looked bored, examined his fingernails. "Hmm. I'm not sure you do. You don't sound like it."

She threw her arms around his knees. "Please, Master? I'll do anything."

He playfully cocked an eyebrow at her. "Anything?"

She eagerly nodded, smiling. "Anything."

I'd noticed his confidence had built since that first time I met him. He also treated Leah differently. Then again, she was greatly changed now, too. Having survived something like that, it shows a person they can take more than they thought. It tempers the soul, and if it doesn't destroy you, it can make you stronger.

Sometimes the old clichés weren't just bullshit.

Seth wasn't hovering over her as Kaden had. I suspected if anyone dared look at her wrong, she'd clock them. Before, Leah would have cowered and needed protection, frozen in fear.

Now, after Kaden's death, Leah would kick Baxter's ass, or anyone else who dared speak to or touch her without her Master's say-so.

Seth dropped the bag and his helmet to the floor, next to Leah's helmet. He shrugged off his bike jacket. He wore a dark charcoal button-up shirt with his black jeans. He slowly started unbuttoning his shirt. "If you really want it, get ready, love."

She jumped to it. She ripped her jacket off and dove for the bag, retrieving two leather cuffs from it.

Ah. That explained the cross.

She fastened the cuffs to her wrists and took out the bullwhip. Then she dropped to her knees again in front of him and offered the whip up to her Master.

"Please?"

He tapped his foot and looked like he was thinking about it. "Why should I?"

"I've been a good girl this week."

"That's true." He made a big show of considering it again, dragging it out for her. "Well, I suppose. Okay." He finished unbuttoning his shirt and dropped it on top of the bag. He took the bullwhip from her. "Go on." He nodded toward the cross.

She jumped to her feet and ran to it, her back to her Master, and clipped her own cuffs to the uprights.

Seth rolled his neck and shoulders and uncoiled the bullwhip. I noticed the new tattoo on his right bicep. A vine design like the one on his left arm, the same one Kaden had, only this one bore Kaden's name, and the dates of his birth and death were worked into the design. I also noticed they were both now wearing small, matching silver vials on chains. They looked like they were engraved with intricate filigree, and I wasn't sure of the significance but I could guess.

He'd really come into his own as his confidence built. I could see Kaden's training and influence in Seth's manner and ways. Still, he was finding his own path with Leah.

From my talks with Kaden over the years, and especially in the weeks before his death, I'd wondered how Seth would change things up. I remembered how freaked out Kaden had been years ago, frantically calling me for advice when Leah first begged him to strip her at the club. I could laugh about it now, and knew Kaden probably would, too, if he was still around. The fact that Seth stood up to her and refused to allow that... I wondered if he understood what a big deal that truly was.

I knew from my talks with Seth that he had an unrealistic view of Kaden as some sort of all-powerful Master. The truth was, most of what Kaden did, Leah had talked him into it even if it didn't seem like it to others. He might have had the title and obviously the demeanor of her Master, but it was all because he loved her and tried to control and heal her pain the only way he thought he could.

Not because he wanted to dominate *her*.

Talk about a reluctant Dom.

Seth cracked the whip. Leah wiggled her ass at him in response. "How many do you think you deserve, love?" Seth asked.

Now a few people had gathered to watch. I kept an eye out and waved some back out of the whip's reach.

"As many as Master wants to give me."

He nailed her in the ass. I knew even through the denim it probably stung a little. She'd obviously love that.

"That wasn't an answer. You don't give me an answer, girl, I'll stop."

"Twenty, please, Master."

His movements were a thing of beauty. Smoothly fluid, confident, sure. He worked her over, the leather bustier taking the brunt of the higher stokes, the rest landing on her ass and thighs, never landing a throw on her bare flesh.

She squirmed against the cross as he finished the set.

"How are we, love?"

"Green, Master." From the sound of her voice, I suspected she wanted at least another thirty strokes, followed by a good, hard fucking.

"Then I guess I can put this away."

"Nooo! Please, Master! Don't stop!"

He laughed and walked up to her, caressed her cheek and whispered something to her no one else could hear. She moaned. An "I reeeeally want to get fucked hard" moan. She nodded.

He laughed and swatted her ass with his bare hand. "All right. I suppose I can give you a few more, love." He returned to his position, checked his clearance, and threw another twenty strokes without hesitation. Every one hit what I suspected was its intended mark.

By this time a small crowd had formed, standing far enough back to avoid the whip.

It was no wonder their classes were always full.

Seth walked back to Leah and talked with her. She nodded. I watched him take a small remote out of his pocket. He thumbed the button before returning it to his pocket.

Ah. The old butterfly.

Leah loudly moaned. Seth returned to his spot, rolled his neck and shoulders again, then cracked the whip. "Twenty more, love?"

"Oh…yes…please, Master!"

She moaned as he nailed her square in the ass. By the tenth stroke I suspected she was close to coming. When she cried out at fifteen, I knew he had her. He quickly finished the set and coiled the whip, used the remote to turn off the vibrator, walked over to her, and freed her.

She wrapped her arms around him, and he tenderly held her for a moment, standing there, a beautiful sight.

A slave and her Master.

When she caught her breath she smiled up at him. The love I saw in her eyes nearly took my breath away.

Damn, he was a lucky bastard.

I'd seen her look at Kaden like that. Now, with the worst of her grief behind her, she looked happy again, almost the way I remembered her being before Kaden's world crashed down around him.

After they finished and packed they walked over to where I stood. Seth casually draped his arm around Leah's shoulders. "Why don't you come over for dinner this weekend? Feel free to bring a friend if you want," Seth invited.

"I'll take you up on it, but I'll be coming solo." We made arrangements, and I followed them outside and chatted briefly before he kissed the top of her head.

"Let's go home, babe. Time for you to pay the piper," he said with a sly smile.

She laughed. "We'll see you later, Tony."

I nodded. "Drive safe."

They donned their gear. Seth secured the duffel bag on the Harley, mounted, and cranked it. Leah waited for his signal to throw her leg over the bike and smoothly slide on behind him. He backed them out as she placed her feet on the pegs and wrapped her arms around him. Then he lifted a hand to me, and they pulled out of the parking lot.

Lucky bastard.

I walked back inside. After having seen them play together my heart wasn't in it anymore for the evening. Tonight there were mostly part-time players, nothing outstanding or even interesting.

How do you even try to compare that to what I just witnessed? It was like trying to choke down a crappy hamburger after getting one bite of the best filet mignon you've ever sampled in your life.

I apologized to Becca for bailing on them and bade my leave.

On the way home, I thought about my talks with Kaden over the final months of his life. I could never claim to be as close a friend as Seth had been to him. I was more a trusted confidant because of our shared lifestyle choices and common interests, but I never deluded myself that he saw me in a different light than he saw Seth.

Frankly, I was surprised and shocked when he asked if I would be his backup in case Seth couldn't be Leah's Master. Kaden never had doubts about her loving Seth and the two of them ending up together as husband and wife. He hadn't been sure at first if Seth could give her the other things she needed.

At the time I'd been involved with someone and agreed to help if I was really needed, partially relieved when Seth stepped into the role.

And, I'll admit, a little disappointed. While I don't mind a purely business arrangement, so to speak, I didn't know if I could handle Leah's grief and the full-time love and care she would obviously need. I also realized that in her heart and mind I never would have been her first choice, only her last option, and only for a very specific reason.

Now...

Well, one day, maybe I'll find the right woman, too.

If I'm lucky.

*   *   *   *

I pulled into their driveway and parked behind the Ridgeline. I suspected Seth would drive Kaden's truck for years, until the wheels fell off.

Leah greeted me at the door, barefoot and dressed in jeans and a blouse. And her collar.

"Hey, come on in." She took the bottle of wine I'd brought and hugged me. "Thank you, you didn't have to do that."

"Is that Tony?" Seth called from the kitchen.

"Yes, hon."

I followed her through the house and slid into my usual seat at the counter. She turned. "Should I put this in the fridge?" she asked.

I shrugged. "Probably wouldn't hurt."

Seth was putting the finishing touches on the salad. "Oh, babe, I put the steaks on. Can you go grab mine before—"

"Done," she said with a smile. She walked out the sliders onto the lanai.

As I watched her, I noticed Seth's sly smile. "How is she? Really?" I asked.

He shrugged. "We have mostly good days now. Both of us. The anniversary was sort of rough, but Kade even planned that, too." He wistfully smiled. "In some ways it's like he's still looking out for us."

"Ever going to redo the vows?"

He shook his head. "No. We both decided we'd rather keep the wedding we had." He smiled again, this time without sadness. "As whacked out and weird as it was, we don't want it any other way. He left messages for my brother and his to watch, so we didn't even have to explain anything. Anyone else, we just tell them we went and got married by a judge."

We both laughed. I pointed at the chain around his neck. "What are those? They're new. If you don't mind me asking."

"They were Leah's idea. She was reading this book where this woman's lover died and she put some of the ashes in something like this. She asked me if she could do that. I sort of liked the idea."

"If it's a comfort then there's nothing wrong with it."

His gaze dropped and he nodded. "Yeah. It's like he's always with us, you know?"

"Yeah." We were quiet for a moment. "So how's school going?" I asked.

A genuine smile lit his face. "She's great. She's wicked smart, man. The only way I'm going to pass those classes is because she's studying with me."

"Do the professors object to you two being in the same classes?"

"No. I doubt most of them realize we're even freaking married. Half of them are clueless."

"Does she like school?"

"She loves it. I'm so glad Kade asked her to take classes with me. She didn't want to, at first. She wanted to stay home. I was afraid she'd start getting depressed again. I didn't want to leave her alone."

"What happens after school?"

"Ed's working with us, teaching us the ropes." He stopped, then laughed. "Well, you know what I mean. We should be managing the properties without him in the next year or so. We've got our eye on another one on Bahia Vista, east of US 41. We might buy if we can get the terms the way we like them. Ed told us to hold out a while longer. As bad as the market is, we can set our own price if we wait."

"That's good. You don't regret changing from nursing?"

He shrugged. "Not that I don't want to do it but..." He paused. "Flashbacks, man," he whispered, glancing at the door. Leah couldn't hear us through the closed sliders. "It hurts to think about those last months. I don't think I could deal with that all the time. I'd see his face every time I was working with someone. At least this way we can work together. It's fun. I get to be with her all the time." He paused, smiled. "It's what he wanted anyway. For us to be together."

We had a great dinner. Seth accidentally dumped wine on his shirt and went to change. To make conversation more than anything, I said to Leah, "You two looked good the other night."

She blushed a little, but smiled. "It's been an adjustment for both of us."

"He's really standing up to you."

She grinned. "You noticed that, huh?"

"Well, the way you led Kaden around. He let you get away with murder. You and I both know that."

She dropped her voice. "Seth put his foot down. He told me if I wanted to get naked in public, other than teaching classes, then I would have to wear a chastity belt for a month first."

I laughed. "He's territorial."

She blushed again. "It's okay though. I mean, he's so different than Kade, but he's not jealous in a bad way. He's protective in a different way. I just wish the three of us had had more time together. I feel bad for him. I sort of get a second chance. He doesn't get another best friend."

"He's got you."

"Yeah, but I'm just his wife. I can never be for him what Kaden was. I don't think anyone can."

Seth returned. After we finished eating, Leah cleared the table and shooed us into the living room. I noticed Seth walked by the bookcase next to the TV, reached out, and gently stroked Kaden's urn before taking his seat. It looked like an automatic action, something he probably wasn't even aware he did anymore.

We shot the shit for a while, then I reached into my back pocket and handed him the envelope. I'd put off doing this for a couple of weeks, considered mailing it to them, but it was as if seeing them at the club the other night was my nudge from the hereafter to make sure I kept my promise to my old friend.

He stared at it for a long moment without speaking before he finally, carefully slipped his thumb under the flap and opened it. Inside, an index card and six small, silver ID tags. Slave collar tags, I suspected.

I never asked Kaden what was in the envelope. It wasn't my business.

Seth wiped his eyes as he read the index card, then laughed and fingered the tags. Then he looked at me, shook his head, and smiled. "I wonder how many more of these he's salted all over the place."

I shrugged. "That's the last one I had."

He rubbed his thumb over the tags. "Kaden the control freak strikes again. How the *hell* did he know?" he mused.

"Know what?"

He handed me one of the tags. Two sets of initials, Kaden's, and... but Seth's wasn't right. I handed it back to him. Seth smiled. "I changed my last name when Leah and I got married. I wouldn't let her change hers. I added Kade's last name to mine, hyphenated it so it wouldn't fuck up my VA benefits." He shook his head, rubbed his thumb over the tags again.

That explained it. How *had* he known? Kaden gave me the sealed envelope months before his death.

Leah walked in, her fingers also brushing the urn before she sat across Seth's lap. "What's that?"

He handed her the card, and she read it. She laid her face on his shoulder, silent tears running down her face. Then he showed her the tags, and she laughed until she cried again.

"He's still looking out for us," she softly said.

"Yeah." He clipped one of the tags to her collar, adding it to the two already there. "I don't have the heart to take the old ones off, babe. Not yet. I'm sorry."

"That's okay. Let's leave them on." She flicked them with her finger, and they made a cheerful tinkling noise as they brushed together. "You can always hear me coming."

All three of us laughed.

I glanced at my watch. "Well, I need to head home. Thank you for dinner, guys. It was great. Really."

"Thank you for all you've done for us," Seth said.

"You both look good together. I mean that. I can't claim to understand what you've been through. I'm sure you're sick of people telling you how sorry they are. Frankly, I don't know how you made it through it. You're both stronger than I am."

Seth patted Leah's thigh. She slung her arm around his shoulders and looked into his eyes.

Lucky bastard.

Seth smiled, never taking his gaze from Leah's face. "It just took the right woman, that's all."

THE END

WWW.TYMBERDALTON.COM

ABOUT THE AUTHOR

Tymber Dalton lives in southwest Florida with her husband (aka "The World's Best Husband™"), son, and too many pets. She loves to hear from readers, so please feel free to drop by her website and sign up for her newsletter to keep abreast of the latest news, views, snarkage, and releases. (Don't forget to look up her writing alter egos Lesli Richardson, Tessa Monroe, and Macy Largo!)

www.tymberdalton.com
www.facebook.com/tymberdalton

For all titles by Tymber Dalton, please visit
www.bookstrand.com/tymber-dalton

For titles by Tymber Dalton
writing as Lesli Richardson, please visit
www.bookstrand.com/lesli-richardson
writing as Tessa Monroe
www.bookstrand.com/tessa-monroe
writing as Macy Largo
www.bookstrand.com/macy-largo

Siren Publishing, Inc.
www.SirenPublishing.com

CPSIA information can be obtained at www.ICGtesting.com
Printed in the USA
LVOW121922061112

306118LV00014B/86/P